THE
JUDGMENT
of CAESAR

THE
JUDGMENT
of CAESAR

A NOVEL OF ANCIENT ROME

STEVEN SAYLOR

Minotaur Books
New York

THE JUDGMENT OF CAESAR. Copyright © 2004 by Steven Saylor. All rights reserved. Printed in the United States of America. For information, address St. Martin's Press, 175 Fifth Avenue, New York, N.Y. 10010.

www.minotaurbooks.com

Library of Congress has cataloged the hardcover edition as follows:

Saylor, Steven, 1956–
The judgment of Caesar : a novel of Ancient Rome / Steven Saylor.
p. cm.
ISBN 978-0-312-27119-0
1. Cleopatra, Queen of Egypt, d. 30 B.C.—Fiction.   2. Gordianus the
Finder (Fictitious character)—Fiction.   3. Romans—Egypt—
Fiction.   4. Rome—History—Civil War, 49–45 B.C.—Fiction.
5. Egypt—History—332–30 B.C.—Fiction. I. Title.
PS3569.A96 J82   2004
813'.54   2003069548

ISBN 978-0-312-58245-6

First published in the United States by Minotaur Books,
an imprint of St. Martin's Publishing Group

First Trade Paperback Edition: January 2012

10   9   8   7   6   5   4   3   2   1

TO THE KA

OF SIR HENRY RIDER HAGGARD,

WHO WROTE OF CLEOPATRA

And

THE WORLD'S DESIRE

Cleopatra:
I am fire, and air; my other elements
I give to baser life.

SHAKESPEARE, *Antony and Cleopatra* V, ii 289–90

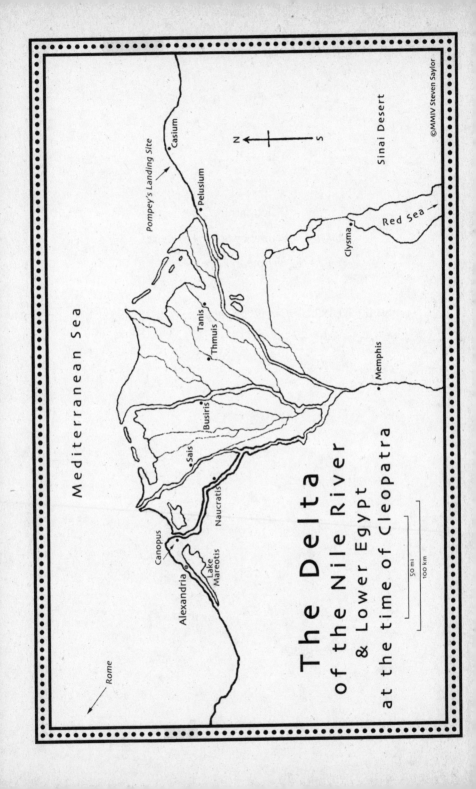

Mediterranean Sea

Rome

Sinai Desert

Red Sea

Clysma

Pelusium

Casium

Pompey's Landing Site

Memphis

Tanis

Thmuis

Busiris

Sais

Naucratis

Canopus

Alexandria

Lake Mareotis

N

S

50 mi
100 km

©MMIV Steven Saylor

The Delta
of the Nile River
& Lower Egypt
at the time of Cleopatra

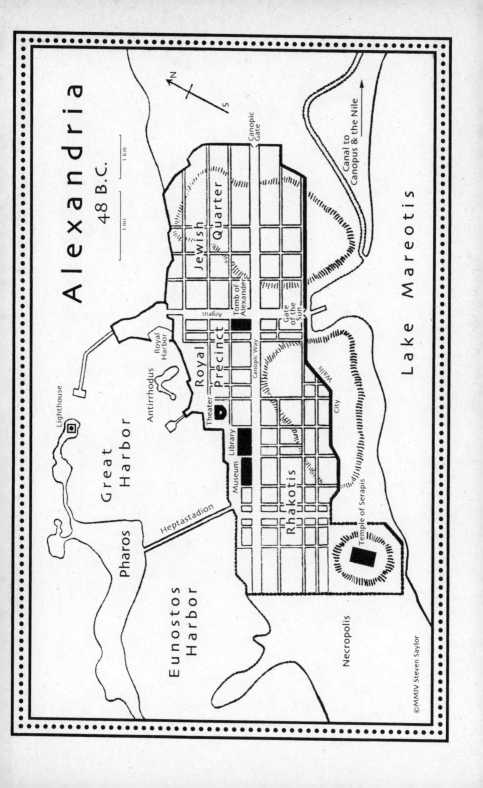

Alexandria

48 B.C.

1 km

1 mi

N

S

Lighthouse

Pharos

Great Harbor

Heptastadion

Eunostos Harbor

Antirrhodus

Royal Harbor

Theater

Museum

Library

Royal Precinct

Argeus

Tomb of Alexander

Jewish Quarter

Canopic Gate

Gate of the Sun

Canopic Way

Walls

Old City

Rhakotis

Temple of Serapis

Necropolis

Lake Mareotis

Canal to Canopus & the Nile

©MMIV Steven Saylor

A NOTE ON DATES

By the year 48 B.C., when this novel takes place, the flawed Roman calendar had drawn some two months ahead of the actual seasons. Thus, although the story begins on the 27th of September by the Roman calendar, the season is actually high summer, and the date, by modern reckoning, is closer to the 23rd of July.

1

"There! Can you see it? The lighthouse!"

Bethesda gripped my arm and pointed to a sparkle of light on the dark horizon. It was the hour before dawn. The deck of the ship rocked gently beneath our feet. I squinted and followed her gaze.

All night Bethesda had stayed awake, awaiting the first glimpse of the great lighthouse of Alexandria. "It could be any minute now," the captain had told us the previous day at twilight, and Bethesda had staked a place at the prow of the ship, her gaze set on the southern horizon, where blue-green sea met azure sky. Slowly the blues darkened to deepest purple and then to black; the sky was pierced with stars, and starlight lit the face of the deep; a sliver of moon traversed the sky, and still the lighthouse did not appear. It seemed we were not quite as close to Alexandria as the captain thought, yet I trusted his navigation; the voyage from Rome had so far been quick and uneventful, and even I could tell from looking at the stars that our course was now due south. The steady breeze at our backs was taking us across a calm sea directly toward Egypt.

All night I stood beside Bethesda, joining in her vigil. The night was warm, but occasionally she shivered, and I held her close. Many years ago we had departed from Alexandria by ship, watching the flame atop the lighthouse for hours as it gradually dwindled and finally vanished from sight. Now we were returning to Alexandria, and again we stood together on a ship, scanning the horizon for a first glimpse of that same undying flame.

"There!" she said, this time in a whisper. I squinted uncertainly; might the glimmer of light be merely a star twinkling just above the water's edge? But no, the light was too steady to be a star, and as we watched, little by little it grew brighter.

"Pharos," I whispered, for that was the name of the lighthouse, as well as the name of the island upon which it was built—the oldest and by far the greatest lighthouse in all the world. With the brightest flame ever produced by men, set atop the tallest tower ever built, for hundreds of years it had guided ships to Alexandria.

"Alexandria!" Bethesda whispered. She had been born there, and there I had met her during my travels as a young man. After I took her home with me to Rome, neither of us had ever returned. But no one forgets Alexandria. Over the years I had dreamed often of the city's broad avenues and magnificent temples. In the last few days, as the ship brought us ever nearer, memories had come flooding back in overwhelming profusion—not only sights and sounds but also flavors and smells and tactile sensations. I swooned, remembering waves of heat from the paving stones of the Canopic Way on a hot day, the dry kiss of a desert breeze through the palm trees, the cool refreshment of a swim in Lake Mareotis under the looming skyline of the city.

During the journey, Bethesda and I made a game of sharing memories, trading them back and forth like children playing tag. Either of us had merely to say a word to spark a memory that sparked yet more memories. Now, with the light of the Pharos twinkling in the distance, she squeezed my hand and whispered, "Scarab."

I sighed. "The jeweler with that little shop just down the hill from the temple of Serapis."

Bethesda nodded. "Yes, the one with the crooked nose."

"No, that was his assistant. The jeweler himself—"

"—had a bald spot and a wattle neck. Yes, I remember now."

"How could you forget, Bethesda? He accused you of stealing that scarab pendant from right under his assistant's crooked nose."

"The assistant's nose wasn't the only thing crooked about him. *He* was the one who took the scarab!"

"As I eventually discovered. The poor fellow should be finishing up his sentence in the salt mines about now."

"Poor fellow? He should never have allowed the blame to fall on an innocent girl." Her eyes flashed, and I saw a glimmer of the mischievous spirit that still dwelled in her, despite the terrible illness that had befallen her. I squeezed her hand. She squeezed it back, and my heart ached at the feebleness of her grip.

Bethesda's illness was our reason for coming to Egypt. For months it had plagued her, sapping her of strength and joy, eluding every cure propounded by every physician we consulted in Rome. At last Bethesda herself proposed a cure: She must return to Egypt. She must bathe in the waters of the Nile. Only then could she be made whole again.

How did Bethesda come to this knowledge? I had no idea. One morning she simply announced that we must be off to Alexandria. Having come into a bit of money, I had no excuse to refuse her. To act as our bodyguard, and because he originally came from Alexandria, we took with us the newest member of my household, a hulking young mute named Rupa. We also brought along my two slave boys, the brothers Mopsus and Androcles; their quickness and cleverness would hopefully outweigh their penchant for getting into trouble. We were the ship's only passengers. In such troubled times, few traveled who could possibly avoid it.

Rupa and the boys slept, as did most of the ship's crew. In the stillness of that final hour before dawn, it seemed that Bethesda and I were the only two people alive, and that the beacon of the Pharos, growing gradually, steadily brighter, shone for us alone.

Little by little the sky lightened. The sea's black luster faded to the color of slate. A faint red glow suffused the eastern horizon. The light of the Pharos seemed to grow fainter, outshone by the sudden flicker of red flame that announced the rising of Helios in his fiery chariot.

I sensed a change on the ship. I looked behind us to see that the deck was now swarming with sailors tending to ropes and riggings. How long had they been there? I seemed to have dozed while watching the dawn, yet I could have sworn that I never closed my eyes. The light of the Pharos had bemused me. I blinked and shook my head. I looked more closely at the sailors. Their expressions were grim, not joyful. Among them I saw the captain; his face was grimmest of all. He was an affable fellow, a grizzled Greek about my own age, sixty or so, and we had become friendly over the course of the voyage. He saw me staring and strode close by me on his way to bark an order at some of his men. Under his breath he muttered, "Red sky. Don't like it."

I turned toward Bethesda. Her eyes narrowed; her lips parted; she continued to stare at the beacon of the Pharos, oblivious to the commotion behind us. For the first time I could barely discern the tower of the lighthouse itself, a tiny sliver of pale stone beneath the bright point of light.

"So close!" Bethesda whispered.

We had only to stay on course and maintain a steady progress, and the tower of the Pharos would little by little grow larger and more distinct—to the height of a fingernail, a finger, a hand. We would begin to make out the fluted stonework that decorated its exterior; we would see the statues of gods and kings that ornamented its base and the balconies of its upper reaches. Beyond the Pharos, we would see the crowded ships in the great harbor and the jumble of rooftops that made up the skyline of Alexandria.

I felt a tug at the sleeve of my tunic and turned to see little Androcles staring up at me. His slightly bigger brother, Mopsus, stood behind him, and looming over them was Rupa, rubbing the sleep from his eyes.

"Master," said Androcles, "what's wrong?"

From amidships the captain spared a glance at me and barked, "Keep those two boys out of the way!" Then, to his sailors: "Down the sail! Raise your oars!"

A sudden wind gusted from the west, ripping a loose flap of sail from the hands of the sailors who were attempting to furl it. The deck abruptly pitched and rocked beneath us. The hull beneath the prow slapped the waves, and we were covered with salty spume. Bethesda blinked and shivered and at last took her eyes from the Pharos. She looked at me dully. "Husband, what's happening?"

"I'm not sure," I said. "Perhaps we should take shelter aft." I took her arm, intending to guide her and my other charges to the small cabin at the stern of the ship. But it was too late. The storm, arising from nowhere, was upon us, and the captain made a frantic gesture ordering us to stay where we were, out of his sailors' way. "Grab hold of whatever you can!" he shouted, his voice barely audible above a sudden shriek of wind. Raindrops stung my face and left grit in my mouth. Sand grated against my teeth; I cursed and spat. I had heard of such storms when I lived at Alexandria but had never experienced one—whirling desert sandstorms that swept out over the sea, combining with furious rainstorms to pelt wind-tossed ships with both water and earth. Once after such a storm a ship had sailed into the harbor at Alexandria weighted down with sand, the broiling sun having burned away the water to leave miniature sand dunes piled high on the decks.

The red light of the rising sun became a memory, banished by howling darkness. Bethesda pressed close to me. I opened my eyes just enough to see that Rupa was nearby, clutching the boys with both arms, yet somehow managing to hold fast to the ship's rail. Mopsus and Androcles hid their faces against his broad chest.

As quickly as it had struck, the lashing wind died down. The howling diminished but did not cease; it seemed merely to draw back in all directions, surrounding us but no longer touching us. A hole opened in the sky above us, showing an incongruous patch of blue amid the swirling darkness all around.

"Can you see the lighthouse?" Bethesda whispered.

I gazed beyond the prow into a mist of deepest purple pierced by flashes of opalescent gray. I saw no hint of the horizon, much less a glimpse of the Pharos beacon. I had the uncanny sensation that Alexandria no longer lay off the prow, anyway; the ship had been so spun about that I couldn't begin to guess which direction was southward. I looked at the captain, who stood amidships, breathing hard but otherwise stock-still, gripping a taut length of rigging with such force that his knuckles were white.

"Have you ever seen a storm like it?" I said, lowering my voice instead of raising it, for the circle of stillness around the ship was unnerving.

The captain made no answer, but from his silence I knew that he was as confounded as I was. "Strange days," he finally said, "in the heavens as on earth."

The comment required no explanation. Everywhere and at all times men were on the lookout for portents and omens. Since the day that Caesar crossed the Rubicon River and marched on Rome with his army, drawing the whole world into ruinous civil war, not a day had passed that could be called normal. I myself had witnessed battles on sea and on land, had been trapped in cities under siege, had been nearly trampled by starving, desperate citizens rioting in the Roman Forum. I had seen men burned alive at sea and men drowned in a tunnel beneath the earth. I had done things of which I had previously thought myself incapable—killed a man in cold blood, disowned my beloved son, fallen in love with a stranger who died in my arms. I had deliberately turned my back on Caesar and his mad ambitions, yet Caesar continued to call me his friend; I had done a better job of alienating Caesar's rival Pompey, who had tried to strangle me with his own hands. Chaos reigned on earth, and in the heavens men beheld its reflection: Birds were seen to fly backwards; temples were struck by lightning; blood-red clouds formed visions of contesting armies. In the days just before we left for Alexandria, word had reached Rome of a momentous turn of events: Caesar and Pompey had met at Pharsalus in Greece, and, if the reports could be trusted, Pompey's forces had been utterly destroyed. The world held its breath, awaiting the next gambit in the great game. It was no surprise, then, that in such an uncanny storm, a man like our captain could not help but see yet another manifestation of the chaos that had been loosed by the dogs of war.

As if to confirm this superstitious dread, the circle of blue sky above us abruptly vanished, and the ship was again lashed by rain. But this rain carried no grit; something larger struck my face, startling me. Bethesda slid downward, eluding my embrace. She knelt to pick up the thing that flopped about on the deck. It slipped from her fingers, but she nimbly retrieved it. I gave a start and shuddered, expecting Bethesda to squeal and cast the wriggling creature away from her, but instead she cradled it in her hands and cooed with delight.

"Do you see what it is, husband? A tiny Nile frog! From out of the sky, and miles from the Delta. Impossible, yet here it is! It must be a sign from the gods, surely!"

"But a sign of what?" I whispered, grunting in disgust as another of the clammy creatures fell from the sky and struck my face. I looked about and saw that the deck was alive with the leaping creatures. Some of the sailors laughed; some wrinkled their noses in disgust; some jumped to avoid being touched by the frogs and bellowed in fright.

A flash of lightning split the sky, followed almost at once by a peal of thunder that rattled my teeth. The frog in Bethesda's hands leaped free, over the parapet and into the void. The deck spun beneath our feet, making me dizzy. I was overwhelmed by a strange illusion that the wind had borne the ship aloft and that we were skimming above the waves, flying through the air.

I lost all sense of time, but hours must have passed while we clutched at one another and braced ourselves against the power of the storm. Then, at last, the sea abruptly grew calm. Black clouds receded in all directions, tumbling back upon themselves so that they seemed to pile up at the distant horizons like mountain walls, steep, polished, and black, tipped along their ragged crests with fire, and opening ever and again with flashes of intolerable splendor, while the bases were scrawled over with lightning like a written scroll. The sun above our heads was small and as red as blood, obscured by a thin, black shroud of vapor. Never in all my travels on land or sea had I beheld anything like the uncanny light that suffused the world in that moment—a lurid glow that seemed to come from no particular direction. But before us, far in the distance, there was one break of clear blue sky on the horizon, where yellow light shone upon a sparkling emerald sea. The captain saw the opening in the gloom and ordered his men to sail toward it.

The sail was unfurled. The oarsmen returned to their places. The break on the horizon was so distinct that I almost expected to emerge from the gloom all at once, as one emerges from the mouth of a cave. Instead, as the oarsmen made steady progress, raising and dipping their oars in unison, we moved gradually from a world of darkness into a world of light. Above our heads the black mist thinned and dispersed, and the sun turned from blood-red to gold. To our right, a strip of low brown land appeared on the horizon; we were proceeding eastward, and the westering sun, warming our rain-soaked shoulders and backs, was at least a couple of hours past midday. I looked over the parapet and saw that the water was a confluence of green and brown, the brown being mud from the Nile. The storm had blown us well past Alexandria, to some point beyond the broad, fan-shaped Delta of the Nile.

So set was the captain on reaching calmer waters that he took no notice of the several ships that lay dead ahead of us, their sails as bright as ivory in the glaring sunlight. Some of the vessels appeared to be warships. Such a group, encountered closer to Alexandria, would have given no cause for alarm, for there the harbor and its guardian fleet would have offered protection from vagabonds and pirates. But our location appeared to be far from any port or harbor of consequence, so that we might as well have been on the open sea. We were acutely vulnerable to robbery and attack. Even as I was considering this, the captain finally appeared to take notice of the vessels ahead of us. He gave an order to veer southward, toward land, even though that arid, featureless strip of shoreline appeared to offer very little in the way of succor or concealment.

But the other ships had already spotted us, and whatever their intentions, seemed unwilling to let us go without an encounter. Two smaller vessels struck out toward us.

The captain maintained a cool expression, only a slight squint betraying his anxiety as he peered toward the pursuing ships; but in his command to the rowers to accelerate, a note of fear rang out as clearly as a trumpet's call. They doubled their speed so abruptly that the deck gave a slight lurch beneath us.

"Rupa!" I said, intending merely to gain his attention; but the hulking mute anticipated my query, and reached into his tunic to discreetly show me that his dagger was readily at hand. Little Mopsus, seeing the glint of Rupa's blade, swallowed hard. His younger brother seized the occasion to give him a teasing nudge. I found myself jealous of Androcles's naive courage. There are few fates more dreaded by travelers than the prospect of being boarded at sea by hostile sailors, far from any prospect of rescue. Even the mercy of the gods is rarely known to be dispensed at sea; perhaps the glint of sunlight on water obscures their view from the heavens. I reached into my tunic to test the grip of my own dagger. If worse came to worst, I might at least be able to spare Bethesda the degradations of capture at sea. With streaks of silver in her black hair, she might no longer be young, but even in her weakened state she was still desirable, at least to my eyes.

We made good speed, but the pursuing ships were faster. As the shoreline drew only slightly closer, the pursuers bore down on us, their white sails full of wind. Armed men populated the decks. They were warships, not trading vessels.

It was no use attempting to elude them, but the captain panicked. Having kept a cool head throughout the storm, which might have capsized the ship and killed us all in an instant, he lost his head when confronted with a human menace. I scowled at his misjudgment; if an encounter was inevitable, forcing the pursuers to give chase would only stir excitement in their blood, making even men with innocuous intentions more dangerous to deal with. He would have been wiser to trim sail and turn about to meet them with whatever dignity and bravado he could muster, but instead he gave a hoarse order to row at full speed.

The shoreline grew nearer, yet showed no more features than before; it was little more than a dun-colored smudge along the horizon, without even a palm tree to betray any sign of life. That hopeless shore mirrored the hopelessness I felt at that moment; but Bethesda squeezed my hand and whispered, "Perhaps these are Caesar's ships, husband. Didn't you say that Caesar himself might head for Egypt next, if the reports of his success in Greece were true?"

"Yes."

"And Caesar has always been your friend, hasn't he, husband—even when you've been less than friendly to him?"

I almost smiled at this sardonic jibe; Bethesda was still capable of needling me, despite the malady that plagued her. Anything that gave evidence of her old spirit was cause for hope.

"You're right," I said. "Those fellows pursuing us have the look of Levantines, but they could well be Caesar's men, or men he's won over from Pompey, if in fact Pompey is vanquished or dead. If that fleet *does* belong to Caesar, and we've encountered him on his way to Alexandria, then . . ."

I left the thought unspoken, for Bethesda knew what I was about to say, and to actually speak his name aloud would be too painful; if he had survived the travails of battle, very likely my adopted son Meto would be by Caesar's side. I had seen him last in Massilia, in Gaul, where I had upbraided him and publicly disowned him for the intrigues and deceits he had practiced on Caesar's behalf. No one in my family, least of all Bethesda, quite understood why I had turned my back on a son I had adopted, who had always been so dear to me; I myself did not quite comprehend the violence of my reaction. If these were Caesar's ships, and if Caesar was among them, and if Meto was with Caesar—what a jest of the gods that would be, to snatch me from a quiet arrival in Alexandria and set me down in the midst of Caesar's fleet, faced with a reunion I could not bear to contemplate.

These thoughts, as gloomy as they were, at least served to distract me from imagining a more dreadful alternative—that the ships pursuing us were not from Caesar after all. These men could be pirates, or renegade soldiers, or something even worse. . . .

Whoever they were, they were practiced sailors with considerable skill at pursuit and capture. Coordinating their movements with admirable precision, they drew apart so as to pull alongside us both to starboard and port, then slowed their speed to match ours. They were close enough now so that I could see the leering faces of the armed men on deck. Were they bent on our destruction, or merely exhilarated by the chase? From the ship to our starboard, an officer called out, "Give it up, captain! We've caught you fair and square. Raise your oars, or else we'll get rid of them for you!"

The threat was literal; I had seen warships employ just such a maneuver, drawing alongside an enemy vessel, veering close, then withdrawing their oars so as to shear off the other ship's still-extended oars, rendering it helpless. With two ships, such a maneuver could be executed on both sides of us simultaneously. Given the skill our pursuers had so far displayed, I had no doubt that they could pull it off.

The captain was still in a panic, frozen to the spot and speechless. His men looked to him for orders, but received none. We proceeded at full speed, the pursuers matching us and drawing closer on either side.

"By Hercules!" I shouted, tearing myself from Bethesda to run to the captain's side. I gripped his arm. "Give the order to raise oars!"

The captain looked at me blankly. I slapped him across the face. He bolted and moved to strike back at me, then the glimmer of reason lit his eyes. He took a deep breath and raised his arms.

"Lift oars!" he cried. "Trim sail!"

The sailors, heaving with exertion, obeyed at once. Our pursuers, with flawless seamanship, mimicked our actions, and all three ships remained side by side even as the waves began to brake our progress.

The ship to our starboard drew even closer. The soldier who had ordered us to stop spoke again, though he was now so close that he hardly needed to raise his voice. I saw that he wore the insignia of a Roman centurion. "Identify yourself!"

The captain cleared his throat. "This is the *Andromeda,* an Athenian ship with a Greek crew."

"And you?"

"Cretheus, owner and captain."

"Why did you flee when we approached?"

"What fool wouldn't have done the same?"

The centurion laughed. At least he was in good humor. "Where do you sail from?"

"Ostia, the port city of Rome."

"Destination?"

"Alexandria. We'd be there now if not for—"

"Just answer the questions! Cargo?"

"Olive oil and wine. In Alexandria we'll be picking up raw linen and—"

"Passengers?"

"Only one party, a fellow and his wife—"

"Is that him, beside you?"

I spoke up. "My name is Gordianus. I'm a Roman citizen."

"Are you now?" The centurion peered at me. "How many in your party?"

"My wife, a bodyguard, two slave boys."

"Are we free to sail on?" said the captain.

"Not yet. All ships without exception are to be boarded and searched, and the names of all passengers passed on to the Great One himself.

Nothing for you to be alarmed about; standard procedure. Now turn about, and we'll escort you to the fleet."

I cast a wistful glance at the bleak, receding shore. We had not fallen into the clutches of Caesar, or pirates, or renegade soldiers. It was much worse than that. Only one man in the whole world presumed to call himself *Magnus,* Great One: Pompey. The Fates had delivered me into the hands of a man who had vowed to see me dead.

2

The "fleet," as the centurion had called it, was a more ragtag assembly than it had appeared to be at a distance. There were a few warships, to be sure, but all seemed to be in varying degrees of disrepair, with thread-bare sails, battered hulls, and mismatched oars. The other ships were transports. The soldiers loaded on their decks had the distracted, ill-disciplined look of conscripted slaves; I had seen enough of those since the outbreak of the war, for both sides in desperate bids for advantage had drafted gladiators, farmhands, and even clerical slaves into their ranks. These soldiers, with their squints and blank expressions and dented armor, were certainly not the crack troops whom Pompey had gathered for his campaign in Greece; those presumably had vanished at Pharsalus, either slain by Caesar's legions or else pardoned and absorbed into Caesar's ranks.

Pompey had escaped from Pharsalus with his life, but not much else. Rumor had it that his defeat had caught him completely by surprise. The engagement had begun at daybreak; as the battle commenced, so certain had Pompey been of victory that he withdrew to his command pavilion to relax and enjoy a midday repast. But Caesar's forces abruptly overran the opposition and sent them fleeing. When they reached Pompey's position, they stormed the ramparts and went streaming into the camp. Caesar himself was the first to reach Pompey's pavilion; when he entered, he found sumptuous furnishings strewn with pillows still warm to the touch, a banquet table set with silver plates piled high with steaming delicacies, and amphorae of fine Falernian wine not yet unsealed. If Pompey had intended a victory banquet, the celebration had been premature; at the last moment, learning that all was lost, the Great One threw off his scarlet cloak and the other badges of his rank, mounted the first horse he could find, and rode through the rear gate of the camp, barely escaping with his life.

And now, here was Pompey with a ragtag fleet of warriors anchored off the coast of Egypt; and here was I, in Pompey's power.

My stomach growled, and I realized that I had grown hungry pacing the deck of the little ship and waiting for word from the centurion, who had diligently recorded my name before rowing off to his commander's ship for further orders. The *Andromeda*'s captain sat nearby, giving me sidelong looks. At last he cleared his throat and spoke up.

"Look, Gordianus, you're not . . . I mean to say, you're not *dangerous*—are you?"

I smiled. "That depends. Do you think I could take you in a fair fight, Cretheus? We're about the same age, the same build—"

"That's not what I meant, and you know it."

"Am I dangerous to know, you mean? Am I dangerous cargo?"

He nodded. "This is Pompey we've run into. I've never had dealings with the man myself, but everyone knows his reputation. He's used to getting what he wants, and stopping at nothing to get it."

I nodded, remembering a famous comment from early in the Great One's career, when he ran roughshod over the Sicilians. They complained of his illegal tactics in bringing order to their island. Pompey's response: "Stop quoting laws to us; we carry swords!" Pompey had always done whatever was necessary to prevail, and throughout his long career he had never tasted defeat—until now.

"Considering what happened at Pharsalus, I imagine the Great One must be in a rather foul mood," I said.

"So you *do* know him, Gordianus?"

I nodded. "Pompey and I are acquainted."

"And will he be pleased or displeased when that officer tells him you're on my ship?"

I laughed without mirth. "Displeased to learn that I'm still breathing. Pleased that he has a chance to do something about that."

The captain wrinkled his brow. "He hates you that much?"

"Yes."

"Because you're a partisan of Caesar?"

I shook my head. "I am not and never was in Caesar's camp, despite the fact that my son—my disowned son . . ." I left the sentence unfinished.

"You have a son who fights with Caesar?"

"They're closer than that. Meto sleeps in the same tent, eats from the same bowl. He helps write the propaganda Caesar passes off as memoirs."

The captain looked at me with fresh eyes. "Who'd have thought . . . ?"

"That such a common-looking fellow as myself would have such a close connection to the world's new lord and master?"

"Something like that. What did you do to offend Pompey, then?"

I leaned against the rail and stared into the water. "That, captain, is my own business."

"My business, if it means Pompey decides to confiscate my ship and throw me overboard, to punish me for taking you as a passenger. I'll ask you again: What did you do to offend the Great One?"

"Even as Caesar was marching on Rome and Pompey was scrambling to escape, a favorite young cousin of Pompey's was murdered. Just before he left Rome, Pompey charged me with finding the killer."

"And you failed to do so?"

"Not exactly. But the Great One was not pleased with the outcome." I thought of Pompey as I had last seen him—his hands around my throat, his eyes bulging, determined to see me dead. He had been in the process of fleeing Italy by ship, disembarking from the port of Brundisium even as Caesar stormed the city. I'd barely managed to escape, wrenching free from Pompey's grip, diving into deep water, surfacing amid flaming flotsam, dragging myself to the shore while Pompey sailed off to fight another day.

I shook my head to clear it. "You've done nothing to insult the Great One's dignity, captain. He has no reason to punish you. If Pompey confiscates your ship, it'll be because he needs more room for that sad-looking bunch of soldiers crowded on these transports. But he'll need someone to sail this ship, so why throw you overboard? Ah, but perhaps we'll know the Great One's intentions soon enough. I see a skiff approaching, and I believe it's carrying our friend, that centurion who detained us."

The skiff pulled alongside. The centurion called up to us. "Ahoy, captain."

"Ahoy, yourself. Your men finished searching my cargo an hour ago. What now? Am I free to go?"

"Not yet. That passenger you're carrying . . ."

I leaned over the rail to show my face. "Are you referring to me, Centurion?"

"I am. Are you the same Gordianus who's called the Finder, who lives in Rome?"

"I suppose there's no point in denying it."

"You must be a rather important fellow, then. The Great One himself would like a word with you. If you'll join us here in the skiff, we'll escort you to his galley."

Bethesda, who had been standing to one side with Rupa and the boys, drew near and gripped my hand.

"Husband—"

"I'll be all right, I'm sure," I said.

She squeezed my fingers and averted her eyes. "We've come so far, husband."

"All the way back to where we first began, you and I. Well, almost all the way. We didn't quite make it to Alexandria, but we did see the lighthouse, didn't we?"

She shook her head. "I should never have insisted on this journey."

"Nonsense! These days, no place is safer than any other. We came to Egypt so that you could bathe in the Nile and cleanse yourself of the malady that plagues you, and so you must. Promise me you will, no matter whether I'm there to see it or—"

"Don't say such a thing!" she whispered.

I took both her hands, but only for a moment. "The Great One doesn't like to be kept waiting," I said, reluctantly letting her fingertips slip from mine. "Look after her while I'm gone, Rupa. And you boys, behave yourselves!" Androcles and Mopsus both looked at me uncertainly, sensing trouble.

A man of my years should never be obliged to climb down a rope ladder into a skiff, but I managed the difficult descent with more grace than I thought possible. Perhaps the gods were watching after all, and thought it fitting to allow an old Roman to retain a shred of dignity on the way to meet his destiny.

"A beautiful day," I said to the centurion. "Not a sign of that storm that blew us here. You'd never know it happened. Nothing but blue skies."

The centurion nodded but did not speak. His reserves of bonhomie were apparently spent. His face was grim.

"Not a very cheerful group," I said, looking at the rowers. They kept their eyes straight ahead and made no response.

We rowed past warships and transports to the center of the little fleet. Pompey's galley stood out from the rest. Its sail was trimmed with crimson, its armored hull gleamed in the sunlight, and the soldiers on the deck were by far the best outfitted of any in sight. It was clearly the handsomest ship in the fleet, and yet, in some intangible way, the gloomiest. Was I only imagining the air of dread that seemed to thicken around us as each stroke of the oars brought us closer?

I was spared the challenge of attempting an ascent by ladder, for the galley was equipped with a ramp that unfolded from the deck. I stepped onto it, swaying a bit. When the centurion gripped my elbow to steady me, I turned to thank him; but the way he averted his eyes, as if the very sight of me might contaminate him, unnerved me. Mustering my courage, I turned and ascended the ramp.

The moment I stepped onto the deck, I was searched. My dagger was discovered and taken from me. I was told to remove my shoes, and those were taken as well; I suppose an enterprising assassin might find some way to conceal a deadly weapon in his shoe. Even the cord I used to belt my tunic was taken. Armed guards escorted me to the cabin at the stern of the galley. Its door stood open, and well before we reached it, I heard Pompey's raised voice from within.

"Tell the brat and his pet eunuch that I'll expect to meet them ashore tomorrow at noon—not an hour earlier and not an hour later. I'll be able to judge how subservient these Egyptians intend to be by what they feed me for lunch. If they spring for crocodile steak and swallows' tongues with a decent Italian wine, I'll tell the boy-king to wipe my bottom for me as well. If they think they can get away with serving Nile mullets and Egyptian beer, I'll know I have my work cut out for me." This was followed by a harsh laugh that made my blood run cold.

Another voice replied, in lower tones, "As you command, Great One," and a moment later an officer emerged from the cabin, wearing full regalia and carrying a plumed helmet under his arm. He spied me and raised an eyebrow. "Is this the one called Gordianus, Centurion Macro?"

"It is, Commander."

"Well, citizen Gordianus, I don't envy you. But then, you probably don't envy me, either. I'm off to the mainland to parlay with that haughty boy-king and his insufferable advisers. The Great One expects to receive a fitting welcome when he goes ashore tomorrow, but one gets the distinct impression that the boy-king had rather be staging another battle against his sister and her rebels in the desert." The officer shook his head. "This sort of thing was so much easier before Pharsalus! I had merely to snap my fingers, and the locals cringed. Now they look at me as if . . ." He seemed to realize he had said too much, and scowled. "Ah, well, perhaps I'll see you again when I get back. Or perhaps not." He gave me a nudge in the ribs that was much too hard to be friendly, and then he pushed past me. I watched the officer descend the ramp and disappear from sight.

While I was distracted, one of the guards had apparently announced my arrival, for without further preamble Centurion Macro pushed me toward the cabin. I stepped inside, and he shut the door behind me.

The little room seemed dark after the bright sunshine. As my eyes adjusted, the first face I saw was that of a young woman, a strikingly beautiful Roman matron who sat in one corner with her hands folded on her lap, fixing me with a condescending stare. Even at sea, she had managed to take considerable pains with her appearance. Her hair was tinted with henna and piled atop her head in a complicated coif. Her wine-dark stola was belted about her shapely torso with chains of gold, and more gold shimmered amid the jewel-encrusted pectoral that adorned her throat and the lapis baubles that dangled from her earlobes. Pompey's young wife had no doubt taken a great deal of jewelry with her when she fled from Rome with her husband; she must have lugged that jewelry from camp to camp as the arena of battle moved. If any woman had learned to look her best while on the move, and if any woman felt she had earned the right to wear her best jewels for any occasion, it was the long-suffering Cornelia.

Pompey was not her first husband. Her previous marriage had been to Publius Crassus, the son of Marcus Crassus, the lifelong rival of Caesar and Pompey. When the elder Crassus set out to conquer Parthia some five years ago, he took his son with him; both perished when the Parthians massacred the invading Romans. Still young and beautiful, and famously well versed in literature, music, geometry, and philosophy, Cornelia had not remained a widow long. Some said her marriage to Pompey was a political union; others said it was a love-match. Whatever the nature of their relationship, through good times and bad she had remained steadfastly at his side.

"So it *is* you, Finder!" The voice, so harsh it gave me a start, came from another corner. Pompey stepped forward, emerging from the deepest shadows in the room.

On the last occasion I saw him, he had been possessed by an almost supernatural fury. There was a glint of that same fury even now in his eyes. He was dressed as if for battle, in gleaming armor, and carried himself stiffly, his chin high, his shoulders erect—a model of Roman dignity and self-control. But along with the glint of fury in his eyes, there was a glimmer of something else—fear, uncertainty, defeat. Those emotions, held carefully in check, nevertheless undermined the stiffly formal facade he presented, and it seemed to me that behind his gleaming armor and scowling countenance, Pompey the Great was a hollow man.

Hollow, I thought—but hardly harmless. He fixed me with a gaze so intense that I had to struggle not to lower my eyes. When he saw that I refused to quail, he barked out a laugh.

"Gordianus! As defiant as ever—or merely stupid? No, not stupid. That can't be, since everyone credits you with being so very, very clever. But cleverness counts for nothing without the favor of the gods, and I think the gods must have deserted you, eh? For here you are, delivered into my hands—the last person on earth I should have thought to see today. And I must be the last person you expected to encounter!"

"We've followed different paths to the same place, Great One. Perhaps it's because the gods have withdrawn their favor from both of us."

He blanched. "You *are* a fool, and I shall see that you end like a fool. I'd thought you dead already when I left Brundisium, drowned like a rat after you jumped from my ship. Then Domitius Ahenobarbus joined me in Greece and told me he'd seen you alive in Massilia. 'Impossible!' I told him. 'You saw the Finder's lemur.' 'No, the man himself,' he assured me. And now you stand before me in the flesh, and it's Domitius who's become a lemur. Marc Antony chased him to ground like a fox at Pharsalus. Damn Antony! Damn Caesar! But who knows? Mark my words, Caesar will yet get his just deserts, and when he least expects it. The gods will abandon Caesar—like that!" He snapped his fingers. "One moment he'll be alive, plotting his next triumph, and the next moment—dead as King Numa! I see you scoff, Finder, but believe me, Caesar will yet receive his due."

What was he talking about? Did he have spies and assassins close to Caesar, plotting to do away with him? I stared back at Pompey and said nothing.

"Lower your eyes, damn you! A man in your position—think of those traveling with you, if not of yourself. You're all at my mercy!"

Would he really harm Bethesda to take vengeance on me? I tried to steady the quaver in my voice. "I'm traveling with a young mute of simple intelligence, two slave boys, and my wife, who is not well. I find it hard to believe that the Great One would stoop to exact vengeance on such—"

"Oh, shut up!" Pompey made a noise of disgust and looked sidelong at his wife. Some unspoken communication passed between them, and the exchange seemed to calm him. I sensed that Cornelia was his anchor, the one thing he could count on now that everything else, including his own judgment, had failed him so miserably.

Pompey now refused to look at me. "Go on, get out!" he said between clenched teeth.

I blinked, not ready to believe that he was dismissing me with my head still on my shoulders.

"Well, what are you waiting for?"

I turned to leave. "But don't think I'm done with you, Finder!" Pompey snapped. "At present I have too much on my mind to fully enjoy seeing the life torn out of you. After I've met with young King Ptolemy and my fortunes have returned to a firmer footing—then I'll summon you again, when I can deal with you at my leisure."

Centurion Macro accompanied me back to the skiff. "You look as pale as a fish belly," he said.

"Do I?"

"Mind your step, getting into the boat. I've been given orders that nothing untoward must happen to you."

"The dagger that was taken from me?"

He laughed. "You won't be seeing that again. Pompey says you mustn't hurt yourself."

3

Night fell. The sea was calm, the sky clear. Far away to the west, beyond the low marshland of the Nile Delta, I imagined I could descry the Pharos, a pinpoint of light upon an uncertain horizon.

"There!" I said to Bethesda, who stood beside me at the ship's rail. "Do you see it? The Pharos."

She squinted and frowned. "No."

"Are you sure?"

"My vision is dim tonight."

I held her close. "Do you feel unwell?"

She grimaced. "It seems such a small thing, now. To have come so far for such a petty purpose—"

"Not petty, wife. You must be well again."

"Toward what end? Our children are all grown."

"Eco and Diana both have given us grandchildren, and now Diana is expecting another."

"And no doubt they'll do a splendid job of raising them, with or without their grandmother. My time on this earth has been good, Master . . ."

Master? What was she thinking, to call me that? Many years had passed since I made her free and married her. From that day forward she had called me husband, and not once had I known her to slip and address me as her master. It was the return to Egypt, I told myself, calling her back to her past, confusing her about the present.

"Your time on this earth is far from over, wife."

"And your time, husband?" She gave no sign of noticing her earlier error. "When you came back today, I gave thanks to Isis, for it seemed a miracle. But the centurion forbade the captain to sail on. That means the Great One isn't done with you."

"The Great One has far greater concerns than me. He's come to seek King Ptolemy's assistance. All Pompey's other allies—the Eastern potentates and moneylenders and mercenaries who gave him their allegiance before Pharsalus—have deserted him. But his ties to Egypt are strong. If he can persuade King Ptolemy to take his side, then he yet has a hope to defeat Caesar. Egypt has grain and gold. Egypt even has a Roman army, garrisoned here for the last seven years to keep the peace."

"Something they've singularly failed to do, if Ptolemy is engaged in a civil war with his sister Cleopatra," said Bethesda.

"So it's ever been in Egypt, at least in our lifetimes. To gain power, the Ptolemaic siblings intermarry, conspire among themselves, even murder one another. Sister marrying brother, brother murdering sister—what a family! As savage and peculiar as those animal-headed gods the locals worship."

"Don't scoff! You're in the realm of those gods now, Master." She had done it again. I made no remark, but sighed and held her closer.

"So you see, Pompey has far too much to think about to be bothered with me." I said the words with all the conviction I could muster.

When sleep is distant, the night is long. Bethesda and I lay together on our little cot in the cramped passenger cabin, separated from Rupa and the boys by a flimsy screen woven from rushes. Rupa snored softly; the boys breathed steadily, submerged in the deep sleep of children. The ship rocked very slightly on the calm sea. I was weary, my mind numb, but sleep would not come.

Had it not been for the storm, we would have been in Alexandria that night, safe and snug in some inn in the Rhakotis district, with a steady floor beneath our feet and a proper roof above our heads, our bellies full of delicacies from the market, our heads awhirl with the sights and sounds of a teeming city I had not seen since I was young. Come the dawn, I would have hired a boat to take us up the long canal to the banks of the Nile. Bethesda would do what she had come to do, and I would do what I had come to do—for I, too, had a reason for visiting the Nile, a purpose about which Bethesda knew nothing. . . .

At the foot of our sleeping cot, where it served each morning as a dressing table for Bethesda and each evening as a dining table for all five of us, was a traveling trunk. Inside the trunk, nestled amid clothing, shoes, coins, and cosmetics, was a sealed bronze urn. Its contents were the ashes of a woman called Cassandra. She had been Rupa's sister, and more than that, his protector, for Rupa was simple as well as mute, and could not make his own way in the world. Cassandra had been very special to me, as well, though our relationship had very nearly proven fatal to us both. I had managed to keep the affair secret from Bethesda only because of her illness, which had dulled her intuition along with her other senses. Cassandra and Rupa had come to Rome from Alexandria; Rupa wanted to return his sister to the land of their youth and to scatter her ashes in the Nile, restoring her remains to the great cycle of earth, air, fire, and water. The urn that contained her ashes loomed in my mind like a fifth passenger among us, unseen and unheard but often in my thoughts.

If all had gone well, tomorrow Bethesda would have bathed in the Nile, and Cassandra's ashes would have been mingled with the river's sacred waters: duties discharged, health restored, the closing of a dark chapter, and, I had hoped, the opening of a brighter one. But that was not how things had turned out.

Was I to blame for my own fate? I had killed a man; disowned my beloved Meto; fallen in love with Cassandra, whose ashes were only a few feet away. Was it any wonder the gods had abandoned me? For sixty-two years they had watched over me and rescued me from one scrape after another, either because they were fond of me, or merely because they were amused by the peculiar twists and turns of my life's story. Had they now grown disinterested, distracted by the grander drama of the war that had swept over the world? Or had they watched my actions, judged me harshly, and found me no longer worthy of life? Surely some god, somewhere, had been laughing that afternoon when Pompey and I met, two broken men brought to the edge of ruin.

Thus ran my thoughts that night, and they kept sleep far away.

Bethesda slept and must have dreamed, to judge by her low murmurs and the occasional twitching of her fingers. Her dreams appeared to be uneasy, but I did not rouse her; wake a sleeper in mid-dream, and the dark phantoms linger; but let a dream run its course, and the sleeper wakes with no memory of it. Soon enough Bethesda might have to face a nightmare from which there would be no waking. How would I die? Would Bethesda be forced to witness the act? Afterwards, how would she remember me? Above all else, a Roman must strive to face his end with dignity. I would have to remember that and think of Bethesda and the last memory of me she would carry, the next time the Great One summoned me.

At some point in the middle of that very long, very dark night, Bethesda stirred and sought my hand with hers. She twined her fingers with mine and squeezed them so tightly that I feared she must be in pain.

"What's wrong?" I whispered.

She rolled toward me and pressed a finger to my lips to silence me. In the darkness I could see the glimmer of her eyes, but I could not make out her expression. I murmured against the finger pressed to my lips. "Bethesda, beloved—"

"Hush!" she whispered.

"But—"

She removed her finger and replaced it with her lips, pressing her mouth to mine in a deep, breathless kiss.

We had not kissed that way in a very long time, not since the onset of her illness. Her kiss reminded me of Cassandra, and for a brief moment I experienced the illusion that it was Cassandra beside me in the bed, her ashes made flesh again. But as the kiss continued, my memory of Cassandra faded, and I was reminded of Bethesda herself, when she and I both had been very young and our passion was so fresh it seemed that such a thing had never before been known in the world—a portal to an undiscovered country.

She pressed herself against me and slid her arms around me. The smell of her hair was intoxicating; neither illness nor travel had stopped her from the ritual of washing, combing, and scenting the great mane of black shot with silver that cascaded almost to her waist. She rolled atop me, and her tresses enclosed me, sweeping across my bare shoulders and over my cheeks, mingling with the tears that abruptly flowed from my eyes.

As the boat swayed gently on the waves, with Rupa and the boys and the urn that contained Cassandra very close, we made love, quietly, slowly, with a depth of feeling we had not shared in a very long time. I feared at first that she might be expending herself beyond her limits, but it was she who set the pace, bringing me quickly to the point of ecstasy and then holding me there at her leisure, stretching each moment to exquisite infinity.

The paroxysm wracked her body, and then again, and on the third occasion I joined her, peaking and melting into oblivion. We separated but remained side by side, breathing as one, and I sensed that her body had relaxed completely—so completely that I gripped her hand, fearing there might be no response. But she squeezed my fingers in return, even as the rest of her remained utterly limp, as if her joints had loosened and her limbs turned as soft as wax. It was only in that moment that I realized just how stiffly, for month after month, she had been holding her body, even when she slept. She released a long sigh of contentment.

"Bethesda," I said quietly.

"Sleep," she whispered.

The word seemed to act as a magical spell. Almost at once I felt consciousness desert me as I sank into the warm, boundless ocean of Somnus. The last things I heard were a high-pitched whisper followed by a stifled giggle. At some point Androcles and Mopsus must have awakened and been richly amused by the noises in the room. In other circumstances I might have been angry, but I must have fallen asleep with a smile on my face, for that was how I awoke.

The smile faded quickly as I remembered exactly where I was. I blinked my eyes at the dim light that leaked around the cabin door. I sensed movement. From outside the cabin I heard the sailors calling to one another. The sail snapped. The oars creaked. The captain had set sail—but to where?

I felt a thrill of hope. Had we somehow, under cover of darkness, escaped from Pompey's fleet? Was Alexandria in sight? I scrambled from the cot, slipping into my tunic as I opened the door and stepped out.

My hopes evaporated in an instant. We were in the midst of Pompey's fleet, surrounded by ships on all sides. They were all in motion, taking advantage of an onshore breeze to draw closer to the coast.

The captain saw me and approached. "Get a good night's sleep?" he asked. "I figured you needed it. Didn't have the heart to wake you."

"What's happening?"

"I'm not entirely sure, but I suspect it has something to do with *them*." He pointed toward the shore. Where on the previous day the beach had been a featureless smear of brown lacking any sign of life, this morning it was thronged with a great multitude of soldiers arrayed in formal ranks, their spears casting long shadows and their armor gleaming in the slanting, early morning sunlight, the plumes atop their helmets appearing to shiver as the leaves of certain trees shiver in the slightest wind. Brightly colored pavilions with streaming pennants had been erected atop the low hills. The largest and most impressive of these pavilions was at the center of the host atop the highest of the hills. Beneath its canopy a throne sat atop a dais—a shimmering chair made of gold ornamented with jewels and worthy to seat a king. At the moment the throne was vacant, and though I squinted, I could not see beyond it into the royal tent.

"King Ptolemy's army," said the captain.

"And the boy-king himself, if that throne is any indication. He's come to parlay with Pompey."

"Some of those soldiers are outfitted like Romans."

"So they are," I said. "A Roman legion was garrisoned here seven years ago, to help the late king Ptolemy hold his throne and keep the peace. Some of those soldiers once served under Pompey, as I recall. They say the Romans stationed here have gone native, taking Egyptian wives and forgetting Roman ways. But they won't have forgotten Pompey. He's counting on them to rally to his side."

The captain, receiving a signal from a nearby ship, called to his men to raise their oars. The fleet had drawn as close to the shore as the shallow water would permit. I turned my eyes toward Pompey's galley and felt my heart sink. The small skiff that had transported me the previous day was headed toward us.

The skiff drew alongside. Centurion Macro did not speak, but merely cocked his head and motioned for me to board.

The captain spoke in my ear. "I hear the others stirring," he said. "Shall I wake them?"

I looked at the cabin door. "No. I said my farewells yesterday . . . and last night."

I descended the rope ladder. Spots swam before my eyes, and my heart began to race. I tried to remember that a Roman's dignity never matters so much as in the moment of his death, and that the substance of a man's life is summed up in the manner in which he faces his end. Stepping into the skiff, I stumbled and caused the boat to rock. Centurion Macro gripped my arm to steady me. None of the rowers smiled or sniggered; instead, they averted their eyes and mumbled prayers to ward off the misfortune portended by such a bad omen.

As we rowed toward Pompey's galley, I was determined to not look back. With that uncanny acumen a man gains over the years, I felt eyes on my back, yet still I kept my gaze straight ahead. But as we pulled alongside the galley, I could not resist a final glance over my shoulder. Quite tiny in the distance, I saw them all standing along the rail—not only the captain and all his sailors, but Rupa, rubbing the sleep from his eyes, and the boys wearing only the loincloths they slept in, and Bethesda in her sleeping gown. At the sight of me looking back, she raised her hands and covered her face.

Centurion Macro escorted me aboard. A crowd of officers had gathered at the prow of the galley, clustered around Pompey himself, to judge from the magnificent purple plume that bristled atop the helmet of the man at the middle of the group, who was hidden by the surrounding throng. I swallowed hard and braced myself to face Pompey, but the centurion gripped my elbow and steered me in the opposite direction, toward the cabin where I had been received the previous day. He rapped on the cabin door. Cornelia herself opened it.

"Come inside, Finder," she said, keeping her voice low. She closed the door behind me.

The room was stuffy from the smoke of burning lamp oil. Against one wall, the coverlet on the bed that Pompey and his wife presumably shared was pulled down and rumpled on one side but untouched on the other.

"You slept well last night?" I said.

She raised an eyebrow. "Well enough, considering."

"But the Great One never went to bed at all."

She followed my gaze to the half-made bed. "My husband told me you're good at noticing such details."

"A bad habit I can't seem to break. I used to make my living by it. These days it only seems to get me into trouble."

"All virtues turn at last to vices, if one lives long enough. My husband is a prime example of that."

"Is he?"

"When I first married him, he was no longer young, but he was nonetheless still brash, fearless, supremely confident that the gods were on his side. Those virtues had earned him a lifetime of victories, and his victories earned him the right to call himself Great and to demand that others address him thusly. But brashness can turn to arrogance, fearlessness to foolhardiness, and confidence can become that vice the Greeks call hubris—an overweening pride that tempts the gods to strike a man down."

"All this is by way of explaining what happened at Pharsalus, I presume?"

She blanched, as Pompey had done the previous day when I said too much. "You're quite capable of hubris yourself, Finder."

"Is it hubris to speak the truth to a fellow mortal? Pompey's not a god. Neither are you. To stand up to either of you gives no insult to heaven."

She breathed in through dilated nostrils, fixing me with a catlike stare. At last she blinked and lowered her eyes. "Do you know what day this is?"

"The date? Three days before the kalends of October, unless I've lost track."

"It's my husband's birthday—and the anniversary of his great triumphal parade in Rome thirteen years ago. He had destroyed the pirates who infested the seas; he had crushed Sertorius in Spain and the Marian rebels in Africa; he had subjugated King Mithridates and a host of lesser

potentates in Asia. With all those victories behind him, he returned to
Rome as Pompey the Great, invincible on land and sea. He rode through
the city in a gem-encrusted chariot, followed by an entourage of Asian
princes and princesses and a gigantic portrait of himself made entirely
of pearls. Caesar was nothing in those days. Pompey had no rivals. He
might have made himself king of Rome. He chose instead to respect the
institutions of his ancestors. It was the greatest day of his life. We always
celebrate with a special dinner on this date, to commemorate the anniversary of that triumph. Perhaps tonight, if all goes well . . ."

She shook her head. "Somehow we strayed from your original observation, that my husband passed yet another night without sleep. He's
hardly slept at all since Pharsalus. He sits there at his worktable, yelling
for slaves to come refill the oil in the lamp, poring over that stack of
documents, sorting bits of parchment, scratching out names, scribbling
notes—and all for nothing! Do you know what's in that pile? Provision
lists for troops that no longer exist, advancement recommendations for
officers who were left to rot in the Greek sun, logistical notes for battles
that will never be fought. To go without sleep unhinges a man; it throws
the four humors inside him out of balance."

"Earth, air, fire, and water," I said.

Cornelia shook her head. "There's nothing but fire inside him now.
He scorches everyone he touches. He shall burn himself out. There'll be
no more Pompey the Great, only a charred husk of flesh that was once a
man."

"But he lives in hope. This meeting with King Ptolemy—"

"As if Egypt could save us!"

"Could it not? All the wealth of the Nile; the armed might of the
Egyptian army, along with the old Roman garrison that's posted here; a
safe haven for the forces scattered at Pharsalus to regroup, along with
Pompey's remaining allies in Africa."

"Yes, perhaps . . . perhaps the situation is not entirely hopeless—provided
that King Ptolemy takes our side."

"Why should he not?"

She shrugged. "The king is hardly more than a boy; he's only fifteen.
Who knows what those half-Egyptian, half-Greek eunuchs who advise

him are thinking? Egypt has managed to maintain its independence this long only by playing Roman against Roman. Take sides with Pompey now, and the die is cast; once the fighting is over, Egypt will belong to Pompey . . . or else to Pompey's rival . . . and Egypt will no longer be Egypt but just another Roman province—so their thinking must go."

"But have they any choice? It's either Pompey now, or else . . ." Since she had not uttered the name Caesar, I did not either. "Surely it's a good sign that the king has arrived in all his splendor to greet the Great One."

Cornelia sighed. "I suppose. But I never imagined it would be like this—here in the middle of nowhere, attended by a fleet of leaky buckets, arriving with our heads bowed like beggars after a storm. And Gnaeus—" Dropping all formality, she spoke of her husband by his first name. "Gnaeus is in such a strait. You should have seen him yesterday after you left. He ranted for an hour, going on and on about the tortures he intends to inflict on you, hoisting you onto the ropes, publicly flaying you, commanding the troops on the other ships to stand at attention and watch. He's lost all sense of proportion. There's a kind of madness in him."

I grew light-headed and strove not to lose my balance. "Why in Hades are you telling me all this? What do you want from me, Cornelia?"

She took something from a cabinet and pressed it into my hand. It was a small vial made of carved alabaster with a cork stopper, the sort of vessel that might ordinarily contain a scented oil.

"What's this?" I said.

"Something I've been saving for myself . . . should the occasion arise. One never knows when a quick, graceful exit might be required."

I held the vial to the light and saw that it contained a pale liquid. "This is your personal trapdoor to oblivion?"

"Yes. But I give it to you, Finder. The man from whom I acquired it calls it Nemesis-in-a-bottle. It acts very quickly, with a minimum of pain."

"How do you know that?"

"Because I tried a sample of the stuff on a slave, of course. She expired with hardly a whimper."

"And now you think—"

"I think that you will be able to maintain your dignity as a Roman much more easily this way, rather than my husband's way. Men think their wills are strong, that they won't cry out or weep, but they forget how weak their bodies are, and how very long those frail bodies can be made to suffer before they give up the lemur. Believe me, Finder, this way will be much better for all concerned."

"Including Pompey."

Her face hardened. "I don't want to see him make a spectacle of your death, especially not with King Ptolemy watching. He'll take out all his rage against Caesar on you. Can you imagine how pathetic that will look? He should know better, but he's lost all judgment."

I stared at the vial in my hand. "He'll be furious if he's deprived of the chance to punish me himself."

"Not if the gods decide to take you first. That's what it will look like. You'll swallow the contents—even the taste is not unpleasant, or so I'm told—and afterwards I'll throw the vial overboard. You'll die suddenly and quietly. You're not a young man, Finder. No one will be surprised that your heart gave out; they'll assume that you were frightened to death by the prospect of facing Pompey's wrath. My husband will be disappointed, but he'll get over it—especially if we do somehow manage to snatch victory from the jaws of defeat. Then there will be countless multitudes upon whom he can vent his rage."

"You intend for me to swallow this now?"

"No, wait. Pompey's about to board a small boat that will take him ashore to parlay with King Ptolemy. Swallow it after he's gone."

"So that I'll be cold by the time he returns?"

She nodded.

"And if I refuse?"

"I'll make you a promise, Finder. Accept this gift from me, and I'll see that no harm befalls your family. I swear by the shades of my ancestors."

I pulled out the cork stopper and stared at the colorless liquid inside: Nemesis-in-a-bottle. I passed the vial beneath my nose and detected only a vaguely sweet, not unpleasant odor. Death by poison was not among the many ways I had imagined dying or had come close to dying over the years. Was this how I was to exit the world of the living—as a favor to a woman who wished me to spare her husband the embarrassment of killing me?

A rap at the door gave me a start. The vial nearly jumped from my fingers. Cornelia gripped my hand and pressed my fingers around it. "Be careful!" she whispered, glaring at me. "Put it away."

I stoppered the vial and slipped it into the pouch sewn inside my tunic.

It was Centurion Macro at the door. "The Great One is almost ready to depart. If you wish to bid him farewell—"

"Of course." Cornelia collected herself, took a deep breath, and stepped out of the cabin. The centurion ushered me out. Keeping my hand inside my tunic, I tightly clutched the alabaster vial.

4

Amidships, Pompey was descending the ramp toward a royal Egyptian skiff that had just arrived. Despite its small size, the craft was ornately decorated; images of crocodiles, cranes, and Nile river-horses were carved around the rim, plated with hammered silver and inlaid with pieces of lapis and turquoise for the eyes. The prow of the ship was carved in the shape of a standing ibis with wings outstretched. Along with the rowers, three soldiers stood in the boat. One of them was clearly an Egyptian of very high rank, to judge by the gold filigree that decorated his silver breastplate. The other two were outfitted not like Egyptians but like Roman centurions; presumably they were officers from the Roman force stationed to keep the peace in Egypt. While the Egyptian officer hung back, the two Romans stepped forward and saluted Pompey as he descended the ramp, addressing him in unison: "Great One!"

Pompey smiled, clearly pleased to be properly addressed. To one of the men he gave a nod of recognition. "Septimius, isn't it?"

The man bowed his head. "Great One, I'm surprised you remember me."

"A good commander never forgets a man who once served under him, even though years may pass. How goes your service in Egypt?"

"These are eventful times, Great One. I can't complain of being bored."

"And you, Centurion? What's your name?"

"Salvius, Great One." The other Roman lowered his eyes, not meeting

Pompey's gaze. Pompey frowned, then looked beyond the centurions to the Egyptian whom they escorted. He was a powerfully built man with broad shoulders and massive limbs. He had the blue eyes of a Greek and the dark complexion of an Egyptian. Nearby, I overheard Centurion Macro speaking into Cornelia's ear: "That's the boy-king's mongrel mastiff; fellow's part Greek, like his master, and part native Egyptian. His name—"

"Achillas," the man said in a booming voice, introducing himself to Pompey. "Captain of the King's Guards. I shall have the honor of escorting you into the presence of King Ptolemy . . . Great One," he added, his voice falling flat on the final syllables.

Pompey merely nodded, then gestured for his party to begin boarding the boat. Only four men accompanied him: Macro and another centurion to act as bodyguards, a slave with a box of writing materials to act as a scribe, and Pompey's loyal freedman Philip, a small, wiry fellow with a neatly trimmed beard who was said to attend all important meetings with the Great One on account of his faculty for never forgetting a name, face, or date.

After the others had boarded, Pompey, assisted by Philip, stepped into the boat. While the others sat, Pompey remained standing for a moment. He turned and scanned the faces of those assembled on the galley to see him off. The crowd parted for Cornelia, who descended the ramp and extended her hand to him. Their fingers briefly touched, then drew apart as the rowers dipped their oars and the skiff set off.

"Remember your manners, my dear," called Cornelia, her voice trembling. "He may be only a boy of fifteen, but he's still a king."

Pompey smiled and made a theatrical gesture of submission, opening his arms wide and making a shallow bow. " 'He that once enters a tyrant's door becomes a slave, though he were free before,' " he quoted.

"A bit of Euripides," muttered one of the officers beside me.

"Sophocles, if I'm not mistaken," I said. The man glowered at me.

Pompey gave Cornelia a final nod of farewell, then moved to sit down, with Philip assisting him. Looking up abruptly, his eyes came to rest on me. It was only for an instant, for the business of settling himself on the moving boat required his attention, but an instant was all that was required for him to convey, in quick order, recognition, mild surprise, a flash of utter hatred, and an implicit promise that he would deal with me later, at his leisure. My throat constricted, and I squeezed the vial in my pocket.

I was worth no more than that single glance; in the next instant, Pompey finished settling himself and turned his attention toward the shore and the company that awaited him at the royal pavilion.

Without a word, those of us on the galley watched the skiff's progress. Everyone on all the other ships watched as well, as did the ranks of soldiers assembled on the shore. The moment became slightly unreal; time seemed to stretch. The water, so close to shore, was quite murky, discolored by mud from the nearby Nile brought down by the rush of the annual floods. The sky was without a cloud but uniformly hazy, its color pearly gray rather than blue. No breeze stirred; the atmosphere was sullen and heavy with humidity. Sounds carried with peculiar clarity; I could clearly hear the noise of Pompey clearing his throat on the receding boat, and the low mutter as he attempted to engage the centurions Septimius and Servius in conversation. They did not answer but only averted their eyes, just as the men who had come for me that morning had averted their eyes. The barren, colorless shore assumed a peculiarly uninviting aspect. The throne set before the royal pavilion remained empty; King Ptolemy still declined to show himself.

Cornelia stepped back from the crowd along the rail and began to pace the deck, keeping her eyes on the royal skiff. She touched her mouth with an anxious gesture.

The tension that hung in the air became so oppressive that I began to think it emanated from me alone. Perhaps the sky, seen through other eyes, was a normal blue, and the moment no stranger than any other—except to me, facing my death. "Quickest done is best done," the Etruscan proverb says. I fingered the vial inside my tunic. A not-unpleasant taste, a little discomfort, and then oblivion . . .

The royal skiff reached the shore, where an honor guard awaited. The oarsmen jumped out and dragged the boat forward until the hull grounded in the sandy surf. Salvius and Achillas stepped out of the boat, followed by Philip, who turned about and offered his hand to Pompey.

Cornelia screamed.

Perhaps she had an instant of precognition. Perhaps she was simply watching more closely than the rest of us. I stared at the boat and at first saw only a confusion of sudden movements. Only afterwards, reviewing those fleeting images in memory, would it become clear to me exactly what happened.

The oarsmen in the surf, joined by soldiers awaiting them on shore, reached for Centurion Macro and Pompey's other bodyguard and pulled them out of the boat. Septimius, standing in the boat behind Pompey, drew his sword from its scabbard. As he raised it to strike, the delayed sound of Macro's cry reached us in the galley, followed, in a weird moment of disconnection, by the scraping noise of Septimius drawing his sword. The blade descended at a sharp angle, plunging between Pompey's shoulder blades. Pompey stiffened and convulsed. In what seemed a bizarre mimicry of his parting gesture to Cornelia, he flung his arms wide.

Philip was seized by soldiers on the beach and pulled back, his mouth open in a cry of anguish. Salvius and Achillas drew swords and clambered back into the boat. On either side, Pompey's two bodyguards were held under the water until their flailing subsided. Inside the boat, while Pompey's scribe cowered and ducked, the Great One collapsed as Achillas, Salvius, and Septimius swarmed over him, their swords flashing in the sun.

Abruptly, the stabbing stopped. While the other two pulled back, their chests heaving and their breastplates spattered with blood, Achillas squatted down in the boat and performed some operation. A few moments later he stood upright, his bloody sword in one hand and the severed head of Pompey held aloft in the other.

Those of us on the deck of Pompey's galley stood frozen and speechless. From the various ships around us, scattered shrieks and cries echoed across the still water, punctuating the unnatural silence. Achillas deliberately made a point of displaying the head of Pompey to the fleet offshore. The Great One's eyes were wide open. His mouth gaped. Gore dripped from his severed neck. Then Achillas turned about to show the head to the troops on shore. In their midst, in front of the royal pavilion, King Ptolemy had at last appeared. At some point during the attack, he had taken his place upon the throne, surrounded by a coterie of attendants. He was small in the distance, his features hard to make out, but he was instantly recognizable by the glittering uraeus crown of the Egyptian pharaohs upon his head, a jewel-encrusted band of gold with a rearing cobra at the center. In his crossed arms the king clutched a flail and a staff with a crook at the end, both made of bands of gold interspersed with bands of lapis lazuli. An adviser spoke in his ear, and the king responded by raising his staff in a salute to Achillas. The assembled Egyptian troops broke into a stunning cheer that swept across the water like a thunderclap.

I turned and looked up at Cornelia. She was as white as ivory, her face contorted like a tragedy mask. The galley's captain ran to her, whispered in her ear, and pointed toward the west. Looking dazed, she turned her head. From the direction of the Nile, a fleet of ships had appeared on the horizon. "Egyptian warships!" I heard the captain say, raising his voice and gripping Cornelia's arm to rouse her from her trance.

She stared at the ships, then at the shore, then again at the approaching fleet. The muscles of her face twitched as if she was trying to speak but could not. She shivered, blinked, and finally cried out, "Weigh anchor! Set sail! *Set sail!*"

Her cry broke the spell that held us frozen. The deck erupted in frenzied movement. Soldiers and sailors rushed this way and that. I was shoved and spun about and almost knocked down.

Amid the chaos I climbed to a higher spot and scanned the nearby ships. All the boats were weighing anchor at once, with oarsmen struggling to turn them about and sailors frantically setting sail. Finally I spotted the *Andromeda*. Bethesda stood at the rail, staring toward Pompey's galley but clearly not seeing me amid the confusion on the deck; she was standing on tiptoes and waving her hands. Even as I watched, Rupa grabbed her from behind and pulled her away from the rail and back toward the cabin, trying to get her out of the way of the sailors running back and forth. I waved my arm and shouted her name, but to no effect; in the next instant she disappeared into the cabin with Rupa and the slave boys.

I jumped onto the deck and ran to the ramp from which Pompey had departed. Sailors were heaving on ropes to raise the ramp clear of the water. I ran to its edge and dove into the waves.

Salt stung my nostrils. My heart pounded in my chest. I broke the surface and drew a desperate breath. All the ships were in motion, confusing me and making me lose my sense of direction. It seemed that every captain was acting on his own, with no coordination among them; hardly more than a stone's throw from Pompey's galley, two smaller boats collided, knocking some of the sailors overboard. I treaded water, turning around and trying to orient myself, searching for the *Andromeda*. I thought I knew the direction where I had last seen her, but my view was blocked by a passing ship. Nonetheless, I set off swimming in that direction, away from the shore.

The motion of so many oars from so many ships created waves that rippled and merged and smacked against one another. Water surged into my nostrils. I swallowed air and breathed in water. Swimming became impossible; just to keep my head above water was a struggle. From nowhere, a galley appeared and went racing by me, the long bank of oars, one after another, crashing into the water beside my head, setting up a turbulence that tossed me this way and that and dragged me under, spinning me upside-down beneath the waves.

By the time I recovered, I was more disoriented than ever, not even sure in which direction the shore lay. It took all my energy just to stay afloat. At some point, I thought I caught a glimpse of the *Andromeda* and tried desperately to swim after it, expending the last measure of my strength to call out Bethesda's name. But it might very well have been some other boat, and in any case my pursuit was hopeless; the ship quickly receded, and with it my hopes of ever seeing Bethesda again.

At last I gave up; or more precisely, gave in. Neptune had his own plans for me, and I relinquished all control to the god. My limbs turned to lead, and I thought that I must surely sink, but the god's hand kept me afloat and upright, with the hot sun on my face. The oar-churned sea grew calmer. The multitude of sails receded into the distance. From somewhere I heard a great commotion of movement, as of an army decamping, but even that noise gradually faded until I heard only the shallow sound of my own breath and the gentle lapping of waves upon a shore. A sandy bank materialized beneath my back; the waves no longer carried me aloft but merely nudged me this way and that. The shallow surf sighed and whispered around me. I let out a groan and closed my eyes.

I may have slept, but probably not for long. Above the sighing of the surf, I heard another sound: the buzzing of flies, a great many of them, somewhere nearby. I opened my eyes and saw a bearded face above me. His eyes were wet with tears. His lips trembled. "Help me," he said. "For the love of Jupiter, please help me!"

I recognized him: Philip, the trusted freedman who had accompanied Pompey ashore.

"Please," he said. "I can't do it myself. He's too heavy. I'm too weary. I saw you on the galley before we left. You were standing with Cornelia. Did you know him well? Did you fight beside him? I thought I knew all his friends, but . . ."

I tried to rise, but my limbs were still made of lead. Philip helped me roll to my side, onto all fours. I rose to my knees, feeling them sink into the wet sand. Philip's hand on my shoulder steadied me.

The beach was deserted. The pavilions were gone; the soldiers had all vanished. The quietness of the place was eerie; I heard only the gentle murmur of waves and the low droning of flies.

I turned my head and gazed at the sea. The same thin haze that blanched the sky obscured the distant horizon. In that uncertain expanse of flat water, there was not a sail to be seen. Earth and sea were both empty, but not so the sky; I looked up and saw carrion birds circling.

Philip slipped his hands under my armpits and lifted, eager to bring me to my feet. He was a small fellow, but obviously quite strong, certainly stronger than I was. He claimed to need my help, but from the look in his eyes, I knew it was my company he wanted, the presence of another living mortal in that place of desolation. Philip didn't want to be alone, and when he led me down the beach to the place where the royal skiff had landed, I saw why.

The skiff was gone. "Where . . . ?" I began to say.

"They loaded it onto a wagon. Can you believe it? They brought it here just to bring Pompey ashore, and when it was over, they cleaned out the blood with buckets of seawater, then turned the boat upside-down and loaded it onto a wagon and carried it off, over those low hills. The whole army did an about-face and vanished in a matter of minutes. It was uncanny, as if they were phantoms. You'd almost think they'd never even been here."

But the army of King Ptolemy had indeed been here, and the proof lay at our feet, surrounded by a swarm of buzzing flies. Someone—Philip, I presumed—had dragged the corpses of Macro and his fellow centurion onto the beach and laid them on their backs, side by side. Next to them was the slave who had accompanied the party to act as scribe. He lay beside his box of writing materials, his tunic stained with blood from several wounds.

"He must have gotten in the way when Achillas and Salvius clambered back aboard the boat with their swords," said Philip. "They had no reason to kill him. They didn't kill me. The poor scribe simply got in the way."

I nodded to show that I understood, then turned my eyes at last upon the sight I had been avoiding. Beside the bodyguards and the scribe lay the naked remains of Pompey the Great, a mangled body without a head. It was around his corpse, and especially around the clotted blood where the neck had been severed, that flies swarmed in greatest profusion.

"They took his head," said Philip, his voice breaking. "They cut it off and carried it away like a trophy! And his finger . . ."

I saw that a finger had been cut from the corpse's right hand; a smaller swarm of flies buzzed about the bloody stump.

"To take his ring, you see. They couldn't just remove it. They cut off his finger and threw it in the sand, or in the surf—who knows where . . . ?" Philip sobbed and in a sudden frenzy stripped off his tunic, using it as a scourge to snap at the flies. They dispersed, only to come back in greater numbers.

Philip gave up the effort and spoke through sobs. "I managed to strip off his clothes. I washed his wounds with seawater. Even so, the flies won't go away. We must build a funeral pyre. There must be enough driftwood, scattered up and down the beach. I've gathered some, but we need more. You'll help me, won't you?"

I gazed at Pompey's corpse and nodded. As a young man, he had been famous for his beauty as well as his bravery. His physique had been that of a young Hercules, his chest and shoulders thick with muscle, his waist narrow, his limbs beautifully molded. Like most men, he had grown softer and thicker with passing time; the sagging lump of flesh at my feet was nothing any sculptor would have seen fit to reproduce in marble. Looking at what remained of Pompey, I felt neither pity nor revulsion. This thing was not Pompey, any more than the head with which the Egyptians had absconded was Pompey. Pompey had been an essence, a force of nature, a will that commanded fantastic wealth, fleets of warships, legions of warriors. The thing at my feet was not Pompey. Nonetheless, it would have to be disposed of. As far as I knew, Neptune himself had saved me from watery oblivion for the singular purpose of paying homage to Pompey's remains.

"He should have died at Pharsalus," said Philip. "Not like this, but at a time and in the manner of his own choosing. When he knew that all was lost, he made up his mind to do so. 'Help me, Philip,' he said. 'Help me keep up my courage. I've lost the game, and I have no stomach for the aftermath. Let this place be the end of me, let the history books say, "The Great One died at Pharsalus."' But at the last instant, he lost his nerve. Pompey the Great quailed and fled, with me running after him to keep up. Only to come to this, with his head carried off as a trophy for the king!"

Philip dropped to his knees on the sand and wept. I turned away and scanned the beach for bits of driftwood.

The sun reached its zenith and sank toward the west, and still we gathered wood, venturing farther and farther up and down the beach. Philip insisted that we build three pyres, one for the murdered scribe, another for the two centurions, and another, conspicuously larger than the others, for Pompey. By the time the pyres were built and the bodies laid atop them, the sun was sinking into the west, and shadows were gathering. Philip started a fire with kindling and flint, and set the pyres alight.

As darkness fell and the flames leaped up, I wondered if Cornelia, aboard her galley, would be able to see her husband's funeral pyre as a speck of light in the far distance. I wondered if Bethesda, wherever she was, would be able to see the same flame, and if it would remind her of the Pharos, and make her weep, as I wept that night, at the twist of fate that had turned a journey of hope into a journey of despair.

5

My body exhausted, my mind numb, I fell asleep that night with the flames of Pompey's funeral pyre dancing on my eyelids and the smell of his charred flesh in my nostrils. I slept like a dead man.

Hunger woke me. I had eaten nothing the previous day, and very little the day before. My stomach growled as I stirred from a dream of fish roasting on an open spit. I smelled cooked fish; the fantasy was so real that it stayed with me even after I opened my eyes.

I was lying on my back on the sand. The sun was high. I blinked at the brightness and raised a hand to shade my eyes, then the figure of a man blocked the sunlight. I saw him only as a looming silhouette, but I knew at once that it was not Philip, for this man was much bigger. I gave a start and skittered back on my elbows, then gave another start as something sharp was poked toward me. My stomach fairly roared with hunger. The thing in the man's hand was a sharpened stick; on the stick was a roasted fish, hot from the flames.

The man above me made a familiar grunt as he poked the fish toward me again in a gesture of offering.

"Rupa?" I whispered. "Is that you?" I shaded my eyes and squinted, and glimpsed his face clearly for only an instant before tears obscured my vision.

I blinked them away and reached for the spit. The next thing I knew, the spit in my hand held only the skeleton of a fish, and my stomach had stopped growling. Above me, Rupa grinned.

I wiped my mouth and looked up the beach, to the spot where Rupa had dug a pit in the sand and filled it with coals from the funeral pyres. Two pieces of driftwood on either side served to hold the spits, upon which more fish were roasting. I looked toward the water and saw Androcles and Mopsus, along with Philip, wading naked in the surf, armed with sharpened sticks and their own tunics to serve as nets. While I watched, Androcles deftly speared a fish and held it proudly aloft, laughing with delight.

I scanned the beach and felt a stab of panic. "But where is—?"

"Here, husband."

I turned my head and saw that Bethesda sat on a hillock of sand behind me, leaning back against our traveling trunk. She gave me a weary smile. I drew myself beside her and rested my head on her lap. She gently stroked my forehead. I sighed and closed my eyes. The sun was warm on my face. The sound of the gentle surf was like a lullaby; gone were the flies of the day before. My body was rested, my hunger satisfied, and Bethesda restored to me, all in the span of a single minute. I blinked and looked up at her. I reached up to touch her face to reassure myself that I was not still asleep and dreaming.

"How?" I said.

She took a deep breath and leaned back against the trunk, settling in to tell the tale. "After we saw Pompey killed, and those Egyptian warships appeared, the captain weighed anchor and fled with all the others. But the Egyptian ships held back. They weren't looking for a battle; they just wanted to scare Pompey's fleet away. Still, we were surrounded on all sides by Pompey's ships, and the captain was afraid to sail off on his own. So he bided his time. When darkness fell, he saw his chance and cut away from the fleet and headed south. No one gave chase.

"As far as I knew, you were still on Pompey's galley with his widow, if indeed he hadn't slain you before he set off to meet King Ptolemy. I wanted the captain to turn back and rejoin the fleet, but he wouldn't. Then we caught sight of the flames on the shore, still very far away. Was it a signal from you? I prayed that it might be, and I was heartbroken, because I thought the captain intended to take us directly to Alexandria, and how would we ever manage to find you again? But the captain wanted to be rid of us as quickly as possible; we're lucky he didn't simply throw us all overboard. He said we must be cursed by the gods and would bring him nothing but trouble as long as any of us were aboard. He sailed straight back to this spot, maybe because it was the nearest patch of land, maybe because the fire served as a beacon.

"By the time we arrived, the fire had died down to embers. The sky was starting to grow light when he rowed us ashore. Then he rowed back to his ship and vanished. When I saw you lying here on the beach, I thought you must be dead. But as I stepped closer, you started to snore, so loudly that I laughed and wept at the same time. I wanted to wake you, but Pompey's freedman begged me not to. He said you were like a dead man when you fell asleep last night, that you desperately needed to rest." She lowered her voice to a conspiratorial whisper, even though Philip was splashing in the surf and could not possibly have overheard. "He seems to be under the impression that you're some sort of important personage, a grizzled old veteran with some special tie to Pompey; he imagines that you were so grief-stricken to see the Great One beheaded that you swam ashore on a mad impulse to mourn for him."

I grunted. "I tried to swim to *you,* but I very nearly drowned instead. I was lucky to make it to shore. That Greek captain's a fool. We're not cursed by the gods, Bethesda, we're blessed by them!" I took one of her hands and pressed it to my lips.

She smiled wanly. "So here I sat and waited all morning, listening to you snore while Rupa and the boys made a meal for us. Would you care for more?"

I saw that Rupa was approaching with another roasted fish. My mouth watered, and my stomach growled again.

"Why don't you have it?" I said.

Bethesda shook her head. "I'm not hungry."

I tried to think of the last time I had seen her eat, and felt a prickle of anxiety. Was she not paler than before, and looking more frail than I had ever seen her? Or was she merely worn out by the events of the last few days, as any woman would be?

I sat up and took the fish from Rupa. I had devoured the first one without thinking, but this one I was able to savor. Bethesda smiled, taking pleasure in my appetite.

I licked my fingers and wiped my hand on my tunic, and felt something in the pouch: the poison Cornelia had given me. Vile stuff! What if I had swallowed it in a moment of weakness and despair? Was Cornelia regretting her gift to me now, wishing she had kept it for herself? *I should pour the contents over Pompey's ashes and throw the alabaster vial into the sea,* I thought; but simple laziness prevented me. It was far more pleasurable to sit beside Bethesda, feel the warmth of the sun on my face, and watch the boys fish in the glinting surf.

That afternoon, Philip and I scouted the vicinity and discovered a small fishing village just around a spit of land to the east. Occupying a territory disputed between Ptolemy and his sister Cleopatra, the war-weary villagers were wary of strangers, but they had no aversion to the Roman sesterces I was able to offer. Times were hard in Egypt, and Roman silver went a long way. For a very reasonable price I was able to hire a wagon and two mules to pull it.

My Egyptian was very rusty, and the villagers spoke nothing else; Philip, fluent in many languages, negotiated the deal, and conveyed the wagon-owner's assurance that the coastal road was well maintained all the way to Alexandria. I asked him how we were to cross the Nile, and he said that at every fording of the many branches of the Delta, there would be ferrymen competing to carry us across. The man had a cousin in the capital; when we arrived, I was to leave the wagon and the mules with him.

Philip stayed in the village, saying he intended to head east, not west, and so we parted company. I gave him some sesterces to see him on his way. He gave me a heartfelt embrace, still harboring the mistaken assumption that I was one of Pompey's devoted veterans.

"Anytime one travels, one must be prepared for changes to the itinerary," I said to the assembled company on the beach that night, over our dinner of warmed-over fish supplemented by flatbread purchased from the villagers. "Granted, we've taken a bit of a detour, but now we shall press on to Alexandria just as planned, except that Bethesda will be able to bathe in the Nile sooner rather than later, since the river lies between us and the city." *And Rupa will be able to scatter the ashes of his sister,* I thought, and silently gave thanks to Cassandra, for it was her legacy to me that was paying for this excursion—the journey by ship, the mules and the wagon, even the morsels of flatbread that Androcles and Mopsus were stuffing into their mouths.

The villagers had told me that Alexandria lay about 150 miles distant—a journey of several days over flat terrain. Wherever the road crossed a branch of the Nile, there would be a village, or at the very least a tavern or an inn. The landscape would consist of flat marshland interspersed with cultivated fields where farmers and slaves would be busy tending to irrigation ditches and waterwheels; for the annual inundation of the river, upon which the life of the country depended, had begun. The trip might be monotonous, but should not be particularly dangerous, and we would be safe sleeping in the wagon alongside the road if we wished; banditry, the villagers maintained, was not a part of the Egyptian character. While this was surely no more than wishful thinking—bandits exist everywhere, as do victims and heroes—it was true that we had arrived in a part of the world that was much older and arguably more civilized than Italy. Brutally beheading a potential conqueror before he could set foot in Egypt was one thing; common banditry was another, and about that I was not to worry.

The next morning, very early, we set out for Alexandria. The weather was hot, the atmosphere muggy, and the sky dotted with puffy clouds. With occasional potholes and crumbling edges, the stone-paved road was definitely not up to Roman standards. Bethesda was jostled about more than I would have liked, but the mules made steady progress.

We reached the easternmost branch of the Nile Delta at the bustling fortress town of Pelusium. The idlers at the shop where we purchased provisions were abuzz with speculation about the war between King Ptolemy and his sister Cleopatra; this I gathered from Bethesda, who was able to understand the locals far better than I. She had grown up in Alexandria, speaking Egyptian, and though she claimed that the dialect spoken by the locals in Pelusium was rough and uncouth, she seemed to have little trouble understanding them. Once we reached Alexandria, everyone would speak at least a little Greek. Greek was the language of the Ptolemies and the official language of the state bureaucracy, and the upper classes spoke nothing else. But outside the capital, the native Egyptians, even after two and a half centuries of Ptolemaic rule, clung stubbornly to their native tongue.

According to Bethesda, word of Pompey's fatal landing had already reached Pelusium, but only as a rumor. Some of the locals believed the story; some did not. Just as we were about to show our purchases to the shopkeeper, a self-important little woman with her nose in the air cut in front of us to purchase a basket of dates, and proceeded to address anyone within earshot.

"Who's this hen?" I whispered to Bethesda.

"The wife of a local magistrate, I imagine."

"What's she saying?"

Bethesda listened for a while, then snorted. "Some nonsense about how Pompey met his end. She claims there was a battle between the Romans and Egyptians, and the boy-king himself wrestled Pompey to the ground and then chopped off his head. Silly hen!"

Catching Bethesda's tone if not understanding her Latin, the woman turned around and flared her nostrils at us. I braced for a scrap, but Bethesda bit her tongue and lowered her eyes, and the woman went on with her story. The moment left me feeling uneasy; it seemed to me yet another symptom of her malady that Bethesda should submit so readily to the babblings of a pompous busybody.

Indeed, it seemed to me that Bethesda became more subdued with each passing mile, so that I regretted putting any extra strain upon her by making her deal with the locals. As our journey continued, an unnatural stillness settled upon her. She stared vacantly at the marshes and the muddy fields. I tried to draw her out with reminiscences, as I had on the sea journey, but she seemed disinterested and distant.

Even about her intentions, she had little to say. We had reached the

Nile, the object of our journey, and I asked her where she intended to bathe and what was needed for the ritual of purification she had in mind.

"Not here," she told me. "Not yet. I'll know the place when we come to it. Osiris will show me where to step into the river. The river will show me what to do."

The farther we traveled, the more uneasy I found the villagers. Word of Pompey's death invariably preceded us and formed the chief topic of conversation. It seemed that the Nile had failed to rise as high as in previous years. A year of low inundation meant fewer crops, with hunger and hardship to follow. To cause such a poor inundation, something must have displeased the god (for in Egypt, the Nile itself is a god). The civil strife between Ptolemy and his sister Cleopatra had previously been blamed, for they, too, were divine, and strife between a god and goddess caused repercussions throughout both the natural and the supernatural worlds. But now it was perceived that the Nile had been withholding its floods in anticipation of an even more cataclysmic event, the murder of the Great One, the only man to claim such a title since Alexander himself. The discord of civil war was everywhere upon the earth, bringing one disaster after another, and the people feared that some even more terrible event was yet to come.

So we passed from Pelusium to Tanis, and thence to Thmuis, and thence to Busiris, at the very center of the Delta. Each day the summer sun grew hotter and the air more stifling and humid. The rank smell of the muddy Nile permeated everything. Along the way, following Bethesda's dictates, we made numerous excursions upriver and downriver, which came to nothing; she would arrive at a spot and declare it suitable, saying she would bathe there the next day, only to change her mind when the next day came. Beyond Busiris, we came to the particularly squalid little village of Sais; saying the sun had grown too bright, Bethesda remained in our private room at the town's shabby little inn, refusing to come out. Rupa, Androcles, Mopsus, and I found little to do in Sais, and I passed several idle days drinking Egyptian beer, stifled by heat, boredom, and a growing sense of foreboding.

At last we pressed on from Sais and came to Naucratis, a village on the westernmost branch of the Nile. We had traversed the entire Delta, and still Bethesda had found no location suitable for the ritual of purification.

Each day, as our journey continued, Bethesda had given me greater cause for concern. She ate almost nothing. When I questioned her about this, she said that fasting was a part of the purification ritual. She sat motionless in the wagon for long hours, and when pressed to move, did so only very slowly and deliberately. She seemed less and less to fully occupy a place in this world, and more and more to reside in some other realm invisible to the rest of us. There were times when I glanced at her and for a startling instant thought I was looking right through her, as if she had become transparent. Then I would blink, and the illusion would pass, and I would tell myself it was merely a trick of the heat and the moisture-heavy air.

6

Beyond Naucratis, the road turned north. The Nile and its Delta were to our right. The road ran parallel to the river, but eventually it would turn to the west and leave the Delta behind.

"Soon?" I asked Bethesda.

She stared at the river, the gleam on the surface lighting her face, her features so impassive that I thought she must not have heard me. But eventually she answered. "Soon," she said, and shut her eyes, as if the simple utterance exhausted her.

At midmorning we came to a stretch of the river where palm trees and date trees grew in great profusion. The river narrowed and ran swiftly between its muddy banks, their exact demarcations obscured by tall reeds. Underground springs fed into the river, making the vegetation especially luxuriant. Low trees grew close together, strewn with vines in great profusion. Reeds encircled miniature lagoons where lotuses and lily pads spread like carpets across the water. Dragonflies flitted, and swarms of midges hovered above the water. The spot teemed with life; it seemed somehow timeless and ancient, a place set apart from the rest of the world.

"Here," said Bethesda, sounding neither happy nor sad.

I stopped the mules. Mopsus and Androcles jumped from the wagon, eager to stretch their limbs. "You're the Cyclops and I'm Ulysses! Catch me if you can!" shouted Androcles, slapping his brother's forehead and racing off. Mopsus gave a yelp and raced after him. Rupa jumped out next, circled to the front of the wagon, and reached up to offer his hand to Bethesda. With my assistance from above and his from below, she alighted from the wagon.

From nearby, Androcles gave a shriek as his brother caught up with him and tackled him on a moss-covered stretch of riverbank. I would have shouted at them to behave, but my eyes were on Bethesda, who strode slowly, but steadily, downriver toward a particularly dense patch of reeds, low trees, and vines. I moved to jump from the wagon and follow her, but Rupa seized my ankle. I tried to shake his grip, but he tightened it. He pointed at the trunk in the wagon. From the plaintive look on his face, I knew what he wanted.

The key hung on a chain around my neck. I slipped the chain over my head and moved to unlock the trunk, but my fingers slipped. I tried to open the lock again, but fumbled. The key seemed determined to thwart me. At last I opened the lock and threw back the lid. It took some digging to reach the urn, which had worked its way to the very bottom of the trunk.

The bronze seemed cool to the touch. I had not held it since packing it away. I had forgotten how heavy it was. All that remained of Cassandra was inside it, the ashes and bits of bone and teeth salvaged from her funeral pyre. I gazed at the urn for a long moment, distracted by memories, then realized Rupa had circled the wagon and was standing just under me, reaching up with both hands. Reluctantly, I leaned over and handed him the urn, then jumped from the wagon.

"This is the place, then?" I asked him.

He nodded.

"Shall I come with you?"

He frowned. It was not unreasonable that he should wish to be alone with his sister's remains while he scattered them in the Nile. From birth they had seldom been parted, and they had loved one another above all else in the world. However strong my passion for her, I had known Cassandra for only a few months before she died; the actual time I had spent with her, however special, had amounted to mere hours. It was right that Rupa, not I, should send her ashes on their final journey to the sea, and if he wished to do so in privacy, I had no right to object.

I put my hand on his shoulder to show him that I understood. He held the bronze urn to his chest and bowed his head over it, tears in his eyes, then turned and began to walk upriver. Afraid they might run after him and disturb him, I called to Androcles and Mopsus to come join me.

Bethesda, meanwhile, had reached the overgrown copse of trees downriver and had been searching for a means of entry. While I watched, she finally located a pathway. Not bothering to look back, she stepped into the foliage and disappeared from sight.

"Come along, boys!" I said, and followed after her.

I reached the copse, and stood baffled before the spot where I had last seen her. Was it possible a pathway had opened and then closed up behind her? Wherever I looked, reeds grew out of the muddy ground, and a tangle of vines hung down to meet them, without any perceptible break.

I called her name. She made no answer.

I searched the soft ground for her footprints. I finally found them, taken aback at how light were the tread marks she left, compared not merely with my footsteps, but also with those of the boys. Truly, in the last few days she had dwindled and faded, so that now she walked upon the earth as lightly as a child.

"She must have gone this way," said Mopsus, staring at the ground.

"No, this way!" insisted Androcles.

"Both of you, step back, before you confuse the track any further," I said, and then I followed her steps back and forth, retracing her faltering search for a way into the copse. I finally found it; a tangle of vines hung just so, obscuring the entrance completely unless one approached it from the correct angle.

"Bethesda!" I called, stepping into the copse.

The boys followed me and recommenced their bickering. "I told you it was this way," said Mopsus.

"No, you didn't! You said . . ." Androcles fell silent as the dappled shadows abruptly closed in around us. The boys sensed what I sensed: that we had entered a place that was not like other places. The gurgling of the river could be heard from nearby, along with the low buzzing of insects and the cries of birds in the treetops.

Ahead, through hanging vines, I glimpsed sunlight on stone. We came to a glade circled by vegetation but open to the sky. The little temple in its midst was lit by a shaft of sunlight; the shaft was so clouded with motes of dust that it seemed a solid thing, and I should not have been surprised to see dragonflies suspended motionless within its light, held fast like insects in amber. But the dragonflies hovered and flitted unimpeded, making way for Bethesda, who approached the temple, mounted the short flight of steps to the colonnaded porch, and disappeared inside.

The temple was of Egyptian design, with a flat roof, squat columns surmounted by capitals carved like lotus leaves, and worn hieroglyphs in riotous profusion on every surface. It betrayed no hint of Greek influence, and so almost certainly predated the conquest of Alexander and the reign of the Ptolemies. It was hundreds, possibly thousands of years old; older than Alexandria, older than Rome, perhaps as old as the Pyramids. Beside it, from a jumble of fern-covered stones, a spring trickled forth, forming a tiny pool.

The spring was life itself; the spring accounted for this lush oasis beside the variable banks of the Nile, and for the sacred spell exerted by the place, and for the temple erected beside it. I gazed at the hieroglyphs on the temple; I listened to the faint gurgle of the spring; I felt warm sunlight on my shoulders, but I shivered, for the place seemed uncannily familiar. I raised a finger to my lips, instructing the boys to maintain their silence, and walked across the clearing to the steps of the temple.

I smelled the perfume of burning myrrh. From within I heard the murmur of two voices. One of them belonged to Bethesda. The other voice might have been male or female; I could not tell. I mounted the steps to the porch, inclined my head toward the opening, and squinted at the gloom within. In brief, uncertain flashes, a flickering lamp illuminated brightly painted walls covered with strange images and glyphs. The grandest of these images was that of the god Osiris: the figure of a tall man swathed in white mummy wrapping, holding a flail and crook in his crossed arms and wearing on his head the atef crown, a tall white cone adorned with ostrich feathers on each side and with a small golden disk at the bulbous top.

I heard the voices from within more clearly, but the language they spoke was strange to me—not any version of Egyptian of which I had any knowledge. To hear Bethesda's voice uttering such alien sounds sent a shiver up my spine; it was as if some other being had claimed her voice, some creature foreign to me. I made no move to enter the temple, but stayed where I was on the threshold.

From inside, the priestess of the place—for little by little I had decided the voice must be that of a woman—took up a chant. The chant grew louder, until I knew the boys must be able to hear it as well. I looked behind me and saw them at the edge of the glade, rooted to the spot, their eyes trained on the opening of the temple, their mouths shut.

How long the chanting lasted I had no way of knowing, for it cast a spell on all of us. Time stopped; even the motes of dust in the air ceased their slow, swirling dance, and the dragonflies, afraid of its magic, dispersed. I closed my eyes and tried to discern whether the chanting carried some message of healing and hope, for had Bethesda not come here to find a cure for her malady? But the words were strange to me, and the feeling the chant inspired in me was not of hope but of resignation. Resignation to what? Not to the Fates or Fortune, but to something even older than those; to whatever unseen force metes out our measure of life beneath the sun.

The gods of Egypt are older than the gods of Rome. A Roman who comes to Egypt finds himself far away from the gods he knows, at the mercy of forces older than life itself, powers that have no names because they existed before men could give them names. I felt stripped of all pretensions to wisdom and worldliness; I was naked before the universe, and I trembled.

The chanting ceased. There was movement within the temple. A silhouette emerged from its uncertain light, and in the next moment Bethesda stood before me.

"It's time," she said.

"Time?"

"For me to bathe in the Nile."

"This temple—you've been here before?"

She nodded. "I know this place."

"But how?"

"Perhaps my mother brought me here once, when I was a child. I'm not sure. Perhaps I've only seen it before in dreams. But it's just as I remember it—or dreamed it."

"It seems to me that I must have been here before, too. But that's impossible."

"Perhaps this is a place everyone sees in dreams, whether they remember those dreams or not." Bethesda seemed satisfied with this explanation, for she smiled very faintly. "I must bathe in the river now, husband."

I stepped aside to let her pass. "I'll come with you," I said.

"No. The wisewoman says that I should go alone."

"The wisewoman?"

A figure stepped from the shadows from which Bethesda had emerged. It was an old woman wearing a simple linen gown with a ragged woolen mantle draped over her shoulders, despite the heat of the day. Her hair was white, pulled into a knot at the back of her head. Her skin was like ancient wood, burned dark by the sun and carved with deep wrinkles. She wore no jewelry. Her gnarled hands, clutching the woolen mantle, looked very small. So did her feet. Her sandals were ragged and worn. A cat, its sleek fur as black as night, followed the old woman out of the shadows and rubbed itself against her ankles.

"Did my wife make a sufficient offering?" I reached toward the coin purse in my pouch.

The woman held up her hand. "The god requires no offering to satisfy your wife's request."

"The god?"

"This place is sacred to Osiris. The spring is wedded to the Nile, and in this place the union of the waters is perpetually blessed by Osiris."

I bowed my head, not understanding, but deferring to the woman's authority. Bethesda walked down the steps. I moved to follow, but she raised her hand. "No, husband. Don't follow. What I have to do, I'll do alone."

"Then at least take the boys with you, to stand by in case you need them. In case anyone else—"

"The place is sacred, husband. No one will disturb me."

I followed her as far as the little grotto formed by the spring. She stepped across the tiny pool and out of sight, following a narrow path that appeared to lead down to the river's edge.

I would have followed her, but some power stopped me. Instead, I found myself staring at the little pool formed by the seeping spring. Patches of sunlight glinted on the surface. Tiny, translucent creatures wriggled under the water.

I heard a loud sigh and looked back at the priestess. She was stooping down, laboriously lowering herself to sit on the temple steps. I hurried back to assist her, then sat down beside her.

The black cat, purring loudly, insinuated itself between us and lifted its chin, inviting the woman to stroke its throat with her gnarled forefinger. Cats were a rarity in Rome and little liked, but in Egypt the creatures were considered divine; once in Alexandria I had witnessed a furious mob tear a man limb from limb for the crime of killing one. The cat looked up at me and mewed loudly, as if commanding me to give it pleasure. I obliged by stroking its back.

The woman nodded toward the far side of the glade. "Those two must give you no end of trouble," she said.

I followed her gaze and saw that Mopsus and Androcles had disappeared. I smiled and shrugged. "They're no worse than other boys their age. Why, I remember when I first adopted Meto—" I caught myself, and fell silent.

"Your son's name causes you pain?" She shivered and pulled her cloak about her.

"I've sworn never to speak it again. Sometimes I forget." I looked at the sun-dappled vines and listened to the chirping of birds. The magic of the place began to fade. The priestess was merely a frail, thin-blooded old woman, after all; the cat was nothing more than an animal; the temple was merely a stone hut constructed by mortals who had died and been forgotten long ago. The spring was hardly more than a seep, and even as I watched, a tiny cloud obscured the sun, and the dappled leaves faded from gold to tarnished brass.

"Your wife loves you very much," the old woman said.

I smiled. Was this what women talked about in secret when one came to the other as suppliant to priestess—domestic affairs? I stroked the cat gently, feeling the vibration of its purring against my palm. "I love her very much in return."

She nodded. "You must be at peace, then. Those who drown in the Nile are especially blessed by Osiris."

Cold fingers clutched my heart. "Surely you mean to say, 'Those who *bathe* in the Nile.'"

The old woman made no reply.

I could not speak. I stood up, feeling dizzy. My head was as light as smoke.

Hearing nothing but the rush of blood in my ears, seeing only lights and shadows, I rushed to the spring. I stamped awkwardly across the little pool and followed the path that Bethesda had taken.

After only a few steps, the path forked. I took the branch to the right.

The path led steadily downhill. Through the tangle of leaves I saw the gleam of the river. But before I reached the water's edge, the foliage became more tangled, and I knew Bethesda could not have come this way. Even so, I pushed through the vines and rushes until I reached the water. I felt sun on my face and sucked in a breath of air. I gazed at the Nile and saw it flowing steadily from right to left.

Suddenly, the water before me became strangely clouded. I gazed at the apparition, confounded, until I realized what it must be. Rupa, somewhere upriver, had only moments before cast his sister's ashes into the water. Instead of vanishing at once in the flood, the ashes somehow held together, changing shape and only slowly dispersing, as clouds change shape and gradually disperse in a hot sky. The ashes of Cassandra passed before me on the water, and in the river's gleam the image of her face stared back at me.

For a long moment I was bemused by the strange illusion; then I was jarred to my senses by the sound of a boyish scream.

The cry came from nearby, a little downriver. It was Androcles, screaming for help: "Master! Oh, Master, come quickly!" Mopsus began to scream, as well: "Anyone! Help us! Come help us, anyone, please!" Along with the screaming, I heard the sound of splashing water.

Hackles rose on the back of my neck.

I bolted upright and doubled back, forcing my way through the foliage until I came again to the fork in the path. I took the left branch and ran toward the water's edge. I collided with something and heard a high-pitched yelp as I tumbled head over heels. It was Mopsus I had run into; on my hands and knees I looked over my shoulder and saw him lying flat on his back, convulsed with weeping. I heard more weeping and turned to see Androcles on the path ahead of me. He was soaking wet.

"What's happened?" I said in a hoarse whisper.

"Gone!" Androcles cried. "She's gone!"

"What do you mean?" I staggered to my feet and grabbed his shoulders.

"We heard you say that we should go with her, so we followed her, even though she wanted to go alone. It was Mopsus's idea. I think he just wanted to watch her bathing—"

"What happened? What did you see? Androcles, speak to me!"

He shivered and clutched himself and blubbered, suddenly weeping so hard he couldn't speak.

I ran past him, down to the water's edge. The place was quiet and secluded, with a leafy canopy overhead and rushes all around. Bethesda was nowhere to be seen. I called her name. The shout rousted a covey of birds, who flapped and cawed and streamed skyward from the undergrowth. I looked at the water and saw the same cloudiness I had seen before, upstream. The ashes of Cassandra were passing by, more diluted and dispersed now, but still discernible. Sunlight glinted on the surface, and I was certain I saw a face in the water. Bethesda? Cassandra? I couldn't tell which. I dropped to my knees and reached into the water, but my hands found only pebbles and moss.

"We watched her from the rushes." It was Mopsus speaking. He must have recovered from the collision and followed me. There was a tremor in his voice, but he was not as hysterical as his little brother. "You said we should come with her, so we did. And *not* to see her bathing, like Androcles says! She didn't take off her clothes, anyway. She knelt by the water for a moment, then stood and walked into the river."

"And then?"

"She just kept walking, until the river . . ." He searched for words. "The river swallowed her up. She just . . . disappeared under the water, and didn't come back! We went in after her, but the water's too deep . . ."

I strode into the river. The solid, sandy bottom quickly gave way to an oozing muck that pulled at my feet. The water rose to my chest, and with another step, to my chin. "Oh, Bethesda!" I whispered, looking downriver. Rushes swayed in the warm breeze. Sunlight glinted on the water. The placid surface of the Nile gave no indication of her passing.

For as long as the daylight lasted, we searched for her.

Mopsus ran to fetch Rupa. He was a strong swimmer. While the boys ran up and down the riverbank, Rupa stripped off his tunic and dove beneath the surface again and again, but he found nothing.

With no spring to feed it, the opposite bank was sandy and relatively barren, but the rushes along the river's edge might nonetheless conceal a body. I swam across and searched that side as well. All day we searched, and found no trace of Bethesda.

At some point, half-mad with grief, I ran back to the temple. I meant to confront the priestess, but she had vanished, along with the cat. Inside the chamber, a single lamp burned very low, its oil almost depleted. By its flickering light I gazed at the images on the walls—gods with the bodies of men and the heads of beasts, hieroglyphs of scarabs and birds and staring eyes that meant nothing to me, and dominating them all, the image of Osiris, the mummified god. What words had passed between the wisewoman and my wife? Had Bethesda intended merely to immerse herself, and met with some mishap? Or had it been her intention all along to sink into the Nile and never emerge?

I stepped out of the temple, into the glade. Again I felt an uncanny shiver of recognition. Had I visited this place before, in dreams afterwards forgotten? If I ever saw the place again in my sleep, it could only be in a nightmare.

Throughout that long, wretched day, from time to time my restless fingers chanced upon the vial Cornelia had given me, still tucked away in my tunic. The thought that I still possessed it was the only comfort left to me.

At last, darkness fell, and further searching became impossible. We retreated to the wagon and made a camp for the night. No one was hungry, but I built a little fire beside the road nonetheless, simply to have something to stare at.

The boys huddled close together and wept. Rupa wept as well, remembering his sister, to whom he had said a final farewell that day; despite his muteness, his quiet sobbing sounded like any other man's. Stunned and exhausted, I did not weep. I merely stared at the fire until, by some miracle of Somnus, sleep came, bringing the gift of oblivion.

7

I was awakened by a spear point poking into my ribs.

A voice spoke in that reedy accent peculiar to the Greek-speakers of Egypt: "I'm telling you, Commander, this is the fellow I saw. He helped the freedman build the funeral pyre."

"Then what's he doing here, all the way across the Delta?" The voice was deep and heavy with authority.

"Good question, sir."

"Let's see how he answers it. You! Wake up! Unless you want this spear poked through your ribs."

I opened my eyes to see two men standing over me. One was resplendent in the uniform of an Egyptian officer, wearing a green tunic beneath a bronze cuirass and a helmet that came to a point; the early morning sunlight glinting off his armor made me blink and shield my eyes. The other man wore a peasant's tunic but had a haughty bearing and a foxlike glint in his eyes; I instantly took him for a spy. More soldiers stood beyond them.

The officer poked me with the spear again.

Suddenly, there was a blur of motion, so startling that I covered my face. I heard a hoarse cry, and then, through laced fingers, I saw two hands seize the spear and yank it from the Egyptian officer's grip. There was a scuffle, and I scrambled to my feet to see a band of soldiers swarming over

Rupa, knocking the spear from his grasp and bending his arms behind his back.

"Don't hurt him!" I cried. "He's my bodyguard. He was only protecting me."

"He attacked an officer of King Ptolemy's guard," sniffed the man who had been poking me, ostentatiously dusting off his forearms. One of his underlings, bowing his head obsequiously, offered him back his spear. The officer snatched it without even a nod of acknowledgment and thrust it against my belly, backing me against the wagon. The point tore through my tunic and scraped naked flesh. I looked down to see a trickle of blood on the bright metal.

"We're peaceful travelers," I protested.

"From Rome, I presume, to judge by that accent. I think you're spies," said the officer.

"Like this fellow?" I eyed the man in the tunic.

"Takes one to know one," said the officer. He turned to the spy. "And *you* should have noticed that the bodyguard was unaccounted for. Probably down at the river relieving himself when we showed up. Sneaking up on us like that, he could have killed me! How many others did you observe in this Roman's party?"

"Just the two slave boys, the ones over there."

Androcles and Mopsus, both heavy sleepers, had been roused by soldiers and were getting to their feet, rubbing their eyes and looking about in confusion.

"And a woman," added the spy. "A bit younger than this fellow, but presumably his spouse." He trained an angry gaze at me, passing on the hostility the officer had vented on him. "Where is your wife, Roman, the one who joined you the day after you burned Pompey? Did you lose her somewhere in the Delta?"

I felt a stab of pain, sharper than the spear point pressing against my belly. As fearful as the last few moments had been, at least, however briefly, thoughts of Bethesda had been driven from my mind.

"My wife . . . went down to bathe in the river yesterday. She didn't come back."

The officer snorted. "A likely story! You arouse my suspicions even more, Roman." He addressed a subordinate. "Take a party of men and search for the woman. She can't have gone far."

"I'm telling you, she disappeared yesterday in the river."

"Perhaps. Or perhaps she's a spy as well, gone off on a mission of her own."

"This is absurd," I said.

"Is it?" The officer poked the spear harder against my flesh. "We have some idea of who you are, Roman."

"Do you? I find that quite unlikely."

The spy spoke up. "Philip told me. Ah, that takes you by surprise, doesn't it?" His snide tone was particularly grating.

"Philip? Pompey's freedman? What are you talking about?"

"You thought the beach was deserted, that afternoon you spent building Pompey's funeral pyre. But when Ptolemy's army withdrew, I stayed behind, to observe. I watched the freedman, wailing over the headless body of his old master. And then you were washed ashore; you could only have come from one of Pompey's ships. I wasn't close enough to hear what you said, but I watched the two of you gather driftwood and build the funeral pyres. And the next day, that merchant ship brought the rest of your party—the woman and the mute and the two boys. Oh yes, there *was* a woman; of that I'm quite sure! And the next day you parted company with Philip, at the fishing village. I had to choose which of you to follow, and Philip seemed the obvious choice. I joined up with some soldiers, and we apprehended him on the road heading east."

"What did you do to him?"

"*We'll* ask the questions, Roman," said the officer, poking me with the spear.

The spy laughed. "Philip wasn't harmed. He's quite comfortable, traveling under guard in Ptolemy's retinue. Who knows what important bits of information he may have to give us, in the coming days? But he already told us about you."

"What could he possibly have told you? I never met Philip before that day."

"Exactly—and that's precisely what I find so intriguing, because Philip says that he saw you on Pompey's galley just before the so-called Great

One came ashore, and you appeared to be on quite close terms with Pompey's wife. Philip says you must be one of Pompey's veterans from the old days—and yet Philip didn't know you, and Philip knew everyone with whom his master associated. How could that be, unless you were one of Pompey's—how shall I say it?—*secret* associates. An agent, traveling incognito. A spy!"

"Ridiculous!" I said, even though the presumption was perfectly logical. I was treading a dagger's edge, trying to decide how much of the truth to tell them. Pompey's spy I certainly was not, but in fact I had worked for Pompey more than once in the past, digging up secrets. How good was the spy's intelligence? Would he recognize the name of Gordianus? Even if he didn't, someone else in King Ptolemy's cadre of spies very likely might have heard of me. If I lied and told the man I didn't know Pompey, he might discover the truth and presume I was hiding some more damaging fact. If I told too much of the truth, he might make his own false assumptions. I shook my head at the irony: Pompey had wanted me dead, and in death he might yet achieve that purpose, condemning me by association.

"My name is Gordianus," I said. The spy showed no reaction to the name. "I'm a Roman, yes. But my wife was born here in Egypt; we met in Alexandria, many years ago. In recent months she fell ill. She came to believe that only a voyage back to Egypt, to bathe in the Nile, could save her. That's why we came here, traveling on a Greek merchant ship. The lighthouse at Pharos was in sight when a storm blew us to the east. That's how I fell in with Pompey. Yes, I knew him, from years gone by, but I certainly wasn't his spy. When he was killed and his fleet set sail, in the confusion I fell overboard. I was lucky to reach the shore alive. Philip asked me to help him build Pompey's funeral pyre. I could hardly refuse."

"And your party? How did they happen to come ashore?"

"The Greek captain was determined to be rid of them, for bringing him bad luck. As soon as we parted with Philip, we headed here, to find this spot by the Nile. There's a temple in that glade, with a priestess who serves Osiris. My wife consulted her yesterday. She went to bathe in the river, alone. She didn't come back." I stared steadily at the spy, my vision blurred by tears.

The man was having none of it. "So, you admit to having been in Egypt before! No doubt that's why you were selected for this mission, because you already know the lay of the land."

"What mission? This is absurd! I haven't set foot in Egypt in over thirty years—"

"So you say. Perhaps your wife, when we find her, will tell a different tale. The temple you speak of has been abandoned for years. The old woman who haunts the place is no priestess; she's some sort of half-mad witch."

The officer interrupted. "This is getting us nowhere. The main body of the army isn't far behind us. I need to push forward with the advance guard. I'll leave behind enough men to secure these prisoners, and you can hand them over to Captain Achillas when he comes through."

"And the woman? What if we fail to find her?"

The officer looked at me for a long moment. The pressure of his spear against me eased. "If you ask me," he said, "I think the Roman is telling the truth, about the woman anyway. But what would I know? I'm just a soldier. I don't have the devious mind of a spy."

He stepped back and lowered his spear, poking the tip against the earth to remove the streaks of my blood. At his signal, soldiers came forward to bind my hands behind my back, as Rupa and the boys had already been bound.

"What about our wagon and mules?" I said.

"Those will be confiscated," said the spy, "along with that trunk you've been carting with you. I'm curious to see what's inside." He ordered soldiers to remove the trunk from the wagon.

"If you insist on sorting through our soiled clothing and my wife's toiletries, may it bring you pleasure," I said.

We were shackled together by our ankles and made to sit in the cart, the boys next to each other at the front, and Rupa and I on either side, opposite one another. The spy emptied the trunk onto the roadside and rummaged through the contents. He turned out to be no better than a common thief, pocketing the coins and the few items of value, such as a silver-and-ebony comb that Bethesda had insisted on bringing with her. He reached into the pouch of my tunic as well, and pulled out the alabaster vial.

"Ah, what's this?" he said.

"A gift from a lady."

"Perfume? Are Roman men scenting themselves like pleasure boys these days?"

"Vials can contain things other than perfume," I said.

He looked as me knowingly. "Poison, I'll wager. Something spies often carry on their persons, in case they wish to make a fast, clean exit. Or were you plotting to use it on someone? On King Ptolemy himself, perhaps? Ha! Whatever's inside, it's a pretty little container," he said, pocketing it along with the coins and the comb.

Soon, I began to hear, from the direction of Naucratis, the distant neighing of horses, shouted commands, the creaking of wagon wheels, the tattoo of military drums, and the tramp of many feet marching in unison. There are few sounds so distinctive, or so unnerving, as the approach of a great army. Birds take to the sky, a buzz throbs upon the air, and the earth itself trembles.

The spy gathered up the items of no use to him and stuffed them back into the trunk, then ordered soldiers to put the trunk back into the wagon. The boys yelped, drawing back their toes to avoid having them crushed, but it was Rupa, with his long legs, who was most inconvenienced.

From my cramped vantage point in the wagon—with my back to the road, facing Rupa opposite and the river beyond—I had to crane my neck to see the streaming pennants and plumed helmets of the approaching army. As they came nearer, the soldiers struck up a marching chant. The words were Egyptian, but hearing them repeated over and over, I was able eventually to make sense of them:

He came to knock on Ptolemy's door,
But never set foot on Egypt's shore.
While he was yet inside the boat,
Captain Achillas cut his throat.
So now he's dead,
The Roman's dead,
As all will know
When they see his head!

Hurrah! Hurrah!
As all will know
When they see the head
Of the so-called Great
Who now is dead!
So-called! So-called!
Like Alexander, he was not;
Pompey was cut, not the Gordian knot!
Hurrah! Hurrah!
This song is short, but the march is long,
And so again we sing the song:
Hurrah! Hurrah!
He came to knock on Ptolemy's door,
But never set foot on Egypt's shore. . . .

Guards remained posted around the wagon, but the spy headed off to meet the advancing troops, and I lost sight of him. The stamp of marching feet grew louder and louder. Iron rings bolted along the top rim of the wagon began to rattle and dance against the wood, so great was the vibration. I would have covered my ears, had my hands been free. I looked at the boys and saw fear in their eyes. Rupa squirmed nervously, his legs bunched up against the trunk. They all looked to me for reassurance, so I struggled to keep my face impassive, despite the thrill of panic I felt. Cranes shot skyward from rushes along the Nile, flapping their wings and emitting shrill cries. I watched their flight, envious.

The army reached us and went rumbling by. The chant was deafening:

Like Alexander, he was not;
Pompey was cut, not the Gordian knot!

On and on it went, as thousands of men marched by. Next came the clatter of hooves from mounted cavalry. After the cavalry came the wagons carrying weapons and provisions. Amid the rumble of wheels, I thought I heard the spy's reedy voice nearby, conferring with someone. It seemed that a decision was reached, for the conversation ended, and a soldier mounted the wagon and drove the mules forward. As we joined the procession of King Ptolemy's army, the spy peeked into the wagon and gave me a sardonic look.

"We never did find any trace of your wife, Roman. She must be quite clever, to cover her tracks so completely. I don't like it when a spy gives me the slip. I'll track her down, sooner or later. And when I do . . ." He curled his lip in an expression that froze my blood, then disappeared.

8

_____

As night fell, the army reached a fortress somewhere to the east of Alexandria.

Vaguely I sensed that the wagon had come to a halt. I dozed, not from physical weariness but from a kind of mental stupor; only by descending into half-formed dreams could my mind escape from an intolerable reality compounded of tedium and dread, physical discomfort and numbing grief.

The shackles on my ankles were loosened. Something sharp poked me into alertness.

"Up, Roman!" The spy, assisted by a few soldiers, rousted us out of the wagon. My bones ached from being jostled all day over a particularly rutted stretch of road. My legs were weak from having been cramped for hours. I staggered like a cripple, with a spear at my back to keep me moving forward.

Great walls with huge ramparts of packed earth surrounded us. In the vast enclosure of the fortress, the army went about the business of unloading provisions and preparing for the night. The buildings within the fortress walls were mostly plain and utilitarian, but one stood out on account of its opulence. Magnificent columns painted in bright colors supported a roof of gleaming copper. It was to this building that the spy drove us.

With Rupa and the boys, I waited outside, ringed by soldiers, while the spy stepped within. He was gone for a considerable time. Above us,

the desert sky was ablaze. The sinking sun illuminated crimson and saffron clouds that glowed like molten metal, then faded to the dull blue of
cooling iron, then darkened into ever-deeper shades of blue fretted by
silver stars. I had forgotten the awesome beauty of an Egyptian sunset,
but the splendor of the dying day brought me only misery. Bethesda was
not there to share it with me.

At length the spy returned, looking pleased with himself.

"What a lucky day for you, Roman! You shall have the great honor of
meeting Captain Achillas himself!"

The murderer? I very nearly said. It was hard to imagine how else the
killing of Pompey could be characterized. Clearly, Achillas was a man
from whom I could expect no mercy.

Serpent-headed lamps atop iron tripods lined a long hallway decorated with a riotous profusion of hieroglyphs. The spy led us into a high-
ceilinged chamber decorated in a fashion more Greek than Egyptian,
with geometric rugs underfoot and vast murals depicting battles painted
on the walls. Scribes and other clerics scurried here and there across the
large space. At the center of all this motion were two men of very different countenance, their heads close together as they engaged in a heated
conversation.

I recognized Achillas at once, from having seen him on Pompey's galley. He was outfitted in the various regalia that marked him as Captain of
the King's Guards, with a red horsetail plume adorning his pointed helmet. His tanned face looked very dark, and his brawny physique seemed
positively bull-like next to the pale, slender figure who stood beside him.
The slighter man had a long face and arresting green eyes. His yellow
linen robes had a hem of gold embroidery, across his forehead he wore a
band of solid gold, and a magnificent pectoral of gold filigree adorned
his narrow chest. He was much too old to be King Ptolemy, yet he had
the look of a man used to giving orders and being obeyed.

As we approached, the two of them looked our way and stopped con-
versing.

The spy bowed so low that his nose almost touched the ground. As a
Roman, I was unused to seeing such displays of servility, which are part
of the very fabric of Egyptian life, and indeed, of life in any state headed

by an absolute ruler. "Your Excellencies," the spy hissed, keeping his eyes lowered, "here is the man I spoke of, the Roman spy whom I apprehended this morning near the abandoned shrine of Osiris, downriver from Naucratis."

The two men looked at me—though the term *man* was not entirely suited to the pale fellow, I thought, as I began to perceive that he was very likely a eunuch—another feature of court life in hereditary monarchies to which Romans are unaccustomed.

Achillas looked at me and scowled. "What did you say he calls himself?"

"Gordanius, Your Excellency."

"Gord*ianus,*" I corrected him. The steady tone of my voice surprised even me. Used to hearing their underlings speak in hushed, toadying voices, Achillas and his companion appeared taken aback to hear a captive speak up for himself while daring to look them in the eye.

The Captain of the King's Guards furrowed his brow. His companion stared at me without blinking.

"Gordianus," Achillas repeated, scowling. "The name means nothing to me."

"As I said, Excellency, he was seen on Pompey's galley, even while you yourself were departing with the so-called Great One on board the royal skiff."

"*I* didn't notice him. Gordianus? Gordianus? Does it mean anything to you, Pothinus?"

The eunuch pressed his fingertips together and pursed his lips. "Perhaps," he said, and clapped his hands. A scribe appeared at once, to whom Pothinus spoke in low tones while staring at me thoughtfully. The scribe disappeared through a curtained doorway.

"And these others?" said Achillas.

"The Roman's traveling companions. As you can see—"

"I wasn't talking to *you,*" snapped the captain. The spy winced and groveled.

I cleared my throat. "The big fellow is called Rupa. Born mute, but not deaf. He was a strongman with a mime troupe in Alexandria before he came to Rome. Through an obligation to his late sister, I adopted him into my family. He's a free man and a Roman citizen now. The two slave boys are brothers. Even among the three of them, I'm not sure one could scrape up the wits to produce a passable spy."

"Master!" protested Mopsus and Androcles in a single high-pitched voice. Rupa wrinkled his brow, not quite following the train of my comment; his simpleness had the virtue of making him a hard man to insult.

Achillas grunted and suppressed a smile. The eunuch's face was impassive, and remained without expression when the scribe came hurrying back, bearing a scroll of papyrus. The scroll had been rolled to a specific passage, to which the scribe pointed as he handed it over to Pothinus.

"'Gordianus, called the Finder,'" Pothinus read. "So you *are* in my book of names, after all. 'Roman, born during the consulship of Spurius Postumius Albinus and Marcus Minucius Rufus in the Year of Rome 643—that would make you, what, sixty-two years old? And looking every day of it, I must say! 'Wife: half-Egyptian, half-Jewish, called Bethesda, formerly his slave (acquired in Alexandria), mother to his daughter. Two sons, both adopted, one freeborn and called Eco, the other slave-born and called Meto—about whom, *see addenda.*'" Pothinus looked pointedly at the scribe, who lowered his head like a scolded dog and ran off to fetch another scroll. The eunuch was about to continue reading when, catching sight of someone behind me, he abruptly assumed a subservient posture, with his hands at his sides and his head bowed. Achillas did the same.

The piping of a flute accompanied the arrival of the young king. All activity in the large chamber ceased. The various scribes and officers stopped whatever they were doing, as if petrified by Medusa. Some hierarchy, unclear to me, apparently allowed some of them to remain standing while others dropped to their knees, and still others prostrated themselves entirely, falling flat on their faces with arms outstretched. If I was in doubt as to the procedure incumbent on me, the spy informed me of it.

"Drop down, you Roman dog! Down on your knees, with your face to the floor!" He punctuated this order with several pokes to my ribs.

I caught only a glimpse of the king, resplendent in robes of gold and silver and wearing the cobra-headed uraeus crown. With my hands tied behind me, it was not easy to drop to my knees and lower my face to the floor. The posture was humiliating. Behind me I heard Androcles whisper to his brother, "Look at the master with his backside stuck up in the air!" This was followed by a tiny yelp as the spy kicked Androcles to remind him that he had assumed the same vulnerable posture. The spy then dropped to his knees, just as the king and his retinue came striding by.

"Captain Achillas, and my Lord Chamberlain," said Ptolemy. A boy he might be, but his voice had already changed into that of a man, for it was lower than I expected.

"Your Majesty," the two said in unison.

"My loyal subjects may rise and go about their business," said Ptolemy.

Pothinus conveyed the order. At once the room was abuzz with movement, as if statues had abruptly sprung to life.

The spy stood. I began to do the same, but he gave me a kick and hissed, "Stay as you are!"

From my position I could see little, but I could hear everything. The piper continued to play, but lowered his volume. It was a curious tune, simple on first hearing but repeated in odd variations. Ptolemy's father had been dubbed Ptolemy Auletes, the Piper, on account of his love of the instrument. Was this one of the late king's compositions? For young Ptolemy to go about accompanied by this link to his father was the sort of device that Roman politicians used; in a struggle to the death with his sister Cleopatra, it behooved the young king to use any means possible to lay claim to his father's legacy.

"I thought you would be refreshing yourself in the royal quarters, Your Majesty, after the rigors of the day's journey," said Pothinus.

Ptolemy did not answer at once. He turned from Pothinus and stepped toward me, until I could sense his presence just above me, so close I could smell the perfumed leather of his sandals. "I'm told you've captured a Roman spy, Lord Chamberlain."

"Perhaps, Your Majesty. Perhaps not. I'm trying to delve to the bottom of the matter. Ah, here's one of my scribes now, with the additional information I called for."

I gathered that another scroll had been delivered. While Pothinus read, muttering to himself, the king remained standing over me. I kept my eyes on a horned beetle that happened to be traversing the patch of floor just in front of my nose.

"Well, Lord Chamberlain?" said the king. "What have you discovered?"

Pothinus cleared his throat. "The man is Gordianus, called the Finder. He's made a career of gathering evidence for advocates in the Roman courts. Thus it appears he's gained the confidence of any number of powerful Romans over the years: Cicero, Marc Antony—"

"And Pompey!" said the spy, standing behind me. There was a moment of awkward silence. The man had spoken out of turn, and I could imagine Pothinus glaring at him.

"Yes, Pompey," said the eunuch dryly. "But according to my sources, the two of them had a severe falling-out at the beginning of the war between Pompey and Caesar. Thus, it's quite unlikely that this Roman was a spy for Pompey, as his captor alleges. Quite the opposite, in all probability!"

"What do you mean, Lord Chamberlain?"

"The fellow has a son, Your Majesty, called Meto, who happens to be one of Caesar's closest confidants; as a matter of fact, the other soldiers refer to him as 'Caesar's tent-mate.' "

I groaned inwardly. Meto's exact relationship with his imperator had long been a puzzlement to me, and a vexation when others gossiped about it. Now it seemed that such speculation had reached even here, to Egypt!

Ptolemy was intrigued. " 'Caesar's tent-mate'? What exactly does that imply, Lord Chamberlain?"

The eunuch sniffed. "The Romans constantly spread vulgar sexual gossip about one another, Your Majesty. Politicians insult their rivals with charges of engaging in this or that demeaning act. Common citizens say anything they please about those who rule them. Soldiers make up riddles and ditties and even marching songs that boast of their commander's sexual conquests, or tease him about his more embarrassing proclivities."

"Tease him? His soldiers . . . *tease* . . . Caesar?"

"The Romans are not like us, Your Majesty. They're rather childish when it comes to sexual matters, and they respect neither one another nor the gods. Their primitive form of government, with every citizen at war with every other in a never-ending struggle for riches and power, has made them as impious as they are brutish."

"Caesar's soldiers are fantastically loyal. They fight to the death for him," said King Ptolemy quietly. "Isn't that what you've told me, Lord Chamberlain?"

"So our intelligence would indicate. There are many examples to prove the point, such as the soldier in the naval engagement at Massilia who continued to fight even after losing several limbs, and died shouting Caesar's name; and also—"

"Yet they feel free to make light of him. How can this be? I had thought his men must be so fiercely devoted to Caesar because they recognized some aspect of godhood in him and willingly subjugated themselves to his divinity; is he not said to be descended from the Roman goddess Venus? But a mortal does not make fun of a god; nor does a god permit his worshippers to ridicule him."

"As I said, Your Majesty, the Romans are an impious people, politically corrupt, sexually unsophisticated, and spiritually polluted. That is why we must take every precaution against them."

Ptolemy stepped even closer to me. The beetle under my nose scurried out of the way to make room for the toe of the king's sandal. His nails, I could not help but notice, were immaculately groomed. His feet smelled of rosewater.

"So, Lord Chamberlain, this man knows Caesar?"

"Yes, Your Majesty. And if he *is* a spy, rather than having been employed by Pompey, it seems more likely, in my judgment, that he was sent here by Caesar to spy upon Pompey and witness his arrival on our shores."

"Then we certainly gave him an eyeful!" said Achillas, abruptly entering the conversation.

"Rise to your knees, Roman," said Ptolemy.

I groaned and felt a stab of pain in my back from the effort of rising without using my hands. The king took a few steps back and looked down his nose at me. I dared to look back at him for a brief moment before lowering my eyes. His face was indeed that of a boy of fifteen. His Greek ancestry was evident in his blue eyes and fair skin. He was not particularly handsome, with a mouth too broad and a nose too large to satisfy Greek ideals of beauty, but his eyes flashed with intelligence, and the twist at the corner of his mouth hinted at an impish sense of humor.

"Gordianus-called-Finder is your name?"

"Yes, Your Majesty."

"The spy who captured you charges that you were in the employ of Pompey. True or false?"

"Not true, Your Majesty."

"My lord chamberlain suggests that you may be in Caesar's employ."

"Nor is that true, Your Majesty."

"But it *is* true that you know Caesar?"

"Yes, Your Majesty." I could see that he was intrigued by Caesar, and that it was my uncertain relationship with Caesar that made him curious about me. I cleared my throat. "If it would please Your Majesty, I might be able to tell him a thing or two about Caesar; provided I am allowed to keep my head, of course."

While not looking directly at him, I could see nonetheless that the corner of his mouth twisted into a crooked smile. The young king of Egypt was amused. "You there, spy. What are you called?"

The man gave a name of numerous syllables that was Egyptian, not Greek. Ptolemy evidently could not be bothered to pronounce it, for he continued to address the man by his profession.

"What caused you to think, spy, that this Roman was Pompey's man?"

The spy, in his reedy voice, proceeded to tell the tale of where and how he had first seen me, and of how he had come upon me again near the temple beside the Nile.

Ptolemy returned his gaze to me. "Well, Gordianus-called-Finder, what do you have to say for yourself?"

I repeated the tale of why I had come to Egypt and how I had fallen in with Pompey's fleet, ending with the disappearance of Bethesda the previous day and my capture that morning.

We had all been speaking Greek. Abruptly, Ptolemy spoke to me in Latin. His accent was odd but his grammar impeccable. "The spy strikes me as a bit of an idiot. What do you say to that, Gordianus-called-Finder?"

From the corner of my eye, I could see that the spy frowned, unable to follow the change of tongues. I answered in Latin. "Who am I to contradict the judgment of Your Majesty?"

"It would seem you are a man of considerable experience, Gordianus-called-Finder. Truly, what do you have to say about this spy? Speak candidly; I command it!"

I cleared my throat. "The man may or may not be an idiot, Your Majesty, but I do know for a fact that he's a thief."

"How so?"

"After I was bound, he rummaged through my traveling trunk, ostensibly to look for evidence to incriminate me. Finding nothing of the sort, he stole the few things of value for himself."

The corner of Ptolemy's mouth twisted in the opposite direction, producing a crooked frown. He fixed his gaze on the spy and resumed speaking in Greek. "What did you steal from this Roman?"

The spy's jaw dropped open and quivered. He was silent for a heartbeat too long. "Nothing, Your Majesty."

"Any spoils taken from an enemy are the property of the king, whose officers may dispense them only in accordance with the king's wishes. Are you not aware of that, spy?"

"Of course I am, Your Majesty. I would never think to . . . that is, I would never dream of taking anything from a prisoner, without first . . . without handing it over directly to—"

In Latin, Ptolemy said to me: "What did he steal from you, Gordianus-called-Finder?"

"Coins, Your Majesty."

"Roman sesterces?"

"Yes, Your Majesty."

"If the man has a few Roman coins on his person, or even a bag full of them, that would hardly constitute proof that he stole them from you."

"I suppose not, Your Majesty."

"To make an unsubstantiated charge of such severity against an agent of the king is an offense worthy of death."

I tried to swallow, but my mouth was as dry as chalk. "There was something else he stole from my trunk."

"What?"

"A comb, Your Majesty. A beautiful thing made of silver and ebony. My wife insisted on bringing it with her . . . for sentimental reasons." My voice caught in my throat.

Ptolemy turned his gaze back to the spy. The man had followed none of our exchange in Latin, but even so he began to tremble and gnash his teeth.

"Captain!"

Achillas stepped forward. "Your Majesty?"

"Have your men strip the spy of his tunic and whatever else he's wearing. Turn out all the pockets and pouches and see what you find."

"At once, Your Majesty."

Soldiers converged. In the bat of an eyelash, the spy was stripped naked. He sputtered at the indignity and blushed crimson from head to foot. I averted my eyes, which chanced to fall on Pothinus. Did I imagine it, or was the eunuch discreetly taking a good look at the naked man's scrotum?

In the background, the piper continued to play. For a while I had ceased to notice his music, though he had never stopped playing the same song in endless variations.

"What did your men find, Captain?"

"Coins, Your Majesty. Bits of parchment. A perfumer's vial, made of alabaster. A few—"

"A comb?"

"Yes, Your Majesty." Achillas held it before the king, who looked down his nose at it but did not touch it.

"A comb made of silver and ebony," observed Ptolemy.

The spy, standing alone and naked, wrung his hands and trembled violently. There was a sound of splashing, and I saw that his bladder was emptying itself. He stood in a pool of his own urine, blushing furiously, biting his lips, and whimpering.

The piper continued to play. The tune changed to a brighter key and a quicker tempo.

"Have mercy on me, Your Majesty, I beg you!" blubbered the spy.

"Captain."

"Your Majesty?"

"Have this man executed at once."

Pothinus stepped forward. "Your Majesty, the man is a valuable agent. He possesses a great store of specialized knowledge. Please consider—"

"This man stole from the king. He lied to the king. You yourself witnessed the lie. Are you saying, Lord Chamberlain, that there is an argument to be made that he should *not* be executed?"

Pothinus lowered his eyes. "No, Your Majesty. The king's words humble me."

"Captain Achillas."

"Your Majesty?"

"Execute the man immediately, where he stands, so that all present may witness the swiftness of the king's justice."

Achillas strode forward. Soldiers seized the spy's arms, not merely to immobilize him but also to keep him upright; his legs had gone soft, and otherwise he would have collapsed to the floor. Achillas put his massive hands around the man's throat and proceeded to strangle him. Where the man's face had been red before, it now turned purple. His body convulsed. Weird sounds came from his mouth until a sickening crunch put a stop to his gurgling. With a snort of disgust, Achillas released him. The man's head flopped to one side, and his limp body crumpled to the floor.

The room fell silent except for the merry tune of the piper.

"Lord Chamberlain."

"Your Majesty?"

"See to it that the Roman and his companions are released from their bonds; that the items stolen from him are returned to his keeping; that he is given suitable quarters and made comfortable. Keep him close at hand, in case the king should wish to speak to him."

Pothinus bowed low. "It shall be as Your Majesty commands."

The same soldiers who had stripped and immobilized the spy now surrounded me and began to untie the cords around my wrists. Meanwhile, to a new and livelier tune from his piper, King Ptolemy made his exit from the room.

Thus I made the acquaintance of the Egyptian king and his advisers, and received my first taste of life in the royal court.

9

Our quarters were simple but adequate: a room made of stone with sleeping cots for all (Mopsus and Androcles sharing), a brass chamber pot in one corner, a rug on the floor, and a small lamp that hung from a hook in the ceiling. There was even a narrow window that looked down on a sandy courtyard where soldiers were camped. Above the curve of the fortress wall beyond, the sky was dark and full of stars.

To eat, we were each given a bowl of lentil soup, a millet biscuit, and a few dried dates and figs. The food disappeared almost at once.

Eventually two soldiers arrived at the door bearing my trunk. They set it in the middle of the room and departed. I opened the lid. Lying on top was Bethesda's silver-and-ebony comb. I picked it up and ran my fingertips over the prongs. Underneath was a bag full of coins, and beside the bag, almost hidden by a fold of cloth, was the alabaster vial that Cornelia had given me.

I extinguished the lamp and lay on my cot, clutching the silver-and-ebony comb. I thought of Diana and Eco back in Rome; they would be devastated when they learned what had happened to Bethesda. How could I bear to tell them? And would I ever have the chance? Rome seemed very far away. A coldness settled over me, and I thought of the alabaster vial. Perhaps it was the will of the gods that I should consume its contents, after all. . . .

Nearby, Mopsus and Androcles chattered to one another in low voices. I was about to tell them to be quiet when Mopsus spoke up.

"Master, is this what Rome will be like?"

"What do you mean, Mopsus?" From outside I heard a sentry give the all-clear. Wind sighed in the tops of the tall palm trees outside the fortress wall. The world had become very quiet and still.

"When Caesar gets back to Rome and makes himself king, is this what Rome will be like?" said Mopsus.

"I still don't know what you mean."

"What he means," said Androcles, seeing that his brother's question needed clarification, "is this: Will everyone have to cringe and fawn and bow to Caesar and call him 'Your Majesty,' even free citizens like you, Master?"

"Yes, Master," said Mopsus, "and will Caesar be able to say, 'I don't like that fellow, so kill him right now!' And the next thing you know, just because King Caesar said so, the man's being strangled to death, like this?" He demonstrated by clamping his hands around his brother's throat. Androcles joined in the demonstration by flailing his arms and legs against the cot and making a gagging noise.

From the cot next to them, I heard Rupa emit a chuckle of amusement, but I saw nothing to laugh at.

"I don't know, boys. When we get back"—I almost said, *If* we get back, but there was no point in planting doubt—"Rome will certainly be different. The Egyptians have always been ruled by a king; before the dynasty of the Ptolemies, there were the pharaohs, whose reigns go back thousands of years, back to the days of the Pyramids. But we've never had a king—well, not in 450 years or so. And no Roman has ever *been* a king, including Caesar. We have no experience of monarchy and no rules to go by. I imagine, like this mess of a war, it will be rather like a play that the players make up as they go along. Now, stop this roughhousing and get to sleep!"

"And if we don't, will you order Rupa to strangle us, Master?"

"Don't test me, Mopsus!"

Eventually they quieted down, until again I heard the sighing breeze in the palm trees. I banished all thoughts of the alabaster vial from my mind; who would see the boys and Rupa through the perilous days ahead, if not me? I clutched the comb until, finally, sleep—blessed sleep, with its blanket of forgetfulness—began to draw near. In my head, the sighing breeze was joined by another sound, and I fell asleep hearing the tune played by Ptolemy's piper, repeated over and over again.

The next morning, we set out for Alexandria.

It appeared that the main body of the army would remain at the fortress, under the command of Achillas, while the king and a smaller, though substantial, armed company would proceed to the capital.

Soldiers loaded my trunk into the wagon. Another soldier was assigned to drive the mules while I rode in the back with Rupa and the boys, not bound as on the day before but free to move about.

The road ran westward, away from the Nile, alongside a wide canal that brought fresh water from the river to the capital and allowed small craft to navigate back and forth. I wondered how Ptolemy would be transported to the city, and assumed he would arrive by chariot, but then, beyond the ranks of marching soldiers, I caught sight of an ornately gilded barge on the canal. It was manned by boatmen who propelled it ahead of the slow current by means of long poles. Stripped to the waist, their muscular shoulders and arms gleaming with sweat, the boatmen worked with graceful efficiency, pushing their poles against the bottom of the canal one after another and then repeating the sequence.

The middle portion of the barge was shaded by a large saffron-colored canopy, beneath which I occasionally caught glimpses of the king and his retinue, including the eunuch Pothinus. Every so often, when a breeze wafted from the direction of the canal, I heard a few notes of music from the king's piper and felt a chill despite the rising heat of the day.

The hour was nearing midday when a soldier on foot approached our wagon.

"Are you Gordianus-called-Finder?" He spoke Egyptian, but so slowly and distinctly that even I could follow.

"I am."

"Come with me."

"Is there trouble?"

"His Majesty ordered me to fetch you."

"And the others in my party?"

"They stay behind. You come with me."

Rupa helped me descend from the wagon. I spoke in his ear. "While I'm gone, take care of the boys. Don't let them get into trouble. They think they're smarter than you, but you're the strong one. Don't be afraid to show them who's boss. Do you understand?"

He looked at me uncertainly, but nodded.

I called to the boys. When they came to the back of the wagon and bent toward me, I grabbed each one by the nearest ear and pulled them close. "You will not, repeat *not*, get into trouble while I'm gone. You'll do as Rupa tells you."

"*Tells* us?" said Mopsus. "But Rupa can't speak—" His words ended in a squeal as I gave his ear a twist.

"You know what I mean. When I return, if I find that you've disobeyed me, I shall twist this ear until it comes off. Do you understand?"

"Yes, Master!" cried Mopsus.

"And you, Androcles?"

His brother, thinking it judicious to keep his mouth shut, simply nodded. I released them both. With a firm grip on my arm, the soldier hurried me off.

"When will you be back?" called Mopsus, rubbing his ear.

"Soon, I'm sure," I called back, though I was not sure of anything.

Threading our way through ranks of marching infantry, the soldier led me across the road and down a ramp set into the embankment of the canal, where the royal barge had pulled alongside a landing spot. The boatmen were taking advantage of the stop to lean against their poles and rest for a moment. As soon as I stepped aboard, the crew leader called out for them to resume their work. The boatmen at the front of the barge on either side raised their poles and brought them down. The barge slowly began to move.

Pothinus peered out from beneath the canopy and gestured for me to follow. Steps led down to the royal accommodations, which were actually below the level of the water; the sunken, shaded area was deliciously

cool. The saffron-colored canopy softened the glaring sunlight; sumptuous carpets underfoot softened my steps. Here and there, courtiers stood
in little groups. Many wore the nemes, a pleated linen head-cloth such as
that worn by sphinxes, with various colors and patterns to denote their
rank, while others wore ceremonial wigs upon their presumably shaved
heads. They stood aside to let me pass, until at the center of the barge,
I saw King Ptolemy seated on his throne. Two other chairs, hardly less
opulent, faced his; both were chased with silver inlaid with bits of ebony
and ivory, and their broad seats were strewn with plump cushions. In one
chair sat Pothinus. The other was empty.

"Sit," said Pothinus.

I sat, and realized that Ptolemy's throne was raised on a dais. The
platform was low, but sufficient to force me to tilt my chin up if I dared
to look at him. If I lowered my eyes, they naturally came to rest upon
a large, covered clay jar next to one of the king's feet. It occurred to me
that the jar was just the right size to contain a man's head.

"Did you sleep well, Gordianus-called-Finder?"

"Quite well, Your Majesty."

"The accommodations were adequate?"

"Yes, Your Majesty."

"Good. Are you hungry?"

"Perhaps, Your Majesty."

"Then you and Pothinus must partake of some food. I myself am
never hungry at midday. Lord Chamberlain, call for food."

Small tables were brought, and atop them were set silver trays heaped
with delicacies—green and black olives stuffed with peppers and nut-
paste, fish cakes sprinkled with poppy seeds, millet cakes sweetened with
honey and soaked in pomegranate wine.

Despite the lavish spread, I had some trouble mustering my appetite,
for I kept imagining what must be inside the clay jar at the king's feet.
While Pothinus and I ate, the king's piper played a tune. The man sat at
a little distance behind Ptolemy, cross-legged on the floor. The tune was
different from the one he had played the night before.

Ptolemy seemed to read my thoughts. "Do you like the music?"

"Very much," I said, which seemed the safe answer. "May I ask who composed the tune?"

"My father."

I nodded. It was as I had thought; Ptolemy went about accompanied by his father's music to reinforce his link to the Piper and thus his legitimacy as the late king's successor. But then he said something that prompted me to reconsider my cynical interpretation of his motives.

"My father possessed a remarkable talent for music. With his playing he could make a man laugh one moment and weep the next. There was a sort of magic in his fingers and lips. This fellow who plays my father's tunes captures the notes, but not always the spirit, of my father's compositions. Still, to hear his music reminds me of my father in a way that nothing else can. Consider: The monuments that men leave behind, even the greatest men, reach out to only one of the five senses, our sight. We look at the image on a coin, or gaze upon a statue, or read the words that were written; we *see*, and we remember. But what about the way a man laughed, or sang, and the sound of his voice? No art can capture those aspects of a man for posterity; once a man is dead, his voice, his song, and his laughter die with him, gone forever, and our memory of them grows less and less exact as time passes. I was lucky, then, that my father made music, and that others, even if not with his precise skill, can reproduce that music. I cannot ever again hear the sound of my father speaking my name, but I can hear the tunes he composed, and so feel his presence persist among the living."

I dared to lift my eyes to gaze into those of Ptolemy, but the king was staring into the middle distance. It seemed strange to hear such a young man utter sentiments so bittersweet; but Ptolemy was not, after all, an ordinary young man. He was the descendant of a long line of kings and queens stretching back to the right-hand man of Alexander the Great; he had been raised to think of himself as semi-divine and the possessor of a unique destiny. Had he ever played with the boyish, careless abandon of Mopsus and Androcles? It seemed unlikely. I had interpreted the presence of his attendant piper as a purely political device, a calculated ploy; in Rome, such would have been the case, but gazing upon Ptolemy through jaded Roman eyes, I had missed something. Could it be that Ptolemy was both more mortal and more kingly than I had thought?

"The bond between father and son is a very special thing," I said quietly, and my thoughts took a dark turn.

Again, Ptolemy seemed to read my mind. "You have two sons, I understand. The one called Eco, who lives in Rome, and the other, called Meto, who travels with Caesar; but the one called Meto you no longer call your son."

"That is correct, Your Majesty."

"You had a falling-out?"

"Yes, Your Majesty. In Massilia—"

For the first time I heard him laugh, though not with joy. "You needn't explain, Gordianus-called-Finder. I've had my share of fallings-out with family members. If my latest military excursion had been successful, I'd be coming back to Alexandria with *two* heads to show the people, not just one!"

Across from me, Pothinus pursed his lips, but if he thought the king spoke carelessly, he said nothing.

The king continued. "Tell me, Gordianus-called-Finder, what do they say about Egypt where you come from? What do the citizens of Rome make of our little domestic squabble?"

This opened treacherous ground. I answered carefully. "Your father was well-known in Rome, of course, since for a period of time he resided there." (In fact, the Piper had been driven out of Egypt by rioting mobs and lived for a while in exile in Rome, while his eldest daughter, Berenice, seized the opportunity to take over the government in his absence.)

"I was very young then," said the king. "Too young to accompany my father. What did the Romans make of him?"

"While he lived there, your father was well-liked. His . . . generosity . . . was much spoken of." (Passing out money and promises of money, the Piper had petitioned the Roman Senate for military assistance to restore him to the throne; in essence, he had ransomed the future wealth of his country to Roman senators and bankers.) "For many months, Your Majesty, Roman politics revolved around 'the Egyptian Question.'" (The question: Put the Piper back on the throne as a Roman puppet, or take

over the country outright and make it a Roman province?) "It was a delicate issue, endlessly debated." (Caesar and Pompey staged a titanic struggle
over who should get the command, but to choose either man threatened to
upset the precarious balance of power in Rome; the Senate finally picked
a relative nonentity, Aulus Gabinius, to pacify Egypt.) "The people of
Rome rejoiced when your father was rightfully restored to his throne."
(Gabinius, with the aid of a dashing young cavalry commander named
Marc Antony, routed the forces of Berenice. Back in power, the Piper as
his first act executed his rebellious daughter; his second act was to raise
taxes, so as to start paying the vast sum in bribes he had promised to Roman senators and bankers. Egypt was impoverished, and the Egyptian
people groaned under the burden, but the sizable Roman garrison left
behind by Gabinius assured that the Piper would remain in power.)

I cleared my throat. "The sudden death of your father two years ago
caused grief and consternation in Rome." (The senators and bankers worried that chaos would overtake Egypt and that further payments from
whomever succeeded the Piper would dry up; there were vicious recrimi-
nations from those who had argued for annexing Egypt outright while
the pickings were easy.)

The king nodded thoughtfully. "And what is the attitude of the citizens of Rome regarding affairs in Egypt since the death of my father?"

The ground became even more treacherous. "To be candid, Your
Majesty, since the death of your father, my knowledge, and, I suspect, the
knowledge of most Romans regarding events in Egypt, are rather hazy.
In the last few years, our own 'domestic squabbles' have occupied all our
attention. Not a great deal of thought is given to affairs in Egypt, at least
not by common citizens."

"But what was said about my father's will, at the time of his death?"

"A man's will is a sacred thing to a Roman. Whatever dispensation
your father decreed would be respected." (In fact, there had been a great
deal of disappointment that the Piper had not bequeathed the governance
of Egypt to the Roman Senate; other monarchs, close to death, massively
in debt to Rome, and wishing to spare their countries from inevitable
war and conquest, had done exactly that. But the Piper had chosen to
leave Egypt to his eldest remaining daughter, Cleopatra, and her younger

brother, Ptolemy, to be ruled jointly by the two of them. Presumably, brother and sister had married one another, as was the custom with co-reigning siblings in the Ptolemy family. Incest was abhorrent to Romans and looked upon as yet another decadent symptom of monarchy, along with court eunuchs, ostentatious pageantry, and capricious executions.)

The king shifted uneasily on his throne and frowned. "My father left Egypt to me—and to my sister Cleopatra. Did you know that, Gordianus-called-Finder?"

"That was my understanding, yes."

"My father dreamed of peace in the family and prosperity for Egypt. But in the world of flesh, even the dreams of a god do not always find fulfillment. The Fates have decreed this to be a time of civil war all across the earth. So it is with Rome. So it is with Egypt. So it is, I take it, even within your own family, Gordianus-called-Finder."

I bowed my head. "You speak again of my son."

"Meto, the tent-mate of Caesar," he said, watching me closely. I bit my lip. "Ah, does that have something to do with your estrangement? Has the eagle taken your son perhaps too much under his wing?"

I sighed. "I find it strange that Your Majesty should show so much interest in the family affairs of a common Roman citizen."

"I am interested in all things having to do with Caesar," he said. The gleam in his eyes was partly that of a curious fifteen-year-old boy, and partly that of a calculating politician.

"For many a Roman," I said, speaking slowly and quietly, "the choice between Caesar and Pompey was not an easy one. Cicero searched frantically for a third way, but found none and finally sided with Pompey—to his regret. Marcus Caelius leaped to Caesar's side, then grew dissatisfied and betrayed him. Milo escaped from exile in Massilia and sought to raise an army of his own—"

"And you have known all these men?" Ptolemy sat forward. "These heroes and adventurers and madmen of whom we hear only echoes here in Egypt?"

I nodded. "Most of them I have known better than I cared to, certainly better than was good for me."

"And you know Caesar as well?"

"Yes."

"And is he not the greatest of them, the nearest to godhood?"

"I know him as a man, not a god."

"A man of great power."

"Yes."

"Yet you begrudge the favoritism he shows your son?"

"The matter is complicated, Your Majesty." I almost smiled as I said this, considering that the person to whom I spoke was married to a sister he loathed and that another of his sisters had been executed by their father. I glanced at the clay jar at Ptolemy's feet. I felt slightly queasy. "If Caesar comes to Egypt," I said, "will you have him beheaded, as you did Pompey?"

The king exchanged a look with Pothinus, who clearly disapproved of this turn in the conversation. "Your Majesty—" he said, intending to change the subject; but the king spoke over him, obliging Pothinus to fall silent.

"He was remarkably easy to kill, wasn't he—Pompey, I mean? The gods deserted him at Pharsalus. By the time he was ready to step ashore here in Egypt, there was not a shred of divinity still clinging to his wretched person. The gods had stripped him of their armor, and when the blades descended, the only resistance they met was feeble flesh. He thought to stride ashore, to remind me of the debts my father owed him, and take command of Egypt, as if our treasury, granaries, and arms were his for the taking. It was not to be. 'Put an end to the so-called Great One before his feet can touch Egyptian soil!'—were those not your exact words, Pothinus? You even quoted that favorite epigram of my tutor Theodotus: 'Dead men don't bite.' I thought long and hard upon this question; in dreams I sought the counsel of Osiris and Serapis. The gods agreed with Pothinus. Had I given succor to Pompey, the same curse that fell upon him would have fallen upon Egypt.

"Caesar may be another matter. I think the gods are still with Caesar. His divinity must grow stronger with every conquest. Will he come to Egypt, Gordianus-called-Finder, seeking our grain and our gold as Pompey did?"

"Perhaps, Your Majesty."

"And if he comes, will he be as easy to kill as Pompey was?"

I made no answer. Ptolemy turned to the eunuch.

"What do *you* think, Lord Chamberlain?"

"I think, Your Majesty," said Pothinus, casting a shrewd glance at the king, "that you promised audiences with certain of your subjects today, here on the royal barge. Perhaps your conversation with this Roman could be postponed while you tend to more-official business."

Ptolemy sighed. "Who comes to me today?"

"Several delegations are here to report on the status of the annual inundation in the regions of the Upper Nile; we have reports from Ombos, Hemonthis, Latopolis, and elsewhere. The news they bring is not good, I fear. There is also a party of merchants from Clysma, on the gulf of the Red Sea, who wish to petition for tax relief; a fire destroyed several warehouses and piers last year, and they need money to rebuild. I've read their reports and petitions, but only you can grant the dispensations they request."

"Must I meet these people *now,* Lord Chamberlain?"

"All these groups have come a very long way, Your Majesty; and I think it would be best to dispose of these matters before we reach Alexandria, where Your Majesty is likely to be greeted by a great many pressing needs that have developed in your absence."

The king closed his eyes. "Very well, Lord Chamberlain."

Pothinus stood. "I shall call for the barge to stop at the next landing, and find a suitable escort to take the Roman back to his—"

"No, let Gordianus-called-Finder stay."

"But, Your Majesty—"

"Let him stay where he is." Ptolemy gave him a severe look.

"As Your Majesty commands."

I had thought, in such a hot climate, that all business would cease in the hours just after midday, but such was not the case. While I sat and struggled not to doze—snoring during a royal audience would surely be frowned on—various envoys were admitted to the king's presence. What impressed me most was Ptolemy's facility with languages and dialects. All the envoys spoke some Greek, but many exhausted their vocabulary after a few ritual greetings, whereupon the king began to converse with perfect fluency in whatever tongue best suited his subjects. All the while, the piper played in the background.

At last the final envoy made obeisance and departed from the king's presence. Pothinus showed the man out. On his way back, he was approached by a messenger, who whispered something in his ear. The message appeared to be quite long and complicated. Hearing it, the eunuch appeared at first alarmed, then amused. At last he hurried to Ptolemy's side.

"Your Majesty! You shall soon have a chance to gaze upon the master of Rome with your own eyes. Your advance guards have reached Alexandria. They send back news: Caesar's ships are in the harbor."

Ptolemy drew a sharp breath. "In the harbor? Does Caesar, like Pompey, await my coming before he steps onto Egyptian soil?"

Pothinus flashed a smile. "Actually, Your Majesty, Caesar arrived some days ago. I am told that he set foot on a public pier and attempted to take a stroll through one of the markets. It seems he wished to awe the people, for he arrived with all the trappings of a Roman consul. He wore his toga with a purple stripe, and twelve armed men called lictors marched before him bearing fasces."

"Fasces?"

"Bundles of birch rods sheathing iron axes—ancient ceremonial weapons that are part of the trappings of a Roman magistrate when he goes about in public. Suitable for Rome, perhaps, but not for Alexandria! Or so the people thought; the crowd was so outraged at this slight to Your Majesty's dignity—that a Roman should strut about the city in the king's absence as if Egypt were a province of Rome—that they raised an outcry and gathered up anything they could find in the market—fruit, vegetables, fish—and proceeded to pelt the Romans until they withdrew to their ships. Now Caesar awaits your arrival before daring to set foot in the city again."

Ptolemy laughed. "It seems there was a battle, and Caesar was forced to retreat! As my father used to say, it never pays to get on the wrong side of the Alexandrian mob. We shall have to consider how to welcome the Roman consul in a more suitable fashion."

He gazed down at the jar at his feet, and smiled.

10

The approach to Alexandria by royal barge was a new experience for me, and bittersweet. Each time I felt a prick of novelty, I also felt a stab of grief, for Bethesda was not there to share the experience.

Fifteen miles east of Alexandria, the canal from the Nile passes through a town called Canopus, notorious as a pleasure resort for the idle rich of the city. I had visited Canopus when I lived in Alexandria as a young man, but in those days even the trinkets in the curio shops were beyond my meager means, and I could only peer into the dining establishments, gambling houses, and brothels along the canal. Forty years later, I again found myself passing through the town, but this time I was seated next to the king himself!

Pleasure-seekers thronged the waterfront to have a look at the royal barge and steal a peek at its occupant. Ptolemy remained seated on his throne at the center of the barge and ignored the waving throng, but I thought I saw a shadow of a smile on his lips when we heard the cheering spectators cry out his name. Egypt might be torn by civil war, but among the pleasure class of Alexandria, Ptolemy's claim to the throne was apparently not in dispute.

From Canopus to Alexandria the canal grew considerably wider, so as to accommodate the numerous barges traveling back and forth. In deference to the royal vessel, all others pulled aside and stopped whenever they met us, so that our progress was unimpeded. Barge after barge we passed, some privately owned and luxuriously outfitted, others serving as common carriers offering various classes of accommodation. As a young man, I had traveled to Canopus standing upright on a barge so crowded I feared it would sink; we passed several of those, and their occupants seemed distinctly less enthusiastic about their monarch than had the diners and gamblers along the waterfront in Canopus. Some of the faces that stared back at us looked positively hostile. Did they favor Ptolemy's sister Cleopatra in the struggle for the succession? Or were they altogether weary of the Ptolemies and the chaos they had inflicted on Egypt in recent years?

Approaching Alexandria, the canal split into two branches, and we took the one to the left. A concentration of palm trees appeared on the flat horizon ahead of us, lining the shore of Lake Mareotis; reflecting the sun overhead, the lake appeared as a scintillating line beyond the silhouettes of tree trunks. The trees grew nearer; the scintillating line became a visible expanse of water. The banks of the canal grew wilder, with rushes on either side. We rounded a small bend and entered Lake Mareotis, more an inland sea than a mere lake. Ahead of us, along the distant shore, was the low, jumbled skyline of Alexandria, with the Pharos lighthouse looming beyond.

Fishing boats and private vessels drew back to make way for the king. Two small warships manned by soldiers in ceremonial armor sailed out to greet us, then turned about and formed an escort for the arrival of the royal barge.

Beneath the city walls, at the busy lakeside harbor, courtiers and soldiers awaited us on a jetty festooned with colorful pennants. The barge pulled beside the landing and came to a gentle stop. Ptolemy rose from his throne, grasping his crook and flail. Courtiers fell in behind him, each seeming to know his exact place in order of rank. I hung back, not sure where I belonged. Pothinus whispered in my ear, "Just follow me, and keep quiet."

A ritual ceremony attended the king's arrival on the jetty, with various members of the court welcoming Ptolemy back to his capital. Then the king stepped into a fabulously decorated litter, its canopy fringed all about with pink-and-yellow tassels, its beams and posts carved of ebony chased with silver, the whole vehicle carried aloft on the shoulders of a team of immensely muscular slaves who were as naked as horses, adorned by nothing more than a few straps of leather and swatches of linen.

Behind the king's litter was another conveyance, almost as magnificent. Pothinus ushered me inside and then joined me. We were hoisted aloft. Surrounded by armed guards and preceded by a veritable orchestra of pipers (playing in unison a festive tune now quite familiar to me), we were carried down the long jetty. The walls of Alexandria stretched to either side of us. Before us loomed the high bronze doors of the Gate of the Sun. The doors swung open. A warm breeze issued from within, as if the city itself released a sigh at the return of its monarch. The royal procession entered the city.

After so many delays and detours, I was back in Alexandria. The scent of the city— for, like a woman, Alexandria has its own perfume, compounded of sea air, flowers, and hot desert breezes—swept over me, and with it a nostalgia far more powerful and all-encompassing than I had anticipated. The flood of memories made me tremble. The absence of Bethesda made me weep. If I had possessed her remains, I could at least have given her, in death, the homecoming she had longed for; but even that small consolation was not possible. I possessed no urn full of ashes, no box containing her mummified remains. Suppressing a sob, I whispered to the air, "Here we are at last, after so many years away!" But there was no one to hear except Pothinus, who gave me a curious sidelong glance and looked away.

We traveled up the Argeus, the principal north-south street of the city, a magnificent promenade one hundred feet wide, with fountains, obelisks, and palm trees down the middle and a colonnade of painted marble statues and fluted columns on each side. Crowds gathered to watch from a safe distance, keeping clear of the armed guards who flanked the king's procession. Many cheered; some drew back, scowling; some shrieked and babbled and prostrated themselves, as if overwhelmed by religious awe. I gathered that Ptolemy was many things to many people: king, hero, usurper, persecutor, god. Would it be so in Rome when Caesar returned there in glory? It was hard to imagine any Roman citizen bowing to another man as if he were divine, but the fate of the world had taken such a tortuous path in recent years that anything seemed possible.

Due to its flat terrain, Alexandria is unusual among great cities for being laid out in a grid, with the streets intersecting at right angles to form rectangular blocks. In Rome, a city of hills and valleys, one comes to a corner where numerous streets intersect, each narrow lane winding off in a different direction, some heading uphill and others downhill; every intersection is unique, and together they offer an endless succession of intriguing sights. In Alexandria the horizon is low, and the broad avenues offer distant views in all directions. The landmark that dominates all else is the Pharos lighthouse, towering impossibly high above the great harbor, its flaming beacon a rival to the sun itself.

It would be hard to say which city seems bigger. Rome is a crowded jumble of shops, tenements, temples, and palaces, with one thing built on top of another and no sense of order or proportion, a once-quaint village grown madly out of control, bustling and swaggering with brash vitality. Alexandria is a city of wide avenues, grand squares, magnificent temples, impressive fountains, and secluded gardens. The precision of its Greek architecture exudes an aura of ancient wealth and a passion for order; even in the humble tenements of the Rhakotis district or the poorer sections of the Jewish Quarter, an invincible tidiness holds squalor at bay. But while the Alexandrians love beauty and precision, the heat of the Egyptian sun induces a certain languor, and the tension between these two things—orderliness and lassitude—gives the city its unique, often puzzling character. To a Roman, Alexandria seems rather sleepy and self-satisfied, and too sophisticated for its own good—sophisticated to the point of world-weariness, like an aging courtesan past caring what others might think. To an Alexandrian, Rome must seem impossibly vulgar, full of loud, brash people, bombastic politicians, clashing architecture, and claustrophobic streets.

We arrived at the great crossroads of the city—the crossroads of the world, some would say—where the Argeus intersects the main east-west avenue, the equally broad Canopic Way, perhaps the longest street in the world. The intersection of these two avenues is a grand square with a magnificent fountain at its center, where marble naiads and dryads cavort with crocodiles and Nile river-horses (or *hippopotami,* as the Greeks call them) around a towering obelisk. The intersection of the Argeus and the Canopic Way marks the beginning of the royal precinct of the city, with its state offices, temples, military barracks, and royal residences. Occupying each of the four corners of the intersection are colonnaded buildings that house the tombs of the Ptolemaic kings and queens of Egypt. The most opulent of these tombs is that of the city's founder, Alexander the Great, whose mummified remains are an object of wonder to visitors who travel from all over the world to gaze upon them. Great tablets adorn the walls of the tomb, with painted reliefs that depict the conqueror's many exploits. On this day, as on every day, a long queue of people stood waiting for their turn to step inside. One by one, they would be allowed to shuffle past the body of Alexander, so as to look for a moment (and at a distance, for the open sarcophagus lies beyond a protective chain and a row of guards) at the face of history's most famous man.

As we passed by the tomb, those in the queue turned to watch the royal procession. On this day, they would catch a glimpse not only of Alexander but also of his living heir.

Beside me in the litter, Pothinus released a heavy sigh. I turned to look at him, and saw that he gazed abstractedly at his fingernails. "At Casium, we almost had her!" he muttered.

I said nothing, but he turned and saw the puzzlement on my face.

"Cleopatra," he explained. "The king's sister. South of the village of Casium, at the outermost eastern frontier, we very nearly had her."

"There was a battle?" I said, striving to show polite interest.

"More precisely, there was *not* a battle," said Pothinus. "Had we been able to confront her in a decisive engagement, that would have been the end of Cleopatra and her ragtag band of bandits and mercenaries. The king's army is bigger, better trained, better equipped—and far more cumbersome. Rather like matching a Nile river-horse against a sparrow; the beast would have no trouble crushing the bird, provided he could catch it first. Time and again they eluded us. We were in the middle of engineering a trap in the hills not far from Casium when word came that Pompey and his fleet had just arrived off the coast."

"You could have crushed Cleopatra first, then met with Pompey."

"That was what Achillas advised. But the risk seemed too great. What if Cleopatra eluded us once again—and it was to her that Pompey made his overture? Then we would have had Cleopatra and Pompey on one side of us, and Caesar on the other. Not a pretty place to be. Better to deal with each threat, one at a time."

"Starting with the one most readily disposed of?" I suggested. What an easy target poor Pompey had turned out to be!

"We considered the threat posed by Pompey, and, as you might say, decided to head him off." Pothinus smiled and looked pleased with himself. It might have been Achillas who struck the blow, but I gathered that Pothinus was the author of the scheme, and not averse to taking credit for it.

"The king himself approved of that decision?"

"Nothing is done in the king's name that does not have the king's approval."

"That sounds rather formulaic."

"But it is true. Don't let the king's youth mislead you. He's very much the son of his father, the culmination of thirteen generations of rulers. I am his voice. Achillas is his sword-hand. But the king possesses a will of his own."

"Is his sister the same?"

"She, too, is the child of her father. If anything, being a few years older, she's even more sure of herself than her brother."

And even less susceptible to the influence of advisers like Pothinus, I thought. Was that why the eunuch had sided with one over the other?

"And so," I said, "having disposed of Pompey . . ."

"We hoped to return at once to the problem of Cleopatra. But the ships that gave chase to Pompey's fleet returned with fresh intelligence about Caesar. He was said to be anchored off the island of Rhodes, planning to come to Alexandria as soon as possible. Once again it seemed prudent to turn our attention to the 'Roman Problem,' and postpone until a later time our dealings with the king's sister."

"Will Caesar then be dealt with as was Pompey?" I felt a quiver of dread, imagining Caesar's head in a basket next to that of the Great One. What would happen to Meto if such a thing came to pass? I cursed myself for wondering. Meto had chosen to live by guile and bloodshed, and his fate had nothing to do with me.

"Caesar presents a more complex challenge," said Pothinus, "requiring a more subtle response."

"Because he arrives in the wake of his triumph at Pharsalus?"

"Clearly, the gods love him," acknowledged Pothinus.

"But isn't Ptolemy a god?"

"The will of the king concerning Caesar shall be made manifest in the fullness of time. First, we shall see what awaits us in the harbor." Pothinus looked at me shrewdly. "They say, Gordianus-called-Finder, that the gods granted you the gift of compelling outspokenness and forthrightness in those you meet. Strangers confide in you. Men like Caesar and Pompey unburden themselves to you. Even the king does not seem immune to this power of compelling candid speech. Even *I* appear to be susceptible to it!"

" '*They* say . . .' " I quoted back to him.

"It's all in your dossier. The king's intelligence is quite extensive. His eyes and ears are everywhere."

"Even in Rome?"

"*Especially* in Rome. Thus your reputation precedes you. The king himself spent an hour last night perusing your dossier and asking questions about you."

"I suppose I should feel flattered."

"Or lucky to still be alive. Ah, but we've arrived at the gates of the royal residence. Time for more formalities, I fear, and an end to our conversation."

Gates opened, and the procession entered the complex of royal residences along the waterfront. It was said that each successive ruler in the line of Ptolemies had felt obliged to add to the royal habitations; thus, over the centuries, the complex had become the most sumptuous concentration of wealth and luxury in the world—a city within the city, with its own temples, courtyards, living quarters, and gardens, honeycombed with hidden chambers and secret passages.

The gates shut behind us. We were in a narrow courtyard surrounded by high walls. The litters were set upon blocks. Pothinus stepped out and attended the king, who emerged from his litter to the greetings of fawning courtiers. For the moment I seemed to have been forgotten, and I sat back against the cushions of the litter, bemused by the twists of fate that had brought me to such a curious place. I felt a prick of anxiety, wondering what had become of Rupa and the boys, and then a sudden overwhelming homesickness for Rome. What was my daughter Diana, pregnant with her second child, doing at that moment? And her son, little Aulus, and her hulking lamb of a husband, Davus? How I missed them! How I wished I was there with them, and with Bethesda, and that the two of us had never left Rome!

Somewhere in the background of my thoughts, I heard the music of Ptolemy's piper echo between the narrow walls and recede into the distance. The courtyard, which had been thronged with attendants, was now almost deserted. I blinked and turned to see a young woman standing beside the litter, staring at me.

Her skin had the hue and luster of polished ebony. Her hair had been styled to take advantage of its natural coarseness so that it formed a circular nimbus around her face, like a floating frame made of black smoke that trailed into wisps along the edges. Her eyes were an unexpected green, a shade I had never seen in a Nubian before, but her high cheekbones and full lips were emblematic of the beauty of Nubian women.

She gave me a demure smile and lowered her eyes. "My name is Merianis," she said, speaking Latin. "If you care to step from the litter, I'll show you to your room."

"I have a room in the palace?"

"You do. Shall I take you there now?"

I took a deep breath and stepped from the litter. "Show me the way."

I followed her through a succession of passages, courtyards, and gardens. We drew closer to the harbor; every now and again through an opening in the walls, I spied a glimpse of sails and the sparkle of sunlight on water, and occasionally, above the rooftops, I saw the Pharos lighthouse looming in the distance. We ascended several flights of steps, then strode down a long hallway, across a bridge of stone between two buildings, and down another long hallway.

"Here," she said, opening a wooden door.

The room was large and simply furnished, with a bed against one wall, a small table and a chair against the other, and a red-and-yellow rug of geometric Greek design on the floor. The lack of ornament was more than made up for by the breathtaking view from the tall window, from which drapes of pale yellow had been pulled back; no painting or mosaic could possibly compete with the majestic image of the Pharos, perfectly framed in the window, and a view of the great harbor dotted with ships in the foreground.

"Magnificent!" I whispered.

"Does Rome have any sight to match it?" asked Merianis.

"Rome has many magnificent sights," I said, "but no other city has a sight such as this. Have you been to Rome?"

"I've never been outside Alexandria."

"But your Latin is excellent."

"Thank you. We can speak Greek, if you like."

"Which do you prefer, Merianis?"

"I appreciate any opportunity to practice my Latin."

"Then it's a pleasure to accommodate you."

She smiled. "You must be famished after the day's journey. Shall I have food brought to you?"

"I'm not hungry."

"Then perhaps I could help to relieve the strains of the day."

I ran my eyes from the lapis-encrusted sandals on her feet, to the sheer linen skirt that left bare her well-proportioned calves, up to the many-pleated linen mantle that clung to her shoulders and shapely breasts. The mantle left her neck uncovered; a necklace strung with lapis baubles nestled against the silky flesh of her throat.

"I'm rather tired, Merianis."

"It will require no expenditure of energy on your part if I simply give you a massage."

I gave her what I imagined to be a very crooked smile. "I think I should simply lie down and rest for a while. What's through there, by the way?" I asked, noticing a narrow door covered by a curtain in the wall beside the bed.

"Quarters for your slaves and for the young man traveling with you."

"Rupa and the boys? Where are they?"

"They'll be here soon, along with your trunk. The wagon in which they traveled and the mules that pulled it will be delivered to the cousin of the owner, as was your intention."

I looked at her more closely, scrutinizing her emerald green eyes. "I took you for a slave, Merianis."

"I *am* a slave—of Isis. I serve the goddess and belong to her completely, body and soul, in this world and in the next."

"You're a priestess?"

"Yes. I'm attached to the temple of Isis within the palace. But in her absence—"

"Absence? Surely Isis isn't off on a trip somewhere."

"As a matter of fact, my mistress *is* away from the palace."

I nodded. "You speak of Queen Cleopatra."

"Who is also Isis. They are one and the same. Queen Cleopatra is the incarnation of Isis, just as King Ptolemy is the incarnation of Osiris."

"I see. Why are you not with her now?"

Merianis hesitated. "When she took her leave, my mistress left the palace . . . rather abruptly. I was unable to accompany her. Besides, my duties keep me here in the palace, close to the temple. Among many other tasks, I see to the comfort of distinguished visitors such as yourself."

I laughed. "I'm not sure what distinguishes me, except a multitude of misfortunes. But I *am* thankful for your hospitality, Merianis."

She bowed her head. "Isis will be pleased."

"Will you be seeing to the comfort of that other distinguished Roman who's come to visit Alexandria?"

She cocked her head quizzically.

I strode to the window. "The one in the harbor. Surely you've noticed that fleet of Roman warships out there?"

She joined me at the window. "There are thirty-five Roman ships in all; I counted them myself. Is it true that you know Caesar?"

I drew breath to answer, then stopped short. Weariness and an excess of emotion had dulled my mind; otherwise, I would have realized, before that moment, the likelihood that the woman who stood beside me—exotic, beautiful, well-spoken, enticingly available—was something more than a servant or priestess. With the king and queen at war with one another, the palace must be filled with spies. Glancing sidelong at Merianis, feeling her nearness, smelling the heady scent of spikenard from her dark flesh, I could easily imagine a man letting down his guard in her presence and saying things better left unsaid.

I turned my gaze to the harbor. The long day was slipping gradually toward nightfall. Ships cast long shadows on flat water pierced by dazzling flashes of reflected sunlight. The Pharos cast the mightiest shadow of all, darkening the entire entrance to the harbor. Beyond, the open sea extended to seeming infinity. I thought of the Nile emptying endlessly into that sea, carrying all that was lost or scattered in its waters. . . .

"I'm weary, Merianis. Leave me now."

"As you wish." She departed without another word, leaving a faint scent of spikenard behind.

How long I stood at the window, I had no idea. The sun continued to sink until it touched a point on the horizon where the earth met the sea; it was then swallowed in a great effulgence of crimson and purple mist. The great harbor grew dark. On the Roman galleys, lamps were lit. Lamps were likewise lit on the great causeway, called the Heptastadion, that swept from the city out to the island of Pharos. Beyond that causeway lay another, smaller harbor to the south, the Eunostos, or Harbor of Good Return; near its center, an archway in the Heptastadion allowed ships to sail from one harbor into the other.

There was a knock at the door. *Merianis,* I thought, and part of me was glad.

But when I opened the door, I saw not the priestess of Isis but the wide-eyed face of Rupa, whose expression declared his astonishment at being inside the royal palace. I lowered my eyes and saw two more astonished faces peering back at me.

"Androcles! Mopsus! You have no idea—"

"How happy we are to see you!" cried the boys in unison, throwing their arms around me. Rupa looked as if he would gladly have hugged me, too, had there been room enough in the narrow doorway.

"But where have you been all this time?" said Androcles.

"And was that really you we caught a glimpse of, on the king's barge?" said Mopsus.

"And look at that!" said Androcles, running to the window. "It's the lighthouse, bigger than a mountain! And all those boats in the harbor! Roman galleys, someone said, with Caesar himself aboard one of them."

Slaves carried my trunk into the room, followed by more slaves bearing trays of steaming food. Until the smell reached my nose, I had no idea how hungry I was.

Mopsus said, "When you were with the king, did he show you Pompey's—"

"Eat now, talk later!" I said, my stomach growling. We would have to be careful when we did speak, for in such a place the floors had ears to listen, and the walls had eyes to watch. But after we ate—great steaming bowls of barley soup, pigeon meat roasted on skewers, spicy lentil wafers, and cups of beer to wash it all down—there was no talk at all, only sleep, as I fell against my pillow and left it to Rupa and the boys to find their own beds.

11

"Thirty-three, thirty-four, thirty-five. Yes! Thirty-five Roman galleys in the harbor," declared Mopsus, who had just counted them for the second time. Morning light glinted on the water and lit the face of the Pharos. The room smelled of the freshly baked bread that slaves had delivered for our breakfast. I sat back against the cushions on my bed, gnawing a piece of hard crust, while the boys stood at the window. Rupa sat on the trunk, shaking his head, amused at the boys and their perpetual squabbling.

"Thirty-five? You missed one. I counted thirty-six!" insisted Androcles.

"Then you miscounted," said Mopsus.

"I did not!"

"You never could count higher than the sum of your fingers and toes," said Mopsus.

"Nonsense! You obviously missed one. Did you count that one with the gorgon head at the prow? I never saw such a fearsome ramming beak on a ship!"

"Where?"

"You can barely see it, because it's mostly blocked by the buildings on that island. What's the name of that island in the harbor, Master?"

"It's called Antirrhodus, and it belongs to the king. Those buildings are his private estate, with their own little harbor within the harbor."

"It must be a fabulous place to visit."

"Can we go there, Master?" said Mopsus.

"I suspect one has to be rather more important than ourselves to receive an invitation to Antirrhodus."

"Yet here we are, with our own room in the palace," noted Androcles. "Imagine that!"

"Maybe Caesar will take over Antirrhodus, and make it his headquarters, and then—"

"Mopsus, hush! You're not to say a word about Caesar while we're here in the palace. Don't even mention his name. Do you understand?"

He frowned, then saw the seriousness of my expression and nodded. Over the last few years, back in Rome, the boys had learned a thing or two about secrecy and espionage. He turned his attention back to the harbor.

"Some of them are cavalry transports," he noted. "Those ships nearest the lighthouse have horses on the decks."

"Imagine bringing horses all the way from Greece," said Androcles. "Do you think they might be the very horses that . . . you-know-who . . . used in the battle at Pharsalus to trample . . . what's-his-name?"

"What's-his-*head,* you mean!" Mopsus laughed.

"But look! More Roman soldiers are disembarking from that larger ship onto the smaller one, the one that keeps sailing out from the palace to bring them to that landing area over there."

"*More* soldiers? Landing area?" I said. "How long has this been going on?"

"Oh, for a while," said Androcles. "The landing area—a sort of big square, on the waterfront—is getting rather full, what with all those Roman soldiers and Egyptian soldiers, and that crowd of people in fancy clothes, and all those banners and pennants. Do you think there's going to be some sort of official meeting between the king and . . . well . . . you-know-who? That could be *him* now, standing amid the soldiers on that Roman galley." He squinted. "He's wearing very fancy-looking armor and a big red cape—like you-know-who."

"*And* he's bald, like you-know-who. The sunlight off his head is blinding me!" Mopsus laughed.

"What are you two going on about?" I got up from the bed to have a look, but before I reached the window, there was a loud rap at the door.

I nodded to Rupa, who sprang up and pulled the door open. Merianis stood in the hall.

Rupa widened his eyes, then pulled himself erect and squared his impressive shoulders. The boys simply gaped.

Merianis wore an extraordinary gown of some sheer green material embroidered with silver threads and cinched beneath her breasts with a silver cord. The green matched her eyes. As before, she wore lapis-encrusted sandals and a lapis necklace, but the stones took on a very different hue when seen next to the green of her gown. The effect, together with her ebony skin, was quite remarkable.

"Can you be ready in half an hour?" she said.

"Ready for what?"

"The lord chamberlain suggests that you wear your best. I assume there's something suitable in that trunk of yours?"

"Nothing remotely as fine as what you're wearing."

"But, Master," said Mopsus, "don't you remember? Before we left the house in Rome, at the very last moment, you decided to bring along your best toga."

"So I did," I said.

"A toga would be splendid!" said Merianis. "The sight of you will make our visitor feel right at home."

"Visitor?"

"Surely you've been watching the assembly gather out on the royal landing? The king desires that you should be in attendance when Caesar arrives."

"I see. I don't suppose I have any choice in the matter?"

"None whatsoever. I'll be back in half an hour to escort you." Merianis smiled, then was gone.

Rupa gave me a look that echoed the question the boys spoke in unison: "Who was *that*?"

"I'll explain while I dress," I said. "Rupa, would you fetch my toga from the trunk? It must be in there somewhere; let's hope it's not too wrinkled. Androcles, Mopsus, attend me. You know the drill." The boys had been helping me put on my toga ever since I acquired them. Except for their inevitable bickering over who should tuck and hold and who should drape and fold, they had perfected the art. Valuable is the slave who has learned to dress a Roman citizen in his toga so that he emerges looking like something other than a pile of rumpled wool.

I had forbidden the boys to speak the name of the man who was about to set foot in Alexandria. But there was another who was likely to make an appearance that morning, and his name the boys already knew better than to utter in my presence. At the prospect of greeting the presumptive master of the Roman world, I felt a curious absence of emotion. But my heart sped up and my brow became clammy when I considered that I might, within the hour, come face-to-face with the man I had once called my son.

How clever the architects of the Ptolemies had been, generation after generation. From without, the palace complex appeared grand, intimidating, and impenetrable. Yet, inside that grandiose edifice, one experienced not a sense of chilly containment, but the simple pleasures of walking through sunlit passageways and quaint courtyards to the music of birdsong and splashing fountains. We might have been strolling through the neatly landscaped gardens and splendidly appointed hallways of some idealized Greek villa, except that the villa went on and on and on. Thus ran my thoughts, all the better to distract me from what was truly on my mind, as I followed Merianis.

"The two slave boys and your mute friend seemed crestfallen when I told them they must stay behind," she remarked.

"I suspect they simply wanted more time to look at you. Especially Rupa."

She smiled. "You look quite splendid yourself."

I laughed. "I'm a gray, wrinkled face peering from a gray, wrinkled toga."

"I think you're rather distinguished."

"And I think you're rather disingenuous, Merianis. But as long as I stand next to you, I don't suppose anyone will notice me anyway. Is it much farther?"

"No. In fact—"

We turned a corner and stepped into a patch of sunlight. I blinked at the bright blue sky above and felt a fresh sea breeze on my face. Before us lay a vast stone-paved square thronged with courtiers in ceremonial wigs or colorful headdresses and elaborate robes. Where the square terminated in steps leading down to the water, a long row of Roman soldiers stood at attention. Companies of Egyptian soldiers were stationed at each corner of the square, and at the very center I saw a canopy with pink-and-yellow tassels, and knew that Ptolemy must be beneath it, seated on his throne.

I assumed we would stay at the edge of the crowd, but Merianis boldly strode forward. When she saw that I hung back, she smiled and took my hand and led me like a child toward the gaudy canopy. Courtiers yielded to her, gatherings of eunuchs stepped back to let her pass, and even the ring of spearmen who circled the king and his retinue broke ranks to let us through. Pothinus stood near the king. He spotted us and strode over.

He spoke in a nervous rush. "At last! What took you so long, Gordianus-called-Finder? The king will be relieved; he was quite insistent that you be here. Watch everything; say nothing. Do you understand?"

I nodded.

"And why on earth are the two of you holding hands?"

Merianis's fingers disengaged from mine.

Pothinus returned to the king's side. There was a blare of trumpets. A small boat had pulled up to the steps. Its occupants disembarked, and through the crowd I caught a glimpse of a familiar balding head. My heart sped up.

The Roman soldiers formed a cordon leading up to the canopy. In the pathway formed by their ranks, a small group came striding toward the king. Foremost among them was Caesar himself. He was dressed not as imperator, in military regalia with a scarlet cape, but as a consul of the Roman people, in a toga with a broad purple border.

I had last seen him in Massilia, on the southern coast of Gaul, on the day his forces entered the city following a lengthy siege. Caesar himself had been off in Spain, defeating his enemies there, and was on his way back to Rome, and thence to Greece for a direct confrontation with Pompey; his stop in Massilia had been little more than a courtesy call, a chance to exhibit his famous penchant for mercy and at the same time to exert beyond question his subjugation of a proud city that had maintained its independence for hundreds of years. Pressed by circumstance, the Massilians had sided with Pompey against Caesar, and had lost everything. I myself had been trapped in the city during the final days of the siege, looking for my son Meto, who I feared was dead. But Meto's disappearance had merely been part of Caesar's scheme for taking the city, and when Caesar made his triumphant appearance, Meto was at his side, beaming with joy. In that moment, the absurdity of the war and the cruelty of my son's deceit had overwhelmed me; instead of embracing Meto, I had rejected him, publicly disowning him before Caesar and the world. Since that moment I had seen neither Meto nor Caesar, though the shadows of both had continually fallen over my life.

Now, half a world away from Massilia, our paths had intersected again. When I had seen him last, Caesar had been flush with victory, a warrior-god doling out grim justice to the Massilians before heading off to face the greatest challenge of his life. He arrived in Alexandria fresh from his triumph at Pharsalus, the undisputed master of the Roman world. His thin lips were set in a straight line, and his jaw was rigid, but his eyes sparkled and betrayed an intense enjoyment of the moment.

His long chin, high cheekbones, and balding pate gave him an austere appearance, but the spring in his step showed the energy of a man half his age. To arrive at such a moment must have been one of the supreme accomplishments of Caesar's long career, the sort of grand occasion that painters and sculptors might celebrate for generations to come. The master of the world's new order was about to meet the ruler of the world's oldest kingdom; the new Alexander was about to confront the heir of Alexander the Great, in the city Alexander himself had founded. In Caesar's countenance I saw a man fully conscious of the moment's import and radiant with confidence.

What of Ptolemy? The king's expression was more obscure. From childhood, he must have been taught to make his face a mask suitable for various formal occasions—dedicating temples, meting out punishments, granting favors, conveying the blessings of the gods—but surely there had never been an occasion quite like this one. His countenance seemed utterly, almost unnaturally devoid of emotion, except for an occasional glint in his eye that betrayed the excited boy beneath the crown. Seated upon his throne, clutching the flail and crook crossed over his chest, he remained absolutely motionless, his stillness befitting a ruler who occupied the unmoving center of the world—except for the toes of his left foot. While I watched, they repeatedly clenched and relaxed against the sole of his jewel-encrusted sandal.

Pothinus stepped forward. Like most Romans, Caesar probably had a distaste for eunuchs, but his face betrayed no reaction. The eunuch spoke in a voice too low for me to hear, no doubt asking Caesar how he wished to be introduced and explaining the protocol for approaching the king; Caesar answered in equally low tones, but from the lilt of his voice, I discerned that the exchange was in Greek.

It appeared there would be an exchange of gifts. Caesar raised his hand and gestured for a member of his retinue to step forward. I drew a sharp breath as I recognized Meto, wearing a gleaming breastplate and garbed in full military regalia.

How young he looks! That was the only coherent thought that crossed my mind, among many others that could not be put into words. I felt a pain in my heart and must have uttered a low cry, for Merianis gave me a puzzled look and touched my hand.

Meto appeared whole, healthy, and alert; it seemed he had emerged unscathed from the battlegrounds of Greece. He carried a box made of hammered silver, with a bronze clasp in the shape of a lion's head. He approached the throne with his arms outstretched. When he reached the dais, he dropped to one knee and bowed his head, presenting the box to Ptolemy. Pothinus accepted the box from him, opened it briefly to peer inside, then smiled.

Meto withdrew. I watched him step backward until he disappeared into the retinue behind Caesar, then turned my gaze again to Pothinus, who had turned toward the throne and was displaying the opened box so that the king could see. The king nodded to show his acceptance of the gift, whereupon Pothinus removed the item from the box and held it aloft. It was a spectacular belt made of thinly hammered pieces of gold in the form of intertwined ivy leaves. The golden leaves shimmered and tinkled in the sea breeze. There were appreciative murmurs from members of the king's retinue.

Pothinus returned the golden belt to the box, handed the box to an underling, then approached Caesar. Their voices carried to my ears.

"A beautiful gift, Consul," said Pothinus, "worthy even of His Majesty. Did it come, I wonder, from the captured possessions of the so-called Great One?"

Caesar's expression barely registered his displeasure at the eunuch's perspicacity. "Actually, yes. It was among the treasures he abandoned in Pharsalus. I'm told that the belt is of royal Parthian origin, a rare item indeed, and that it came into Pompey's possession when he conquered Mithridates. It was one of his longest-held and most prized possessions."

"How fitting!" Pothinus smiled. "The king's gifts to you also came from Pompey. One of these items he owned all his life, and I daresay he treasured it above all his other possessions."

Caesar wrinkled his brow; then the appearance of a small entourage claimed his attention. One of those arriving was Philip, Pompey's freedman. I had not seen him since we parted company after burning the Great One's funeral pyre. He did not look like a man mistreated, but his demeanor was wan and haggard.

"The first gift, Consul," said Pothinus, gesturing for Philip to step forward.

Caesar frowned. "While Philip was once a slave, I believe that Pompey made him a free man. One Roman citizen cannot be given to another as a gift."

Pothinus managed a stiff smile. "Then the gift shall be the pleasure of Philip's company. He is a man of many virtues. May he be as loyal to Caesar as he was to the Roman whom he previously served."

Philip kept his eyes downcast. Caesar regarded him gravely. "You were there with him, at the end?"

"Yes, Consul."

"They say you gave him funeral rites."

"I did what I could, Consul."

Caesar touched the man's shoulder. With a nod, he indicated that Philip should join the others in his retinue.

Following Philip, two courtiers bearing gifts stepped forward. The courtiers themselves were remarkable. One was as black as Merianis and shorter than a child, with child-sized limbs but an old man's face. The other was a bony-browed, hollow-cheeked albino towering at least a head above the next-tallest man present. The tiny one carried a large wicker basket; the giant carried an identical basket in miniature. The grotesqueness of the presentation was unsettling, at least to me; others, including Merianis, found the sight of the mismatched courtiers bearing mismatched burdens amusing. She laughed aloud. Pothinus grinned. Even the king showed the faint indication of a smile.

The albino giant presented his gift first. He held out a long, bare, bony arm, extending the little wicker basket toward Caesar. It was Meto who stepped forward to accept the gift. He looked up at the albino as if searching the giant's colorless face for signs of deviousness, then gave a deferential look to Caesar, who nodded to indicate that Meto should open the basket.

Meto removed the lid, gazed inside for a moment, frowned, then reached into the basket and pulled out a glittering object. I remembered the finger missing from Pompey's corpse—the bloody stump, the swarm of flies—and knew what the object must be, even before my eyes discerned the shape of the ring held between Meto's forefinger and thumb.

Caesar drew a breath, then reached out to take the ring from Meto. He cast a sharp glance at Pothinus, then at the king. Few objects are more sacred to a Roman than his ring. Every citizen possesses one, as a mark of his status; I myself wear a simple band of iron, like most Romans, but those of greater station affect rings of more precious metal, with devices and engravings that proclaim their achievements. Pompey's ring, which I had seen in glimpses, was of gold and bore the single word "MAGNVS," the letters raised in reverse for use as a sealing ring. The ring in Caesar's hand was too far away for me to see in detail, but there could be no doubt, from the expression that crossed his face, that it was Pompey's.

Caesar had already learned of Pompey's demise. But the ring was positive proof of Pompey's death; under no other circumstance could it have been taken from the Great One's finger to be presented as a gift to his rival. Waves of emotion washed over Caesar's countenance. What did he feel? Triumph, surely, for here was tangible proof that the defeat of Pompey was complete and irreversible; but perhaps also a sense of having been cheated, since the fate of Pompey had been taken out of his hands; and perhaps a bit of anger, that a Roman of such stature had been deviously done in by foreigners acting under the orders of a foreign king, and his most treasured possessions treated with such contempt. A ring of citizenship, a symbol of the sacred bond between the Roman state and its individual members, had been reduced to a trophy plundered from a corpse. Was it being presented to Caesar to show the king's esteem, or to send another, more sinister message?

Caesar looked up from the ring in the palm of his hand and cast a searching gaze at King Ptolemy on his throne. Caesar's face was as inscrutable as that of the king, who gazed back at him.

"The king's gift is pleasing to Caesar?" said Pothinus.

Caesar made no answer for a long moment, then said, "Caesar accepts the king's gift."

"Ah, good! But there is another, which I daresay will please Caesar even more; a possession that was even more precious to Pompey than his ring." Pothinus gestured to the black dwarf to step forward. The man did so, carrying his burden awkwardly; the basket was nearly as big as its bearer. He set the basket down at Caesar's feet and then, with a flourish, removed the lid and reached inside.

Suddenly suspicious, Caesar stepped back. Meto stepped forward, gripping the pommel of the sword in his scabbard. Pothinus laughed. The dwarf removed the object in the basket and held it aloft, one hand clutching it by the hair and the other cupping the stump of the severed neck. In a state of excellent preservation—for the Egyptians know all there is to know about embalming dead flesh—the head of Pompey was exhibited for the perusal of Caesar and his company.

Caesar made no attempt to conceal his disgust. His lip curled back to show his teeth. He averted his eyes for a moment, then gazed openly at the head, clearly fascinated by it.

Pothinus inclined his head. "Caesar is pleased?"

Caesar's brow furrowed. A tremor of emotion crossed his face. His eyes glittered, as if suddenly filled with tears.

Pothinus looked from Caesar to the head of Pompey and back. "Caesar accepts the gift?" he said, uncertainly.

"Caesar . . ." Caesar's voice was thick with emotion. "Caesar certainly has no intention of returning this . . . gift . . . into the keeping of those who offer it. Meto! See that the head is returned to the basket, and take the basket to my ship. So far as can be done, have it purified; the coin in the mouth, and the rest, honorably."

As he averted his eyes once again from the head, and also from Pothinus, Caesar's gaze chanced to fall upon me. Perhaps it was the toga I was wearing that caught his attention; the curiosity of a Roman in formal dress amid the throng of Egyptian courtiers piqued his interest. He studied my face, and for a moment gave no sign of acknowledgment; then he exhibited that curious mixture of recognition and doubt that occurs when one sees a familiar face wildly out of context—for surely Gordianus the Finder was the last person he expected to see standing among King Ptolemy's retinue.

Meto was busy collecting the head of Pompey, but when he passed by, Caesar, still looking at me, touched his arm and spoke into his ear. I caught the merest glimpse of motion as Meto began to turn his head toward me. On a sudden impulse I stepped back into the crowd, obscuring the line of sight between Caesar's party and myself.

But I could still see Merianis. Her posture was erect, her expression rapt as she gazed steadily in the direction of Caesar's party, her eyes locked with those of another. I knew at once what had happened: In my absence, Meto's gaze had fallen on Merianis instead. For her, at least—to judge by her expression—the moment was significant.

12

―――――――

" 'When Alexander was fifteen, by chance he passed the place where the wild horse Bucephalus was caged. He heard a terrifying neigh and asked the attendants, "What is that bloodcurdling noise?" The young general Ptolemy replied, "Master, this is the horse Bucephalus that your father the king caged because the beast is a vicious man-eater. No one can tame him, let alone ride him. No man can even approach him safely." Alexander walked to the cage and spoke the name of the horse. Bucephalus, hearing Alexander's voice, neighed again, not in a terrifying way as on every previous occasion, but sweetly and clearly. When Alexander stepped closer, straightaway the horse extended its forefeet to Alexander and licked his hand, recognizing the master that the gods had decreed for him. Whereupon Alexander—' "

"What happens next?" asked Mopsus, sitting on the windowsill and gazing out at the harbor. Both of the boys seemed endlessly fascinated by the doings on Caesar's ships, the comings and goings of the merchant vessels, and the ever-changing play of shadows across the face of the lighthouse. From the abstracted tone of his voice, it was clear that Mopsus's question was not about the narrative I had been reading aloud.

In his lap, purring loudly, sat a gray cat with green eyes. Around his neck the beast sported a collar of solid silver hung with tiny beads of lapis, marking him as a sacred ward of the palace. The cat came and went as he pleased; Mopsus and Androcles had become quite attached to him, and kept scraps of food at hand to lure him to their laps when he deigned to visit us.

Several days had passed since Caesar's arrival. During that time, we had been allowed to move freely about the part of the palace that included our rooms. Our meals were served in a common area where a number of lesser courtiers ate; they kept to themselves and said little to me. Merianis looked in on us every so often, assuring me that the king had not forgotten me and letting me know, subtly but surely, that while I was officially a guest, not a prisoner, I was not to abandon my rooms at the palace. Nonetheless, I was allowed to leave the palace and go about the city as long as I returned by nightfall. But those excursions had grown increasingly problematic.

Alexandria was a city in tumult. Every day since Caesar's arrival, in some part of the city, there had been rioting. Some of the riots were small and easily dispersed by the King's Guards. Others were like whirlwinds that swept through entire quarters, bringing arson, looting, and death. In the bloodiest incident, a company of Roman soldiers on a friendly reconnaissance from the palace to the temple of Serapis had been ambushed and stoned to death, eradicated to the last man despite the fact that they wore armor and carried swords. The fury of an Alexandrian mob is a terrifying thing.

I myself, while out and about in the city, had not been caught in any dangerous situations, but I had seen plumes of smoke and come close enough to some of the disturbances to hear the din of soldiers clashing with rioters. My accent was distinctly Roman, and even the simplest request for directions from a stranger might elicit a hateful glare and a gob of spit at my feet. Rupa, who had lived in Alexandria for many years and still had friends in the city, fared better, but I found it awkward to depend on a mute in every encounter. The boys knew hardly any Greek and no Egyptian, and seemed likely to get themselves—and me—into trouble at any moment.

And so, in recent days, we had taken to staying mostly in our rooms, exchanging words with hardly anyone except Merianis and receiving no other visitors—except, of course, the gray cat that was now curled so contently on Mopsus's lap.

What happens next? Mopsus's query echoed in my head. I sat back against the cushions on my bed and put down the scroll from which I had been reading. Merianis, who had access to the famous Library adjacent to the palace complex, with its 400,000 volumes, had kept me well supplied with reading material. That morning she had brought me a copy of a book I had read as a boy but had never since been able to locate in Rome, *The Wondrous Deeds of Alexander,* by Kleitarchos. Reading aloud helped to pass the time, and I had hoped that the dashing tales of Alexander would prove especially diverting to Rupa and the boys, who badly needed diversion, for we were all growing restless. But even the grand achievements of the conqueror seemed to pale in comparison with the events taking place around us.

I put down the scroll and took a deep breath. We had discussed the uncertain situation in Alexandria many times during the last several days, but the boys seemed to find reassurance in repetition. "What happens next? Hard to say. Caesar's ships effectively control the harbor, and he probably has more ships on the way, so—"

"Is he going to sack Alexandria?" asked Androcles, whose eyes lit up at the prospect of mass destruction. He took a seat opposite his brother on the windowsill, removed the cat from Mopsus's lap, and placed it on his own. The beast emitted a halfhearted mew of complaint, then resumed purring more loudly than before.

"Some of the Alexandrians seem to think so," I said, "but I don't believe that's his intention. Caesar is here to play peacemaker, not warmonger. This conflict between King Ptolemy and Queen Cleopatra needs to be settled once and for all, for Rome's sake as well as Egypt's. The Piper had other children, as well—another daughter, called Arsinoë, who's younger than Cleopatra but older than Ptolemy, and another son, the youngest, who likewise bears his father's name; but those two were left out of the late king's will and seem not to figure much in the conflict. If the royal siblings are incapable of settling their familial dispute, Caesar will act as arbiter. His reward will be stability in Egypt, which will eventually allow for repayment of the debts owed to Rome by the previous king and the resumption of a reliable grain supply from Egypt to feed the hungry citizens back in Rome."

"So King Ptolemy wants him here?" said Mopsus.

"Whether he wants Caesar here or not, Ptolemy may not feel strong enough to expel him; and if he can win Caesar over to his side, that could help to secure the victory over Cleopatra that has so far eluded him. So he's given Caesar a royal welcome and handed over a whole precinct of the palace—"

"Where Caesar's taken up residence and placed his own guards at key points all around the perimeter," said Androcles. "Merianis says that the Egyptians are calling that part of the palace 'Little Rome,' and that the women are afraid to go there because they think the Roman soldiers will molest them. Why aren't *we* staying in Little Rome, Master, along with the other Romans?"

"Because almost certainly we would not be given a room with nearly as good a view of the harbor," I said, giving him a sardonic smile. In fact, since their arrival and installation in the palace, neither Caesar nor Meto had contacted me; nor had I attempted to contact them.

"My turn to hold Alexander!" Mopsus announced.

"Alexander?" I said.

"The cat. That's his new name. We couldn't pronounce his Egyptian name, so Merianis said we could give him a new one, and we decided to call him Alexander. And it's my turn to hold him!" Mopsus took the beast from his brother's lap and placed it in his own. "Do you think Caesar keeps Pompey's head on a nightstand next to his bed?"

I laughed out loud. "Really, Mopsus, I think that might give even Caesar bad dreams. But it does raise a question: Why did King Ptolemy give him the head in the first place?"

"Because he thought it would make Caesar happy," said Mopsus. "Isn't that why anyone gives anyone else a present?"

"Not necessarily," I said. "A gift can be a kind of warning. Fortune is fickle, and Caesar is no more immortal than Pompey was. I think Caesar knows, deep down, that it could just as easily have been *his* head in a wicker basket down on the landing that day, being lugged about and offered as a trophy. I think the king and his advisers wanted to remind Caesar of that fact, even as they pretended to flatter him by handing over the sad remains of his rival."

"Caesar *is* liable to lose his head if he so much as dares to step foot outside the palace," noted Androcles.

"Yes, the streets are unsafe, even for armed men," I noted. "Unsafe, perhaps, even for a god."

"Which supposedly is why you forbid us to go wandering about the city on our own," said Androcles, sulking. "You always allowed us to go out in Rome, even in the worst of times."

"That's not entirely true," I said. "Besides, you both know Rome like the back of your hands; if there's a riot in the Forum, you know all the places to duck and hide. But this is your first visit to Alexandria. You know nothing about the city or the people. You don't even know the language. You're likely to get lost, or kidnapped by some Bedouin slaver, or get into gods know what kind of trouble, and if that were to happen—"

I very nearly said, *If that were to happen, Bethesda would never forgive me.*

Mopsus saw the shadow that crossed my face and gave his brother a glare as if to say, "Stop your childish sulking; see how you've upset the Master!" Rupa, meanwhile, watched the whole exchange in silence and without expression; but I was learning that he missed very little of an emotional nature that occurred around him, and to bring us all out of the moment, he gestured to the scroll in my lap and indicated that I should recommence reading aloud.

I cleared my throat, fiddled with the scroll, and searched for the place where I had left off. "Ah, here it is: 'Straightaway the horse extended its forefeet to Alexander and licked his hand, recognizing the master that the gods had decreed for him. Whereupon Alexander—'"

There was a rap at the door. Merianis had visited us already that morning, and I had no reason to expect her again; and the knock sounded different from hers, louder and more insistent. Alexander the cat sprang from Mopsus's lap onto the floor.

"Rupa, see who it is."

Cautiously, he opened the door, then stepped back to admit an armed Egyptian.

The guard was no common soldier, but dressed in the regalia of the royal retinue. The cat ran between the man's legs and out the door.

The guard gazed about the room, casting suspicious glances at Rupa and the boys, then stepped through the curtain into their room. A moment later he returned and uttered something in Egyptian to another guard in the hallway outside. That guard nodded, then stepped aside to allow Pothinus to enter the room.

The lord chamberlain studied each of us in turn, then walked to the window. Mopsus instinctively ceded his place at the sill. Pothinus gazed at the view for a moment, then turned to me.

"I told them to give you a decent room, but I had no idea you'd been installed in chambers with such a spectacular view of the harbor. I hope you appreciate that, Gordianus-called-Finder. There are visiting diplomats here in the palace who have quarters with views not nearly as impressive."

"I'm grateful for the king's largesse."

Pothinus nodded. "And your meals have been adequate?"

"More than adequate, Lord Chamberlain. Rupa and the boys shall grow fat if they continue to eat all the food made available to them, especially if they do nothing but sit in this room all day."

"But you must have taken some excursions. There's so much for a visitor to see in Alexandria: the Pharos lighthouse, the Library, the Museum, with its world-famous faculty of astronomers and mathematicians, the temple of Serapis, the Tomb of Alexander—"

"On the day we went to see the lighthouse, a disturbance closed the Heptastadion. When we went to see the temple of Serapis, a riot broke out on the Canopic Way. When we went to see the Tomb of Alexander, we were told it was closed to ordinary visitors on that day, for security purposes—"

"Yes, yes, I see your point. These are unsettled days in the city." He shrugged. "All part of the rich fabric of Alexandrian life. I'm sure you recall from the days when you yourself lived here that the Alexandrians are a passionate and highly demonstrative people."

"They appear to have very strong feelings indeed about Caesar's presence in the city."

"There is a certain element of the population who act out of fear and misunderstanding. They believe the rumors that Caesar has come to declare Egypt a Roman province, and that the king intends to allow such a thing. They don't understand that Caesar is a guest of the king."

I smiled. "A guest whose room has an even better view than mine?"

"Perhaps you'd like to see for yourself," said Pothinus. "As a matter of fact, that's why I've called on you this morning. Caesar is aware of your presence in the palace. He's requested me to invite you to dine with him in his chambers this evening."

I stared at the scroll in my hands. I rolled it into a tight cylinder, and made no response.

"The invitation displeases you?" said Pothinus.

"Who else will be present at this dinner?"

"It's not a diplomatic function. No Egyptians will be present, only Romans. Beyond that, I know nothing, except that Caesar stressed the informality of the affair. I suppose it may be limited to his inner circle."

"His inner circle . . ." I repeated, dully.

Pothinus studied me closely. "It was your son who presented the golden belt to the king, wasn't it? And later, the same young officer collected the head of Pompey on Caesar's behalf."

"That young officer is named Meto. At one time he *was* my son. But no longer."

"Of course. Shall I relay to Caesar your desire that Meto should not be present if you're to dine with him?"

"I'm hardly in a position to dictate his choice of dinner companions to Gaius Julius Caesar! Besides, I have no desire to dine with Caesar under any circumstances."

"That seems rather . . . ungracious of you, Gordianus-called-Finder."

"Ungracious? How so? Caesar is not my host."

"Ah, yes, your host is King Ptolemy—and I can assure you that it would be most pleasing to your host if you *did* accept this invitation."

I felt a prickling across the back of my neck. From too many similar experiences in recent years, I sensed the drift of Pothinus's insinuation. When he might have had me killed, King Ptolemy had spared my life. He had done me the tremendous honor of allowing me to enter Alexandria on his royal barge. He had given me accommodations far above my station. In return, he had asked almost nothing of me—until now. Caesar

wished to dine with me. The king would be pleased if I would accept
that invitation. And what would the king expect afterwards? A report on
Caesar's state of mind, a précis of the conversation, the names and ranks
of those present at the dinner and any opinions they might have expressed?

"And if I decline the invitation?"

"Surely, Gordianus-called-Finder, you won't do that. Here you are, far
from home, arriving in Egypt at a time of great uncertainty, even peril,
with three young charges depending for their very survival upon your
judgment, and by the most amazing happenstance, you find yourself under the protection of the king of Egypt himself! Now Caesar, as another
of the king's guests, has asked a favor of His Majesty—that you should
dine with Caesar—and the king, eager to demonstrate his beneficent
hospitality, desires that you should do so. Short of some . . . terrible
accident . . . or a sudden, grave illness threatening you, or one of your
young charges . . . I cannot imagine any reason why you should refuse.
Can you, Gordianus-called-Finder?" The eunuch's bland expression defied me to detect any threat whatsoever in his words.

I shook my head. "No, of course not. I have no reason to deny Caesar
the pleasure of my company. What time shall I be ready?"

13

It was Merianis who came for me that evening. She stood in the doorway and looked me up and down.

"A very handsome tunic," she said. "Dark blue suits you, and the yellow border in that sea-horse pattern is very fashionable. But wouldn't your toga be more suitable?"

I had to laugh. "For a private dinner, in this climate? I think not. Does this mean that you'll be accompanying me?"

"Only as far as the Roman frontier," she said, jokingly referring to the Roman-occupied quarters of the palace. "Once I hand you over to the border guards, my job is done."

"Too bad. A man always feels more confident arriving with a beautiful woman on his arm. But I don't suppose there'll be any women present on this occasion."

"No women have been . . . invited," she said. She seemed to speak with some double meaning, but I could not imagine what.

"Very well, Merianis, if you approve my appearance, then I suppose I'm ready. Rupa, look after the boys. Stay out of trouble, you two!"

We traversed torch-lit corridors, jasmine-scented gardens, and courtyards adorned with Greek statues and Egyptian obelisks. Merianis put her hand on my arm. "It's sweet, the way you fuss over them."

"The boys?"

"And Rupa as well. As if he were your child."

"Technically, he *is* my son, by adoption."

"I see. You took him on as a sort of replacement . . ." She left the sentence unfinished.

"No. I took him into my care because that was the desire of his late sister, a stipulation of her will. It had nothing at all to do with . . ."

She nodded.

"Will Meto be there, tonight?" I said.

"I think not. Pothinus conveyed your sentiments to Caesar. Nonetheless, with or without Meto, Caesar still wishes to dine with you."

I sighed heavily. "I suppose I shall get through the evening somehow. One sits, one eats, one forces a modicum of polite conversation; time passes, and eventually the evening is over, and one may leave."

"Do you dread this meeting with Caesar as much as that? I should love to meet him! There's no man in the world more famous, or ever likely to be. They say he casts a shadow even over Alexander's accomplishments. To be allowed to say just a few words to him would be . . ." Unable to find adequate words, she exhibited an exaggerated shiver instead. I looked at her sidelong and wondered how many men in the world, given the choice, would desire to spend an evening with Caesar rather than with Merianis.

"My only hope is that the evening will be relatively uneventful, and that Caesar won't spring any surprises on me."

She raised an eyebrow. "I shouldn't worry about surprises coming from *that* direction."

"What do you mean?"

She smiled. "Don't men usually enjoy surprises?"

"That depends."

"Upon the man?"

"Upon the surprise. Merianis, why do you keep flashing that coy smile?"

"I suppose I'm in a very good mood tonight."

"And why is that?"

"Ah, but here we are, at the gates of Little Rome." We had entered a courtyard in what must have been one of the older sections of the palace, for the stonework and statuary were noticeably more worn by time. The doorway through which we had just stepped was flanked by Egyptian guards with spears. Flanking the doorway on the opposite side of the courtyard stood their Roman counterparts.

At our approach, the Roman guards exchanged a glance that had nothing to do with me and everything to do with Merianis. They liked what they saw.

"This is Gordianus-called-Finder," she said. "Your master is expecting him."

The senior of the guards snorted. "We're Romans. We don't have a 'master.'"

"Your imperator, then."

The guard glanced at me, then looked Merianis up and down. "But who's expecting *you,* my sweet?"

"Don't be impertinent!" I snapped. "This woman is a priestess in the royal temple of the goddess Isis."

The guard looked at me warily. "I meant no disrespect."

"Then stop wasting our time. Were you not told to expect me?"

"We were."

"Then take me to Caesar at once."

The guard ceded his place to another stationed inside the door and indicated that I should follow him. I glanced over my shoulder at Merianis, who flashed a last, mysterious smile as I stepped around a corner and lost sight of her.

This part of the palace was only a short walk away from the rooms I occupied, and yet I seemed to have stepped into another world. No longer were there whispering courtiers passing in hallways with the sound of sandaled footsteps and the rustle of long linen gowns, leaving the scents of chrysanthemum oil and rosewater in their wake; or the bustle of royal slaves going to and fro, full of self-importance; or the mysterious sounds of music and laughter coming from inaccessible chambers across moonlit courtyards. Instead, I found myself in the brusque, entirely masculine atmosphere of a Roman military camp. I smelled fish stew, heard peals of crude laughter, and felt rough hands searching for concealed weapons in my tunic as I passed through one checkpoint after another. In one of the larger courtyards, tents had been set up to provide the soldiers with accommodations. Priceless statues of Osiris and Serapis loomed incongruously above legionnaires lounging in their undergarments, sitting cross-legged and tossing sheep-bone dice on the ancient mosaic floor.

Eventually the guard passed me into the keeping of a senior officer, who apologized profusely for any indignities I might have suffered and assured me that his imperator was eager to welcome me with all possible attention to my comfort.

We ascended a very long flight of steps, then turned about and ascended more steps. The officer saw that I was slightly winded, and paused for a bit; then we ascended yet more stairs. At the end of a long, colonnaded corridor, tall bronze doors swung open. The officer showed me inside, then discreetly vanished.

The room was stunning. The floor was of dark green marble striated with veins of deep purple and rust orange. Columns of the same extraordinary marble—I had never seen anything like it—supported a ceiling of massive beams painted gold and inlaid with crisscrossing ebony and ivory tesserae. Here and there, rugs with designs of dizzying complexity were thrown on the floor, surrounded by massive pieces of furniture—tripod tables that appeared to be made of solid silver, and chairs and couches inlaid with precious stones and strewn with plump cushions of some shimmering, iridescent fabric. Illumination came from a dozen or more silver lamps hung by chains from the ceiling; each lamp was fashioned in the shape of four ibises flying in different directions, with the tips of their spread wings touching and points of flame flickering from their open beaks. The light was diffused softly and evenly throughout the room, creating an atmosphere of ease and relaxation that muted the magnificence of the appointments. Starlight and moonlight entered through tall windows that opened to views on all four sides of the room; the windows were framed by curtains of green linen hemmed with silver threads. I walked to the nearest window, which faced south, and looked out on a panorama of tiled roofs, hanging gardens, and obelisks, with Lake Mareotis in the background, its still, black face a mirror full of stars.

"Gordianus! In spite of all my entreaties to that wretched eunuch, I still wasn't sure you'd come."

I turned about and saw that Caesar sat in a corner of the room with a coverlet draped over his shoulders, so that only his head was showing. Behind him stood a slave in a green tunic, fussily wielding a comb and a pair of scissors.

"I hope you don't mind, Gordianus, but I'm not quite done having my hair cut. I've been so busy lately that I've rather neglected my grooming. Samuel here is the best barber in the known world; a Jew from Antioch. I conquered Gaul, I bested Pompey, but there's one enemy against whom I find myself powerless: this damned bald spot! It's invincible. Relentless. Merciless. Every month more hairs are lost, the line of battle falls back, and the bald spot claims a wider territory. But if one cannot defeat an enemy, sometimes one can rob him of the trappings of victory, at least. Only Samuel knows the secret of holding this enemy at bay. He cuts and combs my hair just so, and *eureka*! No one would ever know that my bald spot has grown so large."

I raised an eyebrow, tempted to disagree; from where I stood, the shiny spot was glaringly visible, but if Caesar believed that combing a few strands of hair over his naked pate created the illusion of a full head of hair, who was I to disabuse him of the notion?

"There, all done!" announced Samuel. The barber was a tiny fellow, and had to stand upon a block of wood to reach Caesar's head. He stepped off the block, put aside his instruments, pulled the coverlet from Caesar's shoulders, and gave it a shake. I saw with some relief that Caesar was dressed as informally as I was, in a long saffron-colored tunic loosely belted at the waist. He looked quite slender. Meto had once told me that Caesar could boast that he still had the waistline he had possessed at thirty, while Pompey's waistline had doubled with age.

"Perhaps you'd care to avail yourself of Samuel's services?" said Caesar. "You *are* looking a bit ragged, if you don't mind my saying so. In addition to cutting hair, Samuel is also quite adept at tweezing unwanted hair from the nostrils or ears, or from any other part of the body that requires depilation."

"Thank you for the offer, Imperator, but I'll pass."

"As you wish. Off with you, then, Samuel. Tell the servers that I shall take dinner presently. On the terrace, I think." He turned his gaze to me. "No need to address me as a military commander, Gordianus. My mission to Egypt is peaceful. I come as consul of the Roman people."

I nodded. "Very well, Consul."

He began to cross the room. I followed, then stopped in my tracks as my gaze fell upon a life-sized, nude statue of Venus that stood in one corner. The statue was breathtaking, so lifelike and full of sensuality that the marble appeared to breathe. The flesh of the Venus looked warm, not cold; her lips seemed ready to speak, or to kiss; her eyes stared searchingly into my own. Her countenance seemed at once serene and brimming with passion. In Rome, latter-day copies of such masterpieces are strewn about the gardens of the rich, and stuck here and there on public buildings like so many poppy seeds sprinkled on a custard. But a copy is never the same as an original, and this was clearly not a copy; it could only have been fashioned by the hand of one of the great Greek masters of the Golden Age.

Caesar saw my reaction and joined me in front of the Venus. "Impressive, isn't she?"

"I've never seen her equal," I admitted.

"Nor have I. I'm told she was once the property of Alexander himself, and it was he who installed her in the very first royal palace built in Alexandria. Can you imagine? Alexander looked upon her face!"

"And *she* looked upon the face of Alexander," I said, gazing once more into the statue's eyes and feeling irrationally flummoxed that I should be the first to blink and look away.

Caesar nodded. "Upon Alexander's death, Egypt devolved upon his general Ptolemy, and this statue became an heirloom of the new royal family. Do you know, I thought, when I first stepped into this room—knowing that King Ptolemy had chosen it for my personal quarters—I thought that this statue had been brought here especially to impress me, to make me feel at home, since Venus is my ancestor. But if you look at the way the pedestal fits against the floor, it's obvious that she's occupied this room for a very long time, perhaps for generations. So it seems that the guest was fitted to the room, and not the room to the guest." He smiled. "And if you look very closely—here, Gordianus, step closer, she won't bite—you can see that there's a very fine, very slightly discolored line around her neck. Do you see?"

I frowned. "Yes. The head must have been broken off at some point, then reattached."

"Exactly. And when I noticed that, I had to wonder: Did that wretched eunuch give me this room because he knows that Venus is my ancestor, and he wished to flatter me? Or did he install me here so as to give me yet another not-so-subtle reminder that anyone—even a deity—can lose a head?"

I took my eyes from the Venus and stepped toward another of the windows. This one faced east, in the direction of the Jewish Quarter. In the open region beyond the city walls, I discerned the meandering course of the canal that led toward Canopus and the Nile beyond. "You have spectacular views."

"You should see them in the daytime. The harbor on one side, the lake on the other—it's hard to imagine a more ideal location for a city. One can see why Alexander thought that he might someday rule the whole world from this spot, once he finished conquering it."

"But he never had the chance," I said. "Before he could enjoy the fruits of his conquests, he died." A stillness filled the room. Even the Venus seemed to hold her breath, taken aback to hear words of evil omen.

"The evening is warm," Caesar said. "Shall we dine outside, on the terrace overlooking the harbor?"

I followed him onto the flagstone terrace, which was lit by braziers set upon bronze tripods with lion's feet. He took one couch, and I took the other. The moonlight upon the lighthouse skewed my sense of perspective and created the illusion that the tower was a miniature replica, and that if I were to reach out beyond the balustrade, I might lay my hand upon it.

I looked to the west, where a massive structure rose even higher than the room in which Caesar was installed. "What's over there?"

"That's the theater, which presents a steep wall toward the town and opens to the harbor, to which it has access. It's directly adjacent to this building; the space between is quite narrow and could easily be fortified."

"Fortified?"

"Yes, with stones, piled-up rubble, that sort of thing. I've been thinking that the theater could serve very nicely as a citadel, easily defended from attack on the landward side, open for reinforcements from the sea."

"Do you anticipate the need for such a stronghold?"

"Officially? No. But assessing the lay of the land has become second nature to me. Wherever I go, I look for strongholds, points of weakness, hiding places, overlooks." He smiled. "I arrived here in Egypt with a relatively small force, Gordianus, hardly more than an honor guard; but a small number of well-trained men can hold their own against far greater numbers, if their position is carefully chosen."

"Will there be warfare in the city, then?"

"Not if warfare can possibly be avoided. But one must be prepared for all eventualities, especially in a place as volatile as Alexandria."

"I see. There appear to be only two couches here on the terrace. Is it only the two of us for dinner?"

"Why not? Since my arrival in Alexandria, this will be the first night I've dined with anyone who's not a military man, a diplomat, a eunuch, or a spy."

I stiffened at the last word.

Caesar fixed me with a sardonic gaze. "I am right, am I not, Gordianus? You're not . . . a eunuch, are you?"

He laughed. I did my best to laugh with him. He clapped his hands. A moment later the first course arrived, a platter of tilapia fish in a saffron brine. The server was apparently Caesar's taster, as well. As he was displaying the dish for his master's approval, he whispered, "Absolutely delicious!"

Caesar smiled. "This meal is an indulgence for me, Gordianus. Pothinus has been quite stingy with apportioning rations to my men, claiming shortages in the city, though it seems to me that the king's courtiers are quite well fed. But as long as the eunuch starves my men, I eat what they eat—except on a special occasion such as this."

Caesar ate with relish. I had little appetite.

"I still don't understand why you wished to see me," I said.

"Gordianus! You act as if I summoned you here with the intention of interrogating you. I merely asked Pothinus to convey an invitation to dinner, so that we could talk."

"About what?"

"You gave me a bit of a start that day on the landing, when I saw you among the king's retinue. Before I could point you out to Meto, you vanished. Later, I asked Pothinus, and he confirmed that it was indeed Gordianus the Finder I had seen, wearing a toga and standing by that extraordinary female. I'm curious to know how you came to be in Alexandria."

"Did you not ask Pothinus?"

"I did, but I have no reason to believe anything that eunuch tells me. I should prefer to hear the truth from you."

I dropped any pretense of interest in the tilapia and gazed at the lighthouse. "I came to Egypt with my wife, Bethesda. She was ill. She desired to bathe in the Nile, believing its waters would cure her. Instead . . . she was lost in the river."

Caesar gestured for the slave to remove the fish. "Then it's true. Pothinus told me as much. You have my sympathy, Gordianus. I know, from Meto, how dearly you loved your wife." He was silent for a moment. "You must understand that this puts me in a delicate position. Meto doesn't yet realize that you're here in Alexandria."

"No? But that day, on the landing, I saw you speak to him, just after you recognized me. He turned to look in my direction . . ."

"And saw no one, except of course that extraordinary female, who was suddenly standing all alone, because you had disappeared. I never mentioned your name. I merely asked Meto to take a look at the man in the toga and tell me if my eyes deceived me. When he looked and saw no man in a toga, I let the matter drop—you may recall that I was rather busy with another small matter, exchanging greetings with the king of Egypt. Later, meeting privately with Pothinus—without Meto—I inquired about you, and Pothinus gave me an account of your arrival in Egypt. I saw no point in passing the tale on, third-hand, to Meto, at least not until I could speak to you in person. As a result, Meto remains unaware that you're in Alexandria, and he knows nothing of the tragic news about your wife—and it hardly seems fitting that I should tell him, when you're here. Surely the sad news should come from his father."

My heart jumped in my chest. "You didn't invite him to come here tonight, did you?"

"No. Meto doesn't know with whom I'm dining tonight, only that I asked to be given complete privacy." He laughed. "Perhaps he thinks I'm having a liaison with that extraordinary female."

"Her name is Merianis," I said.

Caesar smiled. "As a rule, I prefer to keep Meto close to me at all times. He maintains the official diary of all my comings and goings—without his notes I'd find it impossible to write my memoirs—but I do occasionally draw a breath or eat a meal without him. Your son won't be joining us tonight."

I felt a pain in my chest. "Please don't refer to him as my son."

Caesar shook his head. "Gordianus! The war has been very hard on you, hasn't it? You're rather like Cicero, in that way; you thrived during the old days, when everyone was dragging everyone else into the courts, bending laws to punish their political enemies, flinging reckless accusations, and casting dust in the jurors' eyes. Now all that has changed. Things shall never be the same. I fear that the times we live in no longer suit you. You've become discontented, disgruntled—bitter, even—but you shouldn't take it out on poor Meto. Ah, the second course has arrived: hearts of palm in spiced olive oil. Perhaps you'll like this dish more than you did the tilapia."

Caesar ate. I stared at the food. He had touched on a point that had been troubling my sleep ever since I had seen Meto on the landing. Bethesda had not been kin to Meto by blood, any more than I was; but in every way that mattered she had been a mother to him. Meto would have to be told of her loss. He would want to know exactly what happened; he might have questions that only I could answer, doubts that only I could assuage. Did he not deserve to be told the facts by me, face-to-face?

Caesar took a sip of wine. "Perhaps we should talk of something else. I understand that you witnessed the end of Pompey, and that you even helped to build his funeral pyre."

"Did Philip tell you that?"

"Yes."

"I suppose you had him thoroughly interrogated after Pothinus delivered him to you as a gift."

"That was an unfortunate moment. As a member of Pompey's household—as a renegade and an enemy of the Roman people—Philip should have been delivered to me in a more discreet fashion, along with any other prisoners of war. But I've treated him with great respect. He was never interrogated, in the sense that you suggest; I myself talked to him at length, in private, as you and I are talking now."

"Surely he told you everything you might wish to know about Pompey's final days."

"Philip was revealing about some things, reticent about others. Since you were there, I should very much like to hear the tale from your lips."

"Why? So that you can gloat? Or to help you avoid the same fate at the hands of your Egyptian hosts?"

His expression darkened. "When I looked upon Pompey's head, I wept. He should never have met such an ignominious end."

"He should have been slaughtered by Roman arms, you mean, rather than Egyptian?"

"I would have preferred that he die in battle, yes, rather than by trickery."

"So that you might claim the glory of killing him?"

"I'm sure that death in battle would have been his preference, as well."

"But Pompey had his chance to die fighting, at Pharsalus. Instead, he fled. The end he met was gruesome, but quick. How many of the men you send into battle die as cleanly and as quickly, Consul, and for how many of those men do you weep? You can't possibly weep for them all, or else you'd never be done weeping."

He looked at me coolly, betraying neither anger nor offense. I think he was unused to being spoken to in such a way, and was not sure what to make of it. Perhaps he thought I was a little mad.

"There are other matters we might discuss, Gordianus. For example, during my absence from Rome, my wife has kept me abreast of events in the city. Calpurnia wrote me a particularly interesting letter about the scrape you got into when Milo and Caelius tried to rouse the people against me. She also told me the details of your involvement with that remarkable young woman called Cassandra. I gathered from Pothinus that another of your purposes in coming to Egypt was to allow Cassandra's brother to scatter her ashes in the Nile."

"Yes. That was done on the same day that Bethesda was lost."

"What a dreadful day that must have been for you! I can only imagine the grief you must have felt, given the special bond that developed between you and Cassandra. But I'm glad that my wife was able to facilitate the disposal of Cassandra's belongings after her death. I understand that Calpurnia took special care to see that you accepted Rupa into your household, and that you received the full amount of the bequest Cassandra intended for you."

This was the Caesar I knew: the consummate politician with an unerring ability to find an adversary's weakness, with the aim to either disarm or destroy him. Caesar had no need to destroy me, but if he could disarm my animosity by appealing to my emotions and win me over to his side, he would. His behavior toward me that evening had been above reproach, yet he had managed to prick at the guilt I felt for avoiding Meto, and now, in a single stroke, he was reminding me of the link that Cassandra formed between us and also of the special favor his wife, Calpurnia, had shown me following Cassandra's death. Performing these subtle verbal manipulations came as second nature to him; perhaps he was hardly aware of what he was doing. Yet I felt his words acutely.

"Cassandra was many things," he said, his voice wistful. "Beautiful, gifted, amazingly intelligent. I can well understand how you came to desire her, admire her, perhaps even love her—"

"I had rather not talk about her. Not here. Not with you."

He studied me for a long moment. "Why not? With whom else could you ever talk about Cassandra, except with me? You and I have seen much of the world, Gordianus. We two are survivors. There are so many things we could talk about. We should be friends, not enemies! I still don't know what I ever did to offend you. I took your son into my confidence. I elevated him to a status far above that to which most freedmen could ever dream to aspire. Your son's course in life has thus far been one glorious ascent, thanks to my largesse and his own strong spirit. You should be thankful to me, and proud of him! I don't know what to make of you. Meto is equally baffled. Every Roman desires to please his father, and Meto is no different. Your estrangement causes him great pain—"

"Enough of this, Caesar! Must you win every argument? Must every man in the world give you his love and devotion? I won't do it. I can't. I see the mess the likes of you and Pompey have made of the world, and I feel not love but a deep loathing. My son loves you, Caesar, with all his heart and soul, and with his body as well, or so the gossips insist. Is that not enough for you?"

I stared at Caesar, who stared back at me, speechless. Then both of us, in the same instant, felt the presence of another. We turned our heads in unison.

Meto stood in the doorway.

14

"Father?" whispered Meto. He was dressed for duty, in gleaming armor with a short cape and a sword in a scabbard at his waist. The rigors of war agreed with him; he looked very lean and fit. He was a man of thirty-one now, but he still looked boyish to me and perhaps always would. His broad, handsome face was dark from the sun. His deep tan highlighted the battle scars scattered here and there on his bare arms and legs. Whenever I met him after a long separation, I counted those scars, fearful of finding new ones. I saw none. He had emerged from the Greek campaign and the battle of Pharsalus without a scratch.

I made no reply.

Caesar frowned. "Meto, what are you doing here? I told you I was not to be disturbed."

Meto's eyes traveled back and forth between us. I looked away, unable to bear the confusion on his face. At last Caesar's question seemed to penetrate his consciousness. "You said you were not to be disturbed, Imperator . . . except under one condition."

Caesar's face lit up. His eyes glittered as if reflecting the beacon of the Pharos. "A message from the queen, at last?"

"Not just a message, but a messenger, bearing a gift."

"Where is he?"

"Just outside this room. A big, strapping fellow named Apollodorus. He claims that the gift he bears comes from the queen herself."

"A gift?"

"A rug, rolled up and carried in his arms."

Caesar sat back and pressed his palms together. "Who is this Apollodorus? What do we know about him?"

"According to our intelligence, he's Sicilian by birth. How he came to Alexandria and entered the service of Queen Cleopatra we don't know, but he seems to have become her constant companion."

"A bodyguard?"

"The chatter among the palace coterie loyal to Ptolemy is that Apollodorus is more than a bodyguard to the queen. He *is* an impressive specimen."

"Even so, I think we must discount such innuendos as vicious gossip," suggested Caesar, who himself had been the target of whispering campaigns throughout his political career.

Meto nodded. "Nevertheless, Apollodorus seems never to leave the queen's side."

"He goes with her everywhere?"

Meto nodded.

"I see. How did this fellow get into the palace?"

"He claims he rowed a small boat up to a secluded landing on the waterfront, disembarked with his rug, and made his way through the palace. How he got past Ptolemy's guard, I don't know—he obviously knows his way around the palace, and the place is said to be full of secret passages. He appeared at the Roman checkpoint, handed over a nasty-looking dagger and allowed himself to be searched, then told the guards that the rug he carried was a gift from the queen, who had instructed him to present it to no one but yourself, in person."

"I see. It must be a very fine rug, indeed. I wish to see it. Show him in." When Meto moved to obey, Caesar turned to me. "You don't mind the interruption, do you, Gordianus? Our dinner conversation wasn't going all that smoothly, anyway."

"Perhaps I should leave."

"It's up to you. But do you really want to miss the next few moments?"

"The presentation of a rug?"

"Not just any rug, Gordianus, but a gift from Queen Cleopatra herself!

King Ptolemy—or more accurately, that eunuch, Pothinus—has done everything possible in recent days to seal the palace and to prevent anyone who might represent the queen from approaching me. Courtiers loyal to Cleopatra have been apprehended, the messages they carried confiscated and destroyed, and the courtiers themselves summarily executed. I've protested to the king—how dare he intercept messages addressed to the consul of the Roman people?—but to no avail. The king wants me to hear only one side of this argument between himself and his sister, but I should very much like to meet her. One hears such fascinating things about Cleopatra. Marc Antony met her some years ago, when he helped to restore her father to the throne, and he said the most curious thing . . ."

I nodded. "I think he must have said the same thing to me. Despite the fact that she was then only fourteen years old—about the age her brother is now—there was some quality about her that reminded Antony . . . of *you.*"

Caesar smiled. "Can you imagine?"

I looked at Caesar, a man of fifty-two with wisps of hair combed over his bald spot, a strong, determined jaw, and a hard, calculating glint in his eyes, slightly softened by that veil of world-weariness that falls over men who have seen too much of life. "Not really," I confessed.

"Nor can I! But what man could resist meeting a younger incarnation of himself, especially an incarnation of the opposite gender?"

"It's my understanding that Cleopatra is an incarnation of Isis."

Caesar looked at me archly. "Some philosophers postulate that Isis is actually the Egyptian manifestation of the Greek Aphrodite, who is also the Roman Venus—my ancestor. The world is a small place. If Cleopatra is Isis, and Isis is Venus, then there appears to be a family connection, indeed a divine connection, between Queen Cleopatra and myself."

I smiled uncertainly. Was he serious, or merely indulging in a bit of fancy wordplay? The look on his face was anything but whimsical.

"Imperator!" Meto appeared in the doorway. He studiously kept his eyes from meeting mine. "I present Apollodorus, a servant of Cleopatra, who bears a gift from Her Majesty."

Meto moved aside to permit a tall, imposing figure to step forward. Apollodorus was darkly handsome, with a great mane of black hair swept back from his forehead and a neatly trimmed black beard. He wore a very brief, sleeveless tunic that left bare his long, muscular legs and arms. His biceps were bisected by veins that protruded above the straining muscles as he held aloft a rolled-up rug. I remembered all the steps I had ascended to reach the room; the flesh of Apollodorus was sleek with sweat from the exertion of carrying his burden, but his breath was unlabored.

The rug was bound with slender rope in three places to keep it from unfurling. Apollodorus knelt and set it gently on the floor. "Queen Cleopatra welcomes Gaius Julius Caesar to the city of Alexandria," he said, speaking in Latin, with an ungainly accent that suggested he had memorized the phrase by rote. In Greek, to Meto, he said, "If I may have back my knife, so that I might cut the cords . . ."

"I'll do that myself," said Caesar. Meto pulled his sword from its scabbard and handed it to Caesar. Caesar poked the sharp point against a strand of rope.

Apollodorus gasped. "Please, Caesar, be careful!"

"Is the rug not mine?" said Caesar. He smiled at Meto. "Am I not a man who knows the value of things?"

"You are, Imperator," agreed Meto.

"And am I ever careless with the things that are mine?"

"Never, Imperator."

"Very well, then." Caesar deftly cut the three strands of rope, then stepped back to allow Apollodorus to unfurl the rug.

As the rug was unrolled, it became obvious that there was something inside it—not merely an object, but something alive and moving. I stepped back and let out a gasp, then saw that Caesar and Meto smiled; they were not entirely surprised at the sight of Queen Cleopatra as she rolled forth from the carpet and rose to her feet in a single, fluid motion.

The rolled rug had given no evidence of the prize it concealed; it seemed impossible that its folds could contain a personage who loomed as large in imagination as Cleopatra. But the immensity of the image conjured by her name was curiously out of scale with the actual, physical embodiment of the woman herself. Indeed, she seemed hardly a woman at all, but very much a girl, small and slender with petite hands and feet. Her hair was pulled back and tied in a bun at the nape of her neck—no doubt the most efficient way of styling it for travel inside a rug. It also allowed her to wear a simple diadem set far back on her head, a uraeus crown that featured not a rearing cobra but a sacred vulture's head. Her dark blue gown covered her from her neck to her ankles and was belted with golden sashes around her waist and below her bosom. Small she might be, but her figure was not girlish; the ampleness of her hips and breasts would have pleased the sculptor of the Venus that had so impressed me earlier. Her face might have captivated a master sculptor as well. She was not the most beautiful of young women—Bethesda in her prime had been more beautiful, and so had Cassandra—but there was something intriguing about her large, strong features. Queen Cleopatra had one of those faces that becomes more fascinating the longer one looks at it, for it seemed to change in some subtle way each time the light shifted or whenever she moved her head.

She stood erect, squared her shoulders, and gave a shudder, as if to shake loose the last vestige of her confinement in the rug. She reached behind her head and undid the knots in her hair, shaking it loose and letting it fall past her shoulders, but keeping the diadem in place. She raised her arms and ran her fingers through the tangles. I glanced at Caesar and Meto. They appeared as captivated by her as I was, especially Caesar. What manner of creature was this, who had risked capture and death to smuggle herself into Caesar's presence, and now stood before three strangers preening herself as unselfconsciously as a cat?

She looked at us one by one. The sight of Meto evidently pleased her, for she spent a long moment appraising him from head to foot. I was less interesting to her. Her gaze turned to Caesar and remained upon him. The look they exchanged was of such an intensity that all else in the room seemed to fade; I sensed that I had become a shadow to them.

Caesar smiled. "Meto, what do you think of Queen Cleopatra's present?"

" 'Beware of Greeks bearing gifts,' " Meto quoted. I assumed he was making a joke, facetiously comparing the queen's rug to the Trojan Horse, but when I glanced at his face, I saw that he did not smile.

The queen ignored these comments. She assumed a formal stance, one foot before the other with her head tilted slightly back and her arms spread in a gracious gesture. Her Latin was flawless and without accent. "Welcome to Alexandria, Gaius Julius Caesar. Welcome to my palace."

"*Her* palace?" I heard Meto mutter.

Caesar shot him a sharp look, then spoke to me. "My apologies, Gordianus. I had intended that you and I should dine at our leisure tonight, sharing our thoughts. But one never knows when a matter of state will arise, as it has, however unconventionally, this evening."

"No need to apologize," I said. "I've been a poor guest. My conversation was as weak as my appetite. I'll leave you now."

I strode from the terrace into the grandly appointed room, not looking back. I slowed my pace for a moment as I passed the statue of Venus. There was something about the queen that reminded me of the goddess, some intangible quality to which great artists attune their senses. Ordinary men call it divinity and know it when they encounter it, even if their tongues cannot capture it with words or their hands give shape to it in sculpture. Queen Cleopatra possessed that quality—or was I simply dazzled for the moment, as any man can be dazzled by an object of desire? Surely Cleopatra was no more a goddess than Bethesda had been, and Caesar no more a god than I.

I pushed open the bronze doors and stepped out of the room, and did not realize I was being followed until I heard a voice mutter behind me: "She's trouble."

I stopped and turned around. Meto almost collided with me, then stepped back a respectful distance. "Papa," he whispered, lowering his eyes.

I made no answer. Despite his armor, despite his strong limbs and his battle scars and the thick stubble across his jaw, he looked to me at that moment like a boy, timorous and full of doubt. I bit my lip. I screwed up my courage. "I suppose it's just as well we've met. There's something I must tell you. This won't be easy . . ."

" 'Quickest done is best done,' " Meto said, quoting the proverb I had taught him as a child, suitable for pulling thorns or drinking foul medicine. He kept his eyes lowered, but his lips formed a faint, ingratiating smile. I tried to ignore it.

"The reason I came to Egypt . . ."

He lifted his eyes to meet mine. I looked away.

"Bethesda has been unwell for quite some time," I said. "Some malady the physicians could never put a name to. She conceived a notion, that if only she could bathe in the Nile . . ."

Meto frowned. "Is Bethesda here in Egypt with you?"

My tongue turned to lead. I tried to swallow but could not. "Bethesda came to Egypt. She bathed in the Nile, as she wished. But the river took her from me. She vanished."

"What are you saying, Papa? Did she drown?"

"The river took her. Perhaps it was best, if her sickness was incurable. Perhaps it was what she intended all along."

"Bethesda is dead?" His lips quivered. His brows drew together. The son who was no longer my son, the favorite of Caesar who had seen men die by the thousands, who had hacked his way through drifts of dead bodies and mountains of gore, began to weep.

"Meto!" I whispered his name, but kept my distance.

"I never thought . . ." He shook his head. Tears streamed down his cheeks. "When you're far from home, you can't help but imagine what might be happening there, but you teach yourself to think of only good things. In the field, getting ready for battle, fighting a battle, tending to the aftermath, there's so much terror all around, so much confusion and bloodshed and suffering, that when you think of home you think of everything that's the opposite, a place that's safe and happy, where the people you love are all together and nothing ever changes. But of course that's a dream, a fantasy. Every place is the same as every other place. No one is safe, anywhere. But I never thought . . . that Bethesda . . ." He shot me an angry look. "I didn't even know she was ill. You might have told me in a letter—if you hadn't stopped writing me letters."

I drew back my shoulders and stiffened my spine. "There, then. I've told you. Bethesda is gone. Her body was lost, or else I would have mummified her, as was always her wish."

Meto shook his head, as if dazed. "And Diana? How is she? And little Aulus? And—"

"Your sister—" I corrected myself. "My daughter and her son were well when I left them in Rome. She's expecting another child, or else she might have come herself."

"And Davus? And Eco? And—"

"All are well," I said, wanting to end the conversation.

He sighed. "Papa, I know what a tribulation this must have been for you. I can only—"

"Say no more!" I said. "You needed to be told, and I've told you. Go back to Caesar now."

"Go back?" He laughed without mirth, even as he wiped a tear from his cheek. "Didn't you see the look on his face? And the look on *her* face? She's trouble. It's one thing, dealing with that starstruck boy-king and his eunuch, but I'm afraid Queen Cleopatra may be another matter altogether. I'll give her credit for sheer nerve—"

"I see how long your tears for Bethesda lasted. Now it's back to Caesar and the queen and whatever game the lot of you are up to."

"Papa! That's unfair."

"Think what you wish, but don't address me as your father."

He drew a sharp breath. He winced, as if I had turned a knife in his chest. "Papa!" he whispered, shaking his head. I could have sworn he was a child again, no older than ten or twelve, an uncertain boy clad in the armor of a warrior.

It took the last measure of my resolve to resist embracing him at that moment. Instead, I turned and strode resolutely down the hallway and then down the many flights of steps, leaving Meto to await the pleasure of his imperator and the queen.

15

"You *knew*," I said to Merianis as we walked side by side through court-yards and past bubbling fountains, heading back to my room. She had been waiting for me at the checkpoint marking the boundary of the Roman enclave.

"You knew," I repeated, turning to look at her. "Thus your coy smile earlier. Thus your arch comment about surprises."

"Whatever are you talking about, Gordianus-called-Finder?"

"You knew that another visitor besides myself was going to call on Caesar tonight."

"Who's being coy now?" she said. "Are you saying that you were joined at dinner by an unexpected guest?" She could not suppress a broad smile. Her white teeth, in contrast to the black luster of her flesh, were dazzling.

"A gift for Caesar arrived from an unexpected quarter."

"A gift?"

"A surprise with another surprise hidden inside. It was compared to the Trojan Horse."

Merianis laughed. "Did Caesar say that?"

I frowned. "No, it was one of his men."

"And was this Trojan Horse successfully delivered?"

"It was."

"Did the contents emerge safe and sound?"

"Yes, and just as ready to wreak havoc as those Greek invaders who jumped out of the real Trojan Horse. When I last saw him, Caesar looked poised to surrender to an overwhelming force."

Merianis clapped her hands with delight. "Forgive me for laughing, but the metaphor is so novel. It's always a woman who's described as a city under siege, with gates flung open and walls tumbling down. It makes me laugh to think of mighty Caesar that way."

"He's only human, Merianis."

"For the time being," Merianis said, then muttered something in Egyptian that I took to be a brief, ecstatic prayer of thanksgiving to Isis.

A group of palace guards was waiting outside my room. Before I could step inside, the officer in charge politely, but firmly, ushered me to a place in the midst of his men, and I found myself heading off once again, leaving Merianis behind.

"I'll look in on Rupa and the boys," she called after me.

I was taken to a part of the palace I had not visited before. The corridors grew wider, the gardens more lush, the draperies and other appointments increasingly more magnificent.

The guards escorted me into a large chamber where scores of courtiers were clustered here and there in small groups. The room echoed with the low buzz of many conversations. Curious eyes peered in our direction. The officer in charge disappeared, leaving me to stand idly in the middle of the room with an armed escort surrounding me.

"It's that Roman," I overheard someone say. "The one the king allowed onto his barge. Isn't he a soothsayer?"

"No, some sort of spy, or maybe a famous assassin, I think."

"Looks a bit old for that."

"You never know with Romans. Treacherous, devious types. The older, the wilier."

The officer reappeared and gestured for me to follow. We wended our way through the crowd until we came to a pair of gilded doors. The doors opened. The officer stayed behind but gestured that I should enter. I stepped into a room in which every surface appeared to be covered with gold—golden urns atop golden tables, golden chairs with cushions of gold thread, walls of hammered gold, and a gold-painted ceiling from which hung golden lamps. Even the floor of dazzling white marble had veins of some glittering golden stuff running through it. Sculptures in low relief adorned the walls, depicting the exploits of the first Ptolemy, Alexander's general; these entablatures, though surely carved of stone, were heavily gilded, either painted with gold or covered with gold foil, so that the images shimmered with the reflected light of the golden lamps. Among them I saw the very scene I had read aloud to the boys earlier that day, in which Ptolemy witnessed the first encounter of Alexander and the horse Bucephalus.

It was a room without shadows, for every surface reflected the light. The air itself seemed golden, suffused with a mellow glow of no apparent origin. Carried upon the golden air was the music of a piper playing a familiar tune.

At the far end of the room, upon a gilded throne, sat Ptolemy, dressed in a pleated gown of white linen with a golden mantle over his shoulders. He must have previously attended some religious function in his role as the god Osiris, for he was wearing the atef crown, his young face looking very stern beneath the tall white cone with its plumes of ostrich feathers. Bodyguards stood behind the throne. Scribes sat cross-legged on the floor nearby. Before the throne stood Pothinus, with his arms crossed and his head tilted back, regarding my wonderment with amusement. I had stepped into a room designed to overawe the likes of me, and the room had done its job.

"Your dinner with Caesar was brief," he said.

"The evening was interrupted."

"Ah," said Pothinus. "An unexpected visitor?"

I looked at him sharply. Had everyone but me been expecting the queen's arrival? Then I realized he was referring to Meto, whom he knew I had wished to avoid.

"The man whom I once called my son did in fact make an appearance—"

Ptolemy spoke up. "I think it's sad, this estrangement between yourself and your son. I should give much to have my father back among the living. To look into his eyes again; to hear him laugh; to listen to him play the flute."

Considering that the king's father had killed his oldest sister, and that he himself was at war with his sister-wife, I was not in a mood to have young Ptolemy pass judgment on my familial relationships. But I kept my mouth shut and found myself studying Ptolemy's face, framed by the golden mantle and the atef crown. Having just met his sister, I was struck by the strong resemblance between them. Neither of them was strikingly beautiful in a way that would turn heads, yet both possessed a certain undeniable presence. I felt it more strongly from Cleopatra, but was that only because of my erotic inclinations? The image of her standing erect and shaking loose her hair to let it fall past her shoulders flashed in my mind. . . .

Pothinus loudly cleared his throat. Apparently he had said something that I missed. "If Gordianus-called-Finder can return to the present moment . . ." he said, giving me a condescending look that put me squarely in my place: a befuddled Roman mortal agog in the king's golden room. I bristled.

"Pardon me. I was lost in thought, considering how the king does and does not resemble his sister Cleopatra."

For a moment this comment went over their heads, then simultaneously Pothinus gave a start, and the king lurched forward in his throne.

"What are you saying?" cried Ptolemy.

"The family resemblance is obvious—the nose, the eyes—yet there's a difference, and I can't quite put my finger on it."

"You've seen her? Cleopatra?" Pothinus's voice broke, as the voice of even a mature eunuch sometimes does. "Where? When?"

"Tonight, in Caesar's chambers."

Ptolemy slumped back in his throne and bit the end of one finger. One knee jerked up and down in agitation. "I told you she'd find a way in, Pothinus."

"Impossible, Your Majesty! Every entrance is guarded; every package is examined; every—"

"Obviously not! We left a way open, and she found it. She's like a snake, nosing its way along a wall until it finds the merest breach to slip through."

"Actually, she came by sea," I said. Was I acting rashly, putting the queen and perhaps even Caesar in danger by this revelation? Was I not doing exactly as Pothinus had intended, conveying intelligence back to the king? Perhaps, but the aggravation I was causing them gave me a great deal of pleasure, and I couldn't stop. "A fellow named Apollodorus rowed her across the harbor. The two of them found an unguarded landing somewhere along the waterfront and made their way to the Roman sector of the palace."

"As brazenly as that?" Ptolemy slapped the crown on his head, a gesture most unworthy of a god. "She and that stud-horse Sicilian went traipsing through the palace, right up to Caesar's door?"

Pothinus lowered his voice. "There are ways, as Your Majesty knows, of traversing the palace and its grounds without being seen. Some of those secret passages are very old; there may be some unknown even to me. Once your father, remodeling his private chambers, tore out a wall and came upon a network of tunnels that even he had never suspected—"

"Even so, Pothinus, you assured me that this would not happen!"

"Actually," I said, unable to resist, "the *two* of them didn't traipse anywhere. Apollodorus carried her."

"What?" Pothinus looked at me, confounded. "Carried her? In his arms?"

"Over his shoulder, mostly."

The king and his lord chamberlain looked at me as if I must be mad. One of the bodyguards snickered. The man next to him covered the noise by coughing.

"She was rolled up in a rug," I explained. "Apollodorus carried the rug over his shoulder. He told the Romans he had a gift for Caesar from the queen. I was there when Apollodorus was shown into Caesar's quarters. The rug was unrolled for Caesar's inspection. The queen appeared. Shortly thereafter, I took my leave."

"Who else was in the room?" Pothinus demanded.

I shrugged. "Meto. He left when I did. I'm not sure where Apollodorus went; maybe into one of those secret passages you were talking about."

The king curled his upper lip. "She's *alone* with him?"

"Even as we speak," I said.

Pothinus sighed. "She's like a wine stain on white linen. We'll never get rid of her."

"Best to burn the linen, then, if the stain won't come out." Ptolemy glowered darkly, then drew a shuddering breath and let out a bleating sound. He sniffled, holding back tears. He seemed very much like a boy at that moment, a boy who was not simply furious, but also heartbroken. Learning that his sister was alone with Caesar, Ptolemy wept bitter tears. I gazed at him, confounded.

"Cleopatra!" muttered Pothinus. "Relentless. Ruthless. She's trouble."

Meto had said the same thing.

16

The bodyguards who had shown me to the royal chamber escorted me back to my room. The hour was growing late. The passageways were empty; the palace was quiet. Long before the open doorway of my room came into view, I heard the high-pitched voices of Androcles and Mopsus, breathlessly assailing a visitor with questions.

"Did you kill anyone at Pharsalus?" said Androcles.

"Of course he did! But how many?" said Mopsus. "And did you kill anyone famous?"

"What I want to know," said Androcles, "is this: Were you there with Caesar when he went crashing into Pompey's tent and caught a glimpse of the Great One's backside disappearing out the rear flap? Is it true they were all set up for a banquet, with Greek slave boys strumming lyres and Pompey's best silver laid out?"

I drew closer, and at last heard their visitor's voice, even above the sudden pounding of my heart in my chest. "Boys, boys, how I've missed you! Though I don't know how Papa puts up with all your pestering."

I stopped in the hallway, several steps from the door. "Go!" I whispered to the officer escorting me. "You've delivered me to my room, as you were ordered to do. Don't say a word. Take your men and leave!"

The officer raised an eyebrow, but did as I asked.

I stepped through the open doorway.

Meto leaned against one wall. The boys were gamboling about and gazing up at him until I entered the room, whereupon they collided and almost knocked each other down. Rupa, who had not met Meto before, stood off to himself, near the window; his shy, but good-natured, smile vanished when I looked at him. Merianis stood nearby, holding Alexander the cat in her arms. She saw my expression, put down the cat, and stepped toward the boys, grabbing each by a shoulder to stop their constant motion. The cat disappeared beneath my bed.

"What are you doing here?" I demanded.

Meto gazed at me for a long moment, his expression at first beseeching and then, when I showed no response, exasperated. "Papa, this is madness! I'd beg for your forgiveness—if I even knew what I'd done to offend you."

Had he forgotten the things I said to him at Massilia? I hadn't. Far from it! How many nights had I lain awake while Bethesda tossed and turned beside me, remembering the words that had come tumbling out of me on that occasion? "Words once spoken can never be recalled," as the poet warns, but in the heat of the moment, I had lost all inhibition and the words had rushed forth, delivering me to a decision I had not foreseen.

Meto! First you became a soldier, and you thrived on it, killing Gauls for the glory of Caesar. Burning villages, enslaving children, leaving widows to starve—it always sickened me, though I never spoke against it. Now you've found a new calling, spying for Caesar, destroying others by deceit. It sickens me even more. . . .

What matters most to me? Uncovering the truth! I do it even when there's no point to it, even when it brings only pain. I do it because I must. But you, Meto? What does truth mean to you? You can't abide it, any more than I can abide deceit! We're complete opposites. No wonder you've found your place at the side of a man like Caesar. . . .

This is our last conversation, Meto. From this moment, you are not my son. I disown you. I renounce all concern for you. I take back from you my name. If you need a father, let Caesar adopt you!

Until that day, in Alexandria, those had been the very last words I had spoken to him.

"There's nothing to discuss and no question of forgiveness. It's quite simple: This is my room, at least for the moment, and you don't belong here. You shouldn't have come. I suppose you followed me, or had me followed, since that's your way of doing things—"

"No!" Merianis spoke up. "I brought him here."

"You? But how—?"

"Earlier, when I delivered you for your dinner with Caesar, I waited at the checkpoint. A little later, Apollodorus appeared, bearing the gift for Caesar. Meto came. He recognized me from the other day, when the king officially received Caesar on the landing. We spoke, very briefly—"

"But not so briefly that Meto didn't learn all he needed to know about you. He's become quite expert at extracting valuable information. It's one of his duties." *And one of yours as well?* I thought, but did not say aloud; for it was clear to me now that Merianis was not merely a priestess of Isis, but a spy for the incarnation of Isis, Queen Cleopatra.

Merianis persisted. "Later—after I'd brought you back to this room and the king's men whisked you away—Meto sent a courier requesting me to return to the checkpoint. I met him there. He asked me to show him here, to your room. Was it wrong to do so? Meto is your son, is he not?"

Ptolemy and Pothinus had known of my estrangement from Meto. Had Merianis not also known of it? Perhaps she was more innocent than I thought—or perhaps not. I suddenly found myself full of suspicion, and I loathed the feeling. It was into just such a morass of doubt and double-dealing that I had found myself immersed in Massilia, and the result had been my breach with both Meto and Caesar. The two of them had followed me to Alexandria, bringing their poisonous treachery to a city already riven by deceit. I felt like a man struggling in quicksand, unable to find a foothold. I wanted only to be left alone.

"Go, Merianis."

"Gordianus-called-Finder, if by bringing your son here I have offended you—"

"Go!"

She frowned and wrinkled her brow, then turned and exited through the open doorway.

"As for you, Meto—"

"Papa, don't speak rashly! Please, I beg you—"

"Silence!"

He bit his lip and lowered his eyes, but seemed compelled to speak. "Papa, if it means something to you, I've begun to share your doubts about Caesar." He gazed at me for a moment before looking away, as if taken aback at the enormity and the recklessness of the words he had just uttered.

I stared at him until he returned my gaze. "Elaborate."

He looked sidelong at Rupa.

I nodded. "I see. Your training as a spy has taught you to hold your tongue in front of a stranger. But I won't ask Rupa to leave the room. Or the boys, either. Anything you have to say to me can be said to them as well."

"This is difficult enough for me!" Meto glared at Rupa with an emotion that went beyond mere distrust. I had disowned Meto; I had adopted Rupa. Did Meto feel he had been replaced?

I shook my head. "Say what you have to say."

He drew a deep breath. "Ever since Pharsalus . . . no, even before that. Since the military operations at Dyrrachium . . . or was it when Caesar was last in Rome, using his powers as dictator to settle the problems that had cropped up in his absence? No, even earlier; I think it must have begun when I was reunited with him at Massilia—when you disowned me there in the town square, even as Caesar was basking in the triumph of the city's surrender. The things you said to me, the things you said about Caesar— I thought you'd gone mad, Papa. Quite literally, I thought the strains of the siege had driven you to distraction. Afterwards, Caesar said as much. 'Don't worry,' he told me, 'your father will come to his senses. Give him time.' But perhaps that was the moment I began to come to *my* senses."

He paused, gathering strength to go on. "Was I the one who changed? Or was it Caesar? Don't misunderstand me; he's still the greatest man I've ever encountered in this world. His intellect, his courage, his insight— he towers above the rest of us like a colossus. And yet . . ."

He fell silent for a long moment, then finally shrugged. "It's me. I've simply lost my stomach for it. I've seen too much blood, too much suffering. There's a dream I have over and over, about a little village in Gaul, a tiny place, utterly insignificant compared to Rome or Alexandria, but not so insignificant that it could be ignored when it raised a challenge to Caesar. We circled the village and took them by surprise. There was a

battle, quite short and simple as battles go. We slaughtered every man
who dared to take up arms against us. Those who surrendered we put
in chains. Then we rousted the women and children and the old people
from their homes, and we burned the whole village to the ground. To set
an example, you see. The survivors were sold as slaves, probably to other
Gauls. That was how it worked in Gaul. Surrender and become a Roman
subject; oppose us and become a slave. 'One must always give them a clear,
simple choice,' Caesar told me. 'You are with Rome or against Rome; there
is no middle ground.'

"But when I dream about that village, it's the face of one particular
child I see, a little boy too young to fight, almost too young to understand
what was happening. His father had been killed in the battle; his mother
was mad with grief. The little boy didn't cry at all; he simply watched the
house he'd grown up in as it was eaten by flames. To judge from the work-
shop attached to the house, the boy's father had been a smith. The boy
would probably have grown up to be a smith, too, with a wife and children and a life in the village. But instead, he saw his father die and he was
taken from his mother, to become a slave for the rest of his life. Whatever
money his new master paid for him went to fund more campaigns against
more villages in Gaul, so that more boys like him could be enslaved.
In my dream, I see his face, blank and staring, with the light of the flames
in his eyes.

"His village wasn't destroyed out of simple spite, of course. All that
was done in Gaul was done for a greater purpose; so Caesar always told
me. He has a grand vision. The whole world shall be unified under Rome,
and Rome shall be unified under Caesar; but for that to happen, certain
things must happen first. Gaul had to be pacified and brought under
Rome's sway; and so it was done. When the Senate of Rome turned against
Caesar, the senators had to be run out of Rome, and so it was done. When
Pompey roused the opposition against Caesar, the opposition had to be
destroyed; and so it was done. Now Caesar must decide what is to be done
with Egypt, and who should rule it, and how best to bring it under his
sway. And the glory of Caesar burns brighter than ever. I should be
pleased, having done my part to bring all this about; but I have that
dream, almost every night now. The fire burns, and the boy stares at the

flames, numb with shock. In the great scheme of things it doesn't matter that he was enslaved; Rome shall rule the world, and Caesar shall rule Rome, and to make that happen, that boy's enslavement was one tiny necessity in a great chain of necessities.

"But sometimes . . . sometimes I wake with a mad thought in my head: What if that boy's life mattered as much as anyone else's, even Caesar's? What if I were offered a choice: to doom that boy to the misery of his fate, or to spare him, and by doing so, to wreck all Caesar's ambitions? I'm haunted by that thought—which is ridiculous! It's self-evident that Caesar matters infinitely more than that Gaulish boy; one stands poised to rule the world, and the other is a miserable slave, if he even still lives. Some men are great, others are insignificant, and it behooves those of us who are in-between to ally ourselves with the greatest and to despise the smallest. To even begin to imagine that the Gaulish boy matters as much as Caesar is to presume that some mystical quality resides in every man and makes his life equal to that of any other, and surely the lesson life teaches us is quite the opposite! In strength and intellect, men are anything but equal, and the gods lavish their attention on some more than on others. And yet . . ."

Meto bowed his head, and the rush of words came to a stop. I could see that his distress was genuine, and I was astounded at the course of his thoughts.

"Does Caesar ever harbor such doubts?"

Meto laughed bitterly. "Caesar never questions his good fortune. He loves the gods, and the gods love him. Triumph is its own vindication. So long as a man is triumphant, he need never question his methods or his aims. Once upon a time, that philosophy was enough for me, but now . . ." He shook his head. "Caesar forgets that old Greek word *hubris.*"

It was my turn to laugh. "If Caesar hasn't provoked the gods' wrath before now, then surely—"

"But Caesar never presumed to imagine himself a god, before now."

I looked at him keenly. "What are you saying?"

"Ever since we set sail for Egypt, he's kept bringing it up, jokingly at first. 'These Ptolemies don't merely live like gods,' he'd say, 'they *are* gods; I must see how they put their divinity into practice.' But it's not a joke, is it? With Pompey gone, the Senate made irrelevant, and all the legions united under him, Caesar will need to think long and hard about what it means to rule like a king, whether he calls himself one or not. The example of Alexander doesn't give much guidance; he died too young. It's the Ptolemies who provide the model for a long and successful dynasty, even if their glory has lately dwindled to the two decadent specimens currently vying to run the country."

"You don't think much of King Ptolemy and his sister?"

"You saw that display by the queen tonight! She and her brother both seem to have the same idea: seduce the man to make an ally of the general."

I frowned. "Are you suggesting that young Ptolemy—"

"Is completely smitten by Caesar. It's rather pathetic, actually. You should see the fawning way he behaves when the two of them are together—the way he looks at Caesar, the hero worship in his eyes!"

I nodded, recalling Ptolemy's reaction when I told him that Cleopatra was alone with Caesar. "I suppose Caesar must be immune to that sort of thing, having received the adulation of so many young men over the years." *Including a copious dose from you, Meto,* I thought.

Meto scowled. "You might think so, but with Ptolemy, it's different somehow. Caesar seems equally fascinated by *him.* His face lights up when Ptolemy comes into the room. They put their heads together, share private jokes, laugh, and give each other knowing glances. I can't understand it. It's certainly not because the boy's beautiful. He and his sister are both rather plain, if you ask me." He snorted. "Now we shall have both of them buzzing around him, like flies around a honey pot!"

I considered this revelation. If true, It wouldn't be the first time that Caesar had engaged in a royal romance. His erotic exploits as a young man in the court of King Nicomedes of Bithynia had become the stuff of legend, inspiring vicious gossip among his political rivals and ribald marching songs among Caesar's own men. (Their insatiable imperator was "every woman's husband and every man's husband," according to one refrain.) In the case of King Nicomedes, Caesar had been the younger paramour, and presumably the receptive partner (hence the resulting scandal and the soldiers' teasing, since a Roman male is never supposed to submit to another man, only to play the dominant role). With Caesar and Ptolemy, the roles presumably would be reversed, with Caesar the older, more worldly partner and Ptolemy the wide-eyed youth hungry for experience.

When poets sing of lovers, they celebrate Harmodias and Aristogiton, or Theseus and Ariadne. But lovers need not always be so evenly matched in beauty and youth. I thought of my own affair with Cassandra, a much younger woman, and I comprehended the spark of mutual desire that Caesar and the king might have ignited in one another. Despite all his worldly success, Caesar was at that age when even the most robust of men feel acutely the increasing frailty of their once-invincible bodies, and begin to look with envy (and yes, sometimes lust) upon the firm, vigorous bodies of men younger than themselves. Youth itself becomes an aphrodisiac to the man who no longer possesses it; youth coupled with reciprocal desire becomes irresistible.

To an outsider, such love affairs can appear absurd or demeaning— the doddering man of means hankering after some hapless slave boy. But this was a meeting of two extraordinary men. I thought of Ptolemy's combination of boyish enthusiasm and grave sense of purpose, self-assurance and naïveté. I thought of Caesar's effortless sophistication and supreme confidence, and of his slightly ridiculous vanity, as betrayed by the way he combed his hair to cover his bald spot. Both were not merely men but rulers of men; and yet, not rulers only, but men as well, with appetites, frailties, uncertainties, needs; and not merely men and rulers, but—so they themselves appeared to believe—descendents and incarnations of divinity. Added to this was the fact that Ptolemy had lost his beloved father, and Caesar had never had a son. I could well imagine that Caesar and the king had something unique to offer one another, in a private realm far removed from the public arena of riches, arms, and diplomacy; that in a moment alone with each other, they might share an understanding inaccessible to the rest of us.

Why was Meto so scornful in conveying his suspicions? Had he been as intimate with Caesar as I had often been led to believe? Had that intimacy lessened, or ended altogether? Were his feelings about Caesar's dalliances with the royal siblings tinged with jealousy—and did that jealousy make his assumptions more reliable, or less?

I gave a start, as if waking from a dream. Meto and the way of life he had chosen to follow with Caesar were no longer my concern. Even if what he had just told me was true—that he himself had begun to doubt that way of life—still, it was of no consequence to me. So I told myself.

"You speak as if a gulf has opened between you and Caesar. Yet earlier tonight, I saw with my own eyes how the two of you got along—like the best of old friends, completely at ease. Almost like an old married couple, I daresay."

"Did it look that way? Appearances can be deceiving." He lowered his eyes, and suddenly I felt a stab of doubt. Had Meto grown cagey and dissimulating with Caesar, using the skills of deception that had become second nature to him to put on a face to the man he had once admired but now doubted? Or was I the one being fooled? For all I knew, Meto was still very much Caesar's trusted spy, and I was simply another source of information to be cultivated.

I stiffened my spine and hardened my heart. "You've said what you had to say, and so have I. It's been a long day—too long and too eventful for an old man like me. I need my rest now. Go."

Meto looked crestfallen. "There's so much more I wanted to say. Perhaps . . . next time."

I looked at him without blinking and gestured to the open door.

He gave each of the boys a hug, nodded curtly to Rupa, then turned to leave.

"Meto—wait a moment."

He stopped in the doorway and turned back.

"As long as you're here—Rupa, would you pull the trunk closer to the bed? Open the lid, please." Since we had settled in our rooms, I no longer kept the trunk locked. I sat on the bed and sorted through its contents.

"What are you looking for, Papa?" said Meto.

"Bethesda's things are here. She would have wanted you to have something . . . as a keepsake."

I removed various items from the trunk, spreading them beside me on the bed to sort through them. I came across Bethesda's silver-and-ebony comb. My fingers trembled as I picked it up. Would it mean as much to Meto as it meant to me? Perhaps; but I could not bear to part with it. I would have to find something else to give him.

"What's that?" he asked.

"What?"

"There—that alabaster vial. Was it Bethesda's?"

"No."

"Are you sure? It looks like the sort of thing in which she might have kept a perfume. To be able to smell her scent again—I'd like that."

"That vial was not Bethesda's!"

"You needn't speak so harshly."

I sighed. "The vial was given to me by Cornelia."

He frowned. "Pompey's wife?"

"Yes. The whole story is too complicated to recount, but believe me, that vial does *not* contain perfume."

"Poison?"

I looked at him sharply. "Caesar has indeed taught you to think like a spy."

He shook his head gravely. "Some things I learned from *you,* Papa, whether you like it or not, and a penchant for deduction is one of them. If not perfume, what else would a woman like Cornelia carry in a vial like that? And if she gave it to you . . ."

"She didn't hire me to assassinate someone, if that's what you're thinking."

"I was thinking that she gave it to you out of mercy, or perhaps simple convenience—to spare you a more violent death. The poison was intended for you, wasn't it, Papa?"

I almost smiled; his cleverness pleased me, in spite of myself. "It's something called Nemesis-in-a-bottle, quick and relatively painless, or so Cornelia told me. She claimed it was her personal supply, for her own use if the need should arise."

"Poor Cornelia! She must be missing it now."

"Perhaps, but I doubt it. Cornelia survived Publius Crassus. She survived Pompey. She'll probably survive yet another ill-starred husband."

"If any man would be foolish enough to marry such an ill-starred wife!"

I pulled myself upright and stiffened my jaw. Engaging in banter was not my reason for calling Meto back. Among the objects strewn across the bed, I spotted a small jar made of carved malachite, with a lid of the same stone secured by a brass clamp. I picked it up, gazed at it for a long moment, then handed it to Meto.

"Perhaps you'd like this, to remember her by. The beeswax inside is suffused with the scent Bethesda wore on special occasions. I told her to leave it in Rome, but she insisted on packing it. 'What if we attend a dinner with Queen Cleopatra?' she said. She was being facetious, of course."

He unclamped the lid and held the jar to his nose. The perfume was subtle but unmistakable, its ingredients a secret even to me. I caught a faint whiff. Tears came to my eyes.

Meto clamped the lid. His voice was choked with emotion. "If you're sure you want to give it to me . . ."

"Take it."

"Thank you, Papa."

He turned to go, then turned back. "That vial of poison, Papa—you should get rid of it."

And you should mind your own business, I started to say, but the lump in my throat was too thick. The best I could manage was a curt gesture of dismissal.

Meto stepped through the doorway and disappeared.

Why did I not do as Meto advised? From my window, I could have cast the alabaster vial into the harbor, where it would have sunk like a stone. Instead, I gathered it up with the other things on the bed and stuffed them back into the trunk, then closed the lid and threw myself onto my bed.

Rupa hovered over me. I told him to go to his room. Mopsus approached, clearing his throat to speak. I told him to take Androcles and follow Rupa. They left me alone.

I covered my face with my forearm and wept. As faint as a whisper, Bethesda's perfume lingered on the air.

17

The boys stayed very quiet the next morning, allowing me to sleep late. I was still groggy, my head full of uneasy dreams, when Merianis arrived bearing a scrap of papyrus that had been folded several times and sealed with wax. The impression in the wax was that of Caesar's ring, which bore an image of Venus circled by the letters of his name.

"What's this?" I said.

"I've no idea," said Merianis. "A missive from Little Rome. I'm merely the bearer. Shall I stay, in case you wish to send a reply?"

"Stay, so that I can look upon your beaming face. At least someone in this palace is happy. I don't suppose the return of your mistress has anything to do with your mood this morning?"

She grinned. "While Queen Cleopatra was gone, the temple of Isis was a place without magic."

"And now the magic has returned." I broke the seal and unfolded the papyrus. The letter was in Caesar's own hand.

Gordianus

Apologies for our interrupted dinner. Much was left unsaid. But unexpected encounters bring happy results. There will be a royal reception today that I should very much like you to attend. Call it a lesson in the fine art of reconciliation. Wear your toga and come to the grand reception hall at the eighth hour of the day.

I put down the letter. Merianis looked at me expectantly. "A reception of some sort, later this afternoon," I said.

She nodded to indicate she already knew about it.

"Will you be there?" I said.

"No power in heaven or earth could keep me from attending."

"Then I shall go, as well. Mopsus! Androcles! Stop playing with that cat and lay out my toga for me."

The reception hall was truly grand, the result of hundreds of years of refinements, additions, and adornments by generations of Ptolemies. Here the kings and queens of Egypt received tributes from subjects, announced treaties and trade agreements, celebrated royal weddings, and put on their most magnificent displays of wealth and power. Every surface shone with reflected light, whether from the polished marble of floors and pedestals inlaid with semiprecious stone, or from the burnished silver of brackets and lamps, or from the gold of gilded alcoves filled with gilded statues. The lofty ceiling was supported by a forest of slender columns decorated with lotus motifs and painted in vivid hues.

The room was already buzzing with excitement when Merianis and I arrived. The crowd was made up mostly of Egyptians in ceremonial dress, but there was a large contingent of Romans as well. "A lesson in the fine art of reconciliation," Caesar had remarked in his note to me, and the Roman officers seemed to be following that theme, taking pains to mingle with the locals and engage them in conversation. Among the Egyptians, however, there seemed to be two unequal factions in the room, standing apart from one another. The greater faction I took to be adherents of the king; the lesser group, adherents of his sister. While the Romans moved among both, the two groups of courtiers did not mix, but instead exchanged suspicious, furtive glances.

Merianis took my hand and drew me toward the far end of the room, where four thrones were set upon a low dais. The gilded thrones were upholstered with crocodile flesh, and the arms of the thrones were carved to resemble crocodiles whose open jaws revealed rows of ivory teeth. On the wall behind the thrones, a vast painting depicted the city of Alexandria as it might appear to a bird soaring at a great height, with the Pharos lighthouse looming above all else. Beyond the cityscape and its teeming harbor, an expansive blue sea was scattered with tiny but meticulously rendered ships, and the great islands of Rhodes and Crete (identified by their names in Greek letters beneath them) loomed in the far distance.

A wave of excitement as palpable as a warm breeze passed through the room, with a loud hubbub following in its wake. I saw that an entourage was making its way through the crowd toward the dais. Pothinus was in the forefront, followed by the king, who wore the uraeus crown with a rearing cobra. Caesar came next, dressed as consul of the Roman people in his toga with a purple border. After him, resplendent in a gown of purple, adorned with jewelry, and wearing a uraeus crown with a vulture's head, came Cleopatra.

Following the older siblings came the two members of the royal family I had not seen before, Arsinoë, who was slightly older than the young king, and the youngest of all, a boy who also bore the name Ptolemy, who could not have been more than ten or eleven. These two did not wear diadems, but were dressed in dazzling raiment.

As the royal procession passed by, I tried to read their expressions. Pothinus looked pinched and uneasy, like a man who had swallowed something that disagreed with him. King Ptolemy kept his lips tightly compressed and his gaze straight ahead, as if deliberately putting on an inscrutable face. Caesar looked eminently pleased with himself. And Cleopatra . . .

The previous night I had seen her with her hair in a bun, wearing a practical garment suitable for traveling in rough circumstances, and little other adornment. Even so, she had seemed unmistakably a queen. Now, wearing royal raiment, with a necklace made of golden scarabs adorning her bosom and rings of gold and silver upon her fingers, she seemed to fill the chamber with her presence. I looked about and saw that some of the Egyptians in the room gazed at her with loathing, others with adoration, and that the Roman officers regarded her with expressions that ranged from wonderment to simple curiosity; but every pair of eyes, without exception, looked on Cleopatra as she passed by.

Her expression was as inscrutable as her brother's, but radiated a quality quite different. Ptolemy exuded the tension of a ratcheted catapult;

Cleopatra seemed to flow effortlessly across the room, as a cloud proceeds across the sky.

The king and queen mounted the dais and sat upon the two thrones in the center. To either side of them sat Arsinoë and the younger Ptolemy in thrones only slightly lower and less magnificent. Seeing all the siblings side-by-side, I was struck by how closely the four of them resembled each other. I seemed to be looking at four manifestations of the same being incarnated in bodies of different age and gender, which were nonetheless more alike than different. Had their striking similarity served merely to make the siblings all the more hostile to one another?

Pothinus, facing the king and queen, struck his staff against the floor. The Egyptians in the room bowed their heads and knelt. The Romans hesitated, looking to Caesar for guidance. By a wave of his hand, he indicated that they should do as the Egyptians did, and with considerable grace he dropped to one knee. I followed his example but kept my head up. Caesar, I saw, bowed his head first to Ptolemy, who stared back at him blankly, and then to Cleopatra, who gazed at him with a look that left little doubt, in my mind at least, about what had occurred between the two of them after I left their presence.

" 'History is made at night,' " I muttered.

"What's that you say?" whispered Merianis.

"I was merely quoting an old Etruscan proverb."

Pothinus stood and again struck his staff against the floor. All rose.

Caesar stepped forward. From many years of experience as an orator in the Forum and a commander in the field, he was easily able to fill the vast chamber with his voice.

"Your Majesties, I stand before you today in two capacities: as consul of the Roman people, and as a friend of your late father. Eleven years ago, in the year of my first consulship, your father, driven out of Alexandria by civil strife, came to Rome to seek our help. He received it. The Senate declared him Friend and Ally of the Roman People, a very great honor; in return, he appointed the Roman people to be guardians of his children. Thus Rome and Egypt became bound together by ties of law as well as of friendship.

"The fortunes of private citizens were joined to those of the late king, as well. I myself opened my coffers and exerted all my influence to help sustain him in his exile and eventually to restore him to his throne. His passing was a tragedy for all who knew and loved him, but most especially for this kingdom, which he loved so dearly, and which has since been riven with such turmoil and strife.

"The late king did not die intestate. Indeed, a copy of his will was sent to Rome, to be deposited at the treasury, and another copy was placed under seal here in Alexandria. Alas, the first copy fell into the hands of Pompey, and is lost to us. But since I arrived in Alexandria, I have obtained the second copy of the will, broken the seal, and read it very carefully, although I hardly needed to reacquaint myself with its terms. The dictates of that will were made known upon the king's death and were much discussed in Rome.

"Unfortunately, preoccupied by their own civil strife in recent years, the Roman people were unable to oversee the proper disposition of the late king's will. Arriving here in Egypt, I was dismayed to find that what your father intended had not come to pass. Those who were to have an equal share in the inheritance were instead contesting with one another, by clash of arms, as to who should claim the entire estate. To some extent, the blame for this state of affairs lies with the people of Rome for having failed to carry out their duties as executors of the will and guardians of the royal family; but I now intend to redress that failing. As the embodiment of the will of the Roman people, my authority extends to this matter of executing the late king's will, and I intend to see that its provisions are properly carried out—fairly, amicably, and for the mutual benefit of all concerned.

"When I arrived in Egypt, I was warmly welcomed by Your Majesty, King Ptolemy, and given generous accommodations. I myself have endured some small turmoil and strife of late, and to be admitted into this beautiful city and to be offered safe haven and a respite from my recent struggles were favors I shall not soon forget. I thank you, King Ptolemy. But even dearer to me are the hours that you and I have spent together since my arrival, and the birth between us of what I hope will be an enduring and ever-deepening friendship. In us, Rome and Egypt meet. It is good not only for ourselves but for our peoples that we should forge strong bonds of mutual respect and affection."

Caesar inclined his head to the king, who stared back at him from his throne, his expression more rigid than ever. Caesar paused, apparently waiting for the king to make some gesture of acknowledgment. The moment stretched uncomfortably. Ptolemy's expression remained unchanged, except for a slight tremor of his jaw. At last Caesar cleared his throat and continued.

"My growing friendship with Your Majesty has brought me great joy. But my visit has also been tinged with sorrow born of my dismay over the continuing discord within the royal family. As the playwright says, 'When gods turn one against another, mortals turn brother on brother.' As discord in heaven reverberates upon the earth, so discord in the palace of Alexandria causes distress throughout all of Egypt and even as far as Rome. Not only are the affairs of men disrupted, but the natural order is disarranged, as well. Old men, I am told, have never seen such a low inundation of the Nile as occurred this spring and summer; wise men, I am told, attribute this troubling phenomenon to the river's distress over the discord between Egypt's rightful rulers. Harmony and balance must be restored—as was the intention of your wise father, who provided that Egypt should be jointly ruled by a queen and a king, the elder son and elder daughter of his royal blood.

"To be sure, the late King Ptolemy did not leave affairs in Egypt on an entirely sound footing. The restoration of his throne came at no small price and incurred a considerable debt. Roman arms were called up; Roman blood was spilled. Those Roman troops still reside here in Egypt and now follow orders from an Egyptian commander. The very army that maintains order in Egypt was essentially a gift to the kingdom from the Senate and the People of Rome. Along with this military assistance, Roman gold and silver were lent to your father in considerable amounts, and many other resources were advanced to him upon account. The vast bulk of his financial debt to Rome, including his personal debt to me, remains unpaid. Given the strife and uncertainty that straddle the Nile, it seems impossible that this debt can be repaid until peace and order are restored to Egypt.

"The debt that Egypt owes to Rome casts a shadow upon our friendship; it would be disingenuous of me to deny it. Because of this shadow, there are those here in Egypt who fear that I may have come with more than reconciliation in mind. They fear, following the defeat of Pompey at Pharsalus, that the conqueror of Gaul may have come to Egypt with the intention of challenging the authority of its rightful rulers. Let me assure Your Majesties, here before the members of your royal court and before my own trusted officers, that I have no intention whatsoever of attempting to exert Roman authority over Egypt by force of arms. To do so not only would violate your trust in me, but would go against the express wishes of the Senate and the People of Rome, who desire only peaceful intercourse and friendly commerce between our peoples.

"I come not to bring war but to end war; not to overthrow the heirs of King Ptolemy, but to unite them; not to threaten Egypt, but to embrace her."

Caesar turned toward Cleopatra. "To that end, I welcome back to the city of her ancestors Queen Cleopatra." As he had done before to Ptolemy, Caesar bowed his head. Unlike her brother, the queen returned the gesture and flashed a faint, self-satisfied smile that reminded me of no one so much as Caesar himself.

"The queen has been absent from her capital for many days. Ceremonies and religious invocations that require her attendance have been neglected. Projects begun by her ministers have been set aside. The life of the city and the welfare of its people have suffered. She returned to the palace only last night, guided, so she tells me, by the ingenuity and persistent urgings of the goddess Isis herself. Today, the queen once again sits upon her throne. Her people rejoice, and so do I.

"What of the other siblings, Princess Arsinoë and the young Prince Ptolemy? For them, their father's will made no specific provisions. But I have found them to be of truly regal stature, and I believe they should be granted a territory of their own. Therefore, I decree that the island of Cyprus, which for the last ten years has been a Roman province, shall henceforth return to Ptolemaic rule, and that Princess Arsinoë and the young Prince Ptolemy shall rule there jointly as king and queen. May theirs become a reflection of the harmonious reign of their siblings here in Egypt.

"Let it be thus: that the will of the late king is fulfilled, and his children shall rule together, and there shall be peace in Egypt; and the Senate and the People of Rome shall likewise rejoice, and shall recognize the joint authority of the king and queen—"

"No!" King Ptolemy shouted, his voice cracking. He jumped up from his throne, his arms stiff at his sides and his fists clenched. The inscrutable mask gave way to flashing eyes and twitching lips.

Pothinus rushed toward him and spoke through gritted teeth. "Your Majesty! Distasteful as these proceedings may be, we agreed beforehand—"

"*You* agreed! I said nothing."

"You nodded whenever—"

"I nodded because I was too angry to speak, and too hurt to say what I was really thinking!"

"Your Majesty, please! If there are matters yet to be discussed, that should be done in private. Return to your throne and let me send these people away—"

"No, let them stay! Let them stand here and listen to this nonsense. Let them simper and blow kisses to my whore of a sister and her Roman lover, if that's what they want. It's I who'll leave, so the rest of you can get on with this orgy of self-congratulation!"

Ptolemy strode forward, stumbling slightly as he stepped off the dais. The speechless crowd parted and made way for him. The Egyptian guards at the doorway fell back, genuflecting. He was like the prow of a ship, plowing through waves and wind, deflecting all before him.

Merianis grabbed my arm. "Come!" she whispered.

"Where? What are you thinking of, Merianis?"

"Come! Don't you want to see whatever happens next?"

I looked over my shoulder as we hurried after the disappearing king. Pothinus was pale and grim. Caesar looked utterly at a loss, which was quite out of character. Cleopatra, who had not stirred from her throne and seemed to have no intention of doing so, displayed an inscrutable smile.

"Hurry!" said Merianis, tugging at my arm. She was intent on following the king. His robes billowed behind him as he rushed through the hallways of the palace, never pausing until he came to the courtyard inside the gates. He shouted at the guards to open the gates. When they hesitated, he threatened to have them beheaded. The men rushed to the wheels, and the gates slowly opened.

The king ran into the street. Merianis and I followed, along with a great number of others from the palace.

Ptolemy strode down the wide Argeus. By appearing suddenly, dressed in his crown and robes of state but walking on foot and unattended by any formal retinue, he created a sensation. All who saw him stopped whatever they were doing. Some fell to their knees in awe. Some smiled and cheered. Some simply gawked. All joined in the growing throng that followed at his heels.

At length he arrived at the great intersection of the Argeus and the Canopic Way, where the tombs of his ancestors occupied each of the four corners. The building housing the body of Alexander was his destination. He strode past the sightseers standing in line to view the remains. The guards were taken aback by his sudden appearance, but quickly recovered themselves. They admitted the king but expelled all others, or else I think Merianis would have followed right behind him, dragging me with her. Instead, we stepped into the great square, which was already crowded with people arriving from all directions.

A few moments later the king appeared on a balcony that projected from the upper story of the building. Even at a considerable distance, I could see the streaks of tears on his face.

"People of Egypt!" he shouted. His voice rang through the square. "My beloved people! The Romans have robbed me of my throne! Egypt has been conquered in a single night! We are all the slaves of Rome now!"

There was an uproar all around us. Cries of anger and despair rang in my ears, along with scattered catcalls and peals of laughter. Most in the crowd appeared to love the king, but there were some who despised him.

Ptolemy's voice pierced the cacophony. "Here I stand in the building that houses our venerated Alexander, the greatest of all conquerors, the most beloved of all heroes, the demigod for whom our city is named, from whose authority the Ptolemies for centuries have traced the legitimacy of their divine rule. But now a man has come along who fancies himself greater than even Alexander. He thinks so little of us that he doesn't arrive with a great navy supporting him, or a great army marching at his back; he intends to conquer us by trickery and deceit! I confess to you, my people, for a while he dazzled even me, and I gave to him a warmer welcome than he deserved. I allowed him into the royal palace; I shared food and drink with him; I listened to his vain boasting. But now my eyes are open! If the Roman has his way, he'll throw Alexander's body upon a dung heap, tear down this tomb, and put up a monument to himself! Perhaps he'll even rename the city for himself, and you shall wake up to find yourselves living in Caesaropolis!"

The crowd responded with thunderous shouting. Ptolemy gazed grimly over the square, projecting an authority far beyond his years.

"People of Alexandria, as conniving as Caesar may be, he knows that you will never submit to a Roman who dares to sit openly upon the throne of Egypt—so he seeks to cast me from my throne and put a pretender in my place. Who might that be? What creature with a claim to the royal bloodline would be low enough to conspire with our enemy? I think you know her name! With shame, I call her my sister. For her previous attempts to seize the throne, we drove her out of the city and into the wilderness. Alas, that we didn't cut the serpent in two, for now she's come wriggling back, bloated with venom. To take my throne from me, she'll stop at nothing! Yes, Cleopatra is back in the palace."

At this announcement, there were scattered cheers among the crowd, for Cleopatra as well as Ptolemy had her adherents among the populace. Others booed, and fistfights and shouting matches broke out.

"The serpent has returned," Ptolemy cried. "Last night she made herself a prostitute to Caesar. Today he's giving her the payment due—the crown that should be mine and mine alone!"

"Then what is that cobra sprouting from your forehead?" shouted a wag in the crowd.

"This?" Ptolemy shouted back. "This meaningless toy, this worthless piece of scrap?" He lifted the uraeus crown from his head and cast it down with all his might. The metal rang against the stone balcony.

The crowd reacted with stunned silence, followed by a sudden surge of movement that lifted me off my feet. I looked around and saw Merianis disappear amid a sea of gaping, angry, frightened faces.

"Soldiers, coming from the palace!" someone shouted.

"Roman soldiers! They mean to kill the king!"

"We'll kill them first! Kill every Roman in Alexandria!"

"Long live Cleopatra!"

"Long live Ptolemy! Death to Cleopatra!"

"Death to Caesar!"

"Death to all the Romans!"

Swords flashed. Stones flew through the air. Blood was spattered across paving stones. A woman screamed in my ear. I tripped over a child, and someone helped me stagger back to my feet. I heard the sound of splashing, and realized I was next to the great fountain at the center of the square. Amid the cavorting dryads and gaping crocodiles, a dead body floated facedown, exuding a sickening pinkish murk. A pebble whizzed over my head—too fast to have been thrown by hand, it must have been cast from a slingshot—and struck the helmet of a Roman soldier nearby with a noise that made my ears ring. He furiously slashed his sword in the direction the shot had come from.

I ducked. As I did so, I happened to look over the soldier's head, and saw that the balcony where Ptolemy had stood was now empty. What had become of the king?

And what would become of me? For all I knew, the riot would keep growing until the whole city was in chaos. I stretched to my full height, peering over the heads of those around me, trying to catch a glimpse of the palace. The whole length of the Argeus, from the fountain back to the gates, was packed with an angry mob. As I stood precariously balanced on tiptoes, a group of young men came running by, brandishing sticks. "Get out of the way, old man!" one of them shouted. "The Romans have carried off the king, and they mean to kill him!"

"We'll kill them first!" another shouted.

They jostled me and spun me about and almost knocked me down.

A hand grabbed my shoulder, pulling me upright. It was too strong to be that of Merianis—a man's grip. I tried to shake free and step away, but the grip tightened. The man seized the folds of my toga with strong hands and pulled at it so fiercely, yanking this way and that, that he stripped it off me, leaving me clad only in the thin tunic I wore underneath.

"Rupa!" I cried. "How in Hades did you get here?" I looked past him and saw the white folds of my toga disappear beneath the trampling feet of the mob. "And what in Hades have you done to my toga?"

18

Rupa grunted in reply and pointed toward the building that housed the Tomb of Alexander.

I wrinkled my brow. "I don't understand."

He pointed more insistently, then grabbed my hand and pulled me in the direction in which he was pointing. His sheer size caused a path to open in the crowd; anyone foolish enough to stand in our way he brusquely pushed aside. By nature, Rupa was the gentlest of men, but when called upon, he knew how to wield the strength the gods had given him.

But even Rupa was no match for the gang of toughs who suddenly blocked our way. They appeared to be dockworkers, judging from the huge muscles that popped from their shoulders and arms, not to mention the briny smell that came off their ragged tunics. There were seven or eight of them, and they carried the tools of their trade: iron grappling hooks, lengths of heavy chain, nets made of rope, and barge poles as thick as a man's forearm—lethal weapons in the hands of men like these.

"You, there!" their leader shouted, taking notice of Rupa on account of his size, then casting a disparaging glance at me. "Where did those Romans go, the ones who dared to come and carry off the king?"

"Right," said another, "we're on a Roman hunt! We mean to kill as many of those bastards as we can, and keep killing them until they get out of Egypt and head back to where they came from!"

Rupa looked at them blankly. I suddenly understood why he had stripped me of my toga; the garment that marked me as a Roman would have made me a target of the angry mob. While I had stood confused and uncertain, how deftly Rupa, the native Alexandrian, had grasped the situation!

"What's the matter, too good to talk to the likes of us?" The leader wound a chain around one fist, then pulled the remainder taut. "Or maybe you two actually like these Romans? Maybe you think it's all right for Julius blowhard Caesar to screw the king's sister and start bossing us all around?" He swung the chain through the air, making a whooshing sound.

"He's mute," I started to say, then realized that my accent would give me away. If these men were intent on killing Romans, I had no desire for them to begin with me. Even the smallest of them looked capable of tearing my head from my shoulders.

I grunted and poked Rupa to get his attention, then executed a series of signs, speaking to him in the vocabulary Rupa himself had developed using his hands and facial expressions in lieu of a voice. *Careful,* I said. *These fellows are big!*

I'm not afraid of them, Rupa insisted.

But I am! I gestured.

"What's this?" said the leader, squinting at us suspiciously.

"I think they must be a pair of deaf-mutes," said his friend. "I've got a cousin like that. Married a woman just like him. They talk with their hands."

The leader looked Rupa up and down, then sneered at me. "Ah, well, then. Leave them to it. Now let's go kill some Romans!"

They ran on, in the direction of the palace.

Rupa gestured to me: *I wasn't afraid of them. Really!*

"I can still call them back, if you like," I muttered. "You big, lumbering—"

Rupa grabbed my hand and resumed pulling me toward the building that housed the Tomb of Alexander.

The armed guards who usually flanked the entrance had vanished in the melee, along with the line of sightseers waiting to get in. The huge bronze doors stood wide open.

We stepped inside. The lofty vestibule, opulently decorated with multi-colored marble, was eerily quiet. Our steps echoed around the deserted chamber. The hubbub outside was reduced to a distant roar. A doorway to the left opened into a stairwell, presumably the means by which Ptolemy had ascended to the balcony to address the crowd.

Rupa pulled me through a different doorway and down a long hall-way lined by pillars. We descended a flight of stairs, passed through a small antechamber hewn from solid alabaster, and then stepped into a subterranean vault. The air was cool, as in an underground cellar, and smelled of chrysanthemums. The long, narrow chamber was dimly lit by hanging lamps and dominated by a gilded statue at the far end. The windswept mane of hair, the serene countenance, and the beautifully molded shoulders and limbs made the identity of the statue unmistak-able. Alexander stood naked before us in all his youthful glory, towering over an open sarcophagus in which lay the mummified corpse of the con-queror, draped in glittering robes from head to foot and crowned with a golden laurel wreath. Brought by the many sightseers and strewn about the base of the sarcophagus were bouquets of fresh flowers and wreaths of dried flowers—mandrakes and mallows, irises and poppies, larkspurs and lotus lilies.

But Alexander's was not the only dead body in the room.

The light was so dim, and the images at the far end of the room were so arresting, that I failed to see the obstacle at my feet. I stepped against it and tripped, and only Rupa's strong hand and quick reflexes saved me from falling flat on my face. I staggered back and looked down at the body of an Egyptian soldier. He lay on his back, his open eyes staring at the ceiling and his fist still clutching his sword. If he had put up a fight, he had failed to wound his adversary, for there was no sign of blood on his blade. But of blood there was plenty; it formed a pool around him, flow-ing from a wound in his abdomen.

"Why have you brought me here, Rupa?"

He made no answer, but merely gestured for me to follow. We crossed the room and approached the golden chain that bisected it, beyond which sightseers were not permitted. From its perimeter, the sarcophagus was still several arms' lengths away, but one could clearly see the familiar profile of Alexander and the play of the dim light upon the strands of golden hair tucked beneath the golden laurel wreath. The sight gave me a shiver, and I appreciated the patience of the multitudes who waited for hours to stand in that spot for a brief moment and gaze upon eternity.

Without hesitating, Rupa ducked under the chain and strode directly to the sarcophagus. I felt a pang of superstitious dread, then did likewise. There were no guards to stop us, and the watchful stare of the conqueror's statue showed no signs of displeasure at our invasion of his sanctum.

I stood beside Rupa, and the two of us looked down at the face of Alexander the Great.

I frowned. At such close proximity, the sight of that mummified countenance was not as edifying as it had been when viewed from a few steps farther back. Some semblance of the original flesh remained, but the inner life that had given it beauty had long since fled. The skin was like worn papyrus stretched thin over the bony protrusions of the cheeks and the chin. Those responsible for admitting visitors to the tomb seemed to have gauged exactly how far back to place the golden chain so as to take full advantage of the flattering effects of soft lighting and distance.

"What do you think, Rupa? A bit the worse for wear, isn't he?"

Rupa nodded. Then a youthful voice piped up: "But he's not all that bad when you consider he's three hundred years old!"

I gave a start. "What in Hades—?"

From the dark space between the sarcophagus and the statue beyond, a face popped into view, followed by another.

"Mopsus! Androcles! I might have known. But how—?"

"We came here through the tunnel, of course," said Mopsus.

"What tunnel?"

"The secret tunnel that begins under the rose garden in the palace, runs past the turnoff to the great Library, and then takes you straight on to this place. It comes out just behind that statue. There's a little panel you slide back, some steps to go up—if you're as tall as Rupa, you have to bend a bit and duck your head when you climb out—and then you're here, in Alexander's tomb. It's one of the first passages we discovered."

"*We?*" said Androcles. "*I* was the one who found this passage."

"I said, it was one of the first passages *we* discovered, and we—sometimes you, sometimes me—have discovered quite a few such passages since *we* started exploring the palace," Mopsus insisted.

"Yes, but I'm the one who found *this* passage. I found it with no help from you or anybody else, and then I was generous enough to share the knowledge with you. So, properly, you should say, 'It's one of the first passages Androcles discovered.' Admit it!"

"I'll admit no such thing. You're just being stupid. Isn't he, Master?"

I sighed. "So that's what you've been up to, since we arrived at the palace? Snooping in every nook and corner, looking for trapdoors and sliding panels? You're lucky you're still alive!"

"But no one ever stopped us, Master," said Androcles. "Everyone at the palace seems to like us. Some of the guards even give us bits of sweets when they see us."

"Oh, yes!" said Mopsus. "Especially that guard who's stationed in the garden with the long reflecting pool. Sweet Tooth, we call him, because he always has the best sweets, little honey dabs thickened with flour and flavored with rosewater and rolled in crushed almonds. Delicious!"

I imagined the two of them, smiling and laughing, the picture of innocence, charming their way past every checkpoint in the palace. In time the guards had no doubt grown so used to them that they allowed them to come and go as they pleased, even allowing them to bring along their hulking but harmless friend, Rupa.

I shook my head. "So you've been here before?"

"Oh, yes," said Androcles. "We like to come after sunset, when the tomb is closed to visitors. They lock those doors to the vestibule, and this room is completely empty."

"And dark!" added Mopsus.

"Yes, you have to bring your own lamp. But it's rather nice, being able to wander about and study the murals on the walls, and visit with Alexander the Great with no one else about. They put the lid on the sarcophagus at night, but Rupa is strong enough to lift it off. I think Alexander is in wonderful shape. I only hope that I'll look like that when *I'm* three hundred years old. You can almost imagine that he might sit up and start talking!"

"But I still don't understand how you came to be here today. And where has everyone gone?"

"The three of us were in the palace," said Androcles, "minding our own business—in the rose garden, as it so happened, watching Alexander the cat chase a butterfly—when one of the courtiers ran by, telling everyone that the king was on the balcony at the Tomb of Alexander, rousing the people against the Romans. Suddenly the rose garden was empty, and there we were, sitting on the very bench with the false bottom that lifts up to let you into the secret passage. We *had* to come see what was happening for ourselves, and this was the quickest way. When we came out of the tunnel, this room was empty, except for a single Egyptian guard; everyone had gone outside to listen to the king. We were hiding in the shadows behind one of those big pillars, trying to think of a way to slip past the guard, when suddenly there was a commotion from the vestibule, and then the king himself came rushing in. We could tell it was the king, even though he wasn't wearing his crown. I think he was heading for the secret tunnel. But there were Roman soldiers after him. The Egyptian guard tried to stand in their way. That's him over there, lying in a pool of blood. For a moment we thought the Roman soldiers were going to kill the king as well, and I think the king thought so, too. You should have seen the look on his face!"

"And heard the curses he was shouting against his sister and Caesar!" added Mopsus.

"Anyway, the soldiers fell into a tortoise formation around the king—shields up all around and overhead, and spear points poking out—and went marching out, taking the king with them. Heading back to the palace, I suppose. We stayed out of sight and followed them as far as the vestibule, and then who do you think we ran into?"

"Merianis," I said.

"Exactly! And she told us that you'd been with her, but somehow you were separated, and with everything going on in the square, there was no telling what might happen to you. So we sent Rupa and Merianis to look for you, while Mopsus and I decided to stay right here, so as to be ready to take you straight back to the palace through the secret tunnel."

"Actually," said Mopsus, "we stayed here because Androcles was afraid to go out into the square. He said we might get trampled on, being so small, and it was better to send Rupa out looking for you, because Rupa is big enough to take care of himself."

"I was *not* afraid," insisted Androcles. "Staying here was just part of my plan, and now you can see how cleverly it all worked out."

"Indeed," I said. "But what happened to Merianis?"

I looked at Rupa, who shrugged.

"I suppose you lost her rather quickly in the crowd?"

He frowned and nodded.

"No need to look sheepish, Rupa. If finding me was her priority, Merianis would have been doing that instead of ducking into the vestibule to see what was happening with Ptolemy and the Roman soldiers sent to fetch him. It was good of her to let you know that I might be in danger, but I'm not surprised she slipped off on her own instead of helping Rupa search for me. No doubt she's eager to run ahead of that Roman tortoise and report back to her mistress about everything that took place here. Curious; Merianis must not know about this tunnel leading back to the palace, or else she'd have gone that way." I frowned. "Merianis has been a good friend to us, boys—helpful, thoughtful, full of good humor—but we mustn't forget that her true allegiance lies elsewhere."

"You make her sound like a soldier, Master."

"Because I think she is one, Mopsus, no less than a man who carries a sword and shield."

"She'd never hurt you, Master!" said Androcles.

"I'm sure she won't—as long as I don't run afoul of her mistress. What a joke the gods have played on me this time! I've managed to survive one bloody civil war, only to find myself dropped into the midst of another, about which I care nothing. But from my experience of these conflicts, I know that even the most uncommitted bystander is seldom allowed to remain neutral. The palace is a battleground. Cleopatra and Ptolemy are rival generals, marshaling their forces. Caesar is the strategic stronghold they're both eager to claim; all other battles will count for nothing if one or the other can win over Caesar and the Roman might behind him."

"But, Master, you should have heard the curses the king was screaming against Caesar when the soldiers took him away!" said Androcles. "The king must hate Caesar with all his might."

"I suspect the exact opposite is true. The king may be a Ptolemy to his fingertips, with a regal bearing and a certainty of his own divine place in the world; but he's still a boy not in control of his emotions. When he railed against Caesar, he sounded less like a general rallying his troops, and more like a spurned suitor. As for Caesar, he'd like very much for the siblings to patch up their differences and get on with the business of ruling Egypt and repaying their debts to Rome; then he could congratulate himself on settling the Egyptian Question and go wrap up the loose ends left over from his own civil war. But neither the king nor the queen may be willing to settle for half of Egypt—or half of Caesar. Caesar may finally have to choose one over the other. Before that happens, we may all be forced to take sides, whether we want to or—"

All four of us abruptly turned toward the alabaster antechamber that led up to the vestibule, whence came the sounds of footsteps, a scuffle, and loud shouting.

"Looters?" said Mopsus.

"Soldiers?" said Androcles.

"Or mere sightseers?" I suggested. "In any case, I think it's time for us to head back to the palace. Androcles, show me the passageway."

"Certainly, Master. Step around to the back of the statue."

I gazed into a black void at the foot of the statue. "Is there no light at all in the passage? No air?"

"The first part is rather dark," said Androcles, "but farther on there are grates and vents that let in little patches of light and puffs of fresh air. Here, I'll go first, and lead you by the hand. Mopsus can follow. Rupa can come last and close the panel behind us; it's rather heavy. Just be careful, Master, not to hit . . ."

"Ouch!"

". . . your head!"

19

"People are still rioting all over the city," said Merianis. "Days have passed since the king threw his tantrum, and yet the people remain in a fury. The rabble-rousers claim that Caesar is holding the king captive against his will—"

"A squadron of Roman soldiers did march Ptolemy back to the palace," I observed.

"But they never laid a finger on him! The king returned of his own volition—"

"After one of his guards was slain in the Tomb of Alexander!"

"Someone had to protect the king's person on the way back to the palace; that crowd had turned into a rioting mob, as you saw for yourself, Gordianus. Anyway, once the king was back in the palace, safe and sound, Caesar and Pothinus together managed to calm him. Negotiations between the queen and the king continue, under Caesar's supervision. But the city is in chaos."

"Alexandrians are famous for this sort of thing," I observed. "The Alexandrian mob drove the previous king out of the city; it took a Roman army to get him back in."

"Which is why Ptolemy should have known better than to incite the mob's fury. Most of their anger is directed against the Romans, of course, but even the palace guards are afraid to venture out into the streets.

Alexandria is utterly lawless! The Museum is shut up tight—all those scholars afraid to even look out a window!—and so is the Library. No new books for you, Gordianus! You shall have to reread the ones I already brought."

"Yes, do, Master!" said Mopsus, flinging himself on the bed beside me. "Read the part about Alexander and the Gordian knot again. Is it true that's the origin of your family name? 'In the land of Phrygia there reigned King Gordian, who was born a peasant but became the king because of an oracle—'"

"I see no need to read the tale again if you've memorized it," I said. "As for the origin of the name Gordianus—"

But there was no stopping Mopsus. "'And many years later, Alexander passed through Phrygia and the city of Gordium, named for King Gordian, and he was presented with the Gordian knot; for the oracles claimed that no man could conquer Asia unless first he undid the Gordian knot, which was so deviously tied that even the cleverest man could not undo it, and so tightly tied that even the strongest man could not undo it. Whereupon Alexander—'"

Androcles interrupted, jumping into the middle of the room and pantomiming the action he described. "Whereupon Alexander took out his sword, and with a great whack and a whoosh, he chopped it right in two, and the knot fell apart at his feet, and everyone bowed down to the new king of Asia—hooray!—Alexander, the only man strong enough *and* clever enough to undo the Gordian knot!"

"That's not how it goes!" complained Mopsus.

"Close enough."

"But you left out the part about—"

"I didn't leave out anything important."

"You're just jealous that you don't remember the words."

"It's the story that matters, not the words." Androcles again mimed hacking at a knot with a sword. "With a great *whack* and a *whoosh*, he *chopped* it right in two!"

Mopsus did likewise, jumping about the room and slicing the air with an invisible sword. "With a *whack* and a *whoosh*—"

Rupa made a face and covered his ears. Merianis sighed. "The boys grow restless, trapped inside all day."

"Restless, indeed!" Not only were they unable to go about the city, but I had forbidden them to make any further explorations in the palace's secret passages. "If only I could send them out on some errand. A very long errand."

Merianis smiled. "Perhaps you and I should go out for a bit."

"I think not! The last time I ventured out with you, Merianis, I very nearly got my head staved in by bloodthirsty dockworkers. For all I know, they're still out there hunting for Romans."

"But I have another idea. Come with me, Gordianus."

"Where?"

"Trust me!"

I looked at her askance.

"With a *whack* and a *whoosh*!" shouted Mopsus.

"He *chopped* it in two!" cried Androcles.

I winced. "Very well, Merianis. Take me away from here. Quickly!"

"Where are we going?"

"You'll see."

It seemed at first that we were heading toward the Roman sector, but at some point Merianis turned down an unfamiliar corridor, and I found myself in a part of the palace unknown to me. I was amazed anew at the extent and the opulence of the royal complex.

At last we stepped into the bright sunshine of a garden that fronted the harbor. We crossed the garden, breathing warm, jasmine-scented air, and descended several flights of steps. The cloudless sky was dazzling. The galleys of Caesar's small fleet were scattered here and there across the water, their prows turned to face the harbor entrance, which was barred by a massive chain. Beyond the great harbor, impossibly big, loomed the great lighthouse of Pharos.

Merianis led me to a pier made of stone that projected a considerable distance into the harbor. We passed a series of small buildings, their rooftops decorated with colorful pennants. Beside a squat statue of Bes, the

Egyptian god of pleasure, a flight of steps led down to a little skiff. I sucked in a breath, for the boat was exactly like the one in which Pompey had taken his final journey, its prow carved in the shape of a standing ibis with wings outstretched and its rim decorated with ornate carvings of crocodiles, cranes, and Nile river-horses, the images plated with hammered silver and inlaid with bits of lapis and turquoise for the eyes.

A man wearing only a brief loincloth sat in the boat, leaning back against the prow with his arms behind his head and his eyes closed, basking in the sun. As we stepped closer, I saw that it was Apollodorus, the Sicilian who had delivered Cleopatra to Caesar.

Merianis called his name. He lazily opened one eye.

"Dozing, in the middle of the day?" said Merianis. "What would the queen think of that?"

Apollodorus smiled and placed a hand over his loincloth, splaying his fingers. "Perhaps it's the queen who made me so tired."

"Blasphemer!" said Merianis, but her tone was playful. Apollodorus roused himself, stood in the boat, and shook his great mane of hair as if to untangle it. He cast a heavy-lidded gaze at Merianis and leaned forward with puckered lips. She pretended to reciprocate the gesture, then pulled back at the last moment, so that Apollodorus kissed empty space and almost lost his balance, circling his arms wildly to steady himself.

Merianis gave a deep, throaty laugh. "Summon the boatmen at once, you big lout!"

"Boatmen? Do you think I can't row you there myself?" He made a show of massing his biceps.

"As you wish." Merianis stepped into the boat and reached back to take my hand.

I sat beside her at the prow. "Where are you taking me, Merianis?"

"You'll see."

Apollodorus rowed us away from the pier. Seen from the harbor, the long expanse of the palace complex presented a vista of balconies, shaded alcoves, hanging gardens, and roof terraces. I was able to discern the high room of the building in which I had dined with Caesar and where Cleopatra had been presented to him, and adjacent to that building the great theater with its seats facing the harbor; Roman soldiers armed with spears patrolled the highest tier, and I recalled that Caesar had spoken of the theater's virtues as a possible stronghold in case of attack. Since the riots set off by Ptolemy's harangue, Caesar and his soldiers had begun to fortify the sector of the palace complex that they occupied, closing off streets and barricading the open spaces between buildings with whatever materials were at hand.

The large buildings connected by porticos along the waterfront dominated the skyline, for Alexandria is mostly flat; but there are a few hills, and upon the tallest of these, looming over the western half of the city, stands the great temple of Serapis, the Zeus-like god whom the first Ptolemy elevated to a place in the Egyptian pantheon to rival even Osiris. Above the waterfront rooftops, I could see the temple at a great distance, a majestic building not unlike the Parthenon in Athens and considerably larger, though the hill upon which it sits is not nearly as commanding as the Acropolis.

I felt a catch in my throat. This was the view of Alexandria I would have seen upon our arrival by ship had the storm not blown us off course. This had been my last view of the city, when Bethesda and I departed by ship many years ago, and the view I had expected to share with her upon our return.

"Gordianus-called-Finder, are you unhappy?"

"Why do you ask, Merianis?"

"There's a tear upon your cheek."

"It's nothing. Just a drop of sea-spray," I said, wiping it away and willing the flurry in my chest to subside. "We seem to be approaching Antirrhodus," I said, referring to the largest of the small islands in the harbor, which was reserved for the exclusive use of the royal family; its name declared it, rather fancifully, to be a rival to the great island of Rhodes. The locals sometimes called it the Floating Palace, for the island was so built up with towers, promenades, and balconies that it looked as if a part of the palace complex had detached itself from the mainland and floated into the harbor. To set foot upon Antirrhodus without royal permission carried a sentence of death, and sailors coming and going in the harbor took pains to avoid it. Among ordinary Alexandrians, the island held a special mystique; some said that the late king had held parties of unimaginable debauchery there, while others thought it was the repository of mystical objects and magical talismans handed down from the days of the ancient pharaohs.

"Have you ever been there?" asked Merianis.

I laughed. "No, Merianis. During my last sojourn in Alexandria, many years ago, I was hardly a part of the royal inner circle."

"And yet here you are, about to land on Antirrhodus. You've come up in the world since the days of your youth."

"Or else the world has come down," I said.

Apollodorus rowed us into a small, walled harbor and up to the landing place. The Egyptian guards on patrol raised their spears, then grinned when they saw Merianis.

"I bring a visitor to see the queen," she said, stepping off the boat and reaching for my hand.

"*Another* Roman?" One of the guards, a grizzled veteran with an ugly scar on his cheek, eyed me suspiciously.

"Forgive his tone, Gordianus. Captain Cratipus commands the Queen's Protectors. They're an elite company of warriors who've guarded her person since the day she was born. They shielded her when her sister Berenice usurped the throne, and also when King Ptolemy returned and put Berenice to death. They protected her throughout the turmoil that followed her father's death, and stayed beside her during her exile in the desert. Over the years, no small number of their company have died for her. They're fanatically loyal. For their devotion, the goddess Isis will reward them in the afterlife by allowing them to attend the queen in the Kingdom of the Dead."

"Will the queen still need protection from assassins, even after she's dead?"

Cratipus, taking my comment for sarcasm, growled at me.

Merianis lowered her voice. "Cratipus dislikes you because you're Roman. He thinks all Romans must be very impious. He can't understand why you allow yourselves to be ruled by mere mortals. I must admit, that also puzzles me."

I shrugged. "So far as I know, no god has ever campaigned to get himself elected to a Roman magistracy, probably because election campaigns are so hideously expensive."

Merianis looked at me quizzically, then laughed. "I see; you've made a joke. Anyway, Cratipus resents the queen's reliance on Roman arms, and he distrusts Caesar's judgment. It was Caesar's idea that the queen should retire here to Antirrhodus for the time being, for her own safety. I think it was a splendid idea, but Cratipus thinks it was Ptolemy who should have been removed from the palace, if one or the other of them had to withdraw."

"The location is certainly splendid enough," I said as the guards escorted us away from the landing and we ascended a marble stairway lined by palm trees. Before us loomed the facade of the palace, a curious mixture of Greek columns and Egyptian stonework. "Or does the queen grow lonely, staying here?"

"Caesar visits her daily."

"Daily—or nightly?" I said.

A low, throaty voice, speaking Greek with an elegant accent, came from the shaded portico that led into the palace. "Caesar may visit whenever he wishes. And so may Merianis; for the queen is always pleased to look upon her face."

Cleopatra stepped forth into the sunlight. The guards fell forward onto their faces. Merianis dropped to her knees and bowed her head. I followed her example.

The queen accepted these prostrations as her due. I heard the swishing of her linen gown and watched the movement of her gilded, jewel-encrusted sandals as she strode back and forth before us. Only after a long moment did she utter the words, "You may rise."

Cleopatra proffered her hand to Merianis, who kissed it. "I've brought a visitor, Your Majesty. This is Gordianus of Rome, whom men call the Finder."

Cleopatra turned her gaze to me. "We've met before, have we not?"

"I was present on the occasion when Your Majesty made herself known to the consul of the Roman people."

She nodded. "Ah, yes. My attention was given entirely to Caesar on that occasion, but I do remember seeing you there, very briefly. Meto was also there, but the two of you quickly excused yourselves and disappeared. Since then, I've seen Meto on numerous occasions; Caesar hardly goes anywhere without him. It was only in recent days, and from Merianis, not Caesar, that I learned of your relationship to Meto."

"When he was very young, I adopted him. But he is no longer my son."

"How confusing! I understand that adoption is quite common among the Romans, who put their faith in man-made laws and man-made relationships. In Rome, it seems, two men can be father and son one day, and unrelated to one another the next; such a concept is foreign to us. In Egypt, the bloodline is everything. The bloodline can never be broken."

"Except by death?" I said.

"Not even by death. Sister and brother in this world will be sister and brother in the next. The blood of the Ptolemies runs equally in my veins and in those of my brother. We are joined to one another and to our ancestors for all eternity. But in this realm we inhabit mortal flesh, and at some point death may separate us, if only for the brief span of this mortal lifetime."

"I devoutly hope not, Your Majesty."

She smiled. "If it becomes necessary for one of us to proceed to the next world prematurely, I assure you that it won't be me. Cratipus would never allow that to happen."

"Your Majesty will come to no harm, not as long as there's a single breath left in the body of any man here!" declared Cratipus.

"Your devotion pleases the queen," said Cleopatra. "Now return to the harbor and keep a lookout for other visitors."

"Is Your Majesty expecting someone?" I said.

"Perhaps. But we were speaking of the afterlife." She strolled through the lush gardens surrounding the palace, with Merianis and I following a little behind.

"Having lived in both places, I perceive that Egyptian expectations of an afterlife considerably exceed those of a Roman," I said. "For us, when this life is over, the best has passed. We become shadows who watch the living with envy as we fade into a long, gray eternity."

"Ah, but you have it exactly wrong. For those who attain immortality, this life is but a shadow of the next. The point of this life is to prepare for the life to come. I brought up this subject for a reason, Gordianus. Knowing of Meto's importance to Caesar, knowing of your importance to Meto—and because Merianis has become so fond of you—I have made it my business to know a little about you."

"I find it hard to imagine that anything about myself might interest the queen of Egypt."

"Even so, I know of your reason for coming to Egypt, Gordianus, and I know of your bereavement. Was your wife very ill?"

I sighed. "Is this subject truly of interest to Your Majesty? It causes me pain to speak of it."

"Even so, indulge me."

"Very well. My wife's illness was mysterious to me. Sometimes it seemed to me almost that she must be imagining it. At other times, I feared it would take her from me so suddenly I would have no chance to say farewell."

"She wished to bathe in the Nile, thinking that would cure her?"

"So she said. But . . ."

"You think she might have had another reason for coming to Egypt?"

"I think perhaps she sensed that her death was near, and it was her desire to die in Egypt. She often expressed to me her disdain for Roman funerary rites; she did not care for cremation. Where else but in Egypt could she be properly mummified and given the ancient rites of passage to the afterlife? While that may have been her intention, it was not what happened in the end."

"Your wife was lost in the Nile."

"It happened near a little temple between the road and the river, north of Naucratis."

Cleopatra nodded. "The ancient temple of Osiris, hidden among the vines; I know it well. The place is very ancient, very holy."

"I was told afterward that the temple is abandoned, and that the woman who stays there, pretending to be a priestess, is mad."

The queen raised an eyebrow. "I've met the woman of whom you speak. I found her very wise."

"It was the old crone who told Bethesda to enter the water," I said bitterly.

"But, Gordianus! Do you not understand the significance of a death in the Nile? The river is sacred to Osiris; whom the river claims, the god claims. To drown in the Nile is to be blessed in Osiris. Do you know the story of his death and resurrection? Let me tell it to you.

"It was Osiris who brought the gift of civilization to the world, at the dawn of history. Before Osiris, men were cannibals; Osiris taught them to grow crops and to harvest the fish of the sea, and he gave them much more—the first temples in which to worship the gods, the first cities and laws, even the first instruments with which to make music. The type of flute that my father loved so much to play was invented by Osiris himself.

"Osiris ruled the earth, and all men loved him. But by his very goodness Osiris incurred the jealousy of his wicked brother Set, who devised a plot to destroy him. Set made a wonderful box, and at a banquet of the gods, he promised it to the one whose body best fit the box. When Osiris lay in the box, Set covered it and sealed it with molten lead, then cast the box into the Nile.

"Isis, the sister and wife of Osiris, followed the box and retrieved it. When she opened it, Osiris was dead. But by her magic, Isis made his flesh incorruptible and restored him to life. Osiris might have retaken his throne, but instead he chose to retire beyond this world to the Kingdom of the Dead, where he welcomes the souls of the just."

I bowed my head. "What has this to do with Bethesda?" I whispered.

"We are all composed of four elements: fire, earth, air, and water. To perish in the Nile is to be absolved of the elements of earth and water, which join with the mud of the river. Your wife is all fire and air now. It doesn't matter that she wasn't mummified. If she drowned in the Nile, in emulation of Osiris, she passed from this world directly into the god's embrace. She received the gift of immortality. You should rejoice for her!"

I averted my gaze. "You speak of things about which I know very little. As I said, Roman religion is not as . . . conversant . . . with the afterworld as is the religion of Egypt."

"You may be ignorant of these matters, Gordianus, but clearly, your wife was not. She chose the time and the place and the manner of her going. How many mortals can hope for as much?"

"Unless they have access to Nemesis-in-a-bottle," I muttered under my breath, thinking of the vial Cornelia had given me.

The queen frowned. "What did you say?"

"Nothing, Your Majesty. A passing thought of no importance."

Cratipus came running. "Your Majesty! Other visitors are arriving."

"The guests I invited for the midday meal?"

"Yes, Your Majesty."

"Tell Apollodorus to escort them to the little terrace that faces the city. Caesar likes to dine outside."

"Caesar?" I said. "I should leave now. If Merianis, or someone else, can escort me—"

"Leave? Nonsense! You'll stay, Gordianus, and take the meal with us. My cooks have prepared a poached octopus, and Caesar has promised to bring an amphora of Falernian wine—a rare treat! In recent years, good Italian wines have become as scarce as snowfalls in Egypt. I'm told that this amphora came from Pompey's private store, which Caesar seized when he overran the Great One's camp at Pharsalus."

"Your Majesty, I've no desire to drink a dead man's wine."

"Then I'll have an Egyptian beer decanted for you. Come, Merianis! Show Gordianus the way to the dining terrace."

20

We ascended a flight of marble steps to a flagstone terrace. A railing supported by squat columns overlooked a sheer drop to the water below. On either side, the terrace was flanked by tall palm trees and leafy plants. Behind us rose a windowless wall with a door that gave access to the interior. Dining couches had been set out in a semicircle facing the city, so that each had a view of the sunlit waterfront of Alexandria and its reflection in the harbor.

The queen sat back on the most opulent of the couches, which was strewn with purple cushions. She rested on one elbow and reclined so that one of her feet touched the ground. The pose showed off the lines of her figure; the linen gown clung to her heavy breasts and the sensuous curves of her hips, thighs, and calves. The jewels that adorned her sandals glinted in the dappled sunlight.

Merianis took up a position behind the couch to the queen's left and indicated that I should stand beside her.

A few moments later, Apollodorus appeared. He wore no more clothing than before, but he had ornamented himself with a silver pectoral for the occasion. The hammered metal accentuated the muscles of his bare chest. He made obeisance to the queen. "Your guest has arrived, Your Majesty."

Cleopatra nodded. "You may go, Apollodorus. I'll summon you if I need you."

As Apollodorus turned and disappeared down the steps, the bald pate of Caesar came into view, followed by Caesar's beaming face. He was wearing his consular toga. He mounted the final step and strode onto the terrace. His smile faded, but only a little, at the sight of me.

"The queen of Egypt welcomes the consul of Rome," said Cleopatra. "But where are the consul's lictors?"

"I left them down at the harbor." Caesar approached the queen, making no pretense of bowing. Clearly, in such a setting, there was no need for formality between them. They exchanged a lovers' gaze: relaxed, intimate, confident of reciprocity. She offered her hand; Caesar took it and gave her a lingering kiss, not upon the back of her hand but upon the palm.

Caesar glanced at me. "Do we have another guest?"

"It chanced that Gordianus was here; Merianis brought him, knowing I desired to meet him. Don't worry, there'll be enough octopus for us all. But will there be enough Falernian?"

"Of that, have no fear," said Caesar. A moment later, Meto arrived on the terrace. He was dressed in his finest military regalia, bearing an amphora in his arms as one might carry an infant. He grimaced when he saw me, but said nothing.

I observed the amphora. It was typical in shape, with little handles near the wide-mouthed top and a rounded bottom; it was designed not to stand upright but to be laid lengthwise alongside other amphorae for shipment and storage. The top was stopped with a cork sealed with red wax. Along the side several words had been etched in the clay in letters large enough to be read at a glance:

FALERNIAN
OPEN ONLY IN THE PRESENCE OF
GNAEUS POMPEY MAGNUS

"The wine comes from Pompey's private store," said Caesar. "When we overran his camp at Pharsalus, I found his pavilion abandoned but laid out as if for a great banquet—silver plates, great portions of roasted game, and this very amphora of Falernian wine sitting upright on a stand beside Pompey's dining couch, ready to be unsealed and opened and decanted into pitchers. He escaped at the very last moment, leaving his victory banquet untouched. Pompey must have brought this amphora from his own cellars in Rome, lugging it all over Greece and waiting for the proper occasion to drink from it. You can see his personal seal, the letters 'M-A-G-N-V-S,' impressed in the wax. His ring fits the impression exactly."

Caesar produced the ring King Ptolemy had presented to him, which he kept on a silver chain around his neck. While Meto held the amphora steady, Caesar, holding the ring between his fingers—superstitious about slipping Pompey's signet ring onto his own finger?—demonstrated how the seal had been impressed in the red wax, fitting the ring into the impression.

"Let's open it at once," suggested Cleopatra.

Meto sat on a couch and set the amphora upright into a clay stand on the floor between his knees. He produced a short knife, with which he carefully sliced away the sealing wax. He gently pulled out the cork stopper. Merianis brought a silver pitcher, but before Meto could fill the pitcher with wine, the queen lifted her hand.

"Stop! Before the first pitcher is filled, let Caesar receive the first taste from the amphora itself."

Caesar smiled. "A kind gesture, Your Majesty. But I think the first taste must go to my hostess, the queen of Egypt."

Cleopatra shook her head and smiled. Every exchange between them became a flirtation. "The queen declines. The queen insists that Pompey's conqueror should enjoy the first taste of Pompey's wine. And I know just the cup from which you should drink it! Merianis, fetch the cups of beaten gold I received on my nuptial day."

Merianis disappeared into the palace for a moment, then returned bearing two cups fashioned in the old Greek style—wide, shallow bowls with stout bases and handles, made not of painted clay but of gold.

Rising from her couch, Cleopatra took one of the cups from Merianis and displayed it to Caesar. "These cups were presented to me and my brother on the day of our royal marriage—a gift from the king of Parthia. Are they not beautiful?"

"Quite," said Caesar. "But is it proper that I should drink from one?"

"It is proper if I say it is proper," said the queen. "My brother's lips shall never touch this cup, any more than his lips shall touch my own. There's only one man's lips I want upon this cup; only one man's lips I want to kiss my own." She put her face close to his, and for a moment I thought they would kiss; but at the last instant she drew back and flashed a teasing smile. Merianis laughed, and I recalled that she had done much the same thing to Apollodorus earlier. Which of the women was emulating the other? They both seemed impossibly young to me at that moment—not a goddess-queen and her priestess but two flirtatious girls. Whatever Caesar saw, he liked it; the vaguely stupid look on his face was that of a man so smitten he doesn't care who knows it. Meto, still sitting with the amphora between his knees, saw what I saw, and glowered.

Cleopatra turned to Meto, bearing the golden cup aloft. "Glum Meto! The very picture of the earnest Roman—never a smile for the queen of Egypt!" Meto sought to change his expression and managed an unconvincing, lopsided smile. "Stand up, glum Roman, and pour a splash of wine for your consul!"

Meto stood and lifted the amphora. Pouring a small amount from the long, heavy vessel into the wide cup presented a challenge, but he managed to do so without spilling a drop. When he was done, he replaced the amphora in its stand and put the cork back into the opening.

Cleopatra, walking slowly and carefully, carried the cup to Caesar. He took it in both hands and raised the rim to his lips, smiling at Cleopatra across the dark expanse of wine that reflected both their faces.

Cleopatra smiled back at him; then a shadow crossed her face. "Wait! The wine hasn't been tasted!" She pulled it from Caesar's lips. A tiny portion spilled from the rim and splashed onto the paving stone at her feet.

"Tasted?" said Caesar. "But surely there's no need for that. The wine came from Pompey's private store with the seal intact."

"Seals can be penetrated, and so can cork," said Cleopatra. "What was I thinking? The wine must be tasted first."

"But surely—" said Meto, looking exasperated.

"No! It *must* be tasted. That was one of the first lessons my father ever taught me. All food and drink must be tasted, without exception. Enjoyment of the moment blinded me. Merianis, fetch Zoë!"

Merianis, anticipating the queen's desire, had already stepped inside. She returned a moment later with a demure young slave girl who carried with her an ordinary clay drinking vessel. Cleopatra handed the wine-filled cup to Merianis. Merianis poured a tiny portion of the wine from the gold cup into the clay vessel held by Zoë, since protocol would not permit the lips of the taster to touch the golden cup intended for the queen's consort.

Meto stiffened his jaw; I assumed he was impatient with the queen's intensely suspicious Egyptian ways. Caesar appeared mildly amused, but at the same time slightly disturbed, for the queen seemed to be acting as much upon a premonition as upon the training she had received as a child. Like Caesar, I, too, had seen the agitation on Cleopatra's face when she withdrew the cup from his lips, and the sudden look of fear in her eyes.

Without self-consciousness—for she was used to being watched when she ate—the girl Zoë put the clay vessel to her lips and drank. She lowered the vessel and wiped a bit of red wine from her lips. Her features assumed a curious expression. "Your Majesty . . ."

A wrinkle appeared across Caesar's forehead. Cleopatra peered at the slave girl apprehensively. "Yes, Zoë? What is it?"

"Your Majesty . . ."

I held my breath.

"Your Majesty, I have tasted many wines for you—but never a wine as fine as this one!"

The tension evaporated. Caesar laughed softly. Cleopatra sighed. Meto gave a snort as if to say, "What were you all so worried about?"

Zoë grinned. "Your Majesty, I don't exaggerate! I've never tasted anything like it. Falernian I've tasted before—though not in a long time—but it was never this fine. It's hard to explain. . . ."

"Then I suppose we must find out for ourselves," said the queen. "Go now, Zoë. Come back when the first course is presented."

But the girl did not move. "As I said, Falernian I've tasted before, but never . . . never like this one. . . ." Her eyes, staring straight ahead, took on a glassy look.

"I said that you may go," said Cleopatra sharply.

Zoë ignored her. Her words began to slur together. "The flavor . . . the flavor is like fire . . . like something burning in my throat, and all the way down into my belly. A sweet fire . . . not at all unpleasant . . . but burning nonetheless. Oh, Your Majesty! Oh! I think there was something wrong with that wine!"

Zoë dropped the clay vessel. Everyone drew back, startled by the hollow explosion of the clay shattering on the flagstones.

Zoë fell to her knees, trembling violently. "Your Majesty! Your Majesty, help me, please!"

Cleopatra hurried to the girl's side. She knelt and took Zoë's convulsing body in her arms. Zoë gazed up at her, glassy eyed but with a look of mingled reverence and trust. She lifted her face as if in expectation of a kiss. The queen closed her eyes and put her lips to those of Zoë as the girl released her final exhalation. The convulsions abruptly ceased. The body of Zoë went limp.

Cleopatra held the dead slave girl in her arms, closed her eyes, and chanted softly. The chant was Egyptian, perhaps a song for the dead. For as long as the queen chanted and kept her eyes shut, a spell seemed to be cast over everyone present. No one moved.

I stared, dumbfounded at what I was seeing. Cleopatra was not only the girl's mistress and queen; she was her goddess as well, whose divine agency at the very moment of death might serve to convey a lowly slave to immortality in the lands beyond life.

When Cleopatra opened her eyes, I saw that she had been doing more than chanting. Some furious calculation appeared to have taken place, reflected in the fiery blaze of her eyes. She called to Merianis, who put aside the gold cup, ran to the queen, and knelt beside her. They exchanged hushed, urgent words. Merianis looked over her shoulder at Meto, her expression so wild that I felt a stab of dread. Meto, too, sensed something terrible in her gaze, for I saw him blanch. Caesar caught the looks that shot between them, and on his face I saw a mask of puzzlement.

Merianis appeared to resist whatever Cleopatra was suggesting, until at last the queen raised her voice. "Go, then, and do as I say! Bring Apollodorus!"

Merianis rose to her feet and ran from the terrace.

Caesar looked at the amphora of wine, which had been replaced in the stand on the paving stones. He looked at Meto, who stood over the amphora, then at Cleopatra and the dead slave. "What in Hades just happened here?"

Meto looked down at the amphora. "Poisoned!" he muttered. "It must be. Somehow . . ." He reached down as if to pull out the cork stopper again.

"No!" Caesar shouted. "Don't touch it!" It was understandable that he should speak with alarm, but the look he cast at Meto was tinged with suspicion. He strode toward Cleopatra, but she held up her hand to signal that he should stay back.

"Zoë's *ka*—what you call the lemur—is still not free from her body. I sense it, still clinging to her flesh. Her death was so unexpected that the *ka* remains confused, trapped between this world and the next. Be silent. Don't move."

"But I intend to call for my lictors—"

"Silence!" said Cleopatra, gazing up at him with fire in her eyes. I looked on, amazed, as a twenty-one-year-old girl commanded the world's most powerful man to be still, and he obeyed.

And so we stood, motionless like actors on a stage at the final tableau. Surrounded by stillness, I became conscious of the many sounds of the harbor, muted by distance and the gardens enclosing us—shouts of men working on the waterfront, the shriek of gulls, the susurrant voice of the restless water itself. Dappled sunlight danced upon the flagstones. The moment took on a hard-edged clarity that seemed at once dreamlike and more real than real. I felt light-headed, and despite the queen's command that no one should move, I sat on one of the couches and briefly shut my eyes.

At last Merianis came running up the steps. I could see she had been weeping, no doubt shaken by the turn of events. Apollodorus followed behind her, looking grim.

Cleopatra stood. The body of Zoë slipped from her embrace and crumpled, like a cast-off garment, on the paving stones. Presumably the restless *ka* had been dispatched, for the queen paid no more attention to the corpse.

She raised her arm and pointed at Meto. "I want his person searched."

Meto's face grew long. Caesar stiffened his jaw and nodded. "Of course, Your Majesty. It shall be done. I shall call my lictors and see to it at once."

"No! I summoned Apollodorus for the purpose. Apollodorus shall search him."

Caesar worked his jaw back and forth. "I think, Your Majesty, that in these circumstances, it would be best—"

"This is *my* home," said Cleopatra. "It's my slave who lies dead. It was my cup that was poisoned—"

"A cup intended for *my* lips," said Caesar.

"Filled with wine poured by your man—the same glum-looking Roman who carried the wine here. No, Caesar, I must insist that one of my men perform the task of searching Meto's person."

Caesar considered this for a long moment. He turned toward Meto but did not quite look him in the eye, then turned back to Cleopatra. "Very well, Your Majesty. Let Apollodorus search him. Step forward, Meto. Raise your arms and let the fellow do what he must."

Meto looked indignant, but obeyed. His jaw twitched; I knew he wanted badly to cast a scathing look at the queen, but his discipline held firm, and instead he kept his gaze straight ahead.

Apollodorus ran his hands over Meto's shoulders, limbs, and torso, poking his fingers among the leather straps and buckles. Meto grunted and ground his jaw. Cleopatra stepped closer and watched intently. Caesar's gaze shifted apprehensively from Meto to Cleopatra and back again. Merianis, who had withdrawn to another part of the terrace, hid her face and began to weep.

Apollodorus stiffened. "Your Majesty . . ."

"What is it, Apollodorus? What have you found?"

From between two straps of leather attached to Meto's breastplate, Apollodorus produced a small white object, cylindrical in shape. Caesar leaned forward, as did Cleopatra. I rose from the couch, still light-headed, and moved toward Meto, feeling a sudden premonition of catastrophe.

Apollodorus held the object aloft between his thumb and forefinger. It was a tiny vial made of alabaster.

I could not stop myself; I gasped.

As one, all four turned their gazes on me—Caesar, Cleopatra, Apollodorus, and Meto, whose eyes finally made contact with mine for the first time that day. The look on his face froze my blood.

"Papa!" he whispered hoarsely.

Caesar snatched the vial from Apollodorus. He thrust it under my nose. "What is this, Gordianus?"

I stared at it. The stopper was gone. Though the vial was empty, I caught a faint whiff of the not unpleasant odor I had smelled when I sniffed its contents aboard Pompey's ship. There could be no doubt; this was the vial Cornelia had given me.

Caesar's nose was almost touching mine. "Speak, Finder! I command you! What do you know about this?"

From behind him, I heard the calm, but demanding, voice of Cleopatra. "Yes, Gordianus. Tell us what you know about this alabaster vial that Apollodorus found upon the person of your son."

21

An hour later, in a kind of stupor, I was back in my room, sifting through the contents of my traveling chest. Roman soldiers dispatched by Caesar stood by, watching my every movement. Rupa stood across the room, and the boys sat on the windowsill. I had not yet told them the details of what had transpired, but they knew that something terrible must have occurred. The boys were calming themselves by stroking Alexander the cat, who sat purring between them, oblivious to the tension in the room.

"It's not here," I muttered. Carefully, methodically, I had removed every item from the trunk and spread them across my bed. Now, just as methodically, I replaced each object into the trunk, shaking tunics to make sure nothing was hidden in the folds, opening Bethesda's little trinket boxes to be certain that no alabaster vial was hidden inside.

The search was fruitless. The vial Cornelia had given me was no longer in my possession; Apollodorus had discovered it upon Meto's person. Nonetheless, I had been praying for some miracle whereby I would find the vial in my chest after all, with its stopper and contents intact. Now there could be no doubt. The poison Cornelia had given me—quick to act, relatively painless—must have been the same poison that killed Cleopatra's taster.

My reaction when I first saw the vial in Apollodorus's hand had been so spontaneous, so damning, that dissembling was futile. No lie fabricated on the spot would have satisfied Caesar. Nor was silence an option; refusing to speak would have pitted my will against his, and against the will of Cleopatra as well. Both of them had long experience in obtaining information from unwilling subjects. I might have withstood a degree of suffering, but there were Rupa and the boys to consider. I would not allow harm to be done to them, even for the sake of protecting Meto.

And there lay the bitter irony: After all my protestations that Meto was no longer my son, that our relationship was over, and that he meant nothing to me, my first instinct had been to protect him. Caesar had seen through me at once. "If Meto truly means nothing to you, Finder, then why do you not speak?" he had demanded. "A woman lies dead. But for the queen's action, it would have been me! What do you know about this alabaster vial? Speak! If I have to force you to talk, I will. Neither of us wishes for that to happen, do we, Finder?"

So I told him where the vial had come from and how it had come to be in my possession. When had I last seen it? I couldn't say for certain. (In fact, my last memory of seeing it was the day that Meto had noticed it, when I gave him a keepsake from Bethesda.) How had it come to be in the possession of Meto? I attempted to dissemble, saying I had no idea; but hearing the threat in Caesar's tone, Meto himself spoke up.

"I saw it among Papa's things, on the night I went to visit him in his room. He kept it in his trunk. I told him to get rid of it. I was thinking he might be tempted . . . to use it himself. But from that moment to this, I never saw it again—not until this Sicilian produced it out of thin air, like a magic trick!"

"Are you saying Apollodorus himself was carrying the vial?" said Caesar.

"We know already how talented he is at making things appear from nowhere." Meto glowered at the queen.

"Enough!" said Caesar. "The one thing we know for certain is that father and son both knew of this poison, and here you both are, together with the vial that contained it and the slave who died from drinking it. Meto, Meto! I never imagined . . ."

"Consul, wait!" I shook my head. "Perhaps there's been a mistake."

"What sort of mistake?"

"Let me return to my room and look through my things. An alabaster vial is a common-enough object. Perhaps the one in my room is still there, after all." I tried to speak with conviction, but the chance seemed far-fetched even to me.

Caesar, to his credit, allowed me to pursue the possibility. While his men took Meto into custody, another group of soldiers accompanied me back to the mainland, escorted me to my room, and watched as I conducted a futile search of the things in my trunk. The only result had been to give further evidence that Meto must have purloined the poison at some point after he first saw it in my trunk.

But how had the poison come to be in the wine? And for what purpose? I sat on the bed, numbed by the enormity of what had happened. Was it really possible that my son had attempted to take the life of Julius Caesar?

My son: The words came to my mind unbidden and remained there, unchallenged. As I had wept for Bethesda, now I wept for Meto, knowing he must surely be lost to me forever. I realized in that moment why I had so steadfastly resisted a reconciliation with Meto since seeing him again in Alexandria. It was not stubborn pride, or an irreconcilable disgust for Meto himself; it was my fear of a moment just such as this. Having lost Bethesda, how could I open myself a second time to the chance of losing the person I loved most in the world? Meto, who lived such a perilous existence, who exposed himself again and again to the dangers of war and espionage, who had bound his fate to the fiery comet of Caesar's career—since I had at last shut him out from my life, surely it was better to keep him out for good, or else I might face the intolerable prospect sooner or later of losing him altogether. So it had come to pass, despite all I had done to harden my heart against him. What an ill-starred voyage had brought me to Alexandria!

The soldiers allowed me time to collect myself, but did not withdraw; Caesar had ordered them not to leave my side. Rupa stood before the window, his arms crossed, fretting and frowning. The boys fidgeted, biting their lips and exchanging glances, until at last Mopsus spoke.

"Master, what's going on? What's happened? It's something to do with Meto, isn't it?"

I shook my head. "Boys, boys, it's of no concern to you—"

"No, Master, this isn't right!" Little Androcles stepped forward. "Mopsus and I may be only slaves, and Rupa is—well, he's just Rupa—but we're not children any longer. Something terrible has happened. We want to know what it is. We're clever, Master—"

"And fearless!" piped up Mopsus.

And strong! Rupa tacitly added, massing his bull-like shoulders.

The only occupant of the room who failed to step forward was Alexander the cat, who resettled himself on the windowsill with his back to the room and gazed out at the harbor.

"Perhaps we can help, Master."

I looked at Androcles, manifestly still a child notwithstanding his protestation to the contrary, and I remembered Meto when he was the same age. Between that time and this, Meto had become a man. He had traveled across the world and back, killed other men and very nearly been killed himself, stood beside Caesar and dipped his hands into the tides of history; yet a part of me clung to the absurd notion that Meto was as tender and vulnerable as Androcles, that he was still a boy who needed my protection—and my chiding. In that moment I at last became reconciled to Meto and the man he had chosen to become. I relinquished the false assumption that I had some responsibility for his actions; I acquiesced to his inevitable autonomy; I admitted to myself that I loved him nonetheless. If now he found himself in a dire strait, I would not judge him, and I would do all I could to help him.

"Meto stands accused of trying to kill his imperator, with a poison he obtained from this trunk," I said.

"Oh, no!" said Mopsus.

"It isn't true, is it, Master?"

"The truth, Androcles? I don't know."

"But if Meto did such a thing, Master—"

"Then I shall throw myself upon Caesar's mercy. I shall tear my tunic, pull out my hair, beg him shamelessly; surely all my years around advocates like Cicero have taught me some tools of persuasion. I shall use them now on Meto's behalf."

"But surely Meto is innocent, Master!"

"If he is, Mopsus, then I intend to do everything in my power to absolve him. This is a strange land. Here, justice exists at the whim of those who possess a certain bloodline, and laws are decrees handed down by squabbling rulers. Laws have nothing to do with truth, or justice with proof. Soon it will be the same in Rome, I think; Caesar is taking lessons from these Nile crocodiles and intends to reproduce their habitat along the Tiber. Still, even in Egypt, truth is truth, and proof is proof, and it may be that I can yet do something to save my son."

"And we will help you," insisted Androcles.

"If the gods allow it," I said.

"Did you find it?"

Caesar stood at the eastern window in his high room, gazing over the rooftops of the Jewish Quarter in the direction of the distant Nile.

"No, Consul."

He nodded. Even with his back turned, I could tell that he took no pleasure in the gesture. He stood with his hands clasped behind his back, nervously turning the alabaster vial between two fingers. He turned to face me.

"I've just received disturbing news. How are your eyes, Gordianus?"

"I beg your pardon, Consul?"

"Stand here and look toward the east, beyond the city, at that blur of desert between here and the Nile. What do you see, Gordianus?"

"Not much, Consul. A blur, as you say, further obscured by a great cloud of dust."

"Exactly. That's the dust raised by a marching army. According to my intelligence, the whole of Ptolemy's army has decamped from their fortress in the desert and is now marching this way under the command of a certain Achillas. You've met this fellow, I understand?"

"Not exactly, Consul."

"But you've observed him at close quarters?"

"From a considerable distance, I saw him murder Pompey. Later, practically under my nose, I watched him strangle an Egyptian spy with his bare hands."

"A murderous brute!"

"I believe that both acts were committed at the behest of the king, which would make the killing of Pompey an assassination and the killing of the spy an execution—if one believes that some killings are murder and other killings are not."

Caesar looked at me askance. "I've killed men in battle. Men under my command have caused the death of many others. Would you call *me* a murderer, Gordianus?"

"I would never presume to offer such a judgment, Consul."

He snorted. "Wriggled out of answering that one, didn't you? You remind me more and more of Cicero. The word-twisting, the hand-wringing, the endless equivocations—his ways have rubbed off on you over the years, whether you like it or not."

I kept my voice steady. "The times we live in have led us all down paths not of our choosing."

"Speak for yourself, Gordianus. You spend too much time looking backward. The future lies ahead."

"A future that will soon bring Ptolemy's army to the gates of Alexandria?"

"So it seems. I never intended for Alexandria to become a battleground. I meant to come here, settle affairs between the king and queen, and be on my way. Instead, I now face the prospect of a full-scale war, and I don't like the odds. I've sent for reinforcements, but who knows when those will arrive? As it stands, their numbers are great, and ours are small. Granted, the forces under Achillas's command are highly irregular by Roman standards. The core is made up of the legionnaires who arrived here under Gabinius to restore the late king to his throne and to keep the peace. It seems they've since forgotten their origins and become Egyptianized, marrying local women and adopting native customs. That one of their number would consent to murder Pompey in cold blood tells us just how far they've descended from their honorable beginnings. Added to their ranks are mercenaries, runaway slaves, and foreign criminals. They've no discipline to speak of, and little loyalty; once, when they wanted higher pay, they blockaded the palace to demand it. But they haven't forgotten how to fight. Under a commander as murderous as they are, they may constitute a formidable foe."

He began to pace, turning the alabaster vial in his fingers. It seemed that Meto was far from his thoughts. He spoke again.

"A moment ago, you said that the killing of Pompey was done at the behest of the king. Do you believe that, Gordianus? Did King Ptolemy himself order the assassination? Is he capable of issuing such a command without Pothinus guiding him?"

"Surely you've come to know the king better than I do, Consul. You must be a better judge of his character and capabilities."

"Am I? Do you want the truth, Gordianus? These Ptolemies have me utterly confounded! The two of them have put my head in a spin. It's absurd. The master strategist, the consummate politician, the conqueror of Gaul, the author of Pompey's downfall—stumped by two children!"

I could not restrain a smile. "Cleopatra is hardly a child, Consul, as young as she may seem to men of our years. And—since you asked for my opinion—Ptolemy is no longer a boy. He's very nearly at that age when a Roman youth puts on the toga of manhood and becomes a citizen. Were you not precocious at fifteen, Consul?"

"Precocious, perhaps, but I was hardly ready to run a country like Egypt! When I was the king's age . . ." Caesar's face softened. "That was about the time I lost my father. It happened one morning while he was putting on his shoes. He was a strong, vigorous man in the prime of life; my mentor, my hero. One moment he was alive, tying the straps of his shoes. The next moment, he gave a lurch and tumbled to the floor, as dead as King Numa. His own father had died the same way—suddenly, in middle age, for no apparent reason. Some flaw passed from father to son, perhaps; in which case, I'm already past the span of my allotted years and living on borrowed time. I could die at any moment; perhaps I'll drop dead while we stand here talking!" He gazed at the distant cloud of dust and sighed. "I remember my father every day—every time I put on my shoes. It's a sad thing for a boy on the verge of manhood to lose his father. The same thing happened to Ptolemy, though he was even younger when the Piper died. I think that may be why he craves so strongly the affection and guidance of an older man."

I frowned. "You speak of Pothinus?"

Caesar laughed. "I'll spare you the predictable joke regarding Pothinus's manhood. No, Gordianus, I refer to myself. The other day, in the reception hall, when I spoke of the special friendship between the king and myself, I wasn't just spinning pretty words in the manner of Cicero."

"I think I may understand the king's fascination with Caesar, but I'm not sure I understand . . ."

"Caesar's fascination with the king? Ptolemy is intelligent, passionate, willful, convinced of his divine destiny—"

"Like his sister?"

"Very much like her, though I'm afraid he lacks Cleopatra's sense of humor. Such a serious young man—and what a temper! That tantrum he threw the other day, haranguing the crowd and casting off his diadem!" Caesar shook his head. "I acted too quickly, pressing him to make peace with his sister. I should have anticipated his reaction."

"It seemed to me that the king was behaving like a jealous lover." I gazed steadily at Caesar, wondering if I had spoken too candidly.

He narrowed his eyes. "The intimate relationship between an older man and a youth has always been more warmly regarded in the Greek-speaking world than in our own. Alexander himself had Hephaestion, and then the Persian boy, Bagoas. If the king of Alexander's city has approached me in the same spirit of manly love, should I not be honored? Young men are naturally susceptible to hero worship. The more ambitious or highborn the young man, the more exalted the older man upon whom the youth desires to model himself."

"The king's attention flatters you?"

"Yes; and in a way that his sister's attentions do not."

"They say that Caesar set his sights on a king, when he was young." The steadiness of my voice was inversely proportional to the recklessness of my words. Everyone knew the rumors about Caesar and King Nicomedes of Bithynia. His political enemies had used the tale to ridicule him—but most of those men were dead now. Caesar's soldiers cracked jokes about it—but I was not one of Caesar's comrades in arms. Still, it was Caesar himself who had opened this avenue of conversation.

His response was surprisingly candid. Perhaps, like me, Caesar had reached that point in life when one's own past begins to seem like ancient history—more quaint than quarrel provoking. "Ah, Nico! When I put on my shoes, I think of my father; when I take them off, I think of Nico. I was nineteen, serving on the staff of the praetor Minucius Thermus in the Aegean. Thermus required the help of King Nicomedes's fleet; an emissary was needed to go to the king's court in Bithynia. Thermus chose me. 'I think the two of you may hit it off,' he told me, with a glint in his eye. The old goat was right. Nico and I hit it off so well that I tarried in Bithynia even after Thermus sent a messenger to retrieve me. What a remarkable man Nico was! Born to power, sure of himself, with a voracious appetite for life; a ruler not unlike the one that Ptolemy may yet become. What a lot he had to teach an eager, ambitious young Roman who was no longer a boy but not quite a man. When I think of how naive I was, how wide-eyed and innocent!"

"It's impossible to think of you as naive, Consul."

"Is it? Alas! The youth whom Nico instructed in the ways of the world has long since vanished—but the man remembers those golden days as clearly as if they just happened. I shut my eyes, and I'm in Bithynia again, without a scar on my flesh and with all my life ahead of me. Do you think Ptolemy will remember me that vividly when he grows old, and ruling Egypt has become a tired habit, and that fellow called Caesar has long since turned to dust?"

"I think the world will remember Caesar long after the Ptolemies have been forgotten." I said this matter-of-factly, but Caesar mistook my tone. His gentle mood suddenly evaporated.

"Don't humor me, Gordianus—you, of all people! The last thing I need right now is another sycophant."

The whole time we talked, he had been fiddling with the little vial, turning it over in his hand. Now he gripped it in his fist, so tightly that his knuckles blanched as white as the alabaster. Suddenly he threw it with all his might against the marble wall. Unbroken, the vial ricocheted and struck my leg. The blow was harmless, but still I jumped.

The gesture expended Caesar's fury. He drew a deep breath. "Just when I thought I was on the verge of restoring peace between the king and queen, Achillas marches on Alexandria—and someone attempts to poison me."

"Perhaps the queen was the intended victim."

"Perhaps. But how and when was the wine poisoned, and by whom? We know where the poison came from—and that fact casts a ray of suspicion upon *you*, Gordianus."

"Consul, I didn't even know the vial was missing—"

"So you've already explained. But the possibility remains that you were in collusion with your son—that you provided him with the poison, knowing how he intended to use it. Did you conspire against me?"

I shook my head. "No, Consul."

"Meto claims to know nothing. The queen advises me to torture him. She doesn't understand how strong willed he is. I myself trained Meto to endure interrogation. But if I thought that torture would loosen his tongue—"

"No, Consul! Not that."

"The truth must be discovered."

"Perhaps . . . perhaps I can do so, Consul. If you'll allow me—"

"Why? Meto means nothing to you. In Massilia, you disowned him. I witnessed that moment with my own eyes and ears."

"Consul, please! Let me help my son."

Caesar gazed at me for a long moment. A shadow seemed to dim the light in his eyes, as if some powerful, dark emotion gripped him, but his face remained devoid of expression. At last he spoke. "Over the years, your son has demonstrated great loyalty to me. I've rewarded his devotion with a degree of trust I've given to very few men. And yet, when that slave girl died today, a part of me was not surprised. The worm of deceit starts small, but grows. I think back, and I perceive that a rift has been growing between myself and Meto for quite some time. The signs have been subtle. He never defies me outright, but on his face I've glimpsed a sour, fleeting look; in his voice I've heard a faint note of discord. If Meto *has* betrayed me, he shall be punished accordingly."

I bit my lip. "Caesar has a reputation for clemency."

"Yes, Gordianus, I've shown great clemency to those who've fought against me. Even that rat Domitius Ahenobarbus I forgave, only to see him take up arms against me at Massilia and again at Pharsalus. But for a traitor who resorts to lies and poison, there can be no pardon. I tell you this outright, Gordianus, so that if you harbor any notion of pleading for your son's life, you can spare yourself the indignity. Don't bother to rip your tunic and weep, like one of Cicero's guilty clients playing for sympathy in the courts. If Meto did this thing, my judgment will be harsh and irreversible. Do you understand?"

"Yes, Consul. But what if I can prove to you that he's innocent?"

Again the shadow dimmed his eyes. "If Meto is innocent, then someone else is guilty."

"So I would assume, Consul."

"In which case, the truth is likely to pose a problem."

"I'm not sure I understand."

"The poisoner must have come from one of three camps—my own, or that of the queen, or that of the king. Whatever the truth, the revelation is likely to cause yet more . . . complications. Which is why you will report anything you discover directly to me, and to me alone. Do you understand?"

"Yes, Consul."

Caesar strode across the room, stooped, and picked up the alabaster vial. He held it to the light. "What an irony, if the poison intended for Pompey's widow had taken the life of Pompey's rival! Do you think our poisoner has a sense of humor, Gordianus?"

"I shall take that possibility into account, Consul."

22

I had to stoop to enter through the low doorway. The jailer, one of Caesar's men, shut the door behind me. Meto, sitting on a low cot, sprang to his feet.

He was being held in a small room underground. The walls were dank, and the only light came from a tiny, grated window high above our heads, from which I heard faint, echoing sounds of the harbor—bells, gulls, men calling out, the low murmur of the water.

"Papa! What are you doing here? Caesar can't think that you had anything to do with—"

"I'm not here as a prisoner, Meto. Caesar agreed to let me visit you."

"You looked in your trunk?"

"Yes. The vial wasn't there. I don't know when it was taken. Caesar has it now. He wants to know how it came to be on your person."

"But I never possessed it! The only time I ever saw it was that day in your room, when I told you to get rid of it."

"If only I had!"

Meto shook his head. "This is madness. Why is Caesar holding me here? He can't possibly believe I tried to poison him."

I remembered the darkness in Caesar's eyes. "I'm afraid he does believe it, though it causes him great pain. But if we can prove otherwise—"

Meto was staring at the dank stone wall, not listening. "How the gods must despise me! First, you disowned me, Papa. I thought that nothing could be worse than that. But now Caesar turns against me. All that I've loved and trusted and given my life for has abandoned me. Why did I ever allow myself to expect anything more? I began this life as an orphan and a slave. I shall leave this world in an even lowlier state, branded as a traitor and a criminal, without a father, without a friend, without a name."

"No, Meto! Whatever else may happen, you're still my son."

He looked at me with tears in his eyes. "In Massilia—"

"I repent of the error I made in Massilia! You're my son, Meto. I'm your father. Forgive me."

"Papa!"

I embraced my son. For the first time since Massilia, a place in my heart that had grown numb and cold quickened and sprang to life. I felt an almost palpable relief, as if a jagged stone that had been lodged in my breast was now removed. I had learned to ignore the pain in order to bear it, but now that it was relieved, I realized the grinding, wearing burden of the suffering I had inflicted on myself. I embraced the warm solidity of Meto's body and rejoiced that he was still in the world, alive and whole. But for how much longer? In Egypt, I had lost Bethesda, only to find Meto again; had I now reclaimed Meto only to face losing him forever?

He stepped back. We both took deep breaths and for a moment lowered our eyes, made shy by the emotion of the moment. I cleared my throat.

"I can't stay long. We need to talk, and quickly. And remember, say nothing that can't be safely overheard. These walls appear to be solid stone, but there may be someone watching and listening even now."

"There's nothing I can't say aloud, Papa. I have nothing to hide."

"Even so . . ." I thought of the sentiments he had expressed to me in my room the day he saw the alabaster vial, his doubts about Caesar and the suffering that followed in Caesar's wake; if another of Caesar's men had overheard that conversation, might Meto's words have been construed as sedition? Now that he stood accused of outright treason, anything he said against Caesar would be scrutinized in the worst possible light, so I dared not question him further in such a vein.

For the first time I allowed myself to consider the possibility that Meto might actually be guilty of making an attempt on Caesar's life. It made no sense, unless his resentment against Caesar went far deeper than anything he had expressed to me. But might it be that the poison had been intended for Cleopatra, so as to remove her influence upon Caesar, and that the attempt had somehow gone terribly wrong? I gazed at Meto's face, trying to read the truth in his eyes. Was my son a poisoner, and a bungler as well? In the corner of my heart that had once renounced him, a seed of doubt was stirring.

"Apollodorus found the vial on your person, Meto. How could such a thing have happened?"

"I have no idea, Papa."

"It will take a better answer than that to satisfy Caesar."

"Caesar should be satisfied that I speak the truth! After all we've been through together, it's absurd that he shouldn't trust me."

"Perhaps. But think, Meto. Did Apollodorus simply hold up the vial and claim he'd found it on you? Or was it actually on your person?"

He wrinkled his brow. "I remember that he tugged at it, and when I looked down, I saw it with my own eyes, held between two straps attached to my breastplate. I couldn't believe it! It can't have been there when I put on my armor this morning."

"Could someone besides Apollodorus have planted it on you, earlier in the day?"

He shook his head. "I don't see how. But if such a thing could be done without my knowledge, then who knows when it was done or by whom?"

I nodded. "That amphora of Falernian—where did it come from?"

"It was kept in storage on one of Caesar's ships in the harbor, along with his other personal belongings. This morning, quite early, he sent me to fetch it."

"Did anyone know in advance that he planned to drink from it today?"

"I don't think Caesar himself knew. He decided on a whim. He wanted to impress the queen."

"When you fetched this amphora, did you have any reason to believe it had been tampered with?"

"I don't think it had been touched since it was loaded into the ship. In fact, I had a hard time finding it; it was buried in a corner of the hold, behind a number of other items that were seized from Pompey's tent at Pharsalus—folding chairs, lamps, rugs, coverlets, and such. There was no sign that any of the cargo had been disturbed. And when I did find it, I dusted it off, made sure it was the Falernian Caesar had requested, and inspected the seal to see if it was intact; I checked that quite carefully. After that, the amphora was in my possession and never out of my sight. So, if you're wondering if someone knew in advance that Caesar would want to open that amphora today, and if that person somehow put poison in it before it was opened, you can dismiss such a notion. No one could conceivably have done such a thing . . . except perhaps myself."

"Meto! These walls may have ears. Don't say such a thing, even in jest."

"Why not? If a case is to be made against me, we might as well work out what my accusers will say. And it's true: The person who had the best, perhaps the only, opportunity to poison the amphora beforehand was me. But I didn't. No one did. The seal was intact."

"Seals can be tampered with."

He shook his head. "I understand that you want to consider all possibilities, Papa. But the chain of logic leads directly to the alabaster vial. The vial was there, it was empty, and we know it contained poison." He frowned. "What we don't know is when and how it was poured into the wine, and whether it was poured into the opened amphora, poisoning all the Falernian, or only into the cup that Cleopatra offered to Caesar and then compelled Zoë to taste. Either way, I don't see how it was done without any of us noticing. I broke the seal and opened the amphora myself; I poured the wine into the cup. I can't imagine how the poison could have been added to the amphora; unless, of course, I did it myself."

"Meto!"

"Sorry, Papa. But I did have the opportunity, and I don't see how anyone else could have done it without my knowledge."

"Then perhaps only the cup was poisoned. But when? Think back; let's see if we both remember the sequence of events in the same order. The queen told Merianis to fetch the golden cups. Merianis brought them. The queen showed one of them to Caesar, then held it while you filled it from the amphora. She then presented the cup to Caesar, but before he could drink, she called for the taster. Zoë came. The queen handed the golden cup to Merianis; Merianis poured a bit of the wine from the golden cup into the clay vessel that Zoë had brought with her; Zoë drank from the clay vessel, and quickly succumbed to the poison. Is that how you remember it, Meto?"

He nodded.

I frowned. "But what happened to the wine that remained in the golden cup?"

Meto thought. "Merianis was still holding the cup when Cleopatra went to Zoë. But then Cleopatra called for Merianis, and Merianis put the cup down and ran to her mistress. They talked for a while, too low for the rest of us to hear; then Merianis went to fetch Apollodorus."

"So Merianis put down the cup; but then what became of it?"

Meto shook his head. "It must have been gotten rid of at some point, to be sure no one drank from it. Yes, I remember now! It was after you left the island, Papa, with those men to escort you back to your room. The rest of us remained on the terrace. More men arrived shortly, the ones who brought me to this cell; but before that happened, the queen told Apollodorus to pour the wine from the cup back into the amphora—"

"Numa's balls! Now the whole amphora has been poisoned, whether it was poisoned before or not! The amphora should have been left untouched."

"Does it really matter, Papa?"

"Think, Meto! If only the wine in the golden cup was poisoned, and *not* the wine in the amphora, then we could prove that you didn't poison the amphora and that the poison must have been added to the cup at some later point—a cup that was never in your possession! But now we have no way of knowing if the amphora was previously poisoned or not, since it's surely poisoned now. This was done at the queen's behest?"

"Yes."

"And Caesar did nothing to stop it?"

"Caesar was busy questioning me at that moment. Neither of us took much notice of what was being done with the cup. But now that you ask me, I remember hearing Cleopatra say something about the cup being polluted, and that no one could ever drink from it again, and I remember seeing Apollodorus empty the cup into the amphora, out of the corner of my eye, so to speak."

"Was the amphora saved?"

He wrinkled his brow. "I suppose so. Yes, I remember seeing Apollodorus replace the cork stopper, after he emptied the cup, and at the same time I was led off, I think one of Caesar's men must have carried off the amphora; so I assume it's in Caesar's keeping. But as you say, we know already that it contains poison, if only because the wine in the cup was poured into it."

"You're right; I can't see how the amphora will be of any use to us. I can't see how any of this helps us." *Especially,* I thought, *since all the circumstantial evidence points directly to your guilt, my son!* "Still, it's unthinkable that a man of Caesar's experience and judgment should have stood by and allowed a vital piece of evidence, like the amphora, to become hopelessly tainted."

"Perhaps you haven't noticed, Papa, but Caesar doesn't do his best thinking when he's in the presence of the queen."

"Meto! Keep such thoughts to yourself."

"Does it really matter what I say, Papa, or think, or do? This will be the end of me. I didn't try to poison Caesar, but I shall nevertheless be punished for the crime. Perhaps it's fitting. I stood by and did nothing when that Gaulish boy who haunts my dreams was orphaned and made a slave. No, that's not true—I joined in the slaughter with my sword, and with my stylus I celebrated that slaughter by helping Caesar write his memoirs. Now I shall die for something I never did. Can you hear the gods laughing, Papa? I think the deities who hold sway over Egypt must be just as capricious and cunning as our own gods."

"No, Meto! You will not be punished for a crime you didn't commit."

"If it amuses the gods, if it pleases Caesar, and satisfies Queen Cleopatra—"

"No! I shall find the truth, Meto, and the truth shall save you."

He laughed without mirth and wiped a tear from his eye. "Ah, Papa, I *have* missed you!"

"And I have missed you, Meto."

23

"You understand that I allow this only because Caesar requests it." The queen sat upon her throne in the reception room on the island of Antirrhodus, looking down her nose at me. When I had visited her earlier that day, accompanied by Merianis, I had been admitted informally into her presence; the atmosphere of this second visit was very different. The marble floor was hard against my knees, and I felt a distinct chill in the room, even though the afternoon sun shone brightly outside. "Apollodorus and Merianis are my subjects. You have no right to interrogate them."

"The word *interrogation* implies hostile intent, Your Majesty. I ask only to speak to them. I wish only to establish the truth—"

"The truth is self-evident, Gordianus-called-Finder. For reasons known only to himself, your son sought to poison someone earlier today—perhaps Caesar, perhaps me, perhaps both of us. If you want the truth, interrogate *him.*"

"I've questioned Meto already, Your Majesty. But only by questioning all who were present can I establish the exact sequence of events—"

"Enough! I've told you already that I shall allow this, but only because Caesar himself has asked me to indulge you. Whom would you speak to first?"

"Merianis, I think."

"Very well. Go to the terrace outside. You'll find her there."

. . .

Merianis was leaning against the low railing, gazing at the skyline of the city across the water. She turned at my approach. Gone was the cheerful expression I had come to take for granted. Her face was troubled. "Is it true what they say?"

"What do you mean, Merianis?"

"The army under Achillas is on its way to the city. It could arrive in a matter of hours."

"So Caesar tells me."

"Things are coming to a head, then. There'll be no more of this dancing about. Caesar will have to choose between them. Then we shall see a great deal of dying."

"Caesar's choice would be to see the king and queen reconciled, without bloodshed. He still seems to believe that's possible."

She looked at me for a long moment, then lowered her eyes. "This isn't what you've come to talk about."

"No. I want to understand what happened this morning."

"You were there. You saw. You heard."

"You were there, as well, Merianis. What did you see? What did you hear?"

She turned her gaze back to the city. "I'm sorry about your son, Gordianus."

"Why be sorry for him, if you believe he tried to poison the queen?"

"I'm sorry for your sake, Gordianus. I'm sorry that Egypt has brought you such tribulations."

I tried to look her in the eye, but she kept her face turned from me. "When the queen decided that the wine should be tasted, she sent you to fetch Zoë. Where did you find her?"

"In her room, adjacent to the queen's private quarters."

"Not in the kitchens?"

"Of course not! A taster is never allowed anywhere near the kitchens. A taster must never eat anything that can't be accounted for. Zoë was alone in her room. Like myself, she was attached to the temple of Isis."

"Not a priestess?"

"No, a temple slave. Her life was consecrated to the goddess. Her duty to taste the queen's food was a sacred duty. The rest of her time was spent in contemplation of the goddess."

"The clay vessel Zoë brought with her—where did that come from?"

"It was her private drinking cup, to be touched by no one else. Any liquid Zoë tasted for the queen would first be poured into that cup."

"So the keeping of the cup was one of Zoë's duties?"

"Yes."

"And you never touched it?"

Merianis at last looked me in the eye. "Why do you ask such a question?"

"Why do you not answer?"

"You told the queen this was not an interrogation."

"How do you know that? Were you there, concealed behind a curtain, when I was on my knees in the queen's reception room?"

She stared across the water and made no answer.

"You were! And then you hurried here, so as to be waiting for me." I shook my head at such a petty deceit. "Is that a tear on your cheek?"

Merianis wiped it away.

"Is it Zoë you cry for?"

"No. Her death was a holy death. She earned the gratitude of Isis and the gift of eternal life. I envy her."

"Do you, Merianis? I think perhaps you've done as much, if not more, for the queen."

"What do you mean?"

"You're very loyal to her. Is there nothing you would refuse to do for her?"

"I would die for the queen!"

But would you kill for her? I thought. *Or help to send an innocent man—my son—to his death?* "When Zoë was dying in the queen's arms, Cleopatra called you to her side. You spoke in whispers. What was said?"

"You go too far, Gordianus! You have no business to inquire about words spoken privately between the queen and myself."

"She was telling you something, or asking something of you. I saw the way you looked at Meto. Then you went to fetch Apollodorus. What did the queen say to you, Merianis?"

"To repeat words spoken in confidence by the queen would be to commit sacrilege. Even your great Caesar can't compel me to do that!"

"Caesar isn't asking you. I am."

Merianis shook her head. "If I could save your son, Gordianus—"

"Then something *was* said, something you can't reveal—something that might save Meto."

Merianis sighed, then drew back her shoulders and turned to face me. If some struggle had taken place within her, it was over now. Her expression was serene and opaque, unreadable. "The ways of the gods are sometimes obscure to us mortals, Gordianus, but the righteous submit to their will and learn not to question. Don't ask me again what the queen said to me in that moment."

"Please, Merianis—"

"I understand that you wish to speak to Apollodorus as well. Follow me."

She led me across the terrace and down a series of steps to a shaded spot near the water. Apollodorus was sitting on a stone bench, leaning against the trunk of a palm tree and whittling a small piece of driftwood. He looked up at me sullenly and flicked his wrist. The knife looked very sharp.

I turned to say farewell to Merianis, but she had already vanished.

I looked at the piece of driftwood. It was small enough to fit comfortably in the palm of his hand. The sea had worn it into a curious shape suggestive of a lion's head. With his knife, Apollodorus was enhancing the semblance.

"You're a very clever fellow," I said.

He grunted.

"Should we speak Greek?"

"I speak Latin perfectly well," he said, looking up at me darkly.

His accent was atrocious, but I made no comment. "You come from Sicily, I understand."

"Born there. Egypt suits me better."

"How did you come to join the queen's household?"

He shrugged. "Long story. We've been through a lot, the queen and I."

"She certainly puts great trust in you. I have to say, your relationship strikes me as . . . rather ambiguous."

He bridled. "What does that mean?"

"You're not like Zoë, a slave. Nor are you like Merianis; you don't have—how to put it?—the demeanor of a priest. You're not a military man, like Cratipus; and you're not a court eunuch."

"I certainly am not!" To prove it, he produced a discreet movement that drew my attention to his loincloth, which was draped over his person in such a way as to demonstrate convincingly the difference between himself and a eunuch.

"I'll be candid, Apollodorus. Once, when I was in his presence, the king suggested that your relationship to his sister is not entirely proper."

"Did he? I understand people say the same thing about your son and Caesar." He flashed a nasty grin and whittled another slice from the driftwood.

"She certainly indulges you."

"How so?"

"Here you sit, idling away the afternoon, with no apparent duties—"

"You don't know what you're talking about! When the queen needs me, I'm always there; have been since she was a girl. Good times or bad—and let me tell you, the last year or so has been about as bad as it gets. There were days out there in the desert, with Ptolemy's army on our heels, when even the most stouthearted were ready to give up hope. But never me! I set an example for the others, and if any man needed a kick in the behind, I gave it to him. No, I'm not a priest; but I know what I believe in."

"You believe in the queen?"

"Why not? A man's got to believe in something. The queen's twice as brave as any man I've ever met and three times as smart. She's got the spark, if you know what I mean. So far, I've come across nothing better in this world, and that includes your precious Caesar."

"And King Ptolemy?"

Apollodorus spat on the ground. "He's as useless as that eunuch who leads him around by the balls. What about you? Isn't there something you believe in?"

"I believe my son never put poison in Caesar's cup."

Apollodorus stiffened. He looked at the driftwood in his hand, then tossed it to me. I made an awkward catch to the cackle of his laughter.

"What do you think?" he said.

I turned it about in my hand. He had given the lion a fierce demeanor, with a roaring mouth and exaggerated fangs.

"Been making such things since I was a boy in Syracuse. Used to scrape a living by selling them as souvenirs to wealthy Romans who came to check on their Sicilian estates. And now I look after the queen of Egypt. Imagine that!"

"You're a clever fellow; nimble with your fingers. Did you also learn to do conjuring tricks when you were a boy in Syracuse?"

"What do you mean?"

"Those boys on the waterfront in Syracuse who accost visitors to sell them trinkets—sometimes their nimble fingers go where they shouldn't. A Sicilian urchin stole my coin purse once, and right after I'd been paid handsomely for a bit of work. That purse was heavy, bulky—yet he lifted it so skillfully, I never felt a thing."

Apollodorus shrugged. "There's a trick to it."

I nodded. "And a trick to doing the opposite, as well?"

"What do you mean?"

"Nimble fingers can snatch a purse without the owner feeling a thing. Nimble fingers can plant such a thing upon a man as well—and the victim is never the wiser."

Apollodorus stood and shook the mane of hair from his face. He stepped closer, looming over me, until I felt his breath on my forehead. The smell was sweet, as if he had been chewing cloves.

"I think I've had enough of your questions."

"Come, now. Did the queen not tell you to be candid with me, at Caesar's behest?"

"I'll walk you up the steps. Find Caesar's men and tell them to row you back."

"I thought *you* might do that."

"I'll see you drown, first." He bumped against me, hard enough to make me trip on the first step. As I ascended, I felt his warm breath on the back of my neck.

He escorted me as far as the terrace, then headed back.

"Apollodorus!" I said.

"Yes?" Some paces from me, he turned back, scowling.

"I'm not offended that you should display the fullness of your loin-cloth to me in such a brazen fashion, but I'm not especially impressed, either. It's a pity you feel compelled to augment that which nature gave you."

"What are you babbling about?" He beetled his brow and looked down between his legs, where his scanty loincloth sagged and bulged in an impossibly exaggerated fashion. "What in Hades? I never—"

He reached into the pouch and drew out the carved lion's head, then glared at me darkly, baring his teeth.

I flourished my fingers. "Over the years, I've picked up a few conjur-er's tricks myself. If I could place that object in such an intimate location, without your awareness, then I think it entirely possible that the alabaster vial was planted upon Meto's person by someone who was here on this terrace, in plain sight of everyone present and without Meto's knowledge. The only question is: Was that conjurer you, Apollodorus? Or was it someone else? And what was that person playing at?"

Apollodorus raised his arm. I ducked and heard the lion's head whistle past one ear. The trajectory carried it well beyond the terrace. It landed in the water with a splash.

" 'From driftwood it came, to driftwood it returns,' " I said. The line was from Euripides, as I recalled. I watched the little lion's head bob on the water, and felt a sudden thrill of intuition, as if I had arrived, unex-pectedly and without preparation, on the cusp of a great revelation. What association did that bobbing piece of driftwood recall to my mind, and why was it significant? Like a will-o-the-wisp, some insight hovered, tan-talizingly near but out of reach. If only I could grasp it, I felt certain I would understand everything to do with the poisoning of the cup that morning. I almost had it—and then the insight receded, just as the bob-bing driftwood was suddenly lost to sight amid the waves.

I looked over my shoulder, and saw that Apollodorus had disap-peared.

24

The army headed by Achillas arrived at the city that night. The people of Alexandria opened their gates to the soldiers with mixed emotions. Many thought that the Roman intruders, now greatly outnumbered, would surely be expelled. But at what cost, and with what result? A city is the very worst arena in which to wage a battle. Close quarters thwart strategy; every engagement is reduced to the level of a street fight. Fire and destruction would threaten the people and their city; no one wanted to see Alexandria in flames. And if, after much bloodshed and devastation, Caesar and his men could be annihilated or driven out, what would the Egyptians have gained? They might simply find themselves back where they began, with their country still split between the royal siblings, and the siblings at one another's throats.

Having withdrawn into a defensible portion of the royal precinct, with King Ptolemy and his retinue essentially being held captive, Caesar's forces now ceded the task of maintaining order in the city to Achillas and his motley army. From all indications, rioting and looting continued in many parts of Alexandria. Achillas's attention was split between preparing to lay siege to Caesar's forces and establishing control of the populace. As for the unruly Alexandrian mob, some eagerly welcomed Achillas's troops and even took up arms with them, while others, loyal to Cleopatra, viewed them as an occupying army hardly preferable to that of Caesar and openly defied their authority at every opportunity.

Violently wrenched between all these conflicting powers, volatile even at the best of times, Alexandria seemed poised to fall into utter chaos.

What did the crisis mean for Meto? It seemed, for the time being, at least, that Caesar was distracted from exercising judgment on my son—a good thing, for as yet I had no idea of how to prove Meto's innocence.

With the new impetus of a threatening army, events moved swiftly. To the surprise and relief of many in the palace, Caesar announced that a fresh accord had been reached between the king and queen. A banquet to celebrate the event would be held in the great reception hall. I was called upon to attend.

The room resounded with the music of pipes, horns, drums, and rattles. No doubt it was one of the Piper's tunes that the little orchestra was playing when the guards showed me to my place in a corner quite distant from the dining couches gathered upon the dais, where Caesar sat flanked by the queen on one side and the king on the other. Near to Ptolemy sat Pothinus. Next to Cleopatra was Merianis, with Apollodorus standing watchfully not far off.

There were guards posted all around the perimeter of the room; all the guards were Roman. By mutual consent, both the king's guards and the queen's had been banished. Caesar alone would provide for their protection; Caesar, in a sense, held them both captive. The queen and king had both placed their trust in him, at least for the time being, and the fate of all three hung together.

Girls strolled from couch to couch, pouring wine for the guests. Boys traversed the room with silver platters, offering delicacies. A singer joined the musicians and recited a long ballad in Greek about a band of explorers who sailed up the Nile in search of the river's origin, encountering many wonders along the way.

All around me, people engaged in conversations, leaning forward on couches pulled into circles or reclining with their couches pulled close together, head-to-head, but no one spoke to me. The Egyptians regarded me with suspicion; the Roman officers, knowing who I was, shunned me for fear of picking up Meto's bad fortune. Sitting alone, I pricked up my ears and listened to what others were saying to one another.

"He's obviously scared half out of his wits," said one Egyptian courtier to another. Both appeared quite young, though age is sometimes hard to judge with eunuchs. "Do you recall how cocky he was when he first arrived, all bloated with pride over his victory at Pharsalus, thinking he could remake Egypt with a wave of his hand? Then he saw Pompey's head in a basket, and he's been struggling to keep his own head above water ever since. Now Achillas has arrived, and Caesar knows the game is over. He just hopes to get out of Alexandria alive!"

A Roman officer, overhearing them, interrupted. "You know, you couldn't be more mistaken."

"How's that?" asked the courtier, curling his lip.

"About Caesar. This banquet is just another demonstration of his total mastery of the situation. Think of it as a wedding celebration. Egypt is Rome's new bride, to be put in her place with a sound thrashing if she's naughty, or, if she's sweet and obedient, with a sound—"

"You vile Roman!" snapped the eunuch. The unpleasantness of the encounter seemed about to escalate.

The officer scowled. "You're pretty when you're angry. Maybe you're the one in need of a good, sound—"

Both of the eunuchs shrieked with laughter. The Roman threw back his head and joined them. I realized they knew one another already, and were on friendly terms, at the very least. Thus had the confined, uncertain life in the palace bred unexpected relationships among the Romans and Egyptians.

On the dais, a serving girl had arrived with a fresh pitcher of wine. A protocol had been established whereby the queen would be served first, then the king, then Caesar; but ahead of them all, of course, a cup was poured for a taster, selected and approved, I assumed, by all three of them. The taster was a pretty young girl not unlike the late Zoë, perhaps another consecrated temple slave of Isis. She was situated on a couch in front of the dais and to one side, discreetly out of the way but close at hand and with nothing to impede the line of vision between the royal couple and herself, so that any plate or pitcher from which she safely partook could be taken at once to the king and queen without leaving their sight.

The serving slave poured a splash of wine from the pitcher into the taster's clay vessel; the taster raised the cup to her lips and swallowed.

A vision passed before my eyes. My own cup trembled in my hands. "So *that's* how it was done!" I whispered.

I looked from the taster to Merianis and felt a pain in my heart, compounded of anger and remorse. I would have to share my sudden revelation with Caesar at once. To do so would mean the end of Merianis, and perhaps the end of Cleopatra. What had they intended? Which of them was more culpable? Was it possible that Merianis had acted without her queen's knowledge? It would be up to Caesar to determine the answers to those questions; but whatever he might discover by torture and interrogation, and whatever excuses the guilty might offer, surely even Caesar's much-celebrated clemency could not extend to forgiving the deception that had been perpetrated that day on Antirrhodus. It would not be Meto who fell to harsh Roman justice; I now knew a way to prove his innocence.

I stood unsteadily, my legs trembling. I braced myself and strode across the crowded room, directly toward the dais. Cleopatra was the first to notice my approach. She gave me a withering look that made it clear she thought I had no business being in the room at all. Merianis, sensing her queen's displeasure, followed her gaze and drew a sharp breath when she saw me, then lowered her eyes; did she realize what was about to happen? When Ptolemy saw me he flashed a quizzical smile; had he heard about the poisoning on Antirrhodus and Meto's imprisonment, or had Caesar managed to keep that intelligence from him? That question was answered when I looked at Pothinus, whose cool, appraising glance told me that he was entirely aware of my situation.

At last Caesar noticed my approach. He had been smiling at some quip from Ptolemy, but his smile vanished at once. In the mirror of his face, I saw how terrible my countenance must appear. I was the messenger in the play who arrives bearing news that will shatter all expectations. Guards abruptly converged from either side to check my approach. Caesar raised his hands to order them back.

I stopped at the foot of the dais and looked up at him. A hush had fallen on the room as others noticed my approach and the reactions of those on the dais.

"Do you have something to say to me, Gordianus?"

"Yes, Consul. But not here. If I could speak to you in private . . ." I cast a glance at the queen and Merianis.

"Can this not wait, Gordianus?"

"If I can tell him who poisoned the wine on Antirrhodus, would the consul have me wait?" I lowered my voice as much as I could, but it was impossible to keep those on either side from overhearing. I felt the eyes of the king and queen upon us, and Caesar must have felt them as well.

"Step closer, Gordianus."

I stepped onto the dais. "If we could speak in private—"

He shook his head. "The purpose for this festive occasion takes precedence over all else, Gordianus, including any news you may have for me. I'm on the verge of announcing a glorious peace in Egypt. I will not interrupt the banquet, not even for this. Step closer and whisper into my ear, if you wish."

I dropped to one knee before him. He leaned forward and inclined his head.

"Meto is innocent, Consul. I can prove it, here and now, if you'll allow it."

"How?"

"Bring the amphora of Falernian that Meto brought to Antirrhodus. Have it tasted—"

"And kill another pretty temple slave?"

"The taster will not die, because the amphora was never poisoned. I'll drink from it myself, if you wish."

He drew back, just enough to look me in the eye. "What are you saying, Gordianus?"

"The wine in the amphora was never poisoned."

He thought for a moment. "But at the queen's behest, the wine from the golden cup was poured back into the amphora—"

"Nor was there ever poison in the golden cup the queen presented to Caesar."

Caesar frowned. "And yet, the temple slave Zoë most certainly died."

"Because *her* cup was poisoned—the clay cup from which she and she alone ever drank, and that later was broken when she fell. That cup and *only* that cup was poisoned! Do you remember? When Merianis fetched her, Zoë brought her own cup with her—"

"And Merianis proceeded to fill that cup with wine from the golden cup."

"But the wine itself was untainted. The poison was *already* in Zoë's cup, put there without Zoë's knowledge."

"Put there by whom?"

"Perhaps by the person who fetched her," I said, though it was hard to imagine that Merianis was capable of such cold-blooded treachery.

"But the alabaster vial was later found upon Meto."

"The vial was planted upon Meto by Apollodorus. And who went to fetch Apollodorus?" I kept my eyes lowered, but Caesar looked past me, toward Merianis.

"You're saying both were involved—Merianis *and* Apollodorus?"

"At least those two," I said, thinking of a third but not daring to say her name.

"But why? What was their purpose?"

"Of that I'm not sure, Consul. But consider: Meto distrusted the queen; Meto despaired of the queen's . . . influence . . . upon you. The queen—those near the queen, I mean—might wish to see Meto discredited. How better to do that than to make him appear guilty of a crime against the consul?"

Caesar looked at me gravely. "What you suggest is monstrous, Gordianus. Without naming her, you implicate a certain person in a plot to deceive me. If that should be true, then the purpose of this banquet is negated. I should have to reconsider who should inherit the late king's throne, and whether that throne should be shared." He looked toward Ptolemy and sighed. "Considering whose army has occupied Alexandria, it would certainly be easier to simply . . ."

His voice trailed off. I thought he was lost in thought, until I followed his gaze and saw that someone else was approaching the dais. So I must have appeared, I thought, as I looked upon the face of Samuel, Caesar's barber. The little man threaded his way between the dining couches, resolute but trembling slightly, anxiously shifting his gaze from face to face, looking as if he had swallowed something very bitter.

"What now?" muttered Caesar.

Samuel hurried to the dais. The guards looked to Caesar for instruction and stepped back at his signal.

"What do you want, Samuel?"

"Master, I must speak to you at once." He glanced at Pothinus, who frowned. "In private . . ."

Caesar looked at me askance. "You appear to have a twin tonight, Gordianus, like the Gemini." He looked at the barber. "Come, Samuel. Gordianus has one of my ears. You may have the other."

The little fellow scrambled onto the dais and rushed to his master's side. He knelt and pressed a scrap of papyrus into Caesar's hand. While Caesar read, Samuel whispered in his ear. The barber spoke in a frantic rush, too low for me to hear, and Caesar held the papyrus so that I could not read it, though I caught a glimpse of Greek letters. The news caused the color to drain from Caesar's cheeks.

Caesar lowered the parchment. He raised his hand to Samuel, signaling that he had heard enough. "Pothinus," he said, looking straight ahead. His voice was low and even, but something in his tone chilled my blood.

"Consul?" Pothinus furrowed his brow.

"Come here, Pothinus."

The eunuch cleared his throat. There was a tremor in his voice. "The lord chamberlain of the king of Egypt is not a servant to be summoned by anyone other than the king, not even the consul of—"

"Pothinus, come here!" Caesar's voice was like thunder.

The eunuch stood. Ptolemy looked from Pothinus to Caesar and back. For a brief moment I saw confusion on the king's face, before he assumed the masklike countenance at which he was so adept.

Pothinus stepped toward Caesar, slowly and carefully, as one might approach a lion. "What does the consul require?"

Caesar thrust the papyrus toward him. "Were these words written by your hand, Lord Chamberlain?"

Pothinus flashed a supercilious grin. "The lord chamberlain is accustomed to dictating documents; the actual writing is done by a scribe—"

"Unless the words in a letter are too sensitive to be heard by even the most trusted scribe—or overheard by all the spies who lurk in the walls of this palace."

Pothinus glared at Samuel, and then at Caesar. "I think the consul is no stranger at playing spymaster himself."

Caesar cast a fond glance at Samuel. "Some of my men occasionally make a jest at Samuel's expense. They call him timorous; they say he jumps at the sight of his own shadow. But that fearful quality makes Samuel very observant. Some make fun of his small stature; but that quality, too, has its virtues, for it helps a man to come and go unobserved, and sometimes even to walk through walls."

"Then you admit that this wretch *has* been spying on me!"

"Samuel merely looks out for his master's safety. He needs no instruction from me. But, yes, Samuel has been observing you, Pothinus. He knows your movements. He watched you write this letter, which, at Samuel's request, some of my men seized from your messenger. The messenger can be tortured to divulge the source of the letter—or you can simply admit that you wrote it, Pothinus."

"Lies! The creature has fabricated this elaborate deceit. He's betrayed you, Consul. He makes you look a fool."

"I think not, Pothinus. If a man can't trust his barber, whom can he trust?" Caesar again thrust the letter before Pothinus. "Take it! Read it aloud."

Pothinus took the papyrus. He stared at it and rocked slightly forward and back, as if he were light-headed. He looked desperately at Ptolemy. "Your Majesty!"

The king glowered at him. "Do as the consul says, Lord Chamberlain."

"Read it!" commanded Caesar.

Pothinus gave a start and obeyed. " 'To Achillas, commander of the forces of our rightful king, from Pothinus, Lord Chamberlain, as you may ascertain from the seal on this letter: Greetings.' There, you see! The seal was broken; the wax is missing. There's nothing to prove—"

"Read on, Pothinus," growled Caesar. "Read on, and do not stop until the letter is finished, or I'll have my men skewer you from all sides."

At a nod from Caesar, one of the guards gave Pothinus a poke in the back with his spear. The eunuch yelped. "Please, Consul! Very well, I'll read. 'Though previously I have counseled the king to make a compromise satisfactory to the Roman intruder, if only as a matter of show, I now see that any compromise can lead only to disaster. We must take action, and quickly. I shall do what I can within the palace, but our enemies are well guarded, especially so following an unsuccessful attempt at poison by persons unknown.' Do you see, Consul! The letter proves I had nothing to do with the recent attempt on your life; I have no idea—"

"Read on!"

Pothinus gave another yelp and contorted his back; I could see by a red stain on his robe that the spear had drawn blood. He gasped and continued reading. " 'I will do what I can . . . to solve the problem myself. But meanwhile you must be prepared to wage battle against the enemies who now hold the king hostage. On no account must the king's life be endangered—' There, Your Majesty, do you see the proof of my loyalty to you? Will you not command this Roman to call off his mastiffs?"

Ptolemy regarded Pothinus with an inscrutable gaze. "Read on, Lord Chamberlain."

Pothinus trembled violently. His voice quavered. " 'On no account must the king's life be endangered. But no matter how regrettable, casualties within the palace may be . . . unavoidable. In the event that the worst should come to pass, I have taken steps to smuggle the king's sister Arsinoë out of the palace; she should arrive in your keeping just ahead of this letter. Keep her safe, for to maintain our legitimacy with the populace, at least one member of the royal bloodline must survive the coming battle. Do what you must to eliminate the false queen and to expel the foreign intruder.' Your Majesty, I meant that Caesar himself may kill you, if pressed to desperation by Achillas! I have never been anything less than your most loyal—"

"Silence!" Caesar stood and snatched the letter from Pothinus's trembling hands. "This document clearly spells out your intention to murder me and to assassinate the queen. It also exhorts Achillas to attack the palace, with reckless disregard for the safety of King Ptolemy and in contravention of the peaceful accord reached between the king and his sister. That makes you a would-be assassin, a conspirator, and a traitor, Pothinus."

The eunuch threw himself at Ptolemy's feet. "Your Majesty, do you not see what's happened? Caesar has made you his hostage, and he's forced this accord upon you, to further his own ambitions. It's Cleopatra he's sided with, from the moment he met her. The reason is simple: She can give him a child. When that happens, Caesar will declare himself king of Egypt, with Cleopatra as his queen and the child as their heir, and it will be the end of you, Your Majesty, and the end of your dynasty! Egypt shall be ruled by Romans, and the images of your ancestors will be replaced by images of Caesar."

Ptolemy looked down his long nose at the eunuch. "Caesar is my friend."

"If you believe that, Your Majesty, then put his friendship to the test. Leave the palace. Join Achillas and your army. Let me accompany you—"

"The eunuch wishes only to save his own neck," growled Caesar.

Ptolemy abruptly stood, with such force that he knocked Pothinus aside. The eunuch groveled at his feet. "You've forgotten your place, Lord Chamberlain—though from this moment you no longer occupy that position, so I shall address you simply as Pothinus. You think I'm still a child, easily bent to your will. You fancy yourself the secret ruler of Egypt, and myself a mere puppet upon the throne."

"Your Majesty, where do these notions come from? The Roman has poisoned your mind—"

"Silence! Do you think my mind so feeble that Caesar can shape it at will? Is your estimation of me that low? Yes, I think it is. 'Regrettable'— isn't that the word you used in that letter to describe my death, should Achillas storm the palace and kill me in the process? You shall regret your own death far more, Pothinus."

"No, Your Majesty! Please listen—"

"There is no more to be said, Pothinus! I strip you of your title and your post. I expel you from the privileges of the royal household, now and for all eternity. For your crimes against me, you shall be executed and your body defiled; your flesh shall be fodder for carrion birds. You shall be cursed by the gods; not only your body but your *ka* shall perish forever, and it shall be as if Pothinus never existed. Thus do traitors meet their end."

Pothinus wailed and hid his face.

Caesar stood and stepped to Ptolemy's side. "Your Majesty, since you've cast off the eunuch, and since he has offended against me as well, conspiring to kill me, I ask a favor of you: Let me pass judgment on him, and see to his punishment."

"No!" Pothinus gazed up at the two of them with a woeful expression. "The Roman seeks to take even this prerogative from you, Your Majesty. It's Caesar who treats you as a child—"

"Silence, Pothinus!" The king glared down at him, then turned to Caesar. "Because Caesar requests it, and because Caesar is my dearest friend, I make a gift of this criminal to Caesar, who may do as he wishes with the wretch. The Romans boast of their great love of justice, do they not, Caesar? Perhaps you can teach me a lesson on this subject. How will you dispose of Pothinus?"

Caesar looked down at the cringing eunuch, then turned, briefly, to regard the queen, who had watched the entire episode in silence, wearing an expression as bland as her brother's at his most inscrutable. As he turned back, for a long moment Caesar's eyes met mine, and I saw that he had not forgotten what I had told him.

"Samuel! Go to my quarters. You'll find an amphora there, clearly marked: 'Falernian—Open Only in the Presence of Gnaeus Pompey Magnus.' Bring it to me at once."

The barber nodded, jumped to his feet, and rushed off.

Caesar regarded me, and seeing the expression on my face, he stepped toward me and spoke in a low voice. "You look puzzled, Gordianus."

"What game are you playing at, Consul?"

"Not a game; a test. According to you, the amphora of Falernian was never poisoned, nor was the golden cup; Merianis put poison in the taster's clay vessel, and Apollodorus planted the empty alabaster vial on your son. If that's true, the Falernian was untainted, and remains so, for I had it resealed with wax before I let it out of my sight again. Are you certain of this allegation, Gordianus?"

"It's the only explanation, Consul."

"Unless, of course, Meto poisoned the amphora—in which case the Falernian will kill anyone who drinks it."

I shook my head. "That's not possible, Consul."

"We shall see. I had thought that tonight might be a joyous occasion, a chance to celebrate reconciliation and peace. Instead, it seems I'm fated to learn who are my friends, and who are my foes." He cast a glance at Ptolemy, then at Cleopatra.

Samuel, breathing hard, arrived with the amphora.

Caesar inspected the new seal, which bore the impression of his own ring. Satisfied, he nodded to Samuel, who cut the seal away.

"Pour a cup, Samuel. Here, use mine, since I'm certain no one's tampered with it."

The barber poured a measure of wine into the cup.

"Stand up, Pothinus!"

The eunuch rose to his feet, a mingled look of dread and defiance on his face.

"Consul!" I whispered. "What are you thinking? This isn't Roman justice. This is pure capriciousness."

"The gods are capricious. So must we sometimes be, if we would emulate the gods. It is also a way to determine the truth, Gordianus; and are you not always in favor of that?"

The queen sat forward, frowning. "What do you intend to do, Caesar?"

Merianis looked at her lap and nervously pulled at her fingers. Apollodorus stood with his arms crossed and his jaw thrust forward.

"Yes, Caesar," said Ptolemy. "Why do you not have the traitor strangled, here and now?"

"Because I intend to offer Pothinus a choice, which may yet allow him to live. This is a cup of Falernian wine, Pothinus. It comes from the private stores of Pompey. Falernian wine is legendary; it's the best of all the vintages of Italy. But this amphora may—or may not—contain a deadly poison. Which is it? I should like to know. Rather than test it on a hapless slave, I offer it to you, Pothinus."

"You demean me, Roman!"

"No, Pothinus, I offer you a chance to live—which is far more than you deserve. If the wine is wholesome, and you drink it without ill effect, I shall release you and allow you to join Achillas outside the palace. Gordianus here shall enjoy the second cup, and the rest of us will share a fine Falernian tonight. But if the wine is poisoned . . ."

"You lie! Whether it's poisoned or not, you'll have me killed before I can leave this room."

"I'm a man of my word, eunuch! Make up your mind. Take the cup, or not."

From the shiftiness of Pothinus's eyes, I sensed the debate that raged in his mind. So long as he had his wits and a voice to beg, he might yet contrive some way to win Ptolemy's mercy; but once he drank from the cup, there could be no turning back. I myself felt a sudden tremor of doubt; the logic of my argument to Caesar was compelling, of that I was certain, and yet . . . I recalled the inchoate flash of intuition I had felt when I questioned Apollodorus, somehow tied to the piece of driftwood he had carved into a lion's head; that moment of insight, fleeting and inconclusive, still had seemed to be absolutely authentic—and yet it had no connection to what was happening now. Was I mistaken about the amphora? I found myself almost wishing that Pothinus would refuse to take it.

But at last the prospect of freedom held out by Caesar won Pothinus over. He took the cup, gazed for a moment at his reflection in the wine, then drank it in a single draught.

I looked at those on the dais and saw them all watching with bated breath. I glanced over my shoulder; the guests upon their dining couches looked like silent spectators at a play, intent upon the climax. At the far corner of the room, I glimpsed the two Egyptian courtiers and the Roman who had teased them; the three now sat close together on a single couch, interrupted in their merrymaking and struck dumb by the drama on the dais.

Pothinus thrust the cup back into Caesar's hands and stood erect, turning his head this way and that to glare defiantly at those around him. He licked his lips, ground his teeth, and took a deep breath. He shut his eyes tightly for a moment, then opened them again, smiled, and turned to Caesar.

"There, Roman. Are you satisfied?"

"You feel nothing?"

"Only the satisfaction that comes from drinking a truly fine wine. A pity that the Great One himself was never able to taste it! Well? Are you as good as your word, Caesar? Will you let me go now?"

Caesar tilted his head back and studied Pothinus for a long moment, then turned his gaze to me. He did not look happy. "So, Gordianus, it seems that you were right. The amphora was not poisoned, only the taster's cup. The unpleasant occurrence on Antirrhodus was due to the actions of someone I thought I could trust, someone who's become very close to me." His eyes moved in the direction of the queen, but before his gaze fell upon her, Pothinus made a noise that drew his attention.

The sound came from deep in the eunuch's throat, a grunt that emerged as a stifled gasp. He gave a jerk, as if someone had poked him in a delicate place, and took a step back, putting his hands on his belly. "No!" he whispered. "This isn't happening!" He grimaced and turned toward the king. "You ungrateful little viper! You and your sister deserve one another, and you both deserve the ruin that Caesar has in store for you!"

He dropped to his knees, clutching himself and convulsing. "A curse on you, Caesar! May you die as Pompey died, cut to shreds and covered in blood!" He fell onto his side and drew his knees to his chest. Even as he gave a final twitch, the king stepped forward and gave him a hard kick that sent him rolling off the dais. Limp and lifeless, the eunuch's body fell heavily to the floor.

I looked at Caesar, who stared at the dead body with eyes wide and unblinking. His face was like wax; the eunuch's curse had unnerved him. At last he shuddered and shook off the spell. He looked at me and flashed a rueful smile. "So, Gordianus, it seems you're mistaken. The queen's companions are innocent. The blame for what happened on Antirrhodus falls on your son, after all."

I shook my head. "No, Consul, there must be another explanation—"

"Silence! The king has rid himself of a traitor who managed to climb very high in his esteem. I shall follow the king's example. I shall rid myself of the traitor in my midst. Meto will be executed tomorrow."

I staggered back, as stunned as if Caesar had struck me. Light-headed, I looked at Cleopatra. The queen was smiling.

25

"It was good of Caesar to allow us this final visit," said Meto. He sat on his cot, staring at the dank stones of the opposite wall. From the high, barred window came the sounds of a hot summer morning: the creaking of anchored ships, the cry of hungry gulls, the shouts of Caesar's sailors making sure that nothing was amiss. Achillas had nominal control over most of the city, including the island of Pharos with its lighthouse, as well as the smaller Eunostos Harbor south of the Pharos causeway, but Caesar's control of the great harbor remained unchallenged.

"Good of him?" I shook my head, which was full of cobwebs. I had spent a miserable, sleepless night, struggling in vain to think of some way to save my son. " 'It was good of Caesar to allow us this final visit.' Loyal Meto! Faithful to Caesar to the very last, even as Caesar prepares to put an end to you."

"What else can he do, Papa? Someone tried to poison him on Antirrhodus. Not me; but every bit of evidence points to me. He can't let such an act go unpunished."

"But what point is there in punishing an innocent man—and a man as unfailingly loyal as you? When I think of the sacrifices you've made for that man, the terrible risks you've taken—"

"All done of my own volition. I chose to serve Caesar. He allowed me the privilege. Don't forget that I began life as a slave, Papa. I never forget."

"When I adopted you, all that changed."

"No, Papa. The past never vanishes, not entirely. You made me your son, and a citizen; you changed the course of my life completely, and for that I'm more grateful than you can know. Caesar took me into his confidence, gave me a role to play in his grand scheme, and even gave me a kind of love—and for that, too, I'm grateful. My life has been richer than I could ever have dreamed when I was a boy—all the richer because I had no right and no reason to expect that such wonders awaited me. I never took them for granted! But you disowned me—"

"Meto, forgive me! It was the worst mistake I ever made. If I could undo that moment, I would."

He shrugged. "You did what you felt you had to do. And now Caesar will do what he must. Perhaps he truly believes I tried to poison him; either that, or the alternative is simply unacceptable to him—that the queen, for her own reasons, incriminated me. He must act; and if he must make a choice between Cleopatra and me, then he chooses Cleopatra; and who am I to object? I'm merely a slave who had the good fortune to rise beyond his station; she is the queen of Egypt and the heir of the Ptolemies and, if one believes the Egyptians, a goddess as well. Her destiny is written in the stars; in the great scheme of things, my fate matters not at all."

"No, Meto! I don't accept such a notion. Your life matters as much as anyone else's. I've spent my life stepping through the mess made by these so-called great men and women. They're no better than criminals and madmen, but because they perpetrate their crimes on such a grand scale, the rest of us are expected to bow before them in awe. 'The gods love me,' they say, to excuse their crimes and draw men to their cause; but if the gods so love them, then why do they die so horribly? Look at what happened to Pompey, gutted like a fish on the shores of Egypt. Look at the horrible ends that awaited Milo, Clodius, Marcus Caelius, Catilina, Domitius Ahenobarbus, Curio—the list goes on and on. Mark my words, the same fate will befall Cleopatra, and yes, even your beloved Caesar."

"Are you a soothsayer now, Papa?" Meto laughed without mirth. "This simply brings us back to the same old argument between us, the breach that led you to disown me. You think I give too much blind devotion to a man like Caesar, that I willfully contribute to the mess, as you call it, that he leaves behind in his wake. And perhaps you're right. I share your doubts. I share your resentment that the world should be as it is—so harsh and cruel and full of lies. But in the end, Papa, I've chosen to take part in that world, to embrace the way of the warrior and the spy; and for that I'll now pay the price, just as Caesar will sooner or later pay a price, if what you say is true." He lifted his eyes and scanned the wall. "But should you be giving voice to such seditious thoughts, Papa? It was you who warned me that we should speak discreetly, considering the porousness of these palace walls."

"What does it matter now? Caesar's made up his mind. He's the king of Rome, in fact if not in name, and we are all at his mercy."

"Do you suppose he'll allow me a choice of deaths? I should like to fall upon my sword, like an honorable Roman. Or will he force me to drink from the amphora, to pay for the crime of poisoning it? The way he forced Pothinus to drink, and die, in front of all those people."

I shuddered and fought back tears. "Caesar didn't force him to drink—that was what made his death so terrible! If you could have seen Caesar last night, Meto, lounging up on that dais, dispensing justice willy-nilly like the most decadent Asian potentate. He told me he learned lessons about being a ruler from King Nicomedes, and now he feels disposed to pass on those lessons to young Ptolemy. What sort of example did he set with his treatment of Pothinus? The eunuch was no better than the rest of them, another ruthless schemer with a penchant for murder, but he was no worse, either; he may or may not have deserved a traitor's death, but for Caesar to taunt him in that fashion, pressing him to gamble his own life on a whim to satisfy Caesar's curiosity—the capriciousness of it sickened me. And Caesar knew there was something unseemly about Pothinus's death. You should have seen his face when the eunuch cursed him!"

"Caesar doesn't believe in curses."

"Not even a curse spoken by a dying man with his final breath?"

Meto shook his head. "Curse or no curse, once a man's dead, there's nothing left to fear from him. What was it Pothinus himself said to the king, when he was justifying their plot to murder Pompey? 'Dead men don't bite.'"

I nodded, then stiffened and let out a gasp as I felt a thrill run through me—exactly such a thrill of intuition as I had felt that day when I gazed at Apollodorus's carved piece of driftwood bobbing on the waves. But now, instead of fleeing before I could grasp it, the insight erupted in my consciousness full-blown, inescapable, undeniable.

I turned and banged my fist on the locked door. "Jailer! Come at once!"

Meto rose from the cot. "Papa, you can't leave now. Surely we have more to say—"

"And say it we shall, Meto, at some later date, because this is not our final meeting. Jailer! Let me out! I must be allowed to see Caesar at once!"

I found Caesar dressed not as consul, in his toga, but in the military garb of imperator, with his famous red cape billowing slightly in the sea breeze that swept through the high room from the terrace that faced the light-house. The room had the tense, hurried atmosphere of a commander's tent on a field of battle; thus I remembered encountering Caesar in his camp outside Brundisium just before he drove Pompey from Italy, surrounded by his coterie of young lieutenants all buzzing with questions and reports and running this way and that.

At the sight of me, Caesar held up his hand to silence the officer who happened to have caught his attention a moment before. "Excuse me, officers, but I require a moment alone with this citizen."

Every man in the room knew who I was—the father of the condemned Meto—and from some I received reproving stares, from others looks of sympathy. As a body they collected themselves, rolling up documents and maps, and withdrew to the antechamber. Even after the doors were shut, I could still hear the low roar of their urgent conversations.

I looked at Caesar. "Is there a crisis, Consul? Or should I say, Imperator?"

"A crisis of sorts. Achillas has moved certain of his forces forward and withdrawn others to various parts of the city, in apparent preparation for an attack on our position. It may be that news of Pothinus's death has reached him, and this is his reaction; or perhaps an attack was planned all along. At any rate, we must be prepared for the worst."

"Will Achillas attack without a direct order from King Ptolemy?"

"That remains to be seen. Even as you arrived, we were debating various ways to make the king's will known to Achillas without endangering either the king or our own messengers. Achillas murdered a pair of envoys I dispatched to him earlier. The man's no better than a brigand! He reminds me of the pirates who kidnapped me when I was young."

"And we all know what happened to them." The crucifixion of the pirates was a seminal chapter in the legend of Caesar's career.

"Achillas murdered Pompey with his own sword. I should like nothing better than to see him meet the same fate as his accomplice, the late Pothinus."

"Pompey was killed with the king's consent," I said, "if not at his instigation. Will the king be punished, as well?"

"Don't be absurd, Gordianus. Once certain baleful influences are removed, the king will truly be able to come into his own; I have no doubt that he and his sister will be among Rome's strongest allies." Even as he said this, I saw that some other, contrary thought was at work in his mind; but we had strayed from the purpose of my visit. Caesar abruptly became impatient with our conversation.

"You can see that I'm very busy, Gordianus; I've permitted you an audience only because of the urgency of your request, and because of your assurance that this meeting will bear fruit. I've sent for those you asked me to summon; they should be here at any moment. You say you know conclusively what occurred on Antirrhodus, and that Meto is completely innocent. You'd better be able to prove it."

"Those you summoned know the truth, in bits and pieces. If they'll only admit to what they know, then Caesar shall see the truth in full."

The officer who was manning the door hurried to Caesar's side and spoke in his ear.

"The first of those you asked me to summon is here," said Caesar, then to the officer, "Show him in."

A moment later the doors opened to admit a small, wiry fellow. His hair and his beard were not as neatly trimmed as when I had first seen him on Pompey's ship. Captivity—first as the king's prisoner, now as

Caesar's—did not agree with Pompey's freedman Philip. He had become haggard and disheveled, and had a fretful look in his eye that made me worry that his mind might have become a bit unbalanced.

When he saw me, he frowned. The look in his eyes became even wilder.

"Do you remember me, Philip?" I said. "We gathered driftwood together to build a funeral pyre for your old master."

"Of course I remember you. I remember everything about that accursed day. If only I could forget!" He lowered his eyes. "I see you've fallen into Caesar's clutches, too."

I recalled that he had assumed I was one of Pompey's veterans, so grief-stricken at seeing the Great One struck down that I had leaped overboard and swum ashore, and for that reason he had trusted me. I saw no need to disabuse him of the notion.

"We are all in Caesar's hands now," I said, looking sidelong at Caesar. "Philip, I desperately need your assistance. As I helped you that day on the beach to give the Great One proper rites, will you now help me in return?"

"What do you need from me?"

I drew a deep breath. On the previous night I had felt certain of the scenario I put forth to Caesar to discount Meto's role in the poisoning, and I had been proven utterly, woefully wrong. What if I were mistaken again? Perhaps intuition and judgment alike had deserted me. I saw the apprehensive expression on Caesar's face, and knew that I suddenly looked as wild-eyed as Philip. I fought back the sudden fear and uncertainty that swept over me.

"Philip, you were there with the Great One at Pharsalus, were you not?"

"Yes." He looked shiftily at Caesar, and I could sense the hatred and revulsion he felt for the man who had destroyed his beloved master.

Caesar interrupted. "I've already questioned this man about everything to do with Pharsalus, and with Pompey's murder, and with all that occurred between."

"Yes, Caesar, but I think there may be a matter that escaped your questioning. What was it you said about your interrogation of Philip, the night we dined together? That he was forthcoming about some things, reticent about others. I think I know one of the things he was reluctant to talk about."

Caesar looked at me sharply, then at Philip. "Go on, Gordianus."

"Philip, when Pompey's forces were defeated at Pharsalus, it came as a great shock to him, did it not?"

"Yes."

"But not a complete surprise, I think. He knew that Caesar was a formidable foe; Caesar had already driven him from Italy and crushed Pompey's allies in Spain. Pompey must have had in his mind some idea that he might eventually face defeat. Yes?"

Philip looked at me warily, but finally nodded.

"At Pharsalus," I said, "the battle began early in the day, with Caesar's javelins attacking Pompey's front line. The struggle was bloody and close-fought, but as the day wore on and the sun reached its zenith, Pompey's men panicked and broke the line. Pompey's infantry were encircled. His cavalry gave way and fled. Caesar's cavalry hunted them down and slaughtered a great many, scattering the rest, while the main body of Caesar's infantry converged on Pompey's camp. The rumor goes that the Great One, confident of victory, had retired at midday to his pavilion to eat a meal—a very sumptuous meal, with silver plates and the very finest wine, worthy of a victory banquet. That was the scene Caesar encountered when he entered the camp and strode into Pompey's pavilion, only to find that the Great One had fled moments before. So goes the tale as I heard it in Rome.

"But this is what I think: When Pompey retired to his pavilion, he had no illusions that he had won the battle. Quite the opposite; he stayed long enough to see the tide turn against him, then rode back to his camp knowing that all was lost. He retired to his pavilion to await the inevitable end. He gathered his closest associates—including you, Philip—and demanded that a lavish banquet be served at once. He ordered a very trusted subordinate—was it not you, Philip?—to fetch a very special amphora of Falernian wine that he had been saving for just that occasion, and that occasion alone.

"Do you remember what you said to me, Philip, as you wept for Pompey on the beach? I remember, though at the time I didn't fully understand.

'He should have died at Pharsalus,' you said. 'Not like this, but at a time and in the manner of his own choosing. When he knew that all was lost, he made up his mind to do so.' What were his exact words to you, Philip?"

Philip gazed vacantly, looking beyond me into his memory of that terrible day at Pharsalus. "The Great One said to me: 'Help me, Philip. Help me keep up my courage. I've lost the game. I have no stomach for the aftermath. Let this place be the end of me. Let the history books say, "The Great One died at Pharsalus." ' "

I nodded. "But at the last moment, he lost his nerve; isn't that what you told me, Philip? Pompey the Great quailed and fled, so quickly that you had to run after him to keep up." I shook my head. "I heard, but I misunderstood. I thought you meant he was in the midst of his premature victory banquet when he realized that all was lost, and he looked in vain for the courage to pick up his sword and die fighting, only to lose his nerve and ride off on a horse instead. But even before the banquet began, he knew that he was finished. Indeed, it was when the banquet was served that he asked you to help him find the courage to die as he had previously decided to die, should everything go against him. It wasn't a victory banquet; it was a farewell feast! That carefully sealed amphora of Falernian wine he had been carrying around with him, from battlefield to battlefield, to be opened only in the presence of Pompey himself—what was so very special about that wine, Philip?"

Philip shook his head, not wanting to answer, but Caesar was beginning to understand. "Pompey meant to die by his own choice," Caesar said. "Not by falling on a sword—but by poison?"

I nodded. "With his closest friends around him, surrounded by the trappings of wealth and luxury, and with a fine meal in his stomach. But then the ramparts were overrun, and you yourself came riding through the camp, Consul. Pompey faced a choice he could no longer postpone: capture and humiliation, or a quick, sure death by poison—the same poison his wife kept close at hand, in case she too should face such a choice. He had only to unseal the Falernian, drink a cup, and make his exit to oblivion. That had been his plan. But when the crisis came, he couldn't do it. Was it fear of death? Perhaps. But I think his will to live another day, even in misery and defeat, was simply too strong. He ran from the tent, mounted the first horse he found, and rode off, escaping in the very nick of time. And you rode after him, Philip, leaving the sealed amphora of Falernian behind."

Caesar looked at Philip. "Is this true?"

Philip lowered his eyes and gritted his teeth. His silence was answer enough.

Caesar shook his head. "And to think, had I been of Pompey's ilk, craving luxury and self-indulgence at every turn, instead of overseeing the last stages of the battle, I might have sat down to help myself to a plate of Pompey's venison and a cup of his Falernian—a victory feast!—and I would have died then and there, of poison. Or indeed, I might have died any day since, on any occasion I chose to drink Pompey's Falernian!"

I nodded. "As the Great One himself was well aware. He said as much to me when he summoned me to his ship. 'Caesar may yet get his just deserts,' he told me, 'and when he least expects it. One moment he'll be alive, and the next—dead as King Numa!' I thought that he meant he had an assassin in your midst, or that he was simply raving—but he was talking about the Falernian, which he knew had fallen into your hands, and which, as he hoped, you might any day decide to open and drink."

"Which must have been the hope of this scheming freedman here, as well. Eh, Philip? You knew about the Falernian, yet you never warned me about it. Did you hope that I might yet drink it and die the death Pompey was too craven to claim for himself?"

"Yes!" cried Philip. "To his shame, the Great One discovered he was incapable of suicide, so he came to Egypt instead—which amounted to the same thing. I often wonder if he didn't come here knowing these monsters would do away with him, and thus relieve him of the burden of doing away with himself. But the acts of men live after them, and there was one hope left to me—that sooner or later messengers would come running through the palace, shouting the good news: 'Caesar is dead! No one knows how, no one knows why—he was simply drinking a cup of wine and suddenly dropped dead! Could it be poison? Oh, dear!'" The little man seethed with sarcasm and fury.

"And so it would have been," Caesar said coldly, "had I drunk the wine that day on Antirrhodus. I would have died, struck down by a dead man!"

" 'Dead men don't bite,' " I said. "That was what Pothinus said of Pompey. But he was wrong. Even dead, Pompey might have exacted a final revenge upon you, Caesar. As it happened, the Falernian killed the queen's taster, instead; and the confusion spawned by that event very nearly drove you to do away with Meto—who as you now must realize was innocent all along."

Caesar looked at me sidelong. "But what of the alabaster vial discovered on Meto's person—a vial that we know contained poison, and that was empty when we found it?"

With timing as perfect as that of a messenger in a play, the soldier guarding the door stepped forward to tell Caesar that the others he had summoned had arrived.

"Take this creature away," ordered Caesar, referring to Philip, "and show the others in."

26

Apollodorus entered first, followed by Merianis, both looking grim. I glanced at Caesar and saw that grimness mirrored on his face. Then another expression, hard to discern—consternation, resignation, apprehension?—crossed his countenance as Cleopatra entered the room.

I had asked Caesar to summon her minions without the queen, and without her knowledge if possible; yet here she was. She swept into the room, fully outfitted in royal dress, draped in gold-and-scarlet robes, with the vulture-headed uraeus crown upon her head. Her presence now was very different from that which she projected at ease in her own quarters on Antirrhodus, and more different still from that of the seductress who had emerged from the rug in this very room. Even when I had seen her in her robes of state in the reception room on formal occasions, she had not possessed the air of majesty that radiated from her now.

She cast a singeing glance at me, then turned a softer gaze to Caesar. "The consul desires to question my subjects yet again?"

Caesar cleared his throat. "Gordianus has been able, after all, to cast some light upon the events that occurred on Antirrhodus."

She raised an eyebrow. "Something to do with the freedman Philip, whom I passed in the hall outside?"

"Perhaps. Suffice to say that the amphora of Falernian had been poisoned even before it was opened. We may discuss the details at another time, but for now, that fact has been demonstrated to my satisfaction."

The queen slowly nodded. "Which presents a very awkward question."

"Yes. How did it come to pass that the empty alabaster vial was discovered on Meto's person, when the vial, as it turns out, had nothing to do with the poisoning?"

"A curious situation."

"Curious indeed, Your Majesty, and most distressing. Yet I'm convinced that someone here among us can explain it."

A silence settled over the room. At last the queen spoke. "Is the simplest explanation not the most likely? You say the amphora was already poisoned. But could it not have been doubly poisoned? The vial was found on Meto; the vial was empty. I suggest that Meto acquired the vial from Gordianus—with or without his father's knowledge—and conspired to use it, perhaps against you, Caesar, or perhaps to do away with us both. He fetched the amphora for you, and brought it to Antirrhodus; doing so, he saw his opportunity to use the poison, so he brought that with him as well. When he opened the amphora, he opened the vial at the same time and emptied it into the amphora. None of us noticed, simply because none of us were watching. You say the amphora was already poisoned. It appears that Meto acted in ignorance of that fact, but with no less malice. His crime was no less heinous for being redundant." The queen, in making this assertion, stood erect and kept her voice low and steady, with a gaze that never wavered. Cicero himself, standing in the Forum before a skeptical jury, could not have delivered the argument with greater authority.

But Caesar was not convinced. "What Your Majesty says makes perfect sense, yet the explanation does not satisfy me." He turned his gaze to Merianis, who lowered her eyes and bit her lip. The exuberant, smiling, beautiful young woman who had greeted me when I first arrived at the palace seemed very far away at that moment, replaced by a haggard figure whose shifty eyes and furtive manner reminded me more of Philip. Since the death of Zoë on Antirrhodus, I had not seen a smile on Merianis's face. Each time I saw her, she looked more haunted.

"Perhaps, Merianis, you can offer an explanation that gives more satisfaction?" said Caesar.

She shivered, though the room was warm. She lifted her eyes just enough to cast a questioning look at the queen, who responded with an almost imperceptible nod.

"I confess," said Merianis. Her voice trembled.

"Explain," said Caesar.

"I did what I did . . . to hurt Meto. It was a shameful act, unworthy of a priestess of Isis."

"Go on," said Caesar.

"Yes, Merianis, go on," said the queen, her voice stern.

I shook my head. "Consul, when I asked you to summon the queen's subjects, this was not what I had in mind. This is—"

"Quiet, Gordianus. I shall conduct the questioning. Go on, Merianis. Explain to me what you did that day."

"I had nothing to do with the poisoning. But when Zoë died, and the queen called me to her side . . ."

"Yes, I remember," said Caesar. "You conversed in whispers."

"She merely told me to fetch Apollodorus."

"You conversed at some length, and with noticeable emotion."

"I—I was jarred by what had happened. I was confused and upset. The queen had to repeat herself. She became impatient with me."

Caesar nodded. "And then I saw you look at Meto. Your expression was strange."

"I looked at him strangely because . . . that was the moment I conceived of the plot against him."

"I see. Go on."

"The queen told me to bring Apollodorus. I ran to find him. But first . . . first I went to my room . . . to fetch the vial of poison."

"Then it was you who took the vial from Gordianus's trunk?" said Caesar.

"Yes."

"But how did you even know about the vial's existence, and what it contained?"

"On the day I brought Meto to his room, Gordianus asked me to leave—but I lingered in the hallway outside. I listened to their conversation. I heard what Gordianus said about the vial and the poison inside— and I also heard what Meto told him, to get rid of it! Later, when I had a chance, I took the vial from the trunk—but only because I feared that Gordianus might be tempted to use it against himself, and I could not bear the thought." Her eyes met mine at last. "That's the truth, I swear to you by Isis! I stole the vial only because I wanted to protect you from yourself, Gordianus! Please, believe me!"

I drew a breath to speak, but Caesar raised a hand to silence me. "Go on, Merianis," he said.

"The queen sent me to fetch Apollodorus, but first I ran to my room and found the vial. I emptied it—"

"You hadn't emptied it before?" Caesar asked sharply. "Why did you not empty it when you stole it, if your purpose was to keep the poison from being used?"

Merianis became flustered. "You're right. It was empty already—I forgot. I'm becoming confused again . . ."

"Go on!" Caesar's tone made even Cleopatra wince. Merianis began to weep.

"When I found Apollodorus, I quickly explained what had happened . . . and I told him of my desire: that he should place the empty vial upon the person of Meto, so that Meto would be blamed for the poisoning."

"But why, Merianis? What was your grudge against Meto?"

"Not a grudge; a broken heart! From the moment I saw him, I desired him. He should have desired me in return. I made my feelings plain to him, and he spurned me. I wanted him to suffer!" She shuddered and hid her face in her hands.

"And you, Apollodorus?" Caesar cast a burning gaze at the tall Sicilian. "You went along with this deception?"

Before, in every circumstance, Apollodorus's attitude had been utterly self-assured, even brazenly defiant; but now he lowered his eyes and spoke in a hoarse whisper. "I did what Merianis asked me to do."

"But why, Apollodorus?"

"Because . . ." He spoke through gritted teeth. "Because I love her."

"I see." Caesar nodded gravely. "You must love her very much indeed."

"I do!"

I could no longer remain quiet. "Caesar!" I said—but again he silenced me with his hand and an angry glare. He turned to Cleopatra.

"What does Your Majesty have to say about this?"

Her demeanor was more haughty than ever. Cleopatra seemed as cool and unassailable as a pillar of marble. "Such a deception impugns the dignity of the consul, to be sure. . . ."

"No less than it impugns the majesty of the queen, if she, too, was deceived by her servants!"

"Yes; but their crime is less heinous than that of poisoning. . . ."

"Hardly less heinous, if the result had been the execution of one of my closest lieutenants, an innocent man!" Caesar took a deep breath. "Your Majesty, there must be a reckoning."

A ripple of dismay marred the bland perfection of the queen's composure, like a wind-flaw on flat water. There was a very slight catch in her voice when she spoke. "The consul speaks justly. There must be a reckoning for this deceit, and so there shall be." She turned her gaze first to Merianis, and then to Apollodorus. Something profound was communicated in the look the queen exchanged with these two, the closest of all her subjects. The queen gave them a silent order; in silence they accepted it. The three of them seemed transported to a plane of existence where neither Caesar nor I could follow. Thus I excuse my inaction during the events that immediately followed. They became like actors on the stage, and Caesar and I became mute spectators, able only to watch in horror and awe.

Apollodorus produced a dagger. Later I would wonder why Caesar's guards had not disarmed him. But as we knew already, he was skilled at sleight of hand, and somehow he had slipped the weapon past them.

Apollodorus turned to Merianis, who stood trembling with her eyes shut, as if she knew what would happen next. Her lips moved soundlessly, reciting a prayer. Apollodorus plunged the knife into her heart. I think she died very quickly, for she made only a small, sibilant utterance— "Sweet Isis!"—as she collapsed to the floor. Her body convulsed for a moment, and then became utterly still.

Without hesitation, Apollodorus knelt, planted the long, bloody dagger upright before him, and fell upon it with his full weight. His death was more unseemly than that of Merianis. He grunted, coughed blood on the floor, and expelled a rattling breath. "My queen!" he cried, struggling to lift his eyes to gain a final glimpse of Cleopatra. His eyes rolled back in his head. His jaw gaped. Blood ran from his mouth. He fell onto his side, drawing his knees to his chest. His feet twitched and kicked, and then he lay as still as Merianis.

The guard at the door gave a shout and came running, quickly followed by others. Caesar raised his arm. "Stay back!"

"But, Consul—!" protested the guard.

"Leave us. Now!"

Looking askance at the queen and mumbling among themselves, Caesar's men withdrew.

Cleopatra gazed down at the lifeless bodies at her feet. She drew a sharp breath and let out a cry. Tears ran down her cheeks. For a moment I thought she might lose her composure entirely and fall to the floor weeping. But she stiffened her neck, fought back tears, and turned her glittering eyes to Caesar.

"Is Caesar satisfied?" she asked.

Once more I felt compelled to speak, but Caesar cocked his head, thrust out his jaw, and silenced me with a look. "Caesar . . . is satisfied."

She lowered her eyes. "And this matter is closed?"

"The matter is closed. The queen's subjects have been punished. Meto is absolved and shall be released. We shall never speak again of what happened on Antirrhodus."

"Very well," said the queen. She removed a long linen mantle that was gathered and pinned at one shoulder, shook the garment loose, and laid it over the bodies of Merianis and Apollodorus. "If you will, see that no one touches these remains. Embalmers from the temple of Isis will come very soon to collect them, so that the proper rituals may be observed at each stage of the journey upon which they have embarked."

I could not help myself. My voice trembled. "How terrible, if anything should go amiss and disappoint the queen! Even in the life hereafter, her loyal servants must be ready and waiting for her when the day comes that the queen herself crosses over!"

She gave me a chilly look. "You understand completely, Gordianus. Apollodorus and Merianis worship Isis, and I embody Isis. Their loyalty knows no bounds, and neither does their reward. So it is in this world; so it shall be in the next, and through all eternity. The impious will fall aside and turn to dust, but the righteous shall have life everlasting."

"With you as their queen?"

"Don't worry, Gordianus. I doubt very much that you will be among my subjects in the life hereafter."

With that she collected herself and strode from the room, her head held high.

27

The embalmers came quickly; so quickly, in fact, that it seemed they must have gathered somewhere nearby beforehand, to await the queen's call. The bodies of Merianis and Apollodorus were laid upon biers and carried off.

" 'Caesar is satisfied'!" I said, unable to contain my sarcasm. "*Are* you, Consul? How can you be?"

He looked at me for a long moment before speaking. "I *am* satisfied that I responded as I should have responded to what just took place in this room."

"But you cannot be satisfied that the queen and her subjects told you the truth!"

"That, Gordianus, is another matter."

"Those tears she cried! She used them like a witch to cast a spell over you."

"Perhaps; nonetheless, I think her tears were genuine. Do you not believe that she loved Apollodorus and Merianis, as a queen loves those closest to her? Do you not think that she was profoundly moved by the sacrifice they made for her?"

"Sacrifice, indeed! That nonsense about Merianis being madly in love with Meto, and deciding on a whim to destroy him because he spurned her—and the further nonsense that Apollodorus would go along with such a plot on a moment's notice, without question, behind the queen's back! Apollodorus was a slave to only one woman, and we both know it wasn't Merianis."

Caesar sighed. "In fact, Gordianus, I do happen to know, because Meto told me so at the time, that Merianis did indeed make her affections available to him—"

"As she did to me!"

"—and that Meto declined."

"As did I. But I don't believe for an instant that Merianis decided, on her own initiative, to plant that vial on Meto."

He looked at me gravely. "Nor do I."

"Yet you're satisfied to let the matter rest!"

"Meto will be released, Gordianus. Is that not the result you wished for?"

"I'm a Roman, Consul. Wisely or not, I take justice for granted. But truth also matters to me. While the queen was here, you refused to let me speak. Will you listen to me now?"

He heaved a sigh. "Very well. Because you're Meto's father; because you've suffered much here in Egypt; and also because, whether you realize it or not, I rather like you, Gordianus, I am going to indulge you, and allow you to tell me exactly what you believe to be the truth. Explain to me what occurred on Antirrhodus; and then let us never speak of it again. Do you understand?"

"Yes, Consul."

"Then proceed."

"Will you grant that the amphora of wine was already poisoned, because it was the wine with which Pompey intended to poison himself?"

Caesar nodded. "I grant as much. But what of the alabaster vial?"

"I believe it was taken from my trunk by Merianis, just as she said, and for the reason she gave: She wished to deny me any chance to use the poison on myself. She stole the poison with my best interests at heart. I think that was about the only thing she told us that was true, because there was something Merianis left out. She was a spy for the queen; her eyes and ears belonged to Cleopatra. She told the queen everything, and I believe she told Cleopatra about the alabaster vial, as well. When you asked Merianis about disposing of the poison, she became flustered. I think that was her original intention, but someone ordered her not to—the queen, of course. For a woman like Cleopatra, such a poison might eventually serve a purpose, and so she ordered Merianis to keep the vial and its contents intact.

"Neither of them had any immediate use for the vial; for the moment, they both forgot about it, just as I did. Then came that terrible day on Antirrhodus. When Zoë died from the poisoned wine, the queen was as puzzled and alarmed as the rest of us. But her mind worked very quickly, searching for a way to turn events to her advantage. Because Meto had opened the amphora, he was an obvious suspect, and it may be that Cleopatra actually believed that Meto had poisoned the wine. Meto was her enemy; the queen knew that he disliked her. Whether he had poisoned the wine or not, it would benefit the queen to be rid of him, and she saw an opportunity to deal him a blow—even as she diverted suspicion from herself. A plot formed quickly in her mind, and she put it into action at once.

"While she held the body of Zoë, she called Merianis to her side. What did she say to Merianis? None of us could hear, for they kept their voices low, but did it not seem to you that Merianis balked at the queen's commands? This was what Cleopatra told her to do: first, to fetch the alabaster vial from her room, and to empty the poison from it; then to find Apollodorus, and to convey the queen's desire that he come at once and, when the occasion allowed, that he should plant the empty vial upon Meto. Merianis was appalled; she had no wish to harm Meto, but she had no will to resist the queen's command. Thus the strange look she shot at Meto; thus the shame she exhibited afterward. As for Apollodorus, he obeyed the queen's command without question, and for the very reason he gave today: 'Because I love her,' he said—but he didn't mean Merianis. He meant Cleopatra!"

Caesar rubbed his chin thoughtfully. "And—supposing this version of events is true—this was why you wished the two servants to be called here without their mistress. You hoped they might reveal the truth—and incriminate the queen."

"Yes. But Cleopatra foresaw that possibility. She might simply have refused to cooperate—but she sensed that you must, at some level, be given an explanation, and that someone would have to be punished. Before they came here, the queen told Merianis and Apollodorus exactly what to say, if called upon; and to save her, they lied, knowing it would mean their own deaths." I remembered the look of acquiescence on Merianis's face when Apollodorus delivered the deathblow, and my voice quavered. "If Merianis hadn't stolen the poison from my trunk, desiring only to save me from myself, she might yet be alive."

Caesar nodded. "Strange, how Cornelia's alabaster vial and Pompey's amphora of Falernian wine both seemed to take on a malevolent life of their own, even after their owners abandoned them. Dead men do bite, and so do their widows!"

"You accept my version of events, Consul?"

"It satisfies my curiosity, Gordianus. But it does not satisfy my needs."

"Your needs?"

"I came to Egypt to settle affairs here to my own advantage, and to the advantage of Rome, which amounts to the same thing. Debts must be repaid; for that to happen, the harvests must be gathered and taxes collected; for that to happen, Egypt must have peace. Either the king and queen must be reconciled, or one must be eliminated and the other put upon the throne—and whoever occupies the throne must be a steadfast ally of Rome. Through all that's happened, I've remained committed to carrying out the will of the Piper, namely that both siblings should rule jointly. What occurred on Antirrhodus was unfortunate; but as you yourself assert, the poisoning was accidental, and the queen's response, though regrettable, was not premeditated. To press the queen for answers, to badger her with questions as if she had plotted in some criminal fashion against my person, does not serve the greater purpose—"

"But she *did* plot against you, Consul! Not once, but twice! First, when she sought to falsely incriminate Meto—all the more terrible, if you ask me, precisely because it *was* spontaneous—and again, only moments ago, when she contrived, with complete premeditation, to have her subjects lie to you, even to die, in order to conceal the first deceit!"

"Would you have me call the queen a liar to her face?"

"I would have you call things what they are!"

"Ah, but there we see where you fail to grasp the situation, Gordianus.

You possess knowledge, but you lack understanding. Through these deceits, the queen sought to advance herself, not to endanger me. That is a crucial point, Gordianus, and one that you fail to apprehend. This is a political matter; it has to do with the appearance of things. When the queen was pressed to supply a response that would satisfy appearances, she did precisely that."

"At the expense of two lives! The queen is a monster. To force those two to lie to protect her, and then to stand by and watch as they killed themselves, so that she might save face—"

"So that *I* might save face as well, Gordianus. Do you really believe she forced them to do anything? Quite the contrary, I should think; what they did, they did willingly, even eagerly. What extraordinary devotion! If only I could cultivate such depths of love and loyalty! Men have died for me, yes, but not in the way those two died for their queen. They truly believed her to be a goddess, with the power to grant them everlasting life. Amazing!" There was a note of envy in his wonderment. Would a Roman king ever be able to evoke such total devotion and blind self-sacrifice? I found the notion repellent, but Caesar seemed fascinated by the possibility.

He strode to the window and gazed at the vista that stretched to the distant Nile. "And yet . . ." I heard a note of resignation in his voice. I saw his shoulders sag. "You say that she's bewitched me, Gordianus, and I fear you may be right. I almost believe myself that she's a goddess, if only because she makes me feel like a god. I'm a man of fifty-two, Gordianus. Cleopatra makes me feel like a boy. I've conquered the world, and I feel weary; she offers me a fresh world to conquer, and makes me young again. She offers more than the world; she offers everlasting life. I'm fifty-two, and I've never produced an heir. Cleopatra has promised to give me a son. Can you imagine? A son to rule over not only Egypt, but Rome as well! Together we might found a dynasty to rule the whole world, forever."

I shook my head. Caesar, looking out the window, did not see my reaction, but must have sensed it.

"I suppose," he said, "this is precisely the sort of talk that turned Meto so adamantly against the queen and her influence on me. Do I sound like some deluded Eastern despot? Have I crossed the world, eluding every trap and besting every enemy, only to lose my bearings here in Egypt, to a twenty-one-year-old girl?"

"You say she promises you the world, Consul; yet she lies as easily as she breathes. You say she promises you a son; yet even if she were to announce that she was carrying your child, how could you be certain—"

He raised a hand. "Enough! Some thoughts are better left unspoken."

He clasped his hands behind his back and silently gazed out the window for such a long time that he seemed to have forgotten my presence, until finally he spoke again. The tenor of his voice had changed in some subtle way; in the silent interim, he had come to some decision regarding the queen.

But first he would deal with another matter. He cleared his throat. "I want you to know, Gordianus, that I would never have executed Meto."

"But you told me—"

"I told you what I deemed necessary to tell you, in order to gain the desired result." He turned to face me. "Did the immediate threat to Meto not spur you to find the truth about the poisoned amphora?"

"Perhaps. But still—"

"I know men, Gordianus. If any skill has brought me to the place I occupy today, it's my ability to judge the character and capacity of the men around me. Some men respond to encouragement, some to threats, some to questions about their honor. The trick lies in perceiving the best way to inspire each man to do his utmost. I think I know you, Gordianus, better than you realize. The proof, as always, lies in the result."

I shook my head. "Then you never believed Meto was guilty?"

"Did I say that, Gordianus? I believe I said something slightly different. But the important thing is that Meto shall be freed at once and restored to my side."

"As if nothing had happened?"

"I've learned to forgive my foes, Gordianus. Some of them have even learned to forgive me. Should it not be easier for two friends to forgive one another?"

I gritted my teeth. "You posit a false syllogism, Consul."

"How so?"

"*You* need to be forgiven; Meto has done nothing for which he needs forgiveness."

"Oh, really? How good finally to hear you say that, Gordianus! Your son is blameless after all."

"I meant—"

"I know what you meant. But the choice of how to proceed beyond this . . . unfortunate breach of trust . . . lies with Meto, I think, and not with you. Is your son free to make his own decisions, or will you continue to look over his shoulder and judge him at every turn, holding him hostage to your disapproval? Have my actions toward Meto been any more destructive than your own, when you disowned him? If that breach could be healed, then can this one not be healed as well?"

How deftly Caesar had turned the tables on me, elevating his own decisions above argument while challenging my paternal authority and moral judgment! I chafed at his insinuation, but I could not summon a rebuttal. Either Meto was his own man, or he was not; and if he was, then I had to acknowledge once and for all that he had moved beyond my power to shape his opinions and desires. Would he rush back to Caesar's side, his imperator's "unfortunate breach of trust" forgiven and forgotten? Or had the worm of doubt insinuated itself permanently into Meto's thoughts, and would he never again be able to render to Caesar the loving allegiance the man once had commanded of him? Caesar was right: The choice belonged to Meto, not to me.

But it seemed there was another, more immediate choice at hand, to be made by Caesar. He turned from me and summoned the guard at the door, to whom he issued an instruction in a voice too low for me to hear. He began to pace the room, staring at his reflection in the highly polished marble floor, apparently oblivious of me. Like many of the powerful men I had known, he possessed the ability to move from one preoccupation to another without transition, focusing his entire energies on the problem immediately before him. He had dealt with and was done with me, and though I might linger in his physical presence, for all practical purposes I had already vanished.

I cleared my throat. "If the consul is done with me—"

Caesar looked up, like a sleeper pulled from a dream. "Gordianus! No, stay. I'm about to make a decision too long deferred. Someone should be here to witness the moment. Why not you? Yes, I think Gordianus the Finder is precisely the man to be with me at this moment."

We waited; for what, I wasn't sure. At last, the guard stationed at the door announced that Caesar's visitor had arrived. A moment later, leaving his courtiers in the antechamber outside, the king stepped into the room.

28

I dropped to one knee. Caesar remained standing.

Giving a vague wave of his hand to signal that I might rise, but otherwise showing no acknowledgment of my presence, Ptolemy strode directly to Caesar and stopped a few paces from him. He wore the uraeus crown with a rearing cobra; his bearing was erect. He seemed somehow different—no longer a boy with the attributes of a man, but a man who had left boyhood behind. The gaze he exchanged with Caesar was that of equals, despite the difference in their ages.

"Your Majesty," said Caesar, inclining his head slightly.

"Consul," said Ptolemy, his eyes flashing and a faint smile softening his lips. The resemblance to his sister was more striking than ever.

Caesar sighed. "We've talked before, at great length, about what's to be done. You remain adamant in your position?"

"I shall never share the throne with my sister. Pothinus, whatever his true motives, eventually convinced me to compromise; but Pothinus is no longer here."

I realized the source of the change I saw in Ptolemy; it was due not to something added, but something subtracted. Except for his exhortations from the balcony of the Tomb of Alexander, I had never before seen the king outside the presence of Pothinus. Perhaps those who believed the lord chamberlain had cast an undue influence over the king were right.

With Pothinus gone, Ptolemy seemed to have grown to full manhood overnight.

"Your Majesty realizes the difficulties of the decision I face," said Caesar.

"I do."

"But ultimately, as events have unfolded, and as the character of each of the Piper's children has become clearer to me . . ."

Ptolemy regarded him quizzically. "The consul has made a choice between us?"

"I have."

"And?"

"You know how fervently I desired to reconcile you with your sister. Even now, were it possible, it seems to me the judicious course. And yet it manifestly is *not* possible, and so another choice must be made. . . ."

Ptolemy tilted his head back and narrowed his eyes. "Go on, Consul."

"I have decided, Your Majesty, to support your claim to be the sole ruler of Egypt."

I saw the flash of a boyish grin breaking through the constrained smile of the king. "And my sister?"

"Cleopatra may not readily accept my judgment, but she will be made to see she has no choice; her position in Alexandria relies entirely upon my protection, after all."

The king's smile faded. "What if she should slip out of Alexandria to rejoin her rebels, just as she slipped into the city?"

"That won't happen."

"How can the consul be sure?"

"For one thing, some of her closest confederates—those who assisted her entry to the city—are no longer with her." Caesar glanced at me with a tacit command to say nothing about Apollodorus and Merianis. "For the time being, she'll be returned to the palace on Antirrhodus and confined there. My soldiers will keep a close watch upon her."

"As Caesar's soldiers have kept close watch on me in recent days?" said Ptolemy.

"During the uncertain interim that has just ended, I found it necessary to prepare for all eventualities," said Caesar. "Now that my decision is made, Your Majesty shall of course be free to come and go as he pleases. Cleopatra will not."

"She must be handed over to me for judgment."

"No, Your Majesty. That I cannot do. No harm must come to her."

"If my sister is allowed to live, sooner or later she will escape and raise a revolt. Even in custody, she'll find some way to make mischief. As long as she breathes, she'll never stop plotting my death."

Caesar nodded. "Clearly, Cleopatra cannot be allowed to remain in Egypt. I think it may be best for her to take up residence in Rome—under my watchful protection, of course."

"In Rome? Where she can continue to plot against me?"

"A watch will be kept upon her house. Her movements will be restricted, as will the list of those allowed to visit her."

"Will Caesar be among the visitors who call upon her, in Rome?"

"Perhaps, from time to time."

Ptolemy shook his head. "Alexandria is far from Rome. Caesar will forget his ties to the king of Egypt. The viper will pour poison in your ears and turn you against me!" In the suddenly strident tone of his voice, the boy within the man made a fitful reappearance.

Caesar was adamant. "Your Majesty must trust me on this matter. I will not allow Cleopatra to be harmed. Is it not enough that I recognize your sole claim to the throne of Egypt?"

Ptolemy drew a deep breath. He squared his shoulders. The boy was suppressed; the man reasserted his primacy, and his decision was reached. "Caesar judges wisely. The people of Egypt and their king are lucky to have found such a friend in the consul of the Roman people. But now there is much work to be done. If I'm truly free to come and go . . ."

"You are, Your Majesty."

"Then I shall leave the palace now, to join with Achillas and take charge of my army in the city. I shall inform Achillas of your decision in my favor and order him to call back my troops, so that no more blood will be shed, Roman or Egyptian. Once order is established in the city as well as in the palace, and once my sister and those who wish to stay in her service have departed from Egypt under Caesar's protection, there shall be a ceremony to mark the cessation of hostilities and the affirmation of my rule." His voice softened. "If the consul has time, I should like him to accompany me on a journey up the Nile, so that he may observe the life of the river and witness the many splendors along her shore."

Caesar stepped forward and took the king's hand. "I should like nothing better, Your Majesty. Sooner or later I must leave Egypt; there must be a reckoning with the scattered remnants of Pompey's forces, who are said to be regrouping in Libya under the command of Cato. But I have little to fear from that quarter, and a full and final settlement of affairs in Egypt takes precedence over all other matters of state. To accompany the king on a tour of the Nile—to cement our friendship with such a journey— would please me greatly."

The two exchanged a look of such intimate affection that I felt like an intruder. I cleared my throat.

"In the meantime," said Caesar, resuming a more formal tone, "I shall watch for the cessation of hostilities from Achillas's men, and I shall eagerly await Your Majesty's return."

The king stepped back, pulling his hand from Caesar's grasp. As he turned to go, the look of manly determination on his face wavered; when he turned back, spinning on his heel, it was the boy-king I saw, timorous and uncertain, with tears in his eyes. He rushed back to Caesar and gripped his arm. "Come with me, Caesar! I don't want to leave your side!"

Caesar smiled indulgently at this sudden outburst of emotion. He gently laid his hand over the hand that gripped his arm, and he squeezed it affectionately. "The king has no need of me when it comes to dealing with Achillas. The order to cease hostilities must come from you alone. I would only get in the way."

Ptolemy nodded, but his eyes brimmed with tears. "You're right, of course. What I do now, I must do alone. 'It's a lonely business,' my father used to say, 'being a king.' But never forget one thing, Caesar: The whole of my kingdom is no dearer to me at this moment than the mere sight of you!"

With astonishment, I saw that Caesar, too, had tears in his eyes, and when he spoke, his voice was husky. "If that's true, Your Majesty, then go quickly, that you may return all the more quickly to my side!"

Without another word, his eyes locked with Caesar's until the last possible moment, Ptolemy stepped back, turned away, and withdrew from the room, his linen robes of state rustling in the faint breeze stirred by his passing.

Caesar stood motionless, gazing after him.

"Will you tell her now?" I said.

Caesar gave me such a blank look that I repeated the question. "Will you tell her now? The queen? Or should I say simply, 'Cleopatra,' if she no longer possesses that title?"

"I'm sure she'll retain some sort of title," Caesar said absently, as if my question had distracted him from more-important thoughts. " 'Princess,' I suppose, as she was called when her father was alive; she's still the Piper's daughter, and the sister of the king."

"Though no longer his wife?"

"I'm sure there's a royal law to deal with the dissolution of their marriage," said Caesar. "If not, we'll invent one."

"And will she still be an incarnation of the goddess Isis, even without her crown? To lose one's throne must be terrible; to lose one's divinity—"

"If you're making a jest at the expense of the local religion, Gordianus, it's not amusing."

"Will you tell her now?" I said again.

He drew a deep breath. "There are some tasks that make a coward even of Caesar! But if I put off telling her, she'll find out some other way, and that could lead to trouble. Best to be brave and face the situation head-on. It may be that the queen—the princess, I mean—has left already for Antirrhodus, but perhaps we can catch her before her boat departs."

" 'We,' Consul?"

"Of course I include you, Gordianus. When you witness the beginning of a thing, do you not wish to see it to the end?"

"Perhaps. But does the consul wish me to see it?"

"I've always found it useful to have another pair of eyes and ears to witness important events. My memory is not what it used to be; a second account comes in very handy when I sit down to write my memoirs. Meto has long served that purpose for me."

"I'll make a poor substitute for my son. Perhaps you should summon him to resume his rightful role."

"An excellent suggestion. The cell where he's been confined is close to the pier. I'll send men ahead to release him, so that he can meet us. Having played antagonist to the queen—the princess—Meto deserves to be on hand when I announce my decision to her. Come, Gordianus!"

I walked alongside Caesar as he traversed the palace complex accompanied by his retinue, stopping every so often to issue orders to subordinates along the way. We came to the gardens along the waterfront. Beyond the palm trees and flowering jasmine, out on the stone pier, Cleopatra stood in the company of a few servants, as well as the Roman messenger who had been sent to detain her from boarding the boat that would return her to Antirrhodus.

Closer at hand, I heard a familiar voice. "Caesar!"

The consul, seeing Meto beside the path, stopped and opened his arms wide. "Meto! You look well, thank Venus!"

Meto hung back, but the smile on Caesar's face overcame his hesitation. They embraced.

"The messenger said—"

Caesar nodded. "You've been cleared of all suspicion, thanks to the insights of your father."

"Papa!" Meto hugged me. It was to Caesar he had first spoken, and to Caesar he gave his first embrace; but I tried to think only of the joy I felt at seeing him unharmed and free and out of danger.

"This must mean you found an answer to the question of what happened on Antirrhodus," said Meto, looking quizzically at me and then at Caesar.

"Indeed, your father did exactly that," said Caesar. "But the explanation will have to wait. Cleopatra stands on the pier, and there is something I must tell her."

Caesar led the way, taking long, quick strides.

"Papa, what's happening?" whispered Meto.

I was about to speak, but Caesar looked over his shoulder and silenced me with a glance.

The afternoon sunlight, reflected off the stones of the pier and the water of the harbor, was dazzling. Gulls swooped and cried overhead. Waves lapped against the steps leading down to the royal skiff. Cleopatra, seeing Caesar, smiled at his approach, but as we drew closer, I saw a twist of anxiety at the corner of her mouth. When she saw Meto, the smile remained but grew stiff. She raised her hands to take Caesar's, but he stopped short of stepping close enough, and she was left with an awkward, unfinished gesture of welcome. She drew back her hands and frowned.

"Caesar, what's happening?"

He looked at her gravely. "There's been . . . a development."

"Good or bad? Bad, to judge from the look on your face."

Caesar averted his eyes.

"Caesar? What's happening? Tell me now!" In her suddenly strident tone, I heard the voice of her younger brother.

When he still did not answer, she shifted to a more formal tone. "Consul," she said, and I knew she suspected the truth, for she was testing to see whether Caesar, in response, would formally address her as the queen.

He drew a deep breath and was about to speak when a cry came from one of the Roman watchmen who patrolled the rooftops of the palace behind us. "Warships! Warships! Egyptian warships entering from the Eunostos Harbor!"

All eyes turned toward the Heptastadion. Near the center of the causeway, a tunnel allowed ships to sail from one harbor to the other. With their oars working at a furious pace, one Egyptian warship after another was entering the great harbor. Their decks were crowded with soldiers and catapults and bristled with spears.

Another watchman cried out from the rooftops: "Smoke! Flames! Fire at the barricades next to the royal theater!"

As one, those of us on the pier swung around to witness the cloud of black smoke that rose from the area where Caesar's defenses were most strongly concentrated. At the same time, a heavy, percussive vibration traveled through the air, rattling my teeth—the *boom . . . boom . . . boom* of a distant battering ram. Achillas's forces had launched a coordinated attack by land and by sea on Caesar's position.

I looked at Caesar and saw a series of emotions sweep across his face—consternation, outrage, and bitter disappointment. He saw that I stared at him, and he seized my arm in a painful grip. He drew me aside and hissed in my ear. "Gordianus! You were there. You saw. You heard. Did the king not pledge to call off Achillas and his troops?"

"He did."

"Then what can be happening?"

From the direction of the approaching warships, I heard a loud crack, followed by a recoil. One of the Egyptian warships, slipping past Caesar's galleys, had advanced to a point within firing distance of the pier. Had some eagle-eyed scout spotted Caesar and Cleopatra, or had those in charge of the catapult simply let off a shot at the first available target? Whatever the case, the flaming ball of pitch hurtled towards us. One of Cleopatra's serving girls let out a shriek, and some of those around me scrambled back. But the missile fell short; with a splash and a hiss, it landed in the water some distance from the pier, but close enough to send a spray of hot vapor across my face.

My arm was still captured in Caesar's painful grip. "It's because of her!" he whispered. "It's because I wouldn't let him have her. He hates his sister more than he loves me! He must have issued an order to attack, the moment he reached Achillas. He knows where I've deployed my men and fortified my defenses; he's told Achillas exactly where to mount the assault. The wretched little viper!"

Cleopatra stood a short distance away. Her eyes were not on the approaching warship, but on us. In all the commotion, she had not moved at all. Her expression, if anything, was more composed than before. There was even, unless I imagined it, a slight intimation of a smile on her face. Had she grasped, in an instant, exactly what had transpired? I think so; for the smile on her face was a smile of a queen who has snatched triumph from the jaws of defeat.

"It would appear, Consul, that we are under attack." Her use of the word "we" was not an accident. "I'm surprised that Achillas would mount such an assault, considering that my brother is in your custody."

She *did* know what had happened. She was baiting Caesar to tell her the truth. He did not answer.

The warship drew closer. I could now make out the faces of the Egyptian soldiers on the deck, and I could see that the catapult was being ratcheted back to launch another fireball at us.

"Or could it be," said Cleopatra, "that this assault is being launched at the instigation of my brother?"

Caesar drew a breath. "Your Majesty perceives the situation. Not an hour ago I released your brother and allowed him to join Achillas."

"But why, Consul?"

"Imperator!" cried Meto. "We must withdraw at once! The danger—"

Caesar looked away from the queen long enough to bark an order. "Withdraw to safety! All of you! Now!"

Meto moved to take his arm. "Imperator, you must come as well—"

Caesar shook him off, but curiously, with his other hand, he held me as fast as ever. "Go, Meto. Lead the others to safety. I'll follow in a moment. Go! I order you!"

Reluctantly, Meto turned and gestured for the others to follow him off the pier. I could not have done so had I wanted to; Caesar held me fast in his grip.

He spoke to Cleopatra. "Your brother begged me to let him go to Achillas. He vowed to me that he would order Achillas to withdraw his troops. He promised to return to the palace as soon as that was done."

"And you believed him?"

"I accepted a vow made by the king of Egypt."

"My father was the king of Egypt! My brother is nothing more than a foolish boy."

"I see that now. And if he ever was the king, then, as of this moment, Ptolemy is king no longer, and never will be."

A fire leaped behind Cleopatra's eyes. "What are you saying, Caesar?"

"I abandon all attempts to reconcile you with your brother. As consul of the Roman people, and executor of your father's will, I recognize you as queen of Egypt and sole claimant to the throne."

"And Ptolemy?"

"Ptolemy has betrayed me. In doing so, he's betrayed his people as well, and his own destiny. Once we've defeated him and his army, I shall take whatever steps are necessary to ensure that he can never again lay claim to the throne or do harm to you in any other way."

I heard a loud crack, much closer than before, followed by a recoil. The catapult had launched a second fireball at us. It arced through the air, its trajectory hard to determine from my foreshortened point of view.

"Go, Your Majesty!" said Caesar. "Follow the others to a place of safety."

Cleopatra smiled calmly. She did as Caesar asked and proceeded to leave the pier. Her stride was quick, but she did not run.

"Consul," I said nervously, gazing up at the approaching fireball, "should we not also—"

"Stand fast! I have a good eye for these things, Gordianus. This missile is poorly aimed. We're perfectly safe."

Sure enough, the descending fireball landed harmlessly in the water at a point more distant than the first. Meanwhile, a Roman galley was swiftly approaching to head off the Egyptian warship, which abruptly turned about.

Caesar drew me close. "Did you hear what I told the queen?"

"Every word, Consul." I raised an eyebrow. "You omitted certain details regarding your conversation with her brother."

"Perhaps. But you must never, ever contradict or stray from the exact version of events that I recounted to the queen. Do you understand?"

"I understand, Consul. Cleopatra must never be told that she was your second choice."

He looked toward the head of the pier, where the queen was just joining the little crowd gathered there. He nodded thoughtfully. "I chose between the two of them, and I chose wrongly. But the gods gave me a chance to rectify my mistake before I compounded it further. Cleopatra deceived me, and I lost faith in her. Now I've deceived her in return; and so we're even and may start afresh."

"It seems to me, Consul, that neither of you deceived the other a whit. You each perceived exactly the game played by the other."

"But we shall pretend otherwise; and there you have the essence of statecraft, Gordianus—and of marriage, as well. Cleopatra is a woman, and I am a man; but we are also heads of state. When one of us sets a foot wrong, the other will pretend not to notice. When there is friction, we shall maintain a fiction of harmony; and thereby we shall respect one another's dignity."

"Would it not be wiser, and a great deal less troublesome, in marriage as well as statecraft, to simply be forthright and honest? To admit one's mistakes and ask forgiveness?"

Caesar looked at me and shook his head. "I don't know what sort of husband you made, Gordianus, but you could never have succeeded as a politician or a king."

"I never desired to be either, Consul."

"A good thing! Now, let's get off this damned pier. Where are my officers? Where are my messengers? There's a queen to be defended and a battle to be won!"

29

As it turned out, there were many battles to be waged over the course of the coming months in Alexandria.

Achillas's assault on Caesar's position was only the beginning of what developed into a full-scale war, and a most unusual one, fought almost entirely within the arena of the city and its harbor. The fight on land took place in the close quarters of narrow streets and across adjoining rooftops, rather than on sweeping plains or across mountainous terrain, and therefore it required a strategy very different from the usual tactical deployment of cavalry and infantry. The naval engagements took place within the confines of the harbor, and at times took on the appearance of some vast aquatic spectacle mounted for the dubious amusement of the populace.

Caesar, taken by surprise by Ptolemy's duplicity and outnumbered, was at first hard-pressed to maintain his position. To flee by ship at that time was virtually impossible, due partly to unfavorable winds that made it difficult to leave the harbor, and partly to the extreme hazards attendant upon a withdrawal of all the troops toward the docks and thence by ship through the narrow harbor entrance, all the while under Egyptian attack on land and sea; Pompey, harassed by Caesar, had managed such a naval withdrawal from Brundisium, but just barely. Caesar was effectively trapped in Alexandria, and faced certain destruction should the Egyptians manage to penetrate his defenses. There was considerable grumbling among his officers that he had landed them in a very tight spot, thanks to an uncharacteristic miscalculation of the forces against him and to his love for a treacherous queen; but Caesar himself never betrayed any sign of doubt or gave vent to recrimination. Perhaps Cleopatra had convinced him that together they possessed a divine destiny, and that together they would overcome all obstacles on their path to immortality.

I shall leave it to others to recount all the many incidents of the Alexandrian War. No doubt Caesar himself, with the help of Meto and others, will write a more or less accurate, if entirely self-serving, account. How candid will he be about his relationships with the royal siblings? It will be interesting to read the delicate phrases he uses to justify his decision to allow Ptolemy to leave the palace and join Achillas. But when it comes to recounting events in the military arena, Caesar's memoirs can usually be trusted.

Certain incidents stand out in my memory. Early on, the Egyptians attempted to contaminate the water supply to the palace. In all Alexandria, not a single public fountain is supplied by a well or a spring, and the water of Lake Mareotis is too brackish to drink; all fresh water for the city arrives via the canal from the Nile, and where the canal approaches the city, the water is split into numerous channels to supply various precincts. The Egyptians, having control of the canal, began pumping seawater into the supply that flowed into the areas under Caesar's control. As their water inexplicably grew saltier, Caesar's men came near to panicking; but he assured them that along every coast, underground veins of fresh water could be found. The men devoted themselves to digging at numerous spots, working continuously night and day. And in fact, enough veins of fresh water were struck to produce an adequate supply, and a crisis that might have given the Egyptians an early victory was averted.

Also early on occurred the burning of the warehouses along the harbor, which has since grown into the legend that Caesar burned the whole of the great Library. In fact, when Caesar's men set fire to a number of Egyptian ships anchored in the great harbor, so that the vessels could not later be seized and used against them, the fire spread to some buildings on the waterfront. Among these was a warehouse used by the Library, in which great quantities of papyrus were stored along with an uncertain number of recently acquired or copied scrolls that had not yet been filed in the Library. As many as forty thousand volumes may have been destroyed, but the Library itself was unscathed. Still, Cleopatra gave Caesar much grief about the destruction, and Caesar himself bitterly regretted it, if only because it gave the Egyptians further cause to label him a destroyer and a barbarian.

But the low point of the war, for Caesar, was the day he lost his new purple cape.

Caesar had always worn a blood red cape, proud of the fact that friends and foes alike could easily spot him in the thick of battle. It was Cleopatra who gave Caesar a new cape of a different hue, an equally conspicuous, very regal shade of purple. A few Romans grumbled at this innovation—were they fighting for a consul or a king?—but many appeared to welcome it. Caesar wore the cape on the day he sailed across the harbor with several hundred troops and laid siege to the causeway leading out to the Pharos lighthouse. His object was to gain control of the arch in the causeway that allowed Egyptian ships to attack from the Eunostos Harbor.

The battle went well at first; the island of Pharos itself was seized, as was the causeway, and Caesar's men set about filling the mouth of the tunnel with stones. But the Alexandrians received reinforcements, and the tide of the battle turned. Caesar's men panicked and fled. Caesar himself was forced to retreat to his ship, which was drawn alongside the causeway. So many soldiers streamed onto the ship that it began to founder. Wearing his purple cape, Caesar jumped from the deck and swam toward another ship farther out in the harbor. The heavy folds of the sodden cape threatened to drag him under; struggling in the choppy waves, barely keeping his head above water, he managed to extricate himself from the garment, and for a while he swam with it held between his teeth, for he hated to lose the queen's gift. But in the end the cape slipped from his teeth, and he abandoned it.

The day was a disaster for Caesar. The Alexandrians reclaimed the archway and removed the stones that blocked it; more than eight hundred of Caesar's men were killed by the enemy or drowned, including all those aboard his lost ship; and the triumphant Alexandrians managed to fish his new purple cape out of the water. On the causeway, they danced and shouted and waved the cape like a flag of triumph as Caesar dragged himself sputtering and half-drowned aboard the ship and made an ignominious retreat. Later the Alexandrians attached the tattered, filthy cape to a pole, like a captured banner, and for the rest of the war, they flaunted it on every possible occasion as an insult to Caesar's dignity.

The war continued for months. As in all wars, there were lulls in the fighting as each side regrouped. Caesar used such occasions to consult the many scholars and philosophers who found themselves confined to the precincts of the city under his control, which included the famous Library and the adjacent Museum, the repository of so much of the world's mathematical and astronomical learning. It was during one such lull that Caesar set about devising a new, more reliable calendar, for the venerable Roman calendar had in recent years grown out of step with the actual seasons, so that harvest festivals were taking place long before the actual harvests, and spring holidays occurred while Romans shivered. The world's most esteemed scholars were consulted when Caesar devised the new calendar, and if they did their job well, it may be that the calendar, like the movements of the stars and planets, will outlast Rome itself.

At last the balance between the warring sides was altered by the approach of Caesar's ally, King Mithridates of Pergamum, who arrived at the Egyptian frontier at the head of an army composed of Jewish, Arabian, and Syrian levies. Mithridates took Pelusium, then marched south, toward the apex of the Nile Delta. Hearing of Mithridates's advance, King Ptolemy dispatched a force to intercept him; when this Egyptian force was annihilated, Ptolemy set out himself to do battle with the new invaders. Meanwhile, Caesar, in regular communication with Mithridates, assembled his best troops, left a contingent to hold his position in the city, and sailed out of the harbor. He landed at a point west of Alexandria and circled around Ptolemy's army, marching at such a quick pace that he passed the king and joined Mithridates at the Nile before Ptolemy arrived. Thus the stage was set for the decisive battle of the Alexandrian War, which would not take place in Alexandria, but in the very heart of Egypt on the banks of the great river.

I was not there, but Meto was. Through his eyes I witnessed the end of King Ptolemy.

Ptolemy's army occupied a small village near the river, situated on a hill with a canal on one side to act as a moat; the Egyptians also built earthen ramparts and dug trenches lined with sharp pickets. The position appeared unassailable; but Caesar's men forded the canal by cutting down trees and filling the channel until a makeshift bridge was created, while others of his men swam downstream and emerged on the far side of the village, so that Ptolemy's stronghold was encircled. Still, the fortifications appeared impenetrable until Caesar's scouts noticed a poorly guarded area where the hill upon which the village stood was steepest; apparently the Egyptians assumed the sheerness of the cliff was itself adequate defense. Against that point Caesar launched a sudden and powerful assault, and when the high point was taken, his men went streaming down through the village, driving the Egyptians before them in a panic. The Egyptians were trapped by their own fortifications, falling from the walls, piling atop one another in the trenches, and impaling themselves on the pickets. Those who managed to escape the village faced the Roman soldiers who encircled them, and the army of Ptolemy was slaughtered from within and without.

King Ptolemy, apprised of the disaster as it unfolded, managed to flee by a small boat to take refuge on a royal barge in the Nile. The captain lifted anchor, dipped oars, and began to flee the scene of battle. Meanwhile, hundreds of desperate Egyptian soldiers threw down their weapons, stripped off their armor, and dove into the river. In a great, churning mass they converged on the royal barge and attempted to clamber aboard. Those already on the boat welcomed the first newcomers, then saw that they would quickly be overwhelmed and began to try to fight off their comrades, slashing at them with swords, jabbing them with spears, and firing arrows at those farther off.

The scene was horrific. The banks of the Nile echoed with the screams of the dying and the pleas of the living. The water around the barge grew thick with corpses. But those in the water greatly outnumbered those on the barge, and despite the slaughter, more and more of them managed to climb aboard, until at last the vessel was overloaded. The starboard side was submerged; the opposite side rose into the air. As if tipped by the hand of a Titan, the great barge capsized, emptying its occupants into the water and falling upside down onto the horde of swimmers who had attempted to board her. For a brief moment, the underside of the barge remained visible above the water, and a few dazed, desperate Egyptians managed to climb aboard; then the vessel vanished completely, swallowed by the river.

The army of Ptolemy was annihilated. Caesar's victory was complete.

Or almost complete, for the body of the king was never found. Caesar's troops examined every corpse along the shore, waded through every patch of reeds, pulled nets through the shallows, and dragged poles across every accessible bit of river bottom for miles downstream. Caesar's best swimmers—among them Meto, who led the search—dove repeatedly at the spot where the barge sank, retrieving every corpse mired in the mud or trapped in the debris. It was exhausting, filthy, dangerous work, and it yielded nothing.

Or rather, almost nothing. One diver located the flute that had been played by the king's piper. Another retrieved Ptolemy's cobra-headed uraeus crown and delivered it into Caesar's hands. Meto himself found an even more curious souvenir: a tattered cape, so mud-stained that at first it was difficult to discern its purple hue. It was the cape that Caesar had lost at the battle of the Pharos causeway, when he himself might have perished on a foundering ship. Apparently King Ptolemy had kept it close at hand, intending to use it to rally his troops at some critical juncture or to celebrate his ultimate triumph over the Roman invader. When Meto returned the cape to Caesar, the imperator smiled ruefully but said nothing. He spread the cape on a rock on the riverbank, and when it was sufficiently dry, he laid it upon one of the many pyres that had been lit to dispose of the Roman dead. The purple cape was consumed, and Caesar never spoke of it again.

Hearing the tale of Ptolemy's end, I remembered what Cleopatra had told me regarding those who died in the Nile, and the special blessing they received from Osiris. But it was not the king's existence in the life hereafter that worried Caesar, but the continuation of his existence, real or rumored, in this world. So long as Ptolemy's body was not found, the enemies of the queen might persist in believing that their champion survived, and the peace of Egypt might yet be disturbed by pretenders. There was even the slightest possibility that Ptolemy had indeed survived, and had gone into hiding, disguising himself as a commoner or fleeing to some place beyond the reach of Rome, perhaps to the court of the Parthian king. Caesar would have preferred to return to Alexandria with the lifeless body of the king, so that it could be displayed to Cleopatra as the head of Pompey had been displayed to him—irrefutable proof of the enemy's demise. But in this regard, despite all his efforts, Caesar was to be thwarted.

I shed no tears for young Ptolemy. I had seen him murder men in cold blood; he was anything but innocent. But a victim he was, of those even more ruthless than himself, and the horror of his end filled me with a kind of awe, as had the death of Pompey. History and legend conspire to convince us that there are men who rise above the common lot of humankind, who are set apart from the rest of us by birth or achievement or the favor of the gods; but no man, regardless of his pretensions to greatness, is immune from death, and the death of the so-called great is often more squalid and terrifying than the deaths of their most humble subjects. I thought of the young king and the strange, short life he had led, so full of violence and betrayal and thwarted dreams, and I felt a twinge of pity.

When Caesar returned to Alexandria, news of the king's demise preceded him. Abandoning all resistance, the Alexandrians threw down their weapons and opened the Canopic Gate to Caesar and his retinue. The people put on the tattered clothing of suppliants. Their priests made sacrifices in the temples to appease the wrath of the gods. But Caesar was not wrathful. He forbade his men to make any show of hostility and turned his march through the city into a joyous procession. When he arrived at the royal precinct, the men he had left to garrison the palace received him with ecstatic cheering. Cleopatra strode out to greet him. She had not been seen in public for quite some time, and it appeared to

me, despite the loose gown she wore, that she had grown considerably
larger around the middle. In lieu of her brother's head, Caesar presented
her with the captured crown. Leaving her own diadem in place, she also
fitted the crown of her brother on her brow, so that the vulture's head
and the rearing cobra were side-by-side. The Alexandrians, even those
who previously had cursed and spat at the mention of her name, erupted
in a thunderous cheer and hailed her as their goddess-queen.

The battle at the Nile took place late in the month of Martius, five days
before the kalends of Aprilis (by the old calendar); it was on that very day
that I finally received a letter from my daughter Diana in Rome.

Throughout the war, I had been trapped along with the Roman forces
inside the palace precinct. I had Rupa and the boys for company, and
Meto, when he could take time from attending Caesar. But I had grown
increasingly homesick for Rome.

To assuage that homesickness, I had regularly written long letters to
Diana, apprising her of all that had happened since her mother and I left
Rome, except for the one detail that I could not bear to commit to a letter:
the loss of Bethesda. I told her of my reconciliation with Meto, of my
meetings with the king and queen of Egypt, and of Rupa and the boys
and our curious visit to the Tomb of Alexander. Trade in the harbor had
come to a standstill, but Caesar did occasionally dispatch a ship to carry
messages, and Meto inserted my letters in the consul's official packets.
Whether they ever reached Diana, I had no way of knowing, since no
letters had yet arrived from her—until the day of the battle on the Nile,
when a ship from Rome sailed into the harbor and a little later a messenger knocked upon my door and pressed a sealed roll of parchment into
my hand.

I broke the seal, unrolled the scrap of parchment, and read:

Dearest Father and Mother,

I've written many letters to you, but your own letters give no sign
that you've received them, so I never know quite what to say. At the
risk of repeating myself, know that all is well here in Rome. Eco and
his family seem to be thriving; I think Eco is working in some capacity

for Marc Antony, who is in charge of the city in Caesar's absence, but Eco is so secretive about his work (taking after his father!) that I cannot really tell what he does, though it must be lucrative. Davus and I are looking after the house in your absence. Little Aulus is happy but misses having his grandpapa to tell him stories and his grandmama to tuck him in at night.

But now the real news: The new baby has come! She was delivered on the nones of March—an easy birth—and we have decided to call her Little Bethesda, perhaps simply Beth for short, which I hope will please her grandmother. She is happy, healthy, and very loud! She looks like you, Papa. (I can hear you muttering, "Poor child!," but don't, for she is very pretty.)

We long for you to return home. Your letters say nothing of Mother's search for a cure in the Nile, so we are very anxious to learn about that.

Write soon and let me know that you received this letter. All love to you both, and to Meto, and to Rupa and Androcles and Mopsus. All good fortune to Caesar, that the fighting may soon be over and you can all return to Rome! Neptune bless the ship that brings you this letter, and the ship that brings you back to us!

When I finished reading the letter, Mopsus asked me if I wept for joy or sadness. I could not tell him which.

Diana's new motherhood was very much on my mind when, a few days after Caesar's triumphant return, an official announcement went forth that Queen Cleopatra was expecting a baby. According to Meto, Caesar had no doubt that the child was his. In mid-Aprilis, having settled affairs in Alexandria, the prospective parents set out on a leisurely tour up the Nile, aglow with the triumph of their union and attended by every luxury. I recalled that Ptolemy had proposed just such a journey to Caesar. Instead, Ptolemy had died in the Nile, and it was Ptolemy's sister who showed Caesar the splendid temples and shrines along the river and the source of Egypt's greatness.

30

With the end of the war came peace. Alexandria opened its gates and its harbors. Rupa and the boys and I were free to move about as we wished.

For a few days I wandered about the city, thinking I should see the sights and revisit familiar places before I left, for at my time of life it seemed very unlikely that I would ever return. But the sights and sounds of Alexandria gave me no joy. I asked Meto to arrange a place for me and my charges at the first opportunity on one of Caesar's transport ships sailing to Rome.

Meto did as I asked. On the day before we were set to leave Alexandria, I took Rupa with me and strolled down the Canopic Way, determined at least to have a look inside the temple of Serapis before I left. As we passed by market stalls and public squares and splashing fountains, I fell to musing on the compromises forced upon us by the struggle for survival. In the end, Caesar had chosen Cleopatra, but more because of her brother's default than because of her own virtues. Cleopatra had deceived Caesar, and would have seen Meto executed without experiencing the least qualm of guilt. Caesar had been less than honest with the queen; and what of his relationship with Meto, whom he had imprisoned and threatened with death? I pictured the three of them locked in a circle of deceit, each confronted by the others' betrayals, yet determined, for the sake of expediency, to look the other way. Something about their hardheaded pragmatism left me thoroughly dissatisfied, but who was I to judge them? My rejection of Meto, when I felt betrayed and deceived by him, had brought me only misery, and in the end I recanted, as if I had been the one at fault. As long as things went relatively smoothly, was it wiser to overlook petty treacheries and deceits and disappointments and simply get on with the business of living? What good ever came of issuing ultimatums and passing judgment on others? Thus do we learn to compromise with each other and with our own expectations in an imperfect world.

Such were the thoughts spinning in my head when I saw, across a marketplace, the old priestess who had counseled Bethesda at the temple of Osiris on the Nile.

The market was vast and crowded with people; goods were beginning to flow back into Alexandria, and the populace, in the giddy mood that follows a war, were eager to spend their money. Amid the teeming throng, at a considerable distance, I caught only a fleeting glimpse of the woman; it was only after she moved out of sight that I realized who she was.

I gripped Rupa's arm. "Did you see her?"

He signed with his hands. *Who?*

"The old priestess," I began to say—then remembered that Rupa had had been off scattering Cassandra's ashes in the river when Bethesda sought the counsel of the wisewoman. Rupa had never seen her.

I frowned and squinted, trying to catch another glimpse of her face amid all the others. "Only someone . . . I thought I recognized. But perhaps I was only—no, wait! There she is! Do you see her?" I stood on tiptoes and pointed. "It must be her; she looks exactly the same! The white hair pulled into a knot; the skin like weathered wood; that ragged woolen mantle . . ."

Rupa shook his head, then drew a sharp breath.

"You see her, then?"

He signed: *Look at the younger woman with her. Look!*

"Younger woman? Where? I don't see anyone—unless you mean the woman wearing the cloth headdress and—"

Like Rupa, I drew a sharp breath. The two of us stood stock-still, staring in disbelief.

"It can't be," I whispered, "and yet . . ."

Rupa nodded vigorously, even as he furrowed his brow, as if to say: *It is her. And yet it* can't *be her. . . .*

"It's a trick of the light," I said, squinting at the apparition—for surely the woman in the yellow linen gown, her hair concealed in the folds of a nemes head-cloth, was only a phantom. And yet, the old crone could see her, for the two of them exchanged a few words, apparently about the relative merits of two combs offered by a vendor. They were too far away, I told myself; the Egyptian sun was too bright, making a dazzlement of their distant faces. I was seeing what I wanted to see, not something that was actually there. Yet Rupa seemed to see the same thing. Or did he?

Dissatisfied with both combs, the woman and the crone were moving away. Other, nearer faces intervened. I rose on tiptoes and pitched from side to side, trying to keep her in sight.

"It *is* her, isn't it?" I said. "It's . . ." I pressed my lips together, summoning the strength to speak her name aloud.

Rupa interrupted. He hooked his forefingers together to make the sign that signified his sister, and made the word an exclamation by the look on his face: *Cassandra!*

My jaw froze. The sound died in my throat. I had been about to say a different name.

I was suddenly uncertain. Perhaps the woman *did* look a bit like Cassandra. And yet . . .

Where was she? I had lost sight of the woman, and of the old crone as well. Both of them had vanished into the crowd.

"She was too old to be Cassandra, wasn't she?" I said, my voice hollow. "And Cassandra was blond. We couldn't see her hair, because of the headdress, but this woman had darker features, didn't she?"

Rupa shook his head, looking troubled and confused. I saw tears in his eyes.

No, I thought, it wasn't Cassandra we had seen. That was impossible. Cassandra was ashes now; not even ashes any longer, but ashes dissolved in the Nile—her ephemeral remains merged with the everlasting river, so that Osiris might give her everlasting life.

Had Cassandra believed in such things? I wasn't sure. But Bethesda had. Most certainly, Bethesda had believed in a world beyond this world and in the supernatural power of the great river Nile.

For an hour or more we lingered in the vicinity of that market. I pretended to shop, looking for trinkets and toys to take home as souvenirs to Diana and Aulus and my new granddaughter, but in reality I was hoping for another glimpse of the crone and the woman who accompanied her. But I did not see them again that day.

That night, I asked Meto to cancel my passage on the ship bound for Rome.

"Why, Papa? I thought you couldn't wait to leave."

I shrugged.

"You went sightseeing with Rupa today, didn't you?"

"Yes."

Meto smiled. "Perhaps you enjoyed yourself, after all?"

"Perhaps."

"Good! Alexandria is an amazing city. Take a few more days to relax and see the sights. Shall I arrange passage for you on the next available ship, or the one after that?"

"I'm not sure when I'll be ready to leave. I have a sense of . . . unfinished business . . . here in Alexandria."

"Just let me know when the time is right. But don't wait too long. Once Caesar returns from his cruise up the Nile, it will be time to press on with the war elsewhere, and I'll almost certainly be leaving Alexandria myself."

Day after day I returned to that market, sometimes with Rupa, sometimes with the boys, sometimes alone. I gave every possible reason for doing so, except the real reason.

The vendors at the market soon came to recognize me, for I questioned every one of them about the two women I had seen that day. A few seemed to have some vague notion of whom I was taking about, but none could offer any insight into the identity of the women, their whereabouts, or whether they might return.

Over and over, Meto arranged for me to board ships sailing for Rome, and over and over, at the last moment, I told him to cancel those plans. *One more day at the marketplace,* I told myself; *if I can visit the place just one more day . . .*

Even with all the wonders of Alexandria open to them, Androcles and Mopsus began to grow restless. Caesar and Cleopatra returned from their journey up the Nile. Caesar's inner circle, including Meto, made ready to depart from Alexandria. Meto began to press me about my own arrangements.

"Surely the time has come, Papa. Once I leave, it won't be as easy for you to arrange passage. Shall we set the date?"

"I suppose we should," I said reluctantly.

"Unless you have some compelling reason to stay longer?" He frowned. I was keeping something from him, and he knew it.

"No. Let's set a date and stick to it."

"Good. There's a ship leaving for Rome the day after tomorrow."

I bit my lip and felt a dull pain in my chest. "Very well. I'll be on it."

The next day, which was to be my last full day in Alexandria, I went to the market alone. I arrived very early and stayed there all day. The vendors shook their heads; they were beginning to think I was mad. The old priestess and the other woman never appeared.

The next morning, Rupa and the boys were up early, ready to board the ship for Rome. My trunk was packed. All was ready.

Meto had promised to escort us to the pier. He arrived beaming with excitement. "Can you believe it, Papa? I'm going with you! Caesar's sending me back to Rome. He needs someone to deliver a dossier to Marc Antony, and he says there's no one better for the job. But the fact is, I think he's rewarding me with a trip home in return for . . . well, for a certain amount of unpleasantness that you and I had to endure. It's a good thing you postponed your trip so long, after all, because now I can go with you!"

"Yes, wonderful news," I said, trying to muster some enthusiasm. I could see that Meto was disappointed by my reaction. We proceeded to the harbor.

The sky was cloudless. A favorable wind blew from the south, carrying the dry, sandy smell of the desert. The boys ran onto the deck, despite Meto's caution that they would have to behave themselves aboard a military vessel. Rupa, assisted by one of the sailors, carried my trunk aboard. I lingered on the pier.

"It's time, Papa," said Meto. "The captain's called for everyone to step aboard."

I shook my head. "I'm not going."

"What? Papa, there's no reason for you to stay. I don't understand. Think of Diana! You must be eager to see the baby—"

"Rupa!"

Rupa sat on the trunk he had just carried aboard, catching his breath. He sprang up and came to me.

"Rupa, you have the key to the trunk, don't you?"

He nodded and reached into his tunic to show me the key, which hung from a chain around his neck.

"Good. Open the trunk. On the very top you'll see a leather bag with coins in it. Bring it to me; I'll need some money."

Meto shook his head. "You're actually going to stay, aren't you?"

"Yes."

"But why, Papa? If there's something you must do, let me stay and help you. Or at least keep one of the boys with you, or Rupa—"

"No! The thing I do, I must do alone."

Rupa opened the lid of the trunk. Mopsus and Androcles, with a look of alarm, came running, and a moment later I saw the reason: Peering over the edge of the trunk, his green eyes open wide and his silver collar gleaming in the sunlight, was Alexander the cat.

I raised an eyebrow. "Kidnapping a sacred feline from the royal palace! If Queen Cleopatra finds out, she's liable to throw a couple of slave boys into the harbor."

"Then I suppose the queen must never know," said Meto, smiling crookedly. "I'm sure the captain won't mind; a cat will kill any rats on the ship."

Rupa returned with the bag of coins and handed it to me. Mopsus and Androcles carefully shut the lid of the trunk and looked around the deck to make sure no one else had seen the stowaway.

I embraced Meto, then stepped back. "Look after the others on the journey home, Meto. And when you see Diana, and Eco . . ."

"Yes, Papa, what shall I tell them? They don't yet know about Bethesda. What shall I say about her? What shall I say about *you*?"

"Tell them the truth, as far as you can. Sometimes, Meto, the truth must suffice."

"Diana will be distraught when she finds out about her mother. And am I simply to say that you refused to leave Egypt?"

"Tell them I love them; they know that already. Tell them I shall come home as soon as I can . . . if the gods wish it to be so."

The captain of the ship gave a final call for all to board. Sailors hurried about the deck, preparing to cast off. Never taking his eyes from me, Meto stepped aboard. Rupa and the boys stood beside him. As the ship moved away from the dock, they stared at me in puzzlement.

The ship drew away. Their faces grew smaller and smaller until I could no longer read their expressions. I lifted my eyes to the great lighthouse that towered above the harbor, and thought of the first glimpse I had seen of its flame that night aboard the *Andromeda,* with Bethesda, before the storm struck and swept away all our expectations.

31

I paid a call on Queen Cleopatra. To my surprise, I was admitted to her presence almost at once.

She reclined upon a purple couch strewn with gold cushions. Slaves fanned her with ostrich feathers. The gown she wore was loose and flowing, but did not conceal the fact that she was great with child.

"Gordianus-called-Finder! I thought you were leaving Alexandria for Rome today, along with that irksome son of yours."

"I was supposed to go, Your Majesty. I changed my mind."

She raised an eyebrow. "You've come to visit me instead?"

"Your Majesty once spoke to me of the special circumstances attendant upon a death in the Nile."

She peered at me and nodded slowly. "Those who perish in the Nile are blessed by Osiris. He embraces the *ka* even as the currents and eddies of the river embrace the hollow reed of the body."

I shook my head. "All this talk of the sacred Nile! I've seen the Nile. I wandered up to my neck in its muddy waters, searching for Bethesda's body. I felt the ooze of the bottom suck at my feet. I smelled the stench of rotting plants along the steaming bank. There's nothing beautiful about the Nile. It's fetid, smelly, dark, and dank! The Nile brings death."

"Yet it also brings life!" Cleopatra placed her hand upon her swollen belly. "Some men—squeamish, ignorant fools!—make the same complaints about the sacred delta between a woman's legs. And yet, from that place comes new life. Silly men, turning up your noses at the slippery fluids and strong odors of fertility! You'd rather play with your hard, shiny swords and spears, and watch the blood spurt from each other's wounds! Yes, the Nile is all you say it is—a vast, endless expanse of sluggish water and oozing mud. It spills across Egypt, bringing life and death wherever it goes. That's what gods do. They give life. They give death—and life after death."

"So you say; those who perish in the Nile are reborn. But are they ever resurrected?"

"What do you mean?"

"Do they ever walk again in this world?"

She looked at me darkly. "Are you thinking of my brother? It's true, his body was never located, but—"

"There was another whose body was never found."

She knitted her brow, then nodded. "Your wife?"

"Yes."

"Why do you ask such a question, Gordianus?"

"Let me ask another. You told me you know the old priestess at the temple outside Naucratis."

"I've visited the temple. I've met her."

"Is it possible that I might have seen her here in Alexandria, in one of the markets?"

"She's very old, but there's no reason she shouldn't travel to the city if she wishes. Even a priestess must gather provisions. But if you'd merely seen the priestess, you wouldn't be asking me these questions, would you? You saw someone else."

"I saw a woman with the priestess. So did Rupa. But we didn't see the same woman. He saw his sister, Cassandra, whose ashes he scattered in the Nile. I saw . . . Bethesda. That makes me think . . ."

"That neither of you saw a woman you truly recognized."

"Exactly. Unless . . ."

"Unless you both saw what you thought you saw. Cassandra and Bethesda, somehow joined by the river and risen from the dead."

I shuddered. "Do such things happen in Egypt?"

"Perhaps. But I think you would prefer a more rational, less mystical explanation, wouldn't you, Gordianus? Perhaps the two women shared a stronger resemblance than you realized. Perhaps the woman you and Rupa saw in the market was indeed your wife—who never died, after all."

"But the woman I saw looked younger than Bethesda . . ."

"She was ill when you last saw her, was she not, and had been ill for quite some time? If she's better now, refreshed by the mild Egyptian winter and tanned by the warm Egyptian sun, might she not look younger than before?"

"Bethesda—alive! But how is it possible? We searched and searched—"

"Perhaps she didn't want to be found. Had you done something to offend her?"

I thought of Cassandra. Bethesda had given no indication of knowing what had passed between us, and yet . . .

"Or perhaps something happened to her in the river," said the queen. "Perhaps she forgot herself and became lost."

"But when she came to her senses, she would have looked for me, surely—"

"Looked where? You were carried away by Ptolemy's army; how could she know where you had gone? Even if she did somehow follow you to Alexandria, for many months no one from outside could reach any of us inside the palace. Perhaps, all this time, your wife has been residing at the temple of Osiris beside the Nile, expiating whatever impurity caused her illness, rejuvenating herself and restoring her vitality by serving the priestess."

I drew a ragged breath. "That's what I would like to believe."

"But you fear false hope?"

"Yes!"

"The only solution is to do what you've done all your life: Find the truth for yourself, Gordianus. Go to the temple outside Naucratis. See what you find."

"What if Bethesda isn't there?"

"You'll find her. If not in the temple, then in the river. You must find her, and you must join her, one way or another. Is that not what you want? Is it not your heart's desire?"

"It is!"

"Then overcome your fear. Go to the temple by the Nile. Do whatever you must to be reunited with your wife."

I left the queen's presence, shaken and trembling with doubt, but resolved to do as she counseled. She smiled as I left. Was it because she had shared the sacred wisdom of Isis with me? Or was it because, if I did as she told me, she would have seen the last of me forever?

I made the journey by canal boat, and thence on horseback down the river road. Traveling alone, without the comfort or distraction of companions, I realized that I had not done so in many years. I was reminded of my younger days, when I had set out on journeys without knowing how long they would take or where they would lead, following the road as a man follows his fate, sometimes anxious, sometimes exhausted by the rigors of travel, but more often buoyed by a sense of freedom and the possibility that something surprising and wonderful might lie around the next bend. It was good to be alone with my thoughts, watching the sights along the canal pass by, and then the sights along the road. As I approached the vicinity of the temple, I felt at once calm and filled with anticipation.

The weather was mild. Palm trees swayed in a gentle breeze from the south. Farmers were at work in the fields, tending to irrigation ditches and repairing waterwheels to prepare for the annual inundation. Alexandria seemed far away; Rome, even farther.

This was the Egypt I remembered from my youth, the Egypt I had longed to revisit. I felt the sun on my face, breathed in the smells of the life-giving Nile, and felt transported back in time, as if all the intervening years had never happened. I was the youth I had been when I first arrived in Egypt, owning little, obliged to no one, but confident of the future, as only the young can be confident.

I came to a place where the foliage grew thick and tall between the road and the river. Though I could not see it, I knew the temple must lie somewhere within that dense greenery. I tethered my horse and stretched the stiff, sore legs of an old man not used to riding on horseback. Even that reminder of my body's frailty did not shake the illusion of having stepped back in time.

I passed through a curtain of hanging vines and found a pathway into the foliage. The play of sunlight and shadow confounded my sense of distance. The seclusion of the place cast a spell upon me. The pathway turned this way and that, and I began to think I was hopelessly lost. Then I stepped into a sunlit glade and saw the temple before me. Dragonflies flitted across shafts of sunlight. Water splashed and gurgled in the spring-fed pool beside the temple.

I walked to the steps. I ascended to the porch and entered the sanctum of Osiris.

The smell of burning myrrh enveloped me. The chamber was dimly lit. A figure appeared in the gloom and moved closer until I saw the sere, weathered face of the priestess. I heard the sound of mewing, and looked down to see the black cat stroking itself against her bony ankles.

Was it the same woman I had seen in the market in Alexandria, or had memory played a trick on me?

"Priestess," I said. "I came here many months ago—last summer—with my wife. She was unwell. She sought your counsel. You told her to bathe in the Nile. Do you remember?"

The wisewoman hunched her shoulder against her ear and peered up at my face. "Oh, yes. I remember."

"And then—not long ago, I thought I saw you in a marketplace in Alexandria. Was it you I saw? Were you in the city?"

She looked at me for a long moment, then shook her head. "That's not the question you really want to ask. That's not what you came here to find out."

"No. You're right. I came for Bethesda. Is she here?"

"Your wife was very ill when you came here; more ill than you could know. Her body was weak, but it was her spirit that had grown sick. She was very close to death. There was little I could do, except commend her to the care of the river."

"And did the river heal her?"

"Go to the river. Find the place where you last saw her. Discover the truth for yourself."

Her words echoed those of Cleopatra. I shuddered, as I had shuddered in the queen's presence. I stepped onto the porch of the temple, needing to catch my breath. When I stepped back inside, the priestess had disappeared, and so had the cat. The little room was empty, except for a sputtering lamp and a censer of myrrh that released a final wisp of smoke.

I descended the steps, hopped over the spring-fed pool, and took the path that led to the river. I came to a fork in the path and hesitated, try-ing to remember which way to go. One way had led me to a tangled dead end, I recalled, where I had glimpsed the ashes of Cassandra clouding the flowing water; the other way had led me to the place where Bethesda disappeared. But which was which? Memory failed me, and I stood for a long moment, puzzled. The problem was simple, but my mind was so befuddled that I had to work it out like a child, step-by-step. Bethesda had entered the river downstream from Cassandra's ashes; with the river before me, running from right to left, the path to the left must lead downstream; so that was the way I must take.

The path led steadily downhill. Through the leaves I began to catch glimpses of sparkling sunlight on green water. At last I came to the river's edge. The place was secluded and silent, with a leafy canopy overhead and rushes all around. Bethesda was nowhere to be seen. I called her name. The shout rousted a covey of birds, who flapped and cawed and streamed skyward from the undergrowth.

I stripped off my tunic and loincloth. The angle of the sun was such that the whole of the river seemed to sparkle with dancing light. So many points of light were reflected from the river onto my nakedness that I felt as if I were clothed in a spangled gown of sunlight. The sparkles dazzled my eyes and warmed my flesh.

I strode into the river. The solid, sandy bottom quickly gave way to an oozing muck that sucked at my feet. The water rose to my chest, and with another step, to my chin. "Oh, Bethesda!" I whispered. Rushes swayed in the warm breeze. Sunlight glinted on the water. The placid face of the Nile gave no indication of concern for my fate, or the fate of any mortal; yet at the same time the river seemed to welcome me. Its warm darkness offered solace; its vastness offered an end to mortal vanity; its agelessness offered a doorway to eternity.

Another step, and the water rose above my head. I opened my eyes. The water was murky and green, but the surface above me was like a vast sheet of hammered silver. I opened my mouth to draw the Nile deep into my lungs. A burning fullness flowed into my chest. The silver canopy above me was extinguished. The murky water turned black.

I felt hands upon me. Out of the black murk a face appeared. Cassandra's face! No—the face of Bethesda, her features as soft and smooth as when I first met her in Alexandria. She put her mouth upon mine. Her kiss drew the Nile from my lungs and took my breath away. . . .

I opened my eyes, blinking to expel drops of water from my lashes. I lay upon my back on a sandy riverbank. A canopy of leaves shivered overhead; they appeared to be made of silver. The sky beyond was an unearthly shade of purple shot with streaks of aquamarine and vermilion.

I felt the warmth of a body next to mine; someone lay beside me on the sand. She stirred and rose on one elbow to look down at me.

"Bethesda!" I whispered, and coughed a little. The taste of the Nile was on my tongue.

"Husband," she whispered, in a voice full of love and tenderness. She kissed me.

"Bethesda, where are we?"

She frowned. "Are you so confused, husband, that you don't remember walking into the Nile?"

"Yes, but . . . are we alive—or dead?"

"Does it matter? We're together."

"Yes, but . . . are we immortal yet?"

She laughed. I had not heard her laugh that way, so carefree and relaxed, in a long time. "Don't be silly, husband. Isn't the answer obvious?"

"Not entirely." The sky above me did not look like any sky I could remember. Or was that strange palette of colors simply a phenomenon caused by a meeting of sunlight, sea mist, and a nearby sandstorm? "Where have you been all this time, Bethesda?"

She smiled. "For now, let me ask the questions. Has my granddaughter been born yet?"

"Yes! Diana wrote me a letter—but how did you know it was a girl?"

She shrugged. "A lucky guess. I want to see her. We must get back to Rome, as soon as possible."

I smiled. "Then we *are* alive?"

She raised an eyebrow. "Can't the spirits of the dead go on journeys?"

"I suppose." I cocked my head. "I've heard of haunted ships, but I never expected to haunt one myself! Ah, well. When we were young and poor, we found a way to get to Rome; and we shall find a way to get there now. We shall go together." I took her hand in mine. "Let us go home, Bethesda."

"Yes, husband. Let us go home!"

Author's Note

Long after her lifetime, Cleopatra continued and continues to attract acolytes, admirers, enemies, and victims, especially among dramatists and other writers. In *Antony and Cleopatra,* Shakespeare famously presented the Roman general and the queen as star-crossed lovers. Using the Bard's text (as adapted by Franco Zeffirelli), Samuel Barber composed an opera to inaugurate the Metropolitan Opera House at Lincoln Center in 1966; for his efforts on behalf of the queen, the composer of the immortal *Adagio for Strings* received a devastating critical reception. George Bernard Shaw gave us his *Caesar and Cleopatra,* with a kittenish queen later embodied on screen by Vivien Leigh. In the 1960s, Elizabeth Taylor eclipsed all previous (and subsequent) portrayals in the much-maligned film written and directed by Joseph Mankiewicz, whose involvement with the perilous queen caused him even more suffering than that endured by Samuel Barber. No matter how irresistible her allure, one is wise to approach Cleopatra with caution.

Was Cleopatra beautiful? The historian Dio is unequivocal; this is the translation by Herbert Baldwin Foster:

> She was a woman of surpassing beauty, especially conspicuous at that time because in the prime of youth, with a most delicious voice and a knowledge of how to make herself agreeable to everyone. Being brilliant to look upon and to listen to, with

a power to subjugate even a cold-natured or elderly person, she thought that she might prove exactly to Caesar's tastes and reposed in her beauty all her claims to advancement.

Plutarch, in his *Life of Antony,* equivocates only slightly; this is the Dryden translation:

> Her beauty in itself was not so remarkable that none could be compared with her, or that no one could see her without being struck by it, but the contact of her presence was irresistible; the attraction of her person, joining with the charm of her conversation, and the character that attended all she said or did, was something bewitching.

Unfortunately, we have few images of Cleopatra by which to judge her beauty with our own eyes. Crude coin portraits offer something close to caricature, and the only bust of Cleopatra accepted as genuine, that in the Vatican, is missing its nose. André Malraux said, "Nefertiti is a face without a queen; Cleopatra is a queen without a face."

When I came to study Cleopatra in earnest, my childhood images of her, inspired by the glamorous Elizabeth Taylor portrayal, eventually faded, and I found myself confronted by a profoundly problematic personality. By twenty-first-century supermodel standards, Cleopatra may or may not have been beautiful; but her psyche, by modern standards, was decidedly not pretty. Having been raised to become an absolute ruler, in ruthless competition with her siblings for the affections of their father, the patriarch of an incestuous clan, Cleopatra, one may safely say, came from a dysfunctional family. Just as her father murdered his rebellious eldest daughter, Berenice, so Cleopatra, having eliminated with Caesar's help her brother-husband, Ptolemy, would eventually murder her other siblings, Arsinoë and the younger Ptolemy. We can only wonder at the distorted psychology that created and was created by such violence. There is the added complication that Cleopatra may quite seriously have considered herself to be at least semi-divine. If she were to appear among the glitterati of today, I think we might conservatively classify her as mad, bad, and dangerous to know.

Indeed, the more I study all the dominant individuals of this period—including Pompey and Caesar—the more I am reminded of a comment by the writer L. Sprague de Camp, who, in a different context (reviewing the fantasy novels of E. R. Eddison), wrote:

> In short, Eddison's "great men," even the best of them, are cruel, arrogant bullies. One may admire, in the abstract, the indomitable courage, energy, and ability of such rampant egotists. In the concrete, however, they are like the larger carnivora, best admired with a set of stout bars between them and the viewer.

We have only a vague idea of what Cleopatra looked like; we have no image whatsoever of her brother King Ptolemy. We are not even certain of his age at the time of Caesar's arrival; I have made him fifteen, the oldest age postulated by historians. When writers or filmmakers have bothered to deal with Ptolemy at all, the portrait is not flattering; Mankiewicz cast the boy-king as a petulant brat dominated by the eunuch Pothinus, whom he cast as a simpering queen. But why should we assume that Ptolemy was any less beautiful or charismatic than his elder sister, or that the spell he cast upon Caesar was any less profound? As one of history's losers, Cleopatra was vilified and marginalized by those who triumphed over her. We may assume that the same was done to Ptolemy. Between the lines of Caesar's *The Civil War* is the story of a curious triangular relationship that must have developed between the Roman conqueror and the sibling-spouses amid the hothouse intrigues of their confinement in the palace compound at Alexandria. In this novel, Ptolemy's parting words of love and devotion to Caesar are lifted word for word from Caesar's own account. What did the siblings feel for each other, what did they feel for Caesar, and what did Caesar feel for them in return? It seems to me that historians, blinded by their fascination with Cleopatra (and by the mores of their own times), have ignored the untold story of the decisions, political and personal, that faced Caesar in his struggle to settle affairs of state—and affairs of the heart—in Egypt.

For the tale of Pompey's demise and Caesar's doings in Alexandria, our sources are rich, though not always in agreement. Dio and Appian in their histories of Rome, Plutarch in his lives of Caesar and Pompey, Suetonius in his life of Caesar, Lucan in his epic poem *Pharsalia,* and Caesar in his memoir of the Civil War all recount various aspects of the tale. Pliny gives us exact measurements regarding the inundation of the Nile; this is the translation of H. Rackham: "The largest rise up to date was one of 27 feet . . . and the smallest 7½ feet in the year of the war of Pharsalus, as if the river were trying to avert the murder of Pompey by a sort of portent."

From Strabo, writing in 25 B.C., we learn what little we know of the layout of ancient Alexandria, which remains unexcavated by modern archaeologists; the exact location of the Library and numerous other landmarks is unknown. *The Adventures of Leucippe and Cleitophon* by Achilles Tatius, who wrote in the second century A.D., provides a small clue about the uncertain location of the Tomb of Alexander. Lucan tells us that Caesar visited Alexander's remains. (So did several later Roman emperors; Dio tells us Augustus, wishing to adorn the mummy with a gold crown, inadvertently broke off its nose.)

Among modern historians, I found these books to be of particular interest: Jack Lindsay's *Cleopatra* (Constable & Company Ltd., London, 1971), Arthur Weigall's *The Life and Times of Cleopatra, Queen of Egypt* (G. P. Putnam's Sons, New York & London, 1924), Hans Volkmann's *Cleopatra, A Study in Politics and Propaganda* (Sagamore Press, New York 1958), Jean-Yves Empereur's *Alexandria, Jewel of Egypt* (Abrams, New York, 2002), and volume III of T. Rice Holmes's monumental *The Roman Republic and the Founder of the Empire* (The Clarendon Press, Oxford, 1923). I derived great pleasure from Jane Wilson Joyce's translation of Lucan's *Pharsalia* (Cornell University Press, Ithaca & London, 1993). *Cleopatra of Egypt, from History to Myth* (The British Museum Press, London, 2001), an exhibition catalogue edited by Susan Walker and Peter Higgs, contains a great wealth of images.

My thanks to Penni Kimmel, Rick Solomon, and Rick Lovin for reading the manuscript; to my tireless agent, Alan Nevins; and to my editor at St. Martin's Press, Keith Kahla.

I will close with this observation, which comes from Dio, writing about the volatile situation in Alexandria at the time of Caesar's visit: "The Egyptians," he says (again, in Foster's translation), "are the most excessively religious people on earth and wage wars even against one another on account of their beliefs, since their worship is not a unified system, but different branches of it are diametrically opposed one to another." The hardheaded, endlessly pragmatic Romans, with their affinity for realpolitik, did not know quite what to make of the otherworldly fanaticisms of the Egyptians. It may give us pause that Dio's observation is as true about the inhabitants of the region today as it was in the time of Cleopatra.

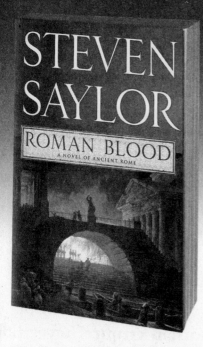

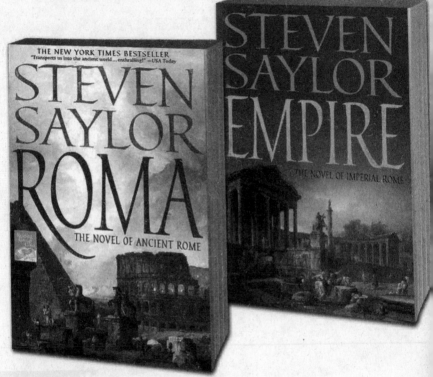